BENEATH THE ALABASTER SPIRE

BOOK TWO
OF THE IMMORTAL ORDERS TRILOGY

Copyright © 2022 by Allison Carr Waechter

All rights reserved.

No part of this book may be reproduced in any form or by any electronic or mechanical means, including information storage and retrieval systems, without written permission from the author, except for the use of brief quotations in a book review.

ISBN: 979-8-9860604-2-2

Cover Image by Christin Engelberth

Book Design by Allison Carr Waechter

Editing by Kenna Kettrick

for the babes who know what it's like to heal in public:
the road is long, the process is nonlinear, and you can do this.

CONTENT WARNINGS

I make every attempt to be sensitive and judicious about the ways in which I include potentially triggering themes in my writing. Please be cautious about the following in this text:

- Descriptions of child abuse
- Descriptions of torture/punishment
- Descriptions of gore/violence
- Descriptions of structural oppression
- Descriptions of trauma responses, mental health struggles, and mention of suicide
- Descriptions of terrorist bombings, some targeted specifically at schools
- One condemned fatphobic comment
- Consensual biting between romantic partners
- Allusions to non-consensual biting/vampiric actions
- Swearing

As a reminder, **all** of my books are written for an adult audience. They include graphic descriptions of sexual encounters, violence and heavy adult themes.

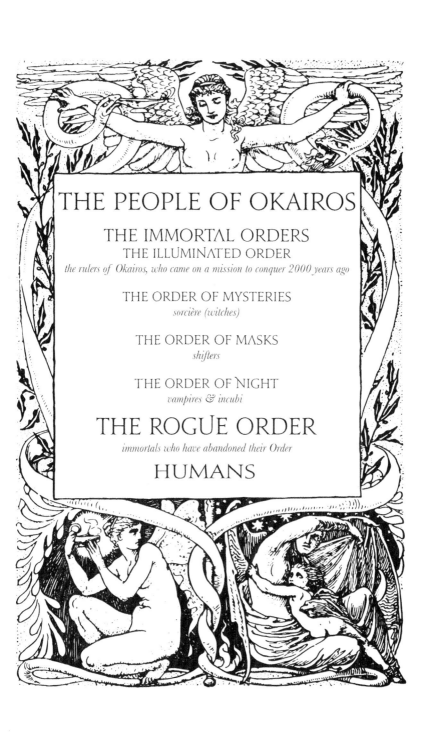

THE PEOPLE OF OKAIROS

THE IMMORTAL ORDERS

THE ILLUMINATED ORDER
the rulers of Okairos, who came on a mission to conquer 2000 years ago

THE ORDER OF MYSTERIES
sorcière (witches)

THE ORDER OF MASKS
shifters

THE ORDER OF NIGHT
vampires & incubi

THE ROGUE ORDER
immortals who have abandoned their Order

HUMANS

PROLOGUE

The chilled air flowing from the vent in the ceiling did nothing to stop the sheen of sweat on Connor McKay's forehead from rolling down one cheek. It was unbearably hot and humid in Nuva Troi. He wiped the offending bodily fluid with his handkerchief and then returned to his phone and his pacing. The reports were infuriating, *impossible*. After over a thousand years of peace, everything was falling apart.

Pasiphae Velarius, arch-chancellor of the Illuminated Order, entered her office in a cloud of rich floral perfume, looking cool as an autumn day despite the oppressive heat outdoors. She offered him a mug of steaming coffee as she sipped from her own, but Connor shook his head.

"Too damn hot already," he remarked, loosening his tie.

Connor regretted his staunch commitment to wearing a three-piece suit to the office every summer, and today was no different. He stared out over Nuva Troi, at Ambracia Bay. Pasiphae's top floor office had a gorgeous view of their city and the ocean, and he never failed to admire it at their weekly breakfast. Boats filled the bay, full of recreating immortals and humans alike, but he didn't feel a lick of resentment towards them. It was a sign that while everything fell apart overseas, at least it was doing so in secret.

He stopped pacing to allow himself a measure of composure, letting the sound of the enormous wall of falling water from Pasiphae's ostentatious fountain soothe him. He'd thought it ridiculous when she'd had it installed a few years back, but now he saw its merits. The quiet sound of moving water was pleasant, and so few things in his life were. Perhaps he needed a fountain downstairs.

His own office was deep in the bowels of the building, a catacombed fortress guarding the hoard of information he'd collected in his over two thousand years on this planet. It was worth it, but he had to admit, he was jealous of this view. The sapphire expanse of water, the people going about their normal lives. It was all so different from what they'd left behind, the carnage of eons of war, the constant rebuilding, the pain of living the same day again and again. This, for all its imperfections, was better. Two thousand years later, he didn't regret his choices. Not when it came to Okairos, anyway. His personal life was another matter entirely.

Pasiphae stood next to him, sipping her coffee in silence. He glanced at her sidelong, wishing to long-dead gods *they'd* fallen in love back in the beginning—that he'd chosen someone smart, ambitious, and shrewd like her, instead of Aislin.

But his bond-mate had been alluring, beautiful. One of the Emperor's favored courtesans and supposedly an expert diplomat, Aislin had ostensibly been sent to aid the envoy in efficiently utilizing the people of Okairos for the empire's endless wars. In reality, she had caused problems between the Emperor and his new wife. Connor had been fool enough to Claim her the first time they'd fucked and had gotten himself stuck. He supposed he should be grateful for Pasiphae's friendship, their alliance in overseeing Okairos, but it was times like these, when she stood next to him quiet and patient, that he truly regretted his choice in partners.

"What are you getting so worked up over?" Pasiphae asked, her voice low, sonorous and seductive as it always was. "I can *feel* you thinking."

Connor's cock jumped in his pants. But she hadn't a hint of arousal in her scent. She wasn't attracted to him in the slightest, nor had she ever been, to his knowledge. He shook his head, shoving his phone into his jacket pocket. "The early readout on the Août security report detailing the riots in Falcyra."

Pasiphae nodded. "They were handled swiftly, and we suppressed most of the news about them. They're nothing but salacious rumors here."

Connor turned from the view and sank into one of the leather chairs that sat opposite to Pasiphae's enormous desk. She drifted to her plush velvet desk chair and wrote in her diary for a while, waiting for him to speak. The familiar sound of her pen on paper always calmed him, and she knew it. This was how it had always been with them: he handled the horrors of their rule, and she governed the public face of their endeavor to keep Okairos safe from the worlds beyond.

He sighed, covering his face with his hands. "*So far,* it's nothing but rumors. The House of Sorath is out of control. Ducare let nests develop all over the country. We shouldn't have allowed the Order of Night a governorship."

Pasiphae shrugged. "They're our closest allies. The shifters and witches will never align with us. Giving the vampires their own country made sense, and Falcyra is isolated. Worry about handling Ducare."

Gerard Ducare had been a problem overseas for nearly a century—ever since the House of Sorath had defected from the House of Remiel's rule. Giving them Falcyra had been an experiment to see if the vampires could handle their own territory. It had seemed safe enough when Ducare defected. After all, Falcyra was a beautiful country, but cold and nearly desolate. It was also far enough from Nytra to keep things under control in Okairos' capital city—but it had all gone wrong at this point. It was only a matter of time before the truth of it reached Nytra, and when it did... Well, they weren't prepared for that. Not yet anyway. He had to buy them some time.

"I sent a legion to Falcyra this morning to impose martial law for the rest of the summer. Does that handle things well enough for you?" Connor couldn't help flashing Pasiphae a crooked grin. He'd meant to be flirtatious, but she didn't even look up from her notes.

Bitch, he thought to himself.

Pasiphae still didn't look at him, continuing to write in her diary. "Who did you send to fix things? Not Penemue, I assume. I saw her at the gym this morning."

"Rakul," Connor said, his voice quiet.

"Oh my." Pasiphae finally looked up, a ferocious smile spreading over her face as her head tilted. She tossed her pen onto the leather blotter on her desk; her luminous brown eyes shone with mirth. "You *are* serious then."

"This isn't a joke," Connor growled. "Everything we've worked for is on the line."

Pasiphae's eyes flashed with cold, furious power. "You think I don't know that, Connor? I read the reports. Ducare was searching out Gene-I. We had the Night's Own's master records wiped clean a month ago—after the incident with the Eastons and your son."

Mark Easton, Harlow Krane's ex-lover and an incubus, had been killed in the House of Remiel's basement on the night of the Solstice Gala. It had been a nightmare to clean up, and the boy's father, Alain, was still on the loose. All evidence pointed to the fact that he too, had been turned into an incubus. Failure after failure had plagued Connor, ever since the Krane girl had re-entered his son's life. She would serve her purpose soon enough, though, and then they could be rid of her once and for all.

Connor shook his head. "And yet, we still haven't found Alain Easton, and there are *riots* in Falcyra. Sending Rakul was the right choice, and I'll bring him back here to handle things if need be."

One of Pasiphae's eyebrows arched dangerously. She'd made her opinions on Rakul's methods clear time and again: allowable for handling things in other countries, but not here, not in Nytra. This was their *home*. "You don't get a say in that, Connor. *I* say what happens in Nytra."

"Of course." Connor gave in immediately. This separation of power was a vital part of their agreement. It kept the peace, and despite what people thought of him, that was the most important thing. No wars, no poverty—only blessed, *peaceful* order.

"I see on socials that your son and his betrothed have been making quite the splash in Nea Sterlis. Are they having trouble? Someone recorded them arguing at a cafe, didn't they?"

Connor rolled his eyes. She was baiting him because her own son had bonded with the rather perfect Thea Krane. "They were arguing over what toppings to get on a pizza. I hardly think that means anything."

Pasiphae's eyebrows lifted. "You had someone parse out the audio?"

"Yes, of course. They're still on track for our plan. It was just foreplay. They fucked twice afterward in a back alley."

The sound of the waterfall was the only noise for a tense few moments. Then Pasiphae smiled. "Watch them carefully, Connor. We need that child if we hope to maintain our hold on Okairos."

Connor's skin crawled at Pasiphae's tone. Hadn't *he* been the one to come up with the plan to push the Krane girl and his son back together? Pasiphae had some nerve. If she were his, he'd punish her for that imperious little mouth. That line of thinking was unproductive though, so he grasped for a change in subject. "Why aren't these humans grateful for all we've done for them? Do they have *any* idea what it's like on other worlds?"

Pasiphae chuckled, and Connor's ire raised a notch higher. "No, Connor, they do not. We've made sure of that, haven't we?"

It was just like her to throw facts in his face. But it *had* worked—keeping the lower Orders at one another's throats, the humans scrambling for prestige, and *everyone* but a precious few ignorant of what the cosmos beyond Okairos was really like—for centuries it had all worked. Now it was falling apart, and Connor was supremely annoyed. He kicked his feet up on Pasiphae's desk because he knew she hated it.

Sure enough, she glared. "Have you ever considered that perhaps they are unhappy in captivity—that this was all inevitable?"

"They aren't *captive*," he sputtered. "They are free to do whatever the hells they please!"

Pasiphae raised her eyebrows. "Humans are free to make as much money as they please, Connor, but their lives are hardly their own. You and I made sure of that."

He hated that she was right. "It's never been ideal, but the alternative..."

"You don't need to school me on the alternative," Pasiphae bit out. "I was there. I remember the price we paid. Never forget that I saw it all—unlike your precious Aislin."

Connor stood in frustration, unable to stay still any longer, and resumed his pacing. He had to get himself under control. Now was not the time for a power struggle with Pasiphae. She served her purpose, and he needed her—for now. "Perhaps we've given the Order of Night too much leeway. Too many privileges."

"I'm certain Rakul's presence in Falcyra will correct that," Pasiphae mused. "Berith Sanvier will not be pleased."

The business with Berith's protégé, Olivia, had been messy, and beyond treasonous once she'd kidnapped Finbar. Finn was troublesome with all his nonsense about helping humans, but he was still Connor's *son*. A foolish son, full of the idealistic vigor of youth, to be sure. But those ideals, Finn's obvious penchant for leadership, and his love for the people of Okairos was exactly what Connor needed to keep the peace. He would be the monster so his son could be the shining hero; he'd always been willing to play that role, and now was no different.

Pasiphae cleared her throat. *Had she asked him a question?* "I said, Berith is already causing problems. There's dissension in the House of Remiel. Some vampires reportedly think we aren't fit to rule. They're discussing it openly."

Connor shook with grim laughter. "Berith won't last the summer. I let him live so that your people could find out all they could about our incubus problem, but I won't suffer a traitor in our midst."

Pasiphae sighed, opening her planner and jotting down a few notes. "Fine. I'll schedule a termination team. Athan as well?"

"End them all. Every single one that questioned the sanctity of our power," Connor replied, releasing the tension that had been building in his chest all morning. Nothing calmed him quite so much as tying up loose ends. Pasiphae pushed his coffee towards him and he took a long sip. He'd finally cooled down.

CHAPTER ONE

T he arched plaster ceiling blurred in Harlow's vision, as
the sound of waves filled her ears. Her skin beaded
with sweat and her head lolled back on the impossibly
soft pile of pillows beneath her. Août had been the hottest
month of summer in Nea Sterlis yet, and she'd gotten a bit too
much sun on her walk back from the Alabaster Citadel. Harlow
had to admit she was ready for fall and missing Nuva Troi. Her
sunburnt shoulders stung against the silky sheets.

Strong hands pushed her dress to her waist, cool fingers
teasing her inner thighs open. "Want me to heal that sunburn?"
Finn asked before pressing his lips to her calf. He could, of
course. All Illuminated could heal minor injuries—cuts, bruises,
and the like.

Her breath caught in her throat as he kissed his way up her
left leg. "Sure," she whimpered as one finger dragged across the
thin fabric of her panties so lightly she wanted to scream.

Her shoulders stopped stinging immediately, a cool rush of
relief, as her core heated beneath his touch. The contrast of hot
and cold, relief and frustration, sent her into a frenzy of desire.

Her head lifted to beg for more, and Finn's eyes, the color of a stormy sea, met hers, sparkling with wicked resolve.

They were meant to be downstairs, in the Vault, training. She was supposed to be trying to turn into the avian creature, the Feriant, that she'd turned into the night of the Solstice Gala. Except nothing they'd tried for the entire summer had worked. No matter what they did, Harlow couldn't shift into the Feriant again. She was supposed to be training her abilities with her shadows, too, but Harlow had come home frustrated. Nothing had turned up at the Citadel libraries today either, and she'd been to three different ones. They'd come to Nea Sterlis to get away from Nuva Troi, yes, but also for information, and so far all they'd done was fail.

They'd spent almost the entire summer in the same routine: Harlow attempted to research sorcière with abilities that were considered outliers to the usual talents, anomalous shifters, limenal magic, anything that might give her a clue how to turn into the Feriant, while Finn tried to find out more via the Knights of Serpens' network. Nothing had turned up, and each passing day was more frustrating than the last in that regard.

She'd left that morning for the Citadel without waking him. He'd been out late, meeting with one of the city's oldest vampires to talk about incubi lore—they were still trying to find out just how the House of Remiel had revived the infamous creatures—and she hadn't wanted to disturb him. But she'd received a series of texts when she broke for lunch that promised this torture, and more, for leaving without so much as a kiss.

Now she closed her eyes, reveling in the way the light touch of his fingers on her inner thighs sent delicious chills up her spine. A drop of sweat rolled down the arch of her back as Finn dragged her panties aside, exposing her to the heat of his breath. The scent of her arousal filled the air, and he groaned as his mouth met her clit.

Apparently, he couldn't wait either. His tongue caressed her, softly at first, then harder as his fingers plunged into her, curling upward to the spot that made her cry out with each thrust into her. He'd been naked, fresh from the shower, when she'd returned to their rooms in Cian Herrington's cliff-side villa, and now she was glad of it.

Her eyes opened as his mouth left her, and she marveled at the way his skin glowed with the effects of the summer sun and his desire for her. Her legs spread wider as he licked his fingers clean of her.

"Touch yourself," he breathed, his deep voice sending a thrill of ecstasy through her as she obliged, rubbing tight circles around her wet clit.

Finn watched, a wanton smile covering his face as he pulled the neckline of her sundress down to expose her breasts. He stroked the length of his cock a few times, liquid beading at the tip, which he swirled over the head as he lowered himself onto her.

He slid into her easily, stretching her open as he moved. His mouth crashed into hers as their bodies met, filling her with his cock, his tongue, his love. Her hips rose as she wrapped her legs and arms around him, letting the friction between them take over the work her hand had been doing. Around her, her shadows gathered as he thrust harder, meeting her wordless begging for *more, harder, faster.*

The light he emitted grew stronger, twining with the magic she produced. Flashes of that light filled her eyes and his fangs scraped her neck, directly above the throbbing artery that begged to be pierced. She knew better than to ask him to bite her now, but she wanted it.

Harlow craved the Claiming more each day, and she knew Finn did too. She felt it in the desperate way he fucked her. They both came hard, her insatiable desire reflected in his eyes as he slowed in her.

She kissed him, squeezing his cock inside her. "We can't go on this way much longer," she murmured. "We both need it."

He brushed a piece of damp hair from her forehead, rocking gently against her, stimulating her swollen, sensitive flesh. Already, she felt him getting harder inside her. Neither of them were fully satisfied with one orgasm, or even two or three anymore. It hadn't been this bad when they first arrived in Nea Sterlis, but the more time they spent together, the closer they got, the more the Claiming seemed to taunt them.

"I know," he replied. "It's not that I don't want to..."

Harlow knew it wasn't. They'd been over this a thousand times—it had started with Finn's worry about the way it would bind them to one another, and what the consequences might be. There wasn't evidence of how the Claiming might affect them both, since she was not one of the Illuminated. They had talked it over with Thea and Alaric a dozen times, but Thea had never triggered Alaric's venom. Apparently, their situation was totally different. As deeply in love with one another as they were, they had experienced nothing like this.

Finn kissed her forehead and then rolled off her, flopping on the bed next to her. Her skin was so sensitive, she nearly cried. He was clearly ready for another round, and so was she. She pulled off her panties, tossing them on the floor as she climbed on top of him.

His breath quickened as she slid her wet center over his hard length, pulling her sundress over her head as her hips moved.

"I missed you," he growled, his cock pushing into her swollen, wet flesh without resistance. He pulled her hips down harder each time she rose and fell above him, her breasts bouncing as her back bowed with the pleasure of riding him as rigorously as she could.

The desire to be Claimed raged through her. She needed more from him. It was all she could think: *more, more, more.* "Shift," she begged. "Please."

The fire in Finn's eyes blazed as his humanoid form fell away. And then beneath her, and inside her, was a creature so powerful she thought she might be able to resist the Claiming another day. She whimpered as his cock grew inside her, filling her so completely she thought she might not be able to take more.

Beneath him, the three sets of wings that she'd first seen on the train from Nuva Troi spread out on the bed, the same opalescent color of his skin in his true form. Harlow blushed for a moment, embarrassed as she remembered that first time she'd seen Finn's true form. She'd thought he had scales, like a dragon. Now she knew that what she'd mistaken for scales, in her exhaustion after the nightmare in the House of Remiel basement, was a part of Finn's illumination she'd never imagined possible. His desire for her lit him up from within, his skin flashing like a fire opal in the dim light of the bedroom.

The Illuminated got their name from the way their eyes and skin glowed in intense, emotional moments in their humanoid alternae, but in their true form, the effect was that much more incandescent. Finn sat up and his wings sprang out—cocooning the two of them as their movement slowed. The flashing light in his wings made her feel like they were at the center of a kaleidoscope. He was stronger and larger in this body, so they had to be careful at first. She rolled her hips slowly, getting used to the increased length inside her.

Finn's long fingers dug into her hair at the nape of her neck with one hand, and pressed against her lower back with the other, sliding down to grab her ass. She arched harder, slamming into him, the reverberations of his giant cock vibrating through her into her bones.

The growl that roared from his throat was primal and his fangs glinted as he pulled her hair, exposing her neck. As he dragged his teeth over her, teasing her with the promise of further exquisite penetration, a long cry built in her chest, tumbling from her lips.

"Claim me," she begged, forgetting all the reasons they had to be cautious. "Make me yours."

She saw it in his eyes. He'd lost his last reservation, or at least his last shred of control. His tongue grazed over her throat. "It will hurt at first," he said, his voice thick with desire as he rooted deeper inside her.

Unable to form words, she nodded her consent. His mouth fell open, his fangs elongating as he pulled her closer. Both their phones blared. It was their family alarm, the one no one was allowed to ignore. Finn's mouth snapped shut as he drew away from her.

Harlow whimpered, her needy body clenching around him. "Please," she murmured. "Can't we just—"

Finn's expression mirrored her anguish and for a moment she thought he'd keep going, but the alarm continued. He shuddered as his arm snaked out to the bedside table, pulling both their phones to him so quickly she barely saw him move.

"It's Indigo," he said. "She and Nox found something. We need to get down to the Vault."

Harlow wanted to scream. The ache inside her, the raw need to connect deeper, was insatiable. She forced new air into her lungs, deep into her belly. "Head down without me. I need to rinse off." When he frowned, she sighed. "I won't wash my hair, but if no one's dying, then I can at least rinse off."

Finn's mouth twisted slightly, as though he wanted to say something. On a rational level, she understood all the reasons they'd waited on the Claiming, but her body told another story entirely. Her muscles, her skin, her blood were all burning, set ablaze with an unquenchable desire for him. She saw it in his eyes, felt it in the way his fingers tightened around her. He felt it too.

"You need a minute," he finally said.

Harlow averted her eyes. "I do. I don't bounce back as quickly as you."

It was true. Every time they were together lately, it didn't matter how many times she came; it was never enough, and it sometimes took her hours to settle down to something normal. Even now, she felt her heartbeat throbbing through her core, pulsing around him. With an expression of the sweetest remorse, he lifted her off him. She did her best to ignore the sight of his enormous alien body, shimmering in the afternoon light with sweat and the slick remains of their encounter.

Finn kissed her eyes and cheeks. "I love you."

Her heart swelled to hear it. "I love you too," she whispered, her heartbeat slowing a measure. This wild desire drove her nearly out of her mind, but the love… The love grounded her in a way nothing ever had.

Finn's wings folded behind him as he kissed her. Then he shifted, moving at that annoying Illuminated speed, zipping through the bedroom until he wore a pair of lightweight joggers, an old surfboard brand's t-shirt and a pair of flip-flops. His skin was golden once more, burnished by the sun. His hair had grown over the summer, and it flopped into his face even more than usual. He'd let Larkin paint his nails black a few nights ago when she did her own, and it was chipping a little already. Harlow sighed as he pushed her toward the bathroom; he looked good enough to eat.

"Shower," he insisted as he slid a pair of horn-rimmed glasses on. He needed them to read, and she thought it was adorable that his Illuminated body didn't somehow correct his eyesight for him. Some things had limits, she supposed.

His gaze lingered on her for a moment longer than necessary, as she smiled at him. "You could join me in the shower."

"*Fuck*," he drawled from the doorway, as if unable to find other words. Then his arms were around her, his mouth on hers, devouring her whole.

He pinned her against the wall, his body caging hers. Her legs went around his waist as she pushed his joggers down. As the head of his cock pushed between her still-drenched folds, their phones both rang again.

Finn groaned in her mouth. "Damn you, sillies." She nodded in agreement as he pulled out of her, rearranging his clothes. His lips brushed her cheek, then her jaw, his tongue grazing the shell of her ear. "Promise you'll think about me in the shower."

Harlow's mouth went dry, but he disappeared so fast she didn't have time to drag him into the bathroom with her. Feeling supremely unsatisfied, Harlow piled her long blonde hair into a messy bun and headed toward the bathroom for a hair tie. Meline had finally taught her how to make it look like all the influencers on socials and she was perpetually pleased that she could pull her hair up without looking like a slob. She turned the shower on before hunting for a hair elastic.

When she found said accoutrement in a drawer of the enormous marble-covered vanity, she fixed the pile of hair atop her head and stepped into the shower, admiring the view of the ocean out the window in their enormous bathroom. Cian Herrington's ancient family villa was nothing short of breathtaking, with a wide view of the cerulean water that surrounded this part of the coast from nearly every window. The best part was that there were nearly a dozen terraces, both covered and uncovered, to lounge and relax on.

To even the keenest observer, it appeared the Kranes were having a rather lovely summer holiday. Finn surfed nearly every day, and the twins sunned frequently on every available terrace, lunching in town with fellow Order darlings most days of the week. Socials, gossips, and the newspapers, alive and well in Nea Sterlis, had gone wild over the twins' sense of style and they were closely followed. The maters attended starlit rituals in the Alabaster Citadel, and dinners hosted by the city's elite sorcière. Thea and Alaric made a big show of enjoying their "elopement" and the media covered them frequently as well.

Harlow was still an object of ridicule, unfortunately. Apparently, the clicks on Section Seven's "Harlow Krane is Over" campaign had been too good *not* to continue trashing everything from her fashion choices to her coffee order. The gossips speculated wildly and incessantly about her and Finn's relationship, and even Axel from time to time. Just last week she and Finn had nearly asphyxiated laughing over what seemed to be an earnest pondering about the cat's life of luxury. What sort of treats did he enjoy? Was he a fan of fresh fish, or was he allergic? It was all too much.

The only piece of luck she could identify was that Mark's death had only been news for about a week. The news claimed he and Olivia died in the House of Remiel fire and that Alain Easton was overseas, deep in mourning, not missing. Harlow was a touch surprised that the humans hadn't seemed that interested in Mark's death, but they often had a strange relationship with their own. One week, a human was interesting to the masses, and the next, they were done with them entirely. Perhaps it was something about the fleeting nature of their lives that caused them to be so fickle, but Harlow was supremely grateful for it. And certainly no one had mentioned the House of Remiel turning humans into incubi. Thankfully, the creatures remained nothing more than scary lore for most of the world.

Harlow rinsed, standing under the water for a few moments longer than necessary to get completely clean. Memories of the night she'd killed her ex haunted her—though not as much as she'd expected. Riley and Enzo both had helped her come to terms with what she'd been forced to do and the nightmares had slowed down, as had the intrusive thoughts, but she couldn't erase the fear she felt that night. The realization that Mark had been changing before they'd even broken up bothered her now —that and the fact that she couldn't shift again.

She'd begged Finn over and over to bite her again, since that had triggered the change the night she'd killed Mark, but he'd refused. He said he was worried about accidentally initiating the

Claiming, but Harlow sensed there was more to it. She understood Finn wasn't maliciously keeping secrets from her. It was more that they'd spent seven years apart, and he had an entire organization's secrets hoarded away, and for good reason.

If the Illuminated knew what the Knights of Serpens were up to with the Haven Project, Harlow feared they'd not only shut it down, but execute everyone involved. It was more than just safe house cafes, like the one in Nuva Troi. There was a network of people who helped those who were victims of the Immortal Orders. It was a noble cause, one she was proud to be a part of, but it could get them all killed.

So she tried to be patient. It was difficult not to grill Finn about everything he was keeping from her when she couldn't do the one thing that might protect all of them: shift into the Feriant. The night of the House of Remiel fire, she hadn't truly understood that a newly made incubus was stronger than one of the Illuminated. But now, after looking through the recorded lore in the Vault about the incubi, it was easy to understand why making them was outlawed: they could cause significant harm to the Illuminated. Maybe even kill them. And with Alain Easton, Mark's father, still unaccounted for, Harlow *needed* to turn into the Feriant.

The glass shower door was cool against her forehead as she shut the water off, forcing air through her lungs in even drafts. *Why couldn't she shift again?* Alain Easton could be *anywhere*, and all signs pointed to the fact that he'd also been turned—and she'd killed his son. Even Alaric, who unfailingly believed the best about people, agreed it was likely that at some point he would come for Harlow and Finn. The possibilities about what might happen if she couldn't shift were dizzying.

Outside the bathroom, she heard a soft knock on the bedroom door. "Come in," she called, forcing herself out of the shower. Quickly, she dried off and slid into one of the long, silky sundresses Enzo was prototyping. This one was a beautiful emerald shade, even though prints were *en vogue* for the summer. All the solid color samples had made their way into her closet, as Harlow did not enjoy loud prints.

When she entered the bedroom, Cian Herrington was standing on the balcony, staring at the sailboats in the little bay. "Your sister found evidence that someone purged the Night's Own Blood Banks' master records. They erased all evidence of families with a history of Gene-I, going back nearly fifty years."

CHAPTER TWO

This was the big news Indi had? They'd assumed something like this would happen, but from the look on Cian's face, it wasn't the full scope of the news. The firedrake shifter was dressed sharply in pressed linen pants, canvas loafers, and a tank top with an artistically rendered alligator on it. Sunglasses rested atop their head, nestled in their shock of silvery blonde hair. Today they wore a little neon yellow eyeliner, just on the inner corners of their eyes.

Harlow sighed. There was no way she'd ever be as effortlessly chic as the ancient immortal. Cian grinned as they turned, leaning on the railing. "I love all these sundresses Enzo's made for you. But why are your sisters all wearing such gaudy prints? All except my precious Larkin, of course."

A small laugh bubbled out of her chest, breaking up the tension the rush of thoughts in the shower had brought up. "Of course, precious Larkin can do no wrong."

Cian raised their eyebrows. "You disagree?"

Harlow bumped Cian's shoulder. "Quite the opposite. I am so glad you and Larkin have grown to be such good friends."

They really had, ever since Harlow's youngest sister had discovered that while Cian did harbor romantic and sexual feelings towards partners, it took them a long time to develop them. As Larkin explored her lack of sexual and romantic feelings, she'd appreciated getting to know the people in her life who experienced something similar. The culture of the Immortal Orders was so focused on pairing and producing progeny that for those who did not have that drive, it could be an isolating experience.

Harlow was glad that Larkin had expressed herself early enough in her life that she could find a strong community of others like herself, even as supported as she was within her own family. Everyone needed friends who understood them deeply, and Larkin was no different. Her friendship with Cian had started with mutual understanding and respect, and grew from there into long talks about their love of classical music and books Harlow considered unbearably dull. She was glad they had each other. Larkin had always struggled to make friends outside their family and it was good to see her connect with someone who shared her interests.

The sound of waves in the small cove beneath the balcony mixed with the whispering of the wind through the needles of the mix of conifers that dotted the rocky cliff face. The scent of the sun-warmed pine needles and salt air combined into a perfume that sent Harlow into a near-instant state of bliss. She was so sensitive to any sensual stimuli these days; everything either grated on her nerves or brought her intense pleasure.

Before the scent of trees could distract her further, she interrupted her own train of thought. "Now, about these 'gaudy' prints... Have you *seen* the curtains in the billiards room?" They were an awful olive green and orange stripe that Aurelia claimed gave her a migraine.

Cian shrugged, keen eyes observing the flush in her cheeks. They pushed away from the railing and headed toward the bedroom door, apparently agreeing to play along with this line of conversation. "I didn't pick them out, my decorator did."

Harlow raised an eyebrow as she followed. "Seventy years ago?"

Cian snorted as they looped her arm through theirs, leading her down the enormous marble staircase at the center of the house. "All right, they're ugly curtains."

Harlow hummed a noncommittal response. Her skin had gone instantly cold inside the house, although it was only mildly cooler than the balcony had been. She shivered.

Cian rubbed her arm, warming her with their hands, but didn't remark on yet another of Harlow's mysterious sensitivities. "They're the *ugliest* curtains. Happy?"

It was Harlow's turn to snort. Like Larkin, she and Cian had fallen into an easy friendship over their summer together, ribbing one another relentlessly like siblings, despite their vast age difference, and laughing late into the evening many nights. Cian felt like family, as much as her sisters or Enzo did.

She tripped over the hem of her dress. Cian caught her before she stumbled down the marble staircase. When she'd righted herself, she asked, "What else did Indi find?"

Next to her, she felt the muscles in Cian's sinewy arm tighten. "There's more trouble in Falcyra."

Nothing seemed amiss on public channels. All the gossips out of Falcyra showed people staying in luxury treehouses overlooking the fjords, partying in Austvanger's glamorous rooftop gardens, or traveling further north to observe the arctic bears and the *limenara borealis*. However, there had been increasing back channel reports on the dark web about what was really happening in Falcyra, though the Wraiths, Arebos and Nox Flynn, hadn't been able to pin anything down—until today, apparently. What they knew for sure was that Falcyra's humans weren't taking their vampire overlord's governing without question anymore, but so far nothing had made it into the mainstream news.

"Something's been confirmed?"

Cian nodded. "Yes, there's rioting in Austvanger. The humans may have burned the Governor's Mansion down last week, but we're still cleaning up the footage. Indi found records of it in the trail she's opened. The Illuminated sent the Dominavus. Rakul took lead."

Harlow's heart skipped a beat. Rakul Kimaris was a legend. He'd spent most of Harlow's life overseas and had led every rumored cleanup for nearly a hundred years. Things rarely went wrong when the Illuminated decreed something should go one way or another, but if they did, the Dominavus—a small, elite crew of immortals—took care of things. When they solved something, it stayed solved. But none of that was why she reacted the way she did.

They'd nearly reached the basement door, where the secret entrance to the Vault was located, and Harlow stopped Cian. "Why is this important to us, other than the fact that the riots in Falcyra are worth watching?"

Cian's pale eyes narrowed. "Because Rakul Kimaris is the only living Knight of Serpens from the envoy. He fought with us in the Great War... And he was the one that sold us all out to the Illuminated."

That shocked Harlow deeply, and it must have shown in the involuntary shudder that passed through her.

"Are you all right?" Cian asked as they opened the door to the basement and pressed their hand to the metal plate next to it.

The door opened with a soft swishing sound. Harlow passed through, descending into the wood paneled staircase that dove deep into the cliff the villa sat on. "I had a strange experience with Rakul when I was a child."

They walked through what appeared to be a wine cellar until

they reached the tasting room. Cian punched numbers into the walk-in refrigerator and, once inside, swung back a shelf to reveal a secret door. Harlow pressed her own hand to the metal plate next to the entryway. It took two verified Knights, or their affiliates, to open the Vault, and Finn had made Harlow an affiliate at the last dark moon. The doors opened and Cian followed her through.

The next set of stairs was much darker, lit by dim sconces on the rough stone wall, and wound deep into the subterranean depths of the Vault—the headquarters of the Knights of Serpens. Over the summer, Harlow had learned much more about their current operations, but still felt she didn't know the extent to which the organization had power. One of the primary policies the Knights adhered to was "just in time" knowledge, meaning that no one knew more than they needed to until exactly the right moment. It was frustrating and occasionally felt unnecessarily secretive, but because their organization was deeply seditious, it made sense.

"What happened?" Cian asked.

"I was on an initiatory trip to the catacombs, under the Order of Mysteries' primary offices, six months before my thirteenth birthday."

Cian smiled fondly. "I bet little witchling Harlow was adorable."

"I was a fool, and an incredibly clumsy child—not much different from now, really. Anyway, Lorcan Greenbriar dared me to walk out onto the Ledge of Wishes..."

"Oh, dear..." Cian said, trailing off.

Lore around the Ledge of Wishes was well known throughout the Orders. The stories said that if you could make it to the end of the Ledge, Ashbourne could hear your voice in the depths of the limen—the realm between all worlds where aether, the force that made magic possible, resided. Supposedly, sound carried straight into the fabled prison of Nihil, where Ashbourne the Warden would grant you a wish. It was a ridiculous legend, come to think of it.

Why would a prison warden grant wishes? It didn't really matter—no one ever made it that far, because the ledge was made of slippery crystal and most witches turned back before it got dangerous. "I wasn't even that far out, but I slid and couldn't stop, heading straight for the edge—and then—like magic, I was caught up in powerful arms and dragged back to my friends."

It made little sense before, how he'd appeared in thin air above her, but now she understood that he'd used his true form. Like Finn, under the humanoid exterior, Rakul Kimaris must have three sets of draconic wings. It had seemed like an absolute miracle. The group of chaperones had chalked it up to Illuminated speed, but Harlow had always known something else was happening. It was satisfying to recognize the truth.

Cian caught her arm, looking shocked. "Are you saying Rakul Kimaris *saved* you from falling off the Ledge?"

Harlow nodded, slightly surprised that Cian didn't expect more from Rakul, but of course, the ancient shifter probably had a much different perspective on him than she did. "Yes, and he said the oddest thing to me. I thought I'd never forget it... I'm actually surprised I didn't remember until now..."

Her brow furrowed. At the time, it had made no sense. She'd just thought Rakul was strange. But now...

"Well," Cian insisted. "What did he say to you?"

"He said, *careful hatchling, your wings aren't yet strong enough to carry you from the abyss.*"

Cian's pale eyes went wide and Harlow thought she glimpsed the silver firedrake that slept inside them, if only for a moment. "Did anyone hear him?"

Harlow shook her head. "I don't think so. Why?"

"There weren't many Knights and Striders like you and Finn in the Feriant Legion. Most of them were deeply platonic partnerships. But a few were in love and had children. They called their children hatchlings. It was... not widely known."

Now Harlow's heart had stopped completely. She looked up to find Finn waiting at the bottom of the stairs, and from the look on his face, he'd heard every word of Harlow's story. Power vibrated through him as his eyes smoldered with lethal force. "Are you suggesting that Rakul Kimaris knows what Harlow is?"

Cian nodded, face grave with concern. "I think we have to assume he does."

Harlow couldn't see the issue. "But he saved me. Wouldn't he have let me fall if he were a traitor like you said? Or have told one of the Illuminated about me?"

Cian sat down on the steps. "Ten minutes ago I would have said yes, without question. But now... Now I wonder."

Finn took Harlow's hand, and she looked up into his worried eyes. "Don't worry," he said. "I can protect you from Rakul, if it comes to that."

"I don't think he'd hurt me, Finn," she said. "He saved my life. He was kind. Strange, but kind."

She didn't think it was a good idea to mention that she'd dreamed of bonding with Rakul for years, before learning just how old he actually was. He hadn't looked a day over twenty-five to her, dashing in his flexible body armor, with long black hair tied in a plait down his back.

"What was he doing in the catacombs, anyway?" Cian asked. "He shouldn't have been allowed in there."

Harlow shrugged. "You'd have to ask the maters."

CHAPTER THREE

Selene passed by, carrying a tray of hot tea from the Vault's state-of-the-art kitchen. She pushed through a pair of steel-paned glass doors, into the conference room, which was really more like a giant living room. "Ask us what?"

"Why was Rakul Kimaris in the Order of Mysteries the day I fell from the Ledge of Wishes?"

Selene sat the tray down on the enormous sun-bleached driftwood coffee table that sat at the center of four buttery soft, navy blue leather couches. The conference room was mostly dark glass and black marble, a bit of sleek modernity in the ancient subterranean archives. The plush red patterned rug that covered the glossy floors was antique, and the couches were obscenely comfortable and could fit their entire entourage, though no one else was here yet.

Selene poured tea into a stoneware mug and handed it to Harlow, while Finn and Cian made themselves comfortable. Her face softened as she looked at her second-eldest daughter, as though remembering the child she'd been. "I'd forgotten about that. He saved you, didn't he?"

Harlow supposed that with over six hundred years of memories and five daughters, Selene Krane was allowed to forget a few things. She'd lost track of the memory herself, after all.

Selene's big green eyes, nearly identical to Harlow's, narrowed as she scraped her memory for information. "If I remember correctly, he was there for the last of the yearly inspections."

Harlow's face twisted in confusion. "Yearly inspections?"

Finn cringed. "Yes, my father used to have Rakul and the Dominavus inspect all the Orders' headquarter buildings once a year as an intimidation technique. It ended when we were children after a rather long bout of negotiations."

Selene nodded, handing Finn and Cian both mugs of their own. "Yes. It's interesting though—now that you mention it, Rakul was always very kind when he came to the Order of Mysteries."

Selene sat, crossing her legs. She too wore one of Enzo's new designs, a long, loose gown with flowing sleeves in a beautiful, dark floral pattern. Cian raised their eyebrows at Harlow as if to say *gaudy print*. Harlow ignored their antics and refocused on what Mama had to say.

"Merhart Locklear used to complain that the Dominavus were unruly and rude at the Order of Masks, but with us, they were polite. Quick about their business and gone. It was an inconvenience, but not nearly as bad as the other Orders made it seem."

Conversation stalled when Indigo and the Wraith, Nox Flynn, entered together carrying laptops. Indigo hardly looked like herself today, or at least the version of herself that had inhabited Nuva Troi last spring. She wore a pair of wide-legged linen pants and a cropped tank top, with her dark hair piled atop her head—and she was wearing her glasses. Over the summer, she'd relaxed more than Harlow had ever seen, no longer looking like the perfectly coiffed society darling that she'd appeared to be in Nuva Troi. Harlow liked the way her sister's style seemed to have evolved into something more comfortable for her. While she'd always been interested in fashion and society happenings, just as Meline was, Harlow had always wondered how much of that was their twin bond, and how much was truly Indi.

Harlow caught Nox checking out Indi's rear as she sat and nearly groaned. The two of them were wild about each other, but unlike Meline and Nox's brother Arebos, who were open about their flirtation whenever Ari reported in, Indi and Nox were desperately pining. Nox caught Harlow watching her, and the tips of her ears got pink and then disappeared completely. The Wraith's faintly arched ears reappeared, and she bit her bottom lip nervously.

Ari and Nox Flynn were rare shifters who could shift into the very scenery of any location, rendering themselves completely invisible, but Harlow hadn't seen either of them use their talents very often. It was adorable to see that the talent could manifest in a moment of embarrassment. Somehow it made Nox, who was imposing otherwise, seem more relatable. Harlow flashed her sister's love interest a conspiratorial grin. She'd never dream of calling either of them out. As open as the twins were about things on their socials, Indi was remarkably private, and she'd be mortified if anyone teased Nox or her for their shy courting.

"Where's Meli?" Harlow asked.

"She, Thea and Larkin are shopping this afternoon," Nox replied, after pulling up the family calendar and checking. Nox had insisted on creating a detailed calendar that coordinated a steady stream of frivolous-looking activity here in Nea Sterlis, especially for the younger Krane girls and the maters, who were all known for being naturally social.

As for Harlow, she wasn't going out much in social situations. Section Seven had been especially cruel about her since the season. While her sisters and the maters were objects of interest and speculation, they seemed to get their kicks out of ridiculing everything from her fashion choices to the expressions she made. They didn't feature her any more or less than anyone else in the family, but the tone they used made it hard to take.

Selene added, "And Li-li is having lunch with the new Order of Mysteries treasury board today, so we'll catch her up later."

The maters had used the summer wisely, gaining supporters in the Order of Mysteries. The plan they'd proposed for dealing with the Illuminated's lax control over the Order of Night was to ally with key members of the Order of Mysteries and the Order of Masks and stage a confrontation and a vote at the Council of Orders that would take place on the Winter Solstice. Harlow had her doubts that having a polite argument with the Illuminated and the vampires was the way to solve Okairos' growing problems, but she understood why the maters wanted to try this route first.

Selene looked around. "Where's Alaric and Petra?"

"Here," Petra said, brushing a kiss to Selene's cheek as she and Alaric rolled in. Selene and Aurelia had essentially adopted Petra since arriving in Nea Sterlis and hearing about how her parents had disowned her. They were the worst of the Illuminated in some ways, ancient, bigoted, and completely removed from the world. Petra's parents rarely socialized with anyone from even the lower Orders, keeping their circle tightly governed to other Illuminated. The little Petra had told Harlow about them was sad—her friend's childhood had been lonely but for her cousin Alaric and Finn, as she hadn't been allowed to make friends from the lower Orders. It warmed Harlow to see Petra accepted into her family.

When everyone settled in, sipping their tea, Indigo caught them up on what she and Nox had uncovered. It was all as Cian had said, but apparently there was more. "The order was there for Rakul and the Dominavus to go to Falcyra, but when we checked into it, he's not there."

Nox watched Indigo closely as she spoke, as though every

word that fell from her lips was a gift from Aphora, before adding, "The Dominavus are in Falcrya. We confirmed that. But no one has seen Rakul."

Next to her on the couch, Harlow felt Finn's muscles tense and his hand gravitated toward her knee. She knew he was thinking of what she'd told Cian just minutes ago. "Where is he?"

"We don't know," Indigo said, her brow wrinkling in frustration. "It's like he's disappeared into thin air. But all we've got is the operatives' accounts right now. Footage from the riots is still processing through the decryption software... There's a lot of it."

Alaric sighed. "That's not like Kimaris. Keep looking."

Nox nodded, getting up. "I'm going to go use the central computer for a while. My laptop doesn't have enough juice for this kind of covert digging in the CCTV archives. The riot footage should be out of decryption shortly."

Indi nodded, checking a timer on her phone. "It's slowed down, but we should have something soon. There's something else..." Indigo hesitated.

"What is it, darling?" Selene asked in a clipped tone, clearly impatient.

Indigo glanced at Nox. "You can explain it better than me."

Nox shook her dark head. "You could explain it just fine."

Indigo blushed and Harlow felt everyone in the room inwardly rolling their eyes with secondhand embarrassment. The two of them were something else. Before anyone could urge them to get to the point, Nox succumbed to Indi's pleading eyes and explained.

"There's been some unique pressure on the wards here at the villa. Someone is probing us." The shifter crossed her legs, looking slightly frustrated. "But they're doing it in a really blunt, obvious way."

"Amateurs?" Alaric asked, one of his dark eyebrows raised.

Indi grimaced a little, her shoulders raising slightly. "Maybe, but the analysis I've done on the probes is anomalous. I'd like to have Enzo look at it when he comes back, if that's okay with you. He's better with complex spellwork than most of us."

Alaric glanced at Harlow and Selene, looking somewhat dubious. Mama nodded. "It's true. Enzo may be a designer, but he's a Weraka, and the entire family has an aptitude for understanding spells. His mother was a prodigy, and she always said he took after her."

Sorcière rarely needed spells, as most pulled aether through the unseen threads of reality that made up all things living and inanimate on Okairos to weave changes, but some workings were too big for that kind of magic. If pulling threads was like embroidering a pillow, then spells were like weaving a giant tapestry. Many threads were engaged, and anchors like herbs, gemstones, and other natural objects had to be used in very specific ways to make spells work. Workings like effectively warding a secret subterranean vault of seditious information, while maintaining the appearance of an average warding, were just the kinds of spells that someone like Enzo needed to look at. Even Aurelia, who was the Kranes' expert in spells, would struggle.

Selene's eyes misted over at the mention of Enzo's mother. Maurice and Clarissa Weraka had been Aurelia and Selene's closest friends before they were killed in a terrible train accident when Enzo and Harlow were in secondary school. Finn placed his hand on Selene's arm, and she patted it, giving him a small smile. He sat forward, making eye contact with Alaric. "It's true. Enzo is as brilliant with spellwork as you are with tech. I think we should have him and Thea look together."

Alaric's head shook slightly. It was the most Harlow had ever seen him disagree with Finn. "We need Thea to stay focused on the restoration of the Merkhov book and the triptych."

Thea had been hard at work restoring the images in the

Merkhov text which they all believed to be a depiction of the relationship between Striders and the Knights of Serpens. She wasn't having much luck with the second and third images. Whatever was done to destroy them was magical in nature and complicated.

Finn nodded once. "All right then, see if you can get Enzo to look at what you've documented about the probes. It should be easy enough for you to work out, shouldn't it?"

Nox smirked at Finn, who had a glint in his eye that told Harlow they'd had conversations like these hundreds of times. She flashed a cocky smile. "Easy as pie."

Indi raised her eyebrows, eyes wide with earnestness. "Pie's kind of hard to make."

Nox's brown eyes went gooey again, like Indi's brand of open seriousness was the most adorable thing she'd ever seen. "Wanna go get back to work?"

Indi nodded, a flush coloring her cheeks pink. They walked off together, laughing softly at some private joke.

Selene checked her watch and then rose from the couch. "Petra, we need to get going if we're going to meet Li-li and the girls for drinks at the Obsidian. Harlow, darling, are you coming?"

The Obsidian was the most popular new club in Nea Sterlis this summer, a collaboration between the Order of Night and one of the human mafia families, if rumors were to be believed. But the way Section Seven had been targeting her lately didn't make it fun for her to go out in the evenings.

Harlow shook her head. "No, I'm going to stay here."

Petra brushed a quick kiss to Harlow's cheek as she followed Selene. "We need a pool day soon."

Harlow nodded and squeezed Petra's hand as she walked away, their arms stretching out between them. Axel passed Petra as she entered, wrapping his long black tail around her slender leg as she went, purring loudly at her in greeting before racing through the room, chasing some invisible prey. He must have come down with Selene earlier, and been napping in the work-room she and Aurelia shared in the back half of the Vault, where there were several rooms for offices and other work.

When it was only Harlow, Alaric, Cian, and Finn, she asked the question she'd been holding in the entire meeting. "Why did the Illuminated let Ducare and the Order of Night have Falcyra?"

Cian sat back, crossing one long leg over the other, their expression pointedly wry. "Well, the climate is perfect for vampires. Cold and cloudy. You know most of them hate a sunny day."

Harlow rolled her eyes. "What? That's not why."

Cian smirked as they kicked Harlow playfully. "No, but it's part of it."

Alaric, ever the diplomat, steered the conversation out of sarcastic territory. "Three hundred years ago, Gerard Ducare was getting out of hand here in Nytra. He wanted to rule the House of Remiel, but of course, the Sanviers wouldn't dream of giving up their power in Nytra."

"And Rosamund Penemue hated the Falcyrans," Finn added. "She was the Illuminated governor there before Ducare."

Harlow knew the name, but had never met Penemue, as she was usually called. "Isn't she some elite warrior?"

Alaric nodded. "Yes, she's one of the original envoy. But she's always said Falcyra is a backward country, obsessed with folklore, and far too liberal with their beliefs about human autonomy."

"But it was the white ash groves that did her in," Cian said. "There were rumors for years that Falcyra somehow has hidden white ash groves."

Harlow narrowed her eyes. "I've never heard that."

Finn shrugged. "The Illuminated don't like it to get around, of course. And we've never been able to find evidence that it was true. Nothing shows up on satellite, nor in any of the extensive ground searches that were done."

"But in Penemue's day, humans kept attempting to kill the Illuminated with weapons made from the stuff," Alaric said. "Eventually, my mother and Petra's parents, who were more involved in governing back then, decided that everyone might be safer if Ducare took over for Penemue."

"Thousands of vampires went with Gerard," Cian added. "Nobody talks about it much, but it made Nytra far safer for humans."

This was why Harlow had hesitated to ask her question in front of the group. She was embarrassed she didn't know all this, or the follow-up question she had. "So, are humans treated badly in other countries? Is that why they're rioting?"

Finn took her hand, his face patient. "Yes. It's much worse than in Nytra."

Harlow nodded, heart sinking. "It's bad enough here, despite...what people say."

"You can say it," Alaric said softly, his usually kind brown eyes hard. "Despite the Illuminated propaganda. Because that is what it has always been: propaganda. *Lies.*"

His words sunk in. Amidst all Alaric's good humor, sometimes he'd say something something so starkly justice-minded, that it shocked Harlow a bit. "We miss it all so easily," Harlow said, letting the idea ruminate a bit. "We look away when we travel. Why?"

Finn sighed deeply, squeezing her hand. "Because none of you are safe from us either."

The air seemed to go out of the room. Harlow appreciated that Finn didn't mask the fact that he too was a part of the threat, just by virtue of being one of the Illuminated, but it did nothing to make her feel better. Perhaps that was the point. Maybe trying to make things *feel better* for too long got everyone into this mess.

Harlow nodded, but Finn's words highlighted exactly why she needed to figure out how to shift, sooner rather than later. A time was coming when they'd have to fight, and she might be among their most effective weapons. Alaric and Cian exchanged glances with Finn, but he shook his head and changed the subject to discussing a tactical operation that one of the Knights' operatives was running in southern Falcyra, to get more information on the situation there. Harlow stopped paying attention.

They were using a lot of jargon she didn't understand, not being well-versed in intelligence gathering. Instead, she went over the little she'd learned about the Feriant in her head, adding her interaction with Rakul Kimaris to her cache of knowledge. She turned the memory over again and again, trying desperately to extract anything from it she might have missed.

CHAPTER FOUR

H arlow didn't realize she'd completely lost track of what was happening around her until she looked up to find that Alaric and Cian had left her alone with Finn. He was reading something on his phone, but when she moved, he looked up at her over his glasses. The lights in the conference room were soft, and the golden glow of the lamps shone on his dark hair.

"You okay?" he asked. "You kind of zoned out there."

She looked around. "Everyone left?"

Finn nodded. "Haven't seen you go deep inside yourself like that since we were kids."

Harlow nodded, feeling absentminded and scattered. "I was thinking about Rakul and the Ledge."

Finn set his phone down, shutting the screen off. "I thought you might be. Did you remember anything new?"

Harlow shook her head. "No, but with Alain Easton unaccounted for, everything going on in Falcyra, and what we're doing here... It seems like we should make my shift more of a priority."

A long moment passed, as though Finn was weighing her words. "I don't want to pressure you."

Of course he didn't. He didn't want her to feel like any of this depended on her. But in some ways, it did. She glanced at the clock hanging on the wall above the console table across from them. "We have time to get a bit of practice in. We could try that new meditation Cian mentioned yesterday."

Cian had been researching different ways to help shifters who'd lost their ability to access their alternae. It was a rare issue, but it happened occasionally, and they believed Harlow might focus her way into shifting.

"You hate the meditations," Finn said.

Harlow let out a wry laugh. "I don't hate them. I'm *terrible* at them."

Finn raised an eyebrow. "I can't understand how someone who can read a romance novel for a whole day can't sit still long enough to meditate."

Harlow rolled her eyes. "Romances are *exciting*, Finbar. Meditating is... not."

He dragged her by her ankle toward him and she let out a little squeal of laughter, but didn't resist as he pulled her into her arms, whispering in her ear, "Yeah? What's so *exciting* in a romance novel?"

The sound of his heart beating was a comfort, as she rested her head on his chest. "Maybe you should read one and find out."

He hummed a little, and his chest vibrated, sending shivers of delight through Harlow. "Only if you get me a smutty one."

"I think Indi and Meline have some of those monster romances. I've heard they're pretty smutty," Harlow said, waggling her eyebrows suggestively.

Finn rolled his eyes. "*Monsters*? Who would want to fuck monsters? Next you'll tell me there are incubi romances."

Harlow almost laughed, but her brain stumbled over what

he'd said. There *were* incubi romances, of course. Ones full of biting and mind control. After her experience with a real incubus last spring, she didn't find them very sexy at the moment. Maybe she'd feel differently in a few years—fiction about the things that scared you most could be healing. But right now, remembering was too much, too raw. Harlow's brain tripped again around the memory. There was something there, even if she didn't particularly want to look.

Thoughts swirled in her head for a moment, uncontrollable and disjointed. When they coalesced, it was so obvious she nearly slapped her forehead. She sat up to face Finn. "You have to bite me."

Finn shifted uncomfortably on the couch. "I'm not ready for the Claiming, Harlow. We've talked about this."

Standing, she tugged on his arm. "I'm not talking about *that*. I'm talking about what we did in the House of Remiel. You bit me."

He sighed. "We've talked about this. It's a dangerous line to walk. If you trigger my desire for you, it could set off the Claiming. I'm not ready for that."

Harlow's jaw clenched. "And if I can't turn into the Feriant, who will kill Alain Easton if he shows up here?"

It was Finn's turn for a clenched jaw, but irritated as it might make him, she knew he couldn't argue. The incubi were the only thing he had to fear, outside his parents. Even with Cian and Alaric here, they'd estimated that the best they could do was hold Alain off while everyone else ran. It was dangerous for her not to be able to shift, and they both knew it.

"We have to try," Harlow said. "You and I both know meditation isn't going to do it. You bit me in the House of Remiel and I shifted."

"It was a foolish move. A gut feeling," he said, looking down at his hands.

"And it's the only thing we haven't tried. If it doesn't work, I won't ask again."

Finn sighed. "Fine."

It surprised her that he agreed so quickly, but it confirmed her worries: they were running out of time to get the upper hand in the conflict that was surely brewing. He stood, and she followed him to the Vault's training room. The ceilings were high, accentuated with cedar beams and gentle lighting that made it feel like being outdoors, rather than deep underground. Mirrors lined three of the walls for practicing form, and the fourth was an arsenal of weaponry.

Finn stood at the center of the room and closed his eyes. "Give me a minute to calm down, and when I motion for you, come stand right here in front of me, just like we were that night."

Harlow nodded. "Then what?"

"I'll bite you—and hopefully the shift will take hold, the way it did on the Solstice. As soon as it does, tap my arm and I'll break my skin for you. Then you'll drink from me... If we've done it right, you'll shift."

"And if I don't?"

"Then stay absolutely still," Finn cautioned. "This is a volatile moment, and I'm going to try my best to stay calm. If my bite doesn't initiate the shift, ask me to stop, okay? But do it quietly, and whatever you do, don't pull away."

Harlow wondered if she ought to ask more questions about why that was necessary, but she was afraid if she did, he'd simply refuse to try this, so she nodded. He closed his eyes and took deep, cleansing breaths. She watched as he rolled his muscular shoulders. Muscle group by muscle group relaxed. Harlow was wretched at meditation, but Finn—well, Finn was great at it. A small smile played on her lips as she watched him. Everything about him was beautiful.

When he flicked a finger at her, she did as he'd asked, walking slowly to stand in front of him, facing the giant mirrors that surrounded them. She'd always thought the mirrors were a little mesmerizing, but now, as she watched Finn's fangs protract, it was difficult to stay calm. It wasn't fear she felt, but she knew she had to tamp her desire down quickly, or Finn would stop.

His eyes were closed as his mouth latched around her neck. The bite was fast and painful, with none of the ecstasy she'd felt in the House of Remiel basement the night she'd killed Mark. This just *hurt*. Finn's fingers dug into her waist as he took draw after draw of her blood. His venom burned through the wound.

Nothing happened on her end. The euphoria she'd experienced the last time they'd done this never appeared. She was practically distraught, but she did as Finn asked and stayed still. "It's not working," she whispered.

He didn't respond. In the mirror, she saw his face, and it scared her. His eyes were predatory, burning with that Illuminated power.

"Finn," she said again, this time more forcefully. "It's not working. Let me go."

But he only gripped her harder. She felt faint.

"Finn!" she shouted, hysteria edging her voice.

Behind her, he snarled. The sound was vicious—like an animal approached while it was *eating*. Vampires lost control sometimes when they fed, becoming more predator than person. Harlow couldn't think through the mechanics of what was happening now. She struggled in Finn's arms, squealing like prey in the throes of death.

An icy voice broke her panic. "Finbar! Let Harlow go."

There was a long, tense moment when she thought Finn wouldn't stop, that perhaps nothing could stop him. His grip on her tightened. Though her vision was hazy, she could just make out his reflection in the mirror. He was staring at whoever was speaking, their eyes locked on one another. Behind her, he paused; his lips slowly pulling away from her skin. When his fangs retracted, her head slumped forward. She could not hold it up.

"Let her go," the voice said. Harlow's vision was still fuzzy, but she vaguely recognized the illustrated alligator floating in front of her. Cian. Cian was here now. "Let Harlow go, Finbar. You don't want to do this."

Finn's fingers loosened, and then she was falling. Before she could hit the floor, Cian caught her in strong, wiry arms. There was a thud behind her, and the sound of muffled cries. She twisted in Cian's grip to see Finn on his knees. He clutched at his hair, and his chest heaved with sobs. He was rocking back and forth, mumbling something to himself.

Not her. Not her. Not her. Not her.

She fought her way out of Cian's arms. They tried to stop her, but she had her arms wrapped around Finn before the fire-drake could catch hold of her. Cian kneeled on the floor next to them, observing as she gathered Finn into her arms.

"I'm so sorry, baby," she whispered.

Whatever had happened, whatever had gone wrong, she'd pushed him to do this, knowing he was scared. And now he crumpled on the floor, sobbing, and she didn't see the grown man she loved; she saw something of the deeply wounded child that lived within him.

His sobs slowed a little as she held him, rocking him gently back and forth. Cian's hand ran through Finn's hair and then moved to Harlow's face. Their silver eyes were full of tears. "He's not ready for this, Harlow. Outside the Claiming, the Illuminated should not consume others' blood."

Harlow's brow knit. "Why not? I thought they were like vampires... Can't they have blood?"

Cian stood. "That is not something I'm permitted to speak about."

Frustration flared through Harlow, rushing through her veins like a monster that raged inside her. She needed to know these things, and all the Knights' wretched policies about secrets meant she wasn't allowed to know, not yet anyway. Cian cupped her face in one of their cool hands. "He loves you, dear girl. More than anything in the world. Please don't initiate anything like this again."

She didn't understand, but there was no way she'd ask Finn for this again. "I won't."

Cian motioned for her to follow them. She didn't want to leave Finn, who was staring vacantly at himself in the training room mirrors, her blood still on his lips, but Cian clearly expected her to follow. She withdrew carefully, watching Finn wrap his arms around his knees and curl into himself.

Out in the hall, Cian hugged her. When they pulled away, they searched her face. "Are you all right?"

Harlow nodded. Her immortal blood healed her quickly, not as quickly as a vampire or one of the Illuminated perhaps, but she was feeling better already. "What was that? What happened to him?"

Cian shook their head. "I cannot tell you that, Harlow... And please, don't ask Finn to tell you either. There are many things he keeps from you. Not to hurt you, but to protect you. This is one such secret."

Harlow let out another huff of frustration. "Wouldn't it be better for me to *know* the dangers?"

Cian shook their head. "Oh, my dear child. You are so young, and so very naïve."

"That's not fair," Harlow bit out.

"It's just the truth, and for what it's worth, I envy your naivete. There are many things I wish I didn't know about the Illuminated." That much Harlow could easily believe. Cian's face held a dark expression that spoke volumes. "Let Finn tell you when he is ready. The things he knows about his people— his family—they are a burden he doesn't want you to carry."

There was something in Cian's countenance that sent

Harlow's heart racing. As they squeezed her arm, she felt the weight of all they *hadn't* said. There were so many things she didn't know about Finn. They'd known one another practically their entire lives, but it wasn't just the years they'd spent apart. There had always been secrets.

She hadn't even known who Cian was until Finn came back into her life, and now couldn't imagine her own life, let alone Finn's, without them. It was suddenly very clear to her that even as children, Finn had only let her see a small portion of who he was and what was happening to him.

"He needs you," Cian said as they disappeared down the hall.

~

WHEN HARLOW RE-ENTERED THE TRAINING ROOM, Finn was standing in front of the weapons rack, fiddling with what looked to be a loose screw. He didn't turn when she approached, though the muscles in his back tensed. She reached towards him, but drew her hand back, not knowing if he'd want to be touched right now.

He caught the motion in the mirror and winced. "You're afraid of me now."

She shook her head. "No, I didn't want to touch you without your permission."

Finn looked down at his hands. "That was unforgivable of me."

Harlow moved to stand next to him, looking up at the helpless expression on his face. She longed to touch him, to brush the hair from his eyes, but she'd meant what she said. She knew what it was like to do something terrible, something that felt simultaneously well within your control, but also desperately beyond it.

"Maybe if this had been your idea, or if you'd just bitten me without my consent. But I pushed you. Am *I* unforgivable?"

A hiss of air rushed through his teeth. "Of course not. You were just trying to figure this out."

Harlow craned her neck, trying to catch his eye. "You were helping... and something went wrong. We pushed things too hard in the wrong direction. You don't have to tell me what that was right now, but I want you to know that when you're ready, I'm here."

"Thank you." His voice was quiet, nearly a whisper. "I need to think this through. I want to tell you these things... It's just..."

"You don't have to tell me anything until you're ready, Finn. We were taught to keep secrets—even in my family—it's how the Orders are. You know it as well as I do. It's going to take time, and we're lucky to have so much of it."

The back of his hand brushed hers, and she pressed her hand into his. "Can I hug you?" he asked, his voice breaking over the words.

Harlow threw herself into his arms, hugging him fiercely, her heart swelling with love. She had no more words in her. A few hot tears slipped down her cheeks as she pressed her face into his chest.

"Are you crying?" he asked. When she didn't answer, he pushed her gently away from him. "You feel guilty for asking me to bite you."

Sometimes it was like he could read her mind. "Yes."

A dark look filled his eyes. "I lost control, Harlow. It wasn't intentional, but I am the one who lost control. You don't need to feel guilty."

Harlow sucked in a shuddering breath. "Maybe neither of us do."

Something new flickered in his eyes, and then a slow smile spread over his face, his eyes crinkling at the corners. "You mean we could just accept that we both fucked up a little and not berate ourselves for days as a result?"

Harlow laughed, pulling him into another hug. "We could try that."

"What will I brood about then?"

"You could try thinking about your poor choices in pizza toppings. That's something to brood about."

"There is *nothing* wrong with pineapple getting hot, Harlow Andromeda Krane," he chided, as he scooped her into his arms. He smiled, but his eyes were still serious as he used his Illuminated speed to whisk them both upstairs.

In their room, he dumped her onto the bed, crawling over her, searching her skin for marks. When he found only a hint of where he'd bitten her, he pressed a soft kiss to her neck. Harlow could feel him worrying.

"Hot pineapple is *disgusting*," she laughed, pulling him down so that his body rested between her legs. Shaken as she still was, she couldn't let either of them dwell on this. Both were prone to overthinking things, and she didn't want to spend the next week tiptoeing around one another. She wrapped her legs around his waist. "I'll forgive you for your poor taste if you finish what you started before we were so rudely interrupted earlier."

Finn paused, as though considering the wisdom of being intimate so soon after feeding on her. He seemed frozen above her, his eyes wide and worried.

"It was an accident, Finn. A mistake. We won't make it again. Make love to me."

He looked down at her as she brushed his hair away from his eyes. When their gazes finally met, his eyes were wet. "Do you think that's safe?"

She nodded. "I trust you. Even if Cian hadn't come in, you would have stopped."

The look on his face told her that nothing she said would convince him, so she pushed him onto his side, rolling over to face him as she laced her legs through his. "We don't have to do anything but be here together," she whispered. "You're safe now, and so am I."

He nodded, his eyes drooping with exhaustion. This was what he needed, to sleep and recuperate. Harlow snuggled closer to him, breathing him in as his arms tightened around her waist. They *were* safe—for now anyway.

CHAPTER FIVE

H arlow woke with a start to find that she and Finn had
slept through dinner, and the entire night. It was
dawn and light was leaking into the bedroom, as
neither of them had closed the curtains. Quietly, Harlow slipped
out of bed and closed all the shades before going to the bathroom and shutting the door. Inside, she looked at her neck in the
mirror.

There were no marks where Finn had bitten her yesterday,
for which she was grateful, but even she did not heal quite so
fast. It was strange, but she didn't let her mind linger long on it.
She showered quickly and threw on another sundress that Enzo
had tailored for her earlier in the summer. It was a beautiful
shade of dark blue-green, and the halter neck was flattering and
comfortable. A pair of sandals and she was ready for her day.

In the bedroom, Finn was still sleeping soundly, though he
murmured something when she pulled her phone from under
his arm. "What was that?"

"You okay today?" he mumbled into the pillow.

Harlow stroked his hair, planting a kiss on his forehead. "I'm
fine. Don't get up—it's early."

"Love you," he said into the pillow.

She didn't respond, waiting for his breathing to even out. When she was sure he was back asleep, she left the bedroom. He was usually a very light sleeper, and she was positive he needed rest right now. She found Axel sleeping against their bedroom door and scooped him up.

"So sorry, sweet boy," she said, pressing a kiss into his fur as she walked downstairs.

Petra was just coming in the front door, heels in her hand. Harlow raised her eyebrows at her and Petra just shook her head, hurrying toward the stairs. "Talk to me at noon. It's been a night."

Harlow shrugged, watching her friend blush and cover a mark on her neck. So it had been *that* kind of night. She chuckled softly as she padded down the marble halls to the kitchen. Axel jumped from her arms and trotted to the terrace door in the kitchen, meowing loudly.

Cian was making espresso. "I'll bring you a latte on the terrace. I have a bag of pastries from Moretti's that I'm willing to share with just you."

"Deal," Harlow said, opening the terrace door for Axel. The human bakery was divine, only open a few random days each week, but the pastries were better than anywhere else in Nea Sterlis.

She followed the cat outside. The terrace was cool and shaded at this time of day. Birds sang and the smell of the sea below mixed with the faint scent of lemons and sun-warmed cypress, making a fragrance unique to Nea Sterlis. The view of the deep green sea from this vantage point was enough to make anyone get emotional.

Harlow folded herself into a big rattan chair and looked around for Axel, who was bumping noses with an enormous auburn cat. *Where did that creature come from?* She jumped up quickly, ready to pull Axel back if the cat were to attack him. But it did nothing of the sort. It blinked at Harlow, its topaz eyes gleaming in the sunlight. And Axel rubbed his head against the gigantic beast's chin.

Harlow had seen nothing like it. The cat had long hair and a fluffy tail, and beautiful lynx tips on its ears. It was so large, it practically looked like a wild animal. It licked Axel's head a few times and then flopped down in the sunshine. Axel joined it, as Harlow stood watching, shaking her head.

Cian interrupted her by handing her a giant latte mug. "Who is that terrific creature?"

"Do you think it's a shifter?" Harlow asked, suddenly anxious. Was this how they were being watched? Could this somehow be the mysterious probe in the wards?

Cian laughed, stepping forward to set their own coffee down on the table between the chairs, along with the bag of pastries they had tucked under their arm. "No, it definitely isn't a shifter. It's just a cat. A huge cat, but gods all bless, what a specimen. Axel seems to like him, and he looks clean and healthy."

"Should I just let them hang out? How did it get up here?"

Cian shrugged. "Who knows with cats? They're having a nice time; why ruin it? Everyone needs friends."

Harlow laughed, feeling silly as she sat down. "I actually thought it might be what was testing the wards."

Cian shrugged. "Valid suspicion, but I don't think that's it. Sometimes a cat is just a cat, Harlow." They picked out a scone and then handed the bag to her. "How are you feeling today?"

Harlow selected a bacon and cheese croissant, then set the bag on the table. "I'm fine. The wound is completely healed."

"Yes, I suppose it would be. Their bites are different somehow—I've never been able to figure it out. I'm glad you've recovered well." Cian was quiet for a few moments, staring out at the slow waves rolling into their little bay. "Are you all right emotionally?"

Harlow drew in a deep breath and held it briefly, knowing

her agitation likely showed on her face. "Yes, but it's going to take some effort to not push Finn to explain what happened."

The firedrake shifted in their chair to better look at her. "We immortals keep too many secrets. There can be no doubt about that. Have you considered that it takes time to build the kind of relationship that can withstand the revelations you're asking for?"

A part of her wanted to argue that Finn had always been able to trust her, that she wasn't the one who'd broken their trust to begin with. But that wasn't quite true, and she knew it. "It's just so frustrating that he has secrets from me."

Cian's head tilted slightly. "It's true; his life, his line of work, they all bank heavily on secrets. But these aren't just secrets, Harlow. This situation is wrapped up in Finn's past, in his child-hood, and that is a much more complicated thing to navigate."

Harlow looked down at her croissant for a moment, tracing the striations in the pastry with her eyes. She remembered how Finn had acted the night of the Statuary party in Nuva Troi, when he'd driven her and Larkin home. The way he'd been in awe of her family's cozy home life stuck with her. "It's probably hard to tell me things about his childhood, isn't it?"

A slim hand took hers. Cian's eyes were sad. "Yes, dear one. The two of you grew up very differently."

"But you were there when he was a child, weren't you?" Harlow asked, wanting to shift the subject slightly. She knew Cian wouldn't reveal any of Finn's secrets, but that didn't mean they couldn't help her know him better.

Cian grinned. "Yes, Finn and I were together a lot when he was a child."

"Why?" It was always fine to be blunt with Cian. They never seemed to mind, and she found it comforting to speak with them, never having to play all the games or go through all the social machinations it took to socialize with most people.

"It's complicated. Long ago, the Illuminated, especially the

McKays, operated much more like the human mafia than they do now. And I was someone who could always find things."

Harlow sipped her coffee. It was perfect, as always. "What kinds of things?"

Cian's mercurial face revealed nothing but mischief. "All kinds. That is of little importance." Harlow doubted that very much, but knew if Cian wanted to tell the story, it would be told. "But I worked for Connor for many years in an affiliated capacity. When Aislin was pregnant with Finbar, she had some trouble with the pregnancy, like many of the Illuminated now, but hers was one of the first in the pattern of their trouble to conceive."

Harlow leaned forward. This was interesting. "What kind of trouble?"

Cian frowned, their brows knitting together. "I was never let completely in, but there was some concern that the pregnancy wouldn't be viable for much longer, and so they hired a hedgewitch."

Harlow nearly gasped in shock. Hedgewitches were human practitioners of magic and were extremely rare, working primarily with earth magics and complex spells that drew aether out. They were often employed as midwives.

"The McKays wanted ingredients for a spell that were difficult to find. So they hired me and I found them."

"What were they?" Harlow was desperate to know. The ingredients might give some clue as to what the issue was, and might give them valuable information on what was stopping the Illuminated from being able to conceive—and why they were so interested in Harlow and Finn having a child together.

Cian shook their head. "They were clever about it. Most of the ingredients were decoys. Connor McKay is always three steps ahead. I could never parse out which they actually used in the spell, but it worked and Finbar was born safely. I brought him a gift on his naming day, and I'd never engaged with a child thus."

Cian's eyes lit up. Harlow kicked the shifter to get their attention. "You're positively dreamy looking. What does that mean?"

Cian smiled, open and genuine. "I never had an opportunity to have children of my own, and I never thought I wanted them. But Finbar was different somehow. Connor and Aislinn asked me to be his godsparent, and I couldn't refuse. I took one look at him and knew that someone had to be in his life who could provide *more* than the two of them."

It all made sense now. Finn had often spoken of his "godsfather" when they were younger. He had been masking Cian's identity even then, protecting them. Harlow didn't bother to ask about that. Whatever it was, there was no way Cian would tell if it were as wrapped up in these family secrets as it seemed to be.

"So you were always there in the background, being his proper family."

Cian nodded, that smile returning to their face. "Raising Finn was a pleasure. And before you ask, he has always loved you, Harlow. From the day the two of you met when you were ten."

Tears sprang to Harlow's eyes. Finn didn't talk about that time much, or what he remembered from their actual childhood, and she stayed away from reminiscing too much, since it seemed to pain him.

"The day he met you and Enzo, he came to my home and we spent hours talking about you both. But mostly you. He's always believed you see the best in him, much as I do."

Harlow took Cian's hand and squeezed. "I love you, you know that?"

Cian looked down at their hands, a faint blush coloring their cheeks. "I love you too, Harlow. I always have, for caring for my boy the way you do. Even when Finn could not be in your life, I did everything I could to make you safe."

Harlow's heart beat faster. "What do you mean?"

A single tear slipped down Cian's cheek. "The night you tried to take your life." They choked on their words, unable to meet her eyes.

Harlow had never known who helped her, but now it was so clear. "You're the one who took me to the hospital. You found me."

Cian nodded, finally looking at her. "I should have been there sooner. I made a mistake, Harlow, and I made more letting things get so bad with Mark Easton. There are so many things I could have done to help you, and I was a coward..."

Harlow shook her head. "You saved me, Cian. You don't even know how much."

Cian's silver eyes filled with tears. "How?"

"I held it in my heart for years that someone cared enough to take me to the hospital. I used the fact that someone thought I was worth saving as armor against trying again more times than I could count back then."

Cian kissed her knuckles. "I wish we could have been friends sooner."

"Me too," Harlow whispered, feeling like Cian had returned a missing part of her heart.

The firedrake squeezed her hand one more time and then changed the subject. "I looked into the Ledge of Wishes last night."

Harlow frowned. "Why?"

Cian shook their head as both Axel and the mysterious red cat rolled into a sunnier spot on the terrace simultaneously. "Before you mentioned it yesterday, I'd never heard of it. Is it a secret with the Order of Mysteries?"

Harlow frowned. "Not that I know of. It's a strange bit of lore though, don't you think? Why would a 'warden' of any kind grant wishes?"

Some of the puffy clouds that were marching across the azure sky shaded the sun, and Cian's face relaxed. "I should have brought sunglasses. Even with the clouds, the sun is hurting my eyes."

Harlow handed them hers, which they put on. Somehow Cian made her giant sunnies look even more fabulous. She tried not to be jealous. This was the way it was with anything Cian touched; it became instantly cool. They leaned back in their chair, stretching their long legs out in front of them. "What's stranger is that there's no record of the Ledge of Wishes or Ashbourne the Warden in the Vault's records."

That *was* odd. "None?"

Cian shook their head. "None."

"What do you think it means?"

Cian sighed. "What do *you* think it means?"

Harlow rolled her eyes, but the grim line of Cian's mouth told her everything she needed to know. "This is another of the Illuminated's secrets?"

Cian shrugged. "I don't know, but we have records of some truly inconsequential lore in the Vault. Why wouldn't we have anything on this?"

"Because the Knights are Illuminated as well, I suppose. But what's the connection between the Illuminated and an aethereal being who supposedly grants wishes and lives under the Order of Mysteries?"

The sigh Cian let out was as exasperated as it was long. "If I knew that, this wouldn't be so intriguing."

"The Sistren of Akatei Library might have something on it," Harlow mused. "If anyone would, they would."

"And you're currently the only one of us with a reader card," Cian replied.

"So, I guess I know what I'm up to today." Harlow stood up, brushing crumbs from the skirt of her dress. "Tell Finn where I went when he gets up."

"Tell me yourself," Finn said from the doorway. He had

mussed hair, and wore the same clothes they'd fallen asleep in the night before.

"I'm headed to the Citadel," she said, brushing a kiss to his lips.

"What for?" Finn asked, pulling her in for a hug. Her heart thumped harder when his fingers grazed the bare skin on her back. She drew away from him, not wanting to be distracted.

"I want to look up the lore about the Ledge of Wishes. The library at Akatei's temple should have texts on it, but the Vault has nothing."

Finn's lips met her hair, then her cheeks, then so softly on her mouth, it nearly brought tears to her eyes. "Okay," he said, his lips moving against her own. "Take my car. It's going to be too hot this afternoon for you to walk."

The Woody was too big to drive around Nea Sterlis—the streets were too narrow, and it made her constantly nervous she was about to hit someone—so it had stayed in the garage all summer. Harlow hated to drive Finn's little vintage sports car. It was gorgeous, irreplaceable, and hard to drive, but he'd insist on taking her if she didn't agree to drive herself. And the last thing she wanted him to do right now was offer to come with her. She'd get nothing done with him in the library.

Even now, his fingers toyed with the zipper of her dress, as though he'd like to yank it down, right in front of Cian. The thought heated her through. She rose before her arousal could mount further.

"Fine," she said, her tone clipped. "I'll take your car."

Finn smirked that arrogant smirk she loved to hate. He knew exactly how wet she was, how much she wanted to take this upstairs, how feverish it made her just thinking of it.

"I'll take it *now*," she emphasized.

"Keys are in the garage," he said with a smile. He plopped down next to Cian, searching for a pastry, and taking a sip of her discarded coffee.

Harlow sighed, wishing she'd thought to bring the coffee with her as he downed the last of it. "This could take a while. I'll have to miss lunch, all right?"

Finn had plans with Kate to surf and go out for a late lunch, and though they'd invited her to come along, she'd found in the past few weeks that it was less comfortable to hang out together than she'd originally hoped it would be.

Finn glanced up, his gaze revealing his worry. "We'll miss you."

"You'll have more fun without me," she said without conviction. She didn't really believe it, even as the words came out, but some plague of insecurity was hounding her lately.

"Not even possible," he replied as she entered the villa. "Want me to bring you something from the restaurant? It's the place with the salad you like, the one with the little flowers in it."

"Sure," she said, though she didn't really want a salad. It was disconcerting how sometimes it felt like he could read her mind, and at others he didn't seem to know her at all. She'd mentioned thinking the salads at the beach cafe were cute with their little edible flower garnishes one time.

Cian must have caught the face she was making, because they rose and placed her sunnies back on her face. "See you when you get back, love."

Harlow pushed the glasses back on her head and then headed to the garage, listening to Cian and Finn's voices echo throughout the villa as she went.

CHAPTER SIX

The old sports car made it up the narrow, winding cobbled streets to the Temple District in the Citadel without giving her much anxiety, and at this time of day there was no traffic. Everyone was soaking up the last days of summer sunshine, not spending time in the Alabaster Citadel's dusty libraries. While Harlow preferred fall to summer, there was always a wistfulness that came over her when seasons changed. Yet this year it felt deeper, rooted in an ache in her chest that refused to dissipate.

Maybe it was the fact that this year was different. After so many months of estrangement with her family, being together here in Nea Sterlis with everyone she loved had been a true balm for her heart. But everyone was already talking about going back to Nuva Troi, and what they planned to do this autumn, though Finn and Harlow hadn't made plans yet.

They had found nothing significant in the Vault to help them discover the Illuminated's motives for manipulating their relationship, though Harlow was invested in learning the history of the Knight of Serpens, regardless. Their role in the War of the Orders had been fascinating. Instead of insisting upon leading, which they might have done with their military superiority, they'd let humans and the lower Orders guide them. Finn held the same value for the Knights now, and he spent a lot of time talking with leaders in the human community about their needs, as well as those in the lower Orders.

The scent of the sun-warmed lemons growing on cedar arbors floated out towards her as she pulled into the Sistren of Akatei Library parking lot. Harlow found a spot easily and sat in the car for an extra moment, looking out at the view of the sea, and Nea Sterlis spread out in tiers below her. The library was at the apex of the Alabaster Citadel, and even the parking lot had views to die for.

Sailboats dotted the rocky coastline and she could see how busy the many terraces and beaches were in the city below. They'd empty in the next few weeks, as everyone traveled back to the city, but for now, Nea Sterlis was bursting at the seams with people and paparazzi. Summer in Nea Sterlis was remarkably similar to the season in Nuva Troi, and Harlow didn't care a whit about any of it. Not the film festival that was in full swing when they'd first arrived, not the wine tastings at the vineyards just outside of town, or the gallery openings. None of it seemed relevant to her—it was all just a beautiful distraction.

The more she learned about the truth of the Immortal Orders, the things the Illuminated had worked so hard to hide, the more uneasy she'd become about the sheltered life she'd led. As she got out of the car to gather her things, she thought she felt eyes on her back, but when she turned, the parking lot was empty. Unease filled her, but she didn't feel she could trust herself.

Harlow had bordered on paranoia since Mark's influence on her in Nuva Troi last spring. She'd missed so many clues that something was going wrong, and now she was jumpy every time she felt even the slightest bit watched. The fact that no one was in sight didn't relieve her a bit. There was still a pressure on her that only her second sight could sense.

Most of the time, it turned out to be paparazzi, just waiting to sell photos of her to the gossips, but now she wasn't sure, so she quickened her pace as she walked through the parking lot. As soon as she passed the library's front gate, relief washed over her in a cool wave. The wards on the library itself didn't allow anyone without a reader's card to enter, and the libraries in the Temple District were strict about vetting their readers. Paparazzi rarely breached the Citadel buildings.

The atrium of the library was made from the same alabaster blocks as the rest of the Citadel buildings, with high arched doorways that led into different wings of the library. One of the Ultima—the Order of Mysteries' warrior class—staffed a heavy wood desk at the center of the atrium. These days, the Ultima were little more than security guards, but during the War of the Orders, they'd been a powerful military force. Harlow showed her reader's card to the fierce sorcière at the desk. She was a tall woman, with dark umber skin, and hair shorn close to her head as all the Alabaster Citadel's guardians had. The hairstyle was an ancient tradition the Ultima still adhered to, and it made them look all the more severe. She wore a simple, close fitting uniform made from flexible material, and a pair of heavy combat boots.

The hammered metal bracelets stacked on each of the warrior's arms showed her rank—she was young like Harlow and didn't have many yet. Harlow thought she noticed a flicker of recognition when she glanced at Harlow's ID, but the stern-faced Ultima said nothing, only nodded as she handed the card back.

I really am getting paranoid, Harlow thought to herself as she settled into one of the carrels, which housed a catalogue computer, and began searching. *Imagine thinking one of the Ultima would have any interest in me.*

There was that strange, discordant, insecure voice in her

head again. Enzo and Riley both thought there might be a kind of psychic residue from Mark's influence that dug deep in places her ex had been cultivating for years. The result, Riley presumed, was a trauma response combined with a nasty bit of magic that made it extra hard to shake. She shook her head and turned her attention back to her search for texts about the Ledge.

When she'd come up with four titles that might have information on the Ledge and the catacombs under the Order of Mysteries' headquarters, she filled out an electronic request form and sent it in, writing her ticket number on a pad of paper left in the carrel for that purpose. Then she headed to the reading room, passing the stern Ultima on her way.

Not even a glance to spare for me, she thought, laughing to herself as she found a seat near the retrieval desk and settled in to wait. *I really am being paranoid.*

Her phone didn't work here. There was poor service all over the library, so she was forced to look around while she waited for her books to arrive. It was no hardship, as the library was a stunning piece of classical architecture. At the opposite end of the reading room, an enormous statue of Akatei, in her three aspects, stood watch. Sunlight filtered in through the glass dome overhead, casting beams of light into the stacks of books that seemed to go on forever.

Four floors of stacks rose above her, librarians flitting back and forth amongst the books and great limestone columns, their feet moving quietly over the stone floors. The only sounds were that of laptop keys clicking, and pages softly turning. Every now and again, a soft cough or sniffle broke the rhythmic sounds of the library.

Harlow took a deep breath in, reveling in the comforting smell of leather-bound books and old paper. Calm settled over her. She was often restless when she was at the villa with her family and Finn, but here everything was well-ordered, and *so* blessedly quiet. Part of her felt guilty for feeling this way. It had taken her a bit to recognize how overstimulating it was to be with everyone nonstop, but quiet moments like these reminded her she *needed* alone time to recharge and think, especially after what had happened with Finn.

Harlow really was all right, but she couldn't deceive herself —the experience had shaken her. Not because Finn seemed to have lost control. She'd meant what she'd said about believing he would have stopped on his own if Cian had not appeared. What had shaken her the most was how different his bite had felt from the night in the House of Remiel basement. It seemed possible that the real problem was that they had started "cold." The night she'd shifted, she'd been scared, all her senses elevated—and he had been too. Those conditions would be difficult to reproduce in a controlled setting, and she wasn't even sure she wanted to.

A soft clacking noise alerted her that the number at the retrieval desk was changing. She glanced down at her piece of paper to double check, but it wasn't her number. Her mind drifted back over the past day, trying to figure out why things felt so different now, so urgent. Harlow knew she was spiraling, trying to pinpoint something that simply needed time to develop. To distract herself from her thoughts, she looked around the reading room. There were several sorcière scattered about, none of whom she knew, a smattering of shifters, and one vampire, who looked as though they were reading something salacious. There were no Illuminated here today.

Not that there had been since she started coming here each week, trying to find more information on the Striders and the Feriant. She was careful about what books she called up, but she *had* to know why she couldn't turn. Thus far, her research had yielded nothing, nor had she been able to find anything of use about the Knights, or anything she didn't already know about the War of the Orders.

It had been dead end after dead end. Aurelia had come with her a few times, watched her process, and called up a few books of her own. But her determination had been that Harlow had the research process more than well enough in hand, and Harlow thought she was secretly enjoying a summer off.

"You have a knack for this, my darling," Mother had said, before excusing herself to meet Selene for a sailboat ride.

It sure didn't feel like she had a knack for this kind of work anymore. So far, she'd read an absurd amount of Okairon lore, but not much of any use. The Orders loved their stories—stories about gods and the heroes of the Golden Age, the time when the Orders first came into their power—and though these were interesting enough, it had become clear to Harlow just how much the Illuminated controlled the way even Order-specific lore was told.

The number at the retrieval desk turned over again, and this time it was Harlow's. She got up to collect the pile of books a librarian had placed in the tray that corresponded with Harlow's number. The witch must have been near a thousand, as her hair had silvered, and she had fine lines etched onto her face.

Harlow took her books and made her way into a brightly lit part of the reading room, near Akatei's foot. She sat down at one of the long bleached oak tables, taking a notebook out of her leather messenger bag. Writing utensils were not allowed near the books, but she could pull threads of aether to take notes. It was an energetic drain, but preserving the books was the most important thing, and Harlow hated to haul the expensive tablet Finn had bought her, with its sleek stylus, to the library.

It had cost nearly three times anything she might have afforded on her own, and was a gorgeous piece of tech, but it made her feel self-conscious. Harlow was fine taking notes the old-fashioned way, with magic, in a paper notebook. She knew it hurt Finn's feelings that she wouldn't take it with her, but it was just so *fancy*. The same company had come out with an intimidating new phone this year that was all the rage. Harlow wasn't that interested in technology, so none of it mattered to her.

The first three books had nothing of interest about the Ledge of Wishes or the Warden. Two focused on the geological aspects of the Ledge, and the third had the same variations of the stories every sorcière heard as a child about people wishing for ridiculous things and then having to make more wishes to fix their terrible first wishes... They were more cautionary tales than anything else.

The fourth volume was slender, with an unremarkable black cover, titled *The Warden*. No author, no description. Harlow glanced back over her request form, which was lying on the table. She most definitely had not called this volume up, but sometimes librarians added related books to retrievals that they found relevant, and certainly the title implied that it was related to Ledge lore.

She placed *The Warden* on the cradle, opened it carefully and examined the book. Though the book was printed by fairly modern means, there were none of the required origin markings that all presses were mandated to emboss on every book, nor was there a copyregister page at the front to show that the book had been approved by the Council for Published Works. This was shocking. The book was likely very rare, and technically, the Sistren of Akatei Library was not allowed to lend out such books without direct supervision and approval of the CPW.

Harlow's heart beat slightly faster. There no way a librarian would breach the rules in such direct conflict with the CPW, which was a powerful organization. The Illuminated knew just exactly how dangerous knowledge and ideas were, and the CPW was one of the most feared of their government organizations. She took a few slow inhalations to calm her breathing, schooling her face into a bland expression. There was no need to draw attention to herself. She took great care as she read, knowing this might be the only copy of the book in existence. The first few pages outlined a war amongst a race of people the author called the "Ventyr," which Harlow knew loosely translated to "wind."

According to the author, the Ventyr were the first people in the cosmos, and were so powerful they would seem like gods to Okairons—*perhaps* even to the Illuminated. At that, Harlow raised an eyebrow. It was as close to treasonous as an author could get away with, without their work being destroyed. Harlow skimmed for a while. The account was interesting enough, even if it was far-fetched. According to the book's unnamed author, the Ventyr were a clannish people and fought many wars in their own realms, which numbered four, originally.

From what Harlow could tell, the author meant different planets, but the book was quite old. There wasn't much else in the text, as far as she could tell, that related to the Ledge of Wishes at all. Perhaps it had been shelved incorrectly and the librarian who'd fetched her books simply included it for the title's relationship to the rest of her books. She was about to close the book and go home when a chapter name toward the end of the book caught her eye: "Ashbourne and the Sixteen." She skipped right to it and began reading.

The two greatest houses of the Ventyr were at war with one another for many a year until both were beleaguered by a heretofore unknown host of incorporeal foes. Though no one could determine what they looked like, all knew quickly after their arrival what they might accomplish. Their presence elevated emotion of all kinds, distracting all they influenced from everyday concerns and matters of state.

When the Ventyr mages determined the scope of the mysterious beings' influence, a truce was struck between House Thuellos and House Anemoi. Despite their ancient grudge, they shared a common enemy, one that neither could defeat alone, as the creatures' presence had an unintended side effect: they drained aether from the land, consuming it at unprecedented rates. While all beings utilize aether to live, essentially consuming it, they also produce it, giving rise to more life. For some reason, the Ravagers, as they were named, did not.

As I am sure you are aware, aethereal energy replenishes itself in all cycles of life, death and destruction, which is why, above all else, a balance must be struck. The Ravagers grew in power for many years, as the Ventyr fought on. When they grew strong enough to leave the Ventyr's realm, the Winged Ones had to admit to themselves that the creatures were an imminent threat to all worlds, as they seemed driven to remake life in their image: creatures that consumed aether, but did not feed the limen in return. This is likely the only reason House Anemos and House Thuellos made the most temporary of alliances.

Winged Ones? Harlow thought of Finn's true form. A sinking feeling came over her. She pretended to look for something in her bag, but glanced around the room. No one was looking her way. She turned back to the beginning of the book to see if there was a detailed description of the Ventyr. Though she couldn't find one, something about the narrative troubled her.

Logic intervened. There was a lot of Okairon folklore about winged creatures—large birdlike creatures with humanoid heads and various humanoids with enormous bird wings were some of the most popular, but they were nothing more than fantasy stories.

Still, *The Warden* wasn't framed as an analysis of folklore, or a collection of fictional tales. It appeared to be a historical account. However, in the century before, there had been a rash of pseudo-historical novels published by underground presses. Aurelia had a small collection of these types of tales, and had always said that their value was in disseminating actual knowledge about the cosmos that the Illuminated suppressed, so it was possible that *The Warden* was such a text. If so, it was not supposed to be here, and she should not have access to it.

As casually as possible, Harlow glanced around. She couldn't help but wonder if the book's inclusion was some kind of trap? But no one was paying even the slightest bit of attention to her. These episodes of paranoia had been happening a lot when she was out by herself lately, and she was determined not to let them get the best of her. *The Warden* was an odd book, to be sure, but to believe its inclusion was anything other than one of the librarians helping her with what was clearly her area of research was ludicrous. She turned back to the book and kept reading.

The two houses' scholars and mages devised a plan to imprison the Ravagers in the only place with enough raw aether to create a container that might hold them: Nihil, the center of the limen. As you know, of course, Nihil is not technically the center of anything in the limen, as it is a realm without shape, without true form. But Nihil is the birthplace of aether, and therefore the most logical place to imprison indestructible beings. It is also obviously the most dangerous, since the creatures were capable of consuming aethereal power at such a destructive rate. But the alliance saw no other way.

The first problem was wrangling the creatures into Nihil, and the second was keeping them there. For once the doors to Nihil closed, it would be dangerous to open them again, lest the creatures escape. The mages determined that at least a dozen immortals would be needed to control the spell that would keep the creatures contained. But neither House would volunteer their own to spend eternity with the creatures.

That tracked with what Harlow knew about the limen. Though no sorcière had ever *been* to the world between worlds, where all aethereal power originated, there was plenty of theoretical work on the matter. Most scholars of metaphysics agreed that the limen was an actual place, and that it likely touched all inhabited worlds, as aether was integral for life to exist on a planet. Realms without aether could not sustain any life, and certainly had no access to magic.

Harlow made a note to look up more about the kind of spellwork that would be needed for such a feat later. Perhaps a vascularity of some kind? Vascularities were most often used in industrial applications these days, but she guessed one might connect the guardians to form a network of extra strong wards. If anything, it was a fascinating idea; perhaps the book itself said more. She read on.

> *During the alliance between Thuellos and Anemos, fraterniza-tion amongst the houses was forbidden, which was to make it easier to resume the war once they had dealt with the Ravagers. The two noble houses agreed to work together to avoid the destruction of the known realms, but anything more was as forbidden to them as intermingling with humans too closely would be for us. Despite this, Ashbourne of House Thuellos fell irrevocably in love with Lumina of House Anemos, and she with him.*

Harlow flipped the page, and found that it had been torn. Bits of the story remained; from what she could discern, the Ventyr had found a way to temporarily subdue the Ravagers but in doing so Lumina and Ashbourne were somehow discovered, and her family imprisoned her at their estate.

> *Together, he and his sixteen generals led seventeen legions of House Thuellos on a campaign to regain his love and her free-dom, but his father, Notus, had not approved the campaign. When Ashbourne's legions attacked, they slaughtered many of House Anemos, but failed to reclaim Lumina. Had they done so, Notus might have let them go unpunished, for the Ventyr loved*

nothing more than a fight well-won, with the reward of a good woman at the end.

For his son's unforgivable failure, Notus appointed Ashbourne as Warden to the newly constructed prison for the Ravagers, deep within the limen, along with the companions who helped him. Of course, House Anemos wanted retribution as well, so this served their purposes nicely, as each House had agreed to appoint half of the guardians needed to maintain the Nihil prison for eternity. Being that it would take exceptional warriors to accomplish such a feat, each house had been reluctant to elect their best and brightest to the position. Ashbourne and his generals made this choice easy for everyone.

But House Thuellos wanted reassurances that their connection to House Anemos was well and truly severed. Their greatest fear was that Lumina might escape her family's imprisonment and tempt Ashbourne to find a way out of Nihil. Their first petition asked that Lumina be immediately executed, but House Anemos summarily refused.

It seemed, for a time, that the two Houses had come to a stalemate. Soon though, Notus devised a devious plan to end this diplomatic conflict so that the great Houses might return to the nobler enterprise of eternal war. As Lumina valued her freedom so highly, second only to her love for Ashbourne, Notus suggested she be exiled to the realm of Sirin—a dark world, populated by creatures so ingenious that the Ventyr could not conquer them. And so Lumina and Ashbourne were separated for all time.

And there the story ended, though Harlow eagerly flipped the page, hoping that perhaps there might be a happier ending for all concerned. The next page was the start of another story about the conflicts between the two Houses, not the continuation of Lumina and Ashbourne's story. Someone had removed about thirty pages from the book with a sharp instrument.

Harlow sighed. It was like this with many books that

revealed too much information, or used a defamatory tone about the Illuminated. Sections would be missing or redacted. As this might be the only copy of *The Warden* in existence, there was little chance she'd find out the whole story, if someone had already removed it. She wondered why that particular bit had been removed, but the rest was allowed to stay. What did the end of the story reveal? And why had this book found its way into her possession?

Nearby, someone dropped their tablet, swearing softly, and the noise startled Harlow. She turned her attention back to *The Warden*, returning to the beginning of the chapter to read the preface to the tale several more times, taking notes. The mention of relations between humans and what Harlow assumed to be immortals gave her an idea of when the book had been written. Until just a few centuries ago, it was forbidden for immortals to fraternize in any way considered intimate with humans, whether that be friendship or more.

She wasn't sure how the story might help her at this point. It was more of a tragic love story than an explanation of how the Ledge of Wishes came to be, or what Ashbourne's connection to it was. What she *was* certain of was that Ashbourne was one and the same with the character who granted wishes in Okairon lore, but why had anyone come to that conclusion, if this was the truth of his story?

Perhaps the early part of the story had been left in to allow scholars to make sense of the legend. She skimmed the rest of the book quickly. There was no mention of the Ledge of Wishes itself or what was beneath it, but this was a solid lead. Harlow gathered her things. She wanted to use their secure server in the Vault to look a few terms up before examining *The Warden* more closely, and she wanted to show the story itself to Finn and Cian.

Harlow made her way to the small chamber right off the reading room, which housed a copy machine that had to be thirty years old. The machine had a hand scanner that would be perfect for preserving the delicate book, though, and she could quickly make a hard copy of the chapter on Lumina and Ashbourne. She nearly groaned when she entered the chamber; a gigantic sign reading "Out of Order" was stuck to the copy machine. She would have to come back another day.

Harlow had two options: return the book and try requesting it again at another time, or ask the librarian at the retrieval desk to hold it for her until the copy machine was fixed. She eyed her little stack of books and tucked *The Warden* in the middle of the rest.

At the retrieval desk, she filled out a hold form, indicating that she wanted to hold the books from being re-shelved or lent out to readers until the copy machine was fixed.

The witch at the retrieval desk smiled at her, read her request and whispered, "We should have the machine fixed in three to four business days. At least that's what the repair shop said."

Harlow smiled back at the librarian. "I'm in no rush."

"We'll email you when it's fixed, dear."

"Thank you," Harlow whispered back, and then made her way out of the library.

CHAPTER SEVEN

The early evening air was cool and damp on her skin, a sure sign that autumn was coming. It would bring rainstorms to this area for a few months, while Nuva Troi would enjoy the golden light of autumn. The phenomenon was called "reversal of the rains," and it signaled the end to summer's vibrant social season in Nea Sterlis and the return of Aphelion University's students, which inevitably changed the entire feel of the town, though Harlow had never visited during fall or winter. Harlow glanced upwards. Aphelion was located in the Alabaster Citadel, and there was a view of its high walls, covered in climbing roses, from the library's courtyard.

Finn had fled here after secondary school, to Nea Sterlis and Aphelion, rarely coming home to Nuva Troi for years. It had occurred to her more than once this summer that he rarely spoke of his university days, but that he'd lived here for seven years. She didn't even know where he'd lived during that time. *Had he lived on campus, or did he stay at the villa with Cian?* She shook her questions off as best she could. Cian was right; they had plenty of time to discuss these things. It wasn't necessary that she know everything at once.

Harlow wound through the courtyard of the library, amongst gigantic palm fronds and fragrant blooms, enjoying the last smells of summer. While she was missing Nuva Troi, she was happy enough not to be there this time of year. Summer here had been glorious, and until this month, the heat had been mild. The crunch of footsteps on gravel caused her to turn, but when she did, the courtyard was empty—save for the fountain, a rendition of Akatei weaving the first threads of aether.

Harlow looked at it closely for the first time since she'd arrived in Nea Sterlis. The pose was familiar to her. It was a common enough way to depict Akatei, but there was something different about this one. Typically, the "First Weaving" imagery featured Akatei drawing sigils in front of her body, but this statue was different—the goddess' arms stretched out in front of her, reaching upwards. Something about the difference caught Harlow's attention, though she'd walked by the fountain dozens of times this summer.

There was something written on the palms of Akatei's hands. Harlow leaned so far over she nearly fell in the fountain. There was no way to read the words without actually getting in. A librarian passed by just then, likely the source of the footsteps. They smiled placidly at Harlow as they went, their eyebrows knitting slightly as they observed the close attention she was paying the fountain.

Harlow smiled at the librarian. "My parents were affianced here. I've always wanted to see it."

The wrinkles in the librarian's brow smoothed. "How lovely." They moved on without another glance back. There was no way to examine the statue more closely right now, curious as it was. Perhaps she could look again when she came back to copy *The Warden*.

When she finally made her way to the parking lot, Finn was waiting by the car, leaning against it as the light of the setting sun set his skin aglow. He was looking at his phone, but the way the muscles in his forearms clenched as she approached told her he knew she was coming. He'd probably smelled her as soon as she'd left the library. Damn Illuminated and their weird sense of smell.

"Thought you were getting me a salad," she said as she approached.

He looked up, nodding toward the takeaway bag in the back. His smile was sheepish. "Got you gyros instead. Kate said they're your favorite."

Harlow's breath caught. It put her off-kilter, the way Kate remembered so much about her. She desperately wanted to be the kind of person who was completely cool with this, but she was struggling with Kate and Finn's friendship more than she'd expected to.

At first it had seemed so wonderful that they were already friendly with one another and that Finn wasn't the least bit jealous, but after spending a handful of coffee dates and brunches together when they'd first arrived in town, Harlow found that the two of them were better friends than she'd expected and she mostly felt left out—and a little resentful about it. She didn't particularly like this, but wasn't sure how to make the feeling go away.

Finn pushed off the hood of his car. The motion was casual, full of ease, but Harlow saw the intensity burning in his eyes. He'd noticed her reaction. "What is it?"

Harlow had to suppress the urge to cringe, reminding herself that even though he'd been upset about the incident in the Vault, he wasn't upset with her... And that even if he had been upset with her, Finn would not act the way Mark had when he was angry with her. This was the hardest holdover from their relationship to break.

All Harlow wanted right now was those gyros and to feel just slightly normal again. She took a deep breath, tossing her bag into the car. "Nothing. I'm just edgy today. It's about time for my bleed and I'm getting hormonal."

His nostrils flared, and she rolled her eyes. She slapped his arm, though her breath caught as a flush of damp heat spread into her core. "Stop smelling me, you creeper!" The looming feeling that something was still wrong between them cleared; the constriction in her chest loosening as she watched him visibly relax back into their usual dynamic.

Finn's left eyebrow raised. He laughed as he brushed a kiss to her forehead, then buried his face in the crook of her neck, his breath hot against her skin as his tongue grazed the shell of her ear as he laughed. "But you smell *delicious*."

That laugh combined vulnerability and longing, and the mixture shot right to Harlow's heart. All her worries melted into the core of her, now aching with need. Desire licked over her, spreading like wildfire. With Finn, it was easy to go from burdened with worries to *this*.

As though feeding off her arousal, his arms were around her waist before she could say a word, turning her, pushing her toward the car, grazing her hips and belly as he went, as though he couldn't quite help himself. She gasped, leaning into him. Some modicum of propriety and sense kept her from bending over the hood of the car and lifting the skirt of her dress, though the thought thrilled her.

What if he fucked her right here, in the parking lot of the library?

Finn helped her into the car, murmuring, "Let's get out of here. *Now*."

His voice rumbled with the same ravenous passion that roared through her as he closed her door behind her and hopped into the driver's seat. He started the little sports car and was out of the parking lot in a flash. The cobblestone streets of the Citadel were blessedly empty and the slight nausea Harlow often felt going down the switchbacks was tempered by Finn's hand on her thigh, and the hitch in his breath.

The movement of his thumb on her inner thigh sent a rush of chills through her. In a nearly involuntary motion, her legs parted as her back arched.

"*Damnit, Harlow*," he growled, glancing at her sidelong.

"Keep your eyes on the road," she pleaded, her voice breathless.

She pulled the hem of her dress up and Finn's hand slid under, grazing the bare skin of her thigh. Her legs parted wider, giving him easier access to her. The sound of his tortured groan filled the car as he caught the scent of her mounting lust.

"How wet are you?" he bit out, glancing away from the road again.

"Find out," she begged as his fingers grazed the outside of her panties.

He was so quick she barely felt his fingers move the thin fabric, but her sensitive flesh lit on fire as the tip of his fingers pushed between her swollen folds, sliding easily inside her.

"Yes," she hissed.

His arm was at an awkward angle and the stroke of his fingers inside her was excruciatingly slow and gentle, where she wanted to be filled hard and fast. It wasn't enough for him either. She could sense it in the tension in his forearm, the way he couldn't keep his eyes on the road. There was a scenic over-look ahead, and thank Aphora, Finn pulled into it.

No other cars were there, but the traffic to and from the Citadel was picking up. Evening events and devotional services were starting, as archival and museum staff changed shifts. Finn adjusted slightly, and switched hands, sucking his fingers slowly, then kissing her deeply so she tasted herself on his tongue.

"I can't get enough of you," he murmured as one set of fingers twined into her hair, while the other teased her, letting her panties cover her once more.

The tips of his fingers dragged over the wet spot in her panties. She wanted his fingers inside her so badly she thought she might reach down and push them in herself. Beneath the thin fabric of her undergarments, she felt her lips open for him. He pressed one finger a little harder into the now very damp spot between her legs. The fabric of her panties dragged against her flesh, tantalizing her, promising some of the blessed friction she desired as his mouth met hers.

Finn's tongue against hers made promises about what he could do to the rest of her. The finger between her legs pressed the fabric of her panties a little harder, increasing the pressure on her clit. Her hips lifted, trying to get more of the sweet relief she was desperate for.

"What do you need?" Finn's question was all command, and she was eager to comply.

"Release," she moaned.

Finn rewarded her with another breathtaking kiss and an increase in pressure. The wetness between her legs pooled, soaking the fabric of her panties.

Finn's voice came out in a growl. "Release?"

She nodded as he pulled her hair, and she yanked the bodice of her dress down to expose her bare breasts. His mouth closed over one nipple and as he moved to the other, he asked, "You need me to make you come?"

"Yes," she begged.

His lips covered her other nipple, and he nipped it lightly. A cool breeze drifted in through the cracked window, making her exposed nipple pebble into a stiff, damp peak. She whimpered with need, pushing her molten core hard into his teasing hand.

"Please," she begged.

"Please, what?" he teased, nipping her neck, her ears, her bottom lip. "What do you want?"

"I want you inside me," she begged.

He pushed his seat all the way back in one fluid motion, his hands leaving her desperate for contact, and then he deftly dragged her into his lap, where he'd freed his cock, which was now pressed hard against her wet center, only the thin fabric of her panties between them. It was a flagrant display of his immortal strength and agility, and it only aroused Harlow further.

"How much do you like these panties?" Finn asked, pulling her hips down so his cock rubbed hard against her clit.

"Not a bit," she answered, and he ripped them off her like they were made of sodden paper. As soon as the wet folds of her slid against his bare cock, she lifted her hips.

"Just like that," he said, one hand sliding up her back to pull her hair out of its bun so he could dig his fingers into her hair. "Tell me again how you want me inside you."

The head of his cock teased her entrance now, but he was holding her firmly in place, not letting her slam down on him as she wanted to. Every nerve in her was alight as her lips caressed the head of his cock, wanting desperately to suck him inside her until he hit that place that would make her scream.

"Tell me, baby girl."

"I want you inside me," Harlow begged, but he shook his head, a mischievous glint in his now-glowing eyes. He wanted more. His hips moved and his cock shifted slightly, slick with her arousal, to press against her clit, then dragged back to her entrance. She didn't know how it was possible for him to make such precise movements. Maybe it was just a Finn thing, but it was driving her wild.

"I want you to fill me with that huge cock," she snarled, nearly feral with lust. "I want you to fuck me so hard I can't walk straight. Bury your cock in me. *Now*, McKay."

His eyes blazed with clear golden light as he pulled her hips down hard, giving her exactly what she asked for. She ground herself against him, every thrust pushing her closer and closer to the edge she desperately wanted to fall over.

"You're everything I've ever wanted," he said.

His words caused every muscle in her body to tighten around him. She was pulled apart with this wild need for him to be deeper inside her, for them to join on some other level she couldn't yet attain. Pleasure mixed with the intense need for *more,* as the tease of release remained just out of reach.

The warm rush of his orgasm, the wet heat of their union, pushed her over the edge. Her shadows released, twining with the bright light Finn emitted as he continued to ride her wave of pleasure as well as his own. When their bodies finally slowed, he stayed buried deep inside her and she rested her head on his chest.

Harlow loved the feeling of Finn rooted in her, of the second round of desire she felt brewing, even as he softened inside her. She knew that all she'd have to do was rock her hips a little, or lean back and touch herself, and he'd be ready to go again. She wanted to desperately, already wanting more of him.

But before she could start another round of things, another car pulled up, followed quickly by another, and a pack of fox shifters piled out of the cars, taking photos of the dying sunset over the sea. Harlow pulled her dress back up over her breasts and ducked slightly, attempting to hide the fact that she was on Finn's lap. The shifters were several spots away, at the end of the overlook parking lot, by a set of stairs that led to an observation deck. None of them spared a look for Harlow and Finn, but all they had to do was turn.

Finn's cock hardened inside her, growing rapidly as he too registered they might be caught. His breath quickened, and she saw the question in his eyes, *Stay and fuck again, or go home like respectable people?*

Harlow rocked against Finn, pressing her breasts, which had grown heavy and aching, against his hard chest as she clenched around him.

"Yes," he hissed as he grabbed her ass.

She glanced at the shifters, who were still not paying a lick of attention to them as they spread a blanket out on the observation deck. Finn followed her gaze as she moved slowly above him, tightening herself around his cock as she moved. When his eyes turned back to her, she pulled her dress down again, pinching her nipples.

"You are so fucking hot," he groaned.

The sun slipped further down into the sea, and the parking lot was nearly dark. The shifters were unpacking a picnic dinner and had lit a few lanterns. Someone was playing a guitar, and the soft sound of their voices faded away as Harlow pulled her dress off. She honestly didn't care who saw, or smelled, what they were doing.

Finn's eyes glowed in the twilight of the parking lot. He cupped her face in his hands as she undulated above him, her breasts and belly moving in time with his slow thrusts into her. She didn't pull away in order to slam down on him, as she'd done before. Now they moved languidly as he pushed deeper still inside her.

She realized his girth was growing, as well as his length, but the rest of him was still in his humanoid form. "Did you let your glamour drop on just your cock?"

Finn grinned. "I can't believe I never thought to try it before."

He kissed her, his tongue dancing against hers for a moment before he pushed her back into an upright position. "You're the most gorgeous thing I've ever seen," he said as his hands slid down her neck, his fingers grazing reverently over her collarbones and the top of her breasts. He cupped them firmly, his thumbs rubbing over her sensitive nipples for a few blissful moments.

"Don't stop," he begged. She hadn't realized she'd paused, but she moved against him again as he dragged his hands down her sides, grazing her hips and thighs. "Rub your clit for me."

She'd been bracing herself on his chest as she moved her hips, and released one hand to do as he asked. She leaned backwards slightly so he could see her better.

"You smell so good," he grunted. "I wish you were sitting on my face."

She moved the fingers she'd been using to touch herself into his mouth. He sucked them, his tongue massaging them with a sensual grace that showed her exactly what he wanted to do to her clit. She'd discovered he loved to go down on her more than just about any other act and the scent of her arousal was enough to have him between her legs within moments if they were alone.

As he sucked her fingers, she pulled his shirt up. He released her fingers to yank his shirt off, tossing it in back. He was sweating under it. When she had him free, he pulled her against him, their damp bodies sliding against one another. His cock was so big inside her now, and Harlow felt it pulse with Finn's increased arousal. This was one of her favorite parts of his true form, something that differed from his humanoid anatomy. Sometimes, if they moved slowly like this, his cock pulsed in a low vibration that buzzed through her in a way that no toy could ever achieve.

His fingers pressed hard into the full flesh of her ass cheeks as the intensity of the encounter heightened. She knew better than to ask him to bite her now. That wasn't an option, though she still wanted it desperately. The low vibration reached the base of Finn's cock and traveled into his pubic bone, straight into Harlow's clit.

Her back arched hard as he pressed her ass harder into him, grinding her against him as he writhed beneath her, the muscles in his chest and abdomen rippling with the effort. Now her breasts were in his face and as he rode his pleasure, he latched onto one of her nipples, sucking hard as he came. Harlow's toes curled as she moaned Finn's name over and over, moving her body fast and rough against his. In his true form, orgasms lasted for minutes, not seconds, and could be intensified by increased speed and pressure. Though he hadn't shifted entirely, this still seemed to be true.

He pushed her back into a seated position as he crested his wave of pleasure, rubbing her clit with his thumb. A few of the fox shifters had glanced their way now, and Harlow was sure they knew what was going on, but she couldn't seem to care. She pinched her nipples and screamed Finn's name as he released fully inside her, the furious rush of his orgasm filling her, sending her over the edge.

When the haze of her pleasure cleared, the fox shifters were gone, and she and Finn collapsed against one another, sweaty and come-drunk as teenagers. "Holy Raia." He pressed a kiss to her damp hair. "You are a goddess, you know that?"

Harlow wrapped her arms around his neck, boneless and spent. "I love you, McKay," she muttered as she fell asleep. She was mildly aware of him wrapping her in the picnic blanket he kept in the backseat and the kiss he brushed on her brow.

"Love you to the end of everything, baby girl," he said, so softly she wondered if he was talking to himself. The last thing she heard before falling into a deep, restful sleep was the rumble of the car coming to life, and then all went blissfully dark.

CHAPTER EIGHT

T he next morning, as Harlow was feeding Axel and most of the household was gathering for breakfast, Nox rushed upstairs in her pajamas, followed closely by Indigo. The footage they had been working on decrypting had finally finished processing, and what it showed was apparently so shocking that neither could describe it. Riley and Enzo had come over for breakfast, so everyone gathered around the cozy kitchen table overlooking the bay to watch.

Nox had a few bracing sips of the latte Aurelia handed her and explained that at first it had appeared the video was only footage of humans in Falcyra burning the Governor's Mansion to the ground, but once decrypted, the true revelation was why they'd done it. Someone had leaked a video onto the dark web, filmed by a group claiming to be resistance fighters in Falcyra. Nox and Indi had already put together a full dossier on the ones they could identify. All had radical political leanings and were associated with a loosely formed group calling themselves "Humanists."

Alaric skimmed over the report as Nox was talking. "All your evidence points to them being a disorganized group of humans disgruntled about vampiric rule—easy to ignore."

Nox shook her head. "Doesn't line up with what you're about to see. There's something else happening here."

Finn raised an eyebrow as Nox paused, looking exhausted. The shifter smiled sheepishly and opened her laptop. When the video played, the smile slid off her face. It was clear she and Indi had both seen it already, because they immediately looked away as the video began. Under the table, Indi took Nox's hand in hers.

The footage was blurry at first. Whoever was holding the camera was running in a group of three people, all wearing ski masks. Then the footage cleared, though the camera was pointed at the ground, and the camera person spoke softly. "We got word a month ago that this was happening—and we—"

"Shut up," a harsh voice cut in.

"I'm just trying to tell them what we're looking at," explained the first voice.

"We're in the Governor's Mansion, that's all they need to know," a third voice chimed in. "We're going down into the fourth sub-basement to see if we can get our people out."

"No more than that," the harsh voice barked. "If what's down here is what we think it is, the rest will be obvious."

The first voice started to say something but the harsh voice interrupted again: "Got the sample? It's asking for it."

There was a shuffle, and the camera angle changed, showing a computer screen for a moment. Alaric said, "It's got a DNA lock. Old school—has to come right from the finger."

A freshly severed hand came into the frame for a moment. Selene turned green, burying her face in Aurelia's shoulder. The elevator door opened, and the Humanists were running again, this time down a long wood-paneled hallway. A few broke off at the first door on the left, as the harsh voice rang out, "Search all Ducare's files. Scan what you can. You. You're with me."

The camera jostled a little as the camera person ran alongside the person who was clearly their leader. Another door opened and the harsh voice spoke again. "Zoom in on them."

The footage was blurry for a moment, but when focused, showed a decadently decorated room. Humans lay about, in various stages of undress, barely moving, but clearly still alive.

"What is wrong with them?" Enzo asked, his voice breaking a little. His empathy had to be going wild. Harlow reached across the table and squeezed his hand.

The harsh voice answered, as though they'd heard Enzo's question. "Ducare and his cronies have been fucking and sucking down here for months. There's a reason there's no food, no money for schools, roads or clean water. They've been frittering it all away on this. On *orgies.*"

One of the humans laying on a crimson velvet settee opened her eyes, a lazy smile on her face. "Calm down, man. Everybody here is having a good time."

The harsh voice growled, then pulled the camera towards their face. They yanked a mask off, revealing a handsome face, with the eyes of a vampire, surrounded by a crown of wavy golden hair. The Humanists had vampires among them, *helping* them. "Ducare is out of control. We have reported back to Nuva Troi a hundred times about this shit, and you do *nothing.* Help us. Help these people."

The human woman laughed at the speech. "We have everything we need." She slumped over on the settee, losing balance as her silk robe came untied; she struggled to tie it.

The vampire shook his head at someone standing behind the camera person. "Get them out of here." He stared into the camera again. "Let's go."

The camera person and the vampire ran back down the hall, stopping at the office they'd left part of their party in before. Two masked figures sorted through a pile of papers, using hand scanners. One looked up, handing a small pile to the vampire.

Through the mask, Harlow could see their eyes were the brilliant blue of a cetacean shifter. They rarely left water or used their humanoid form.

"The Humanists have shifters among them," Cian said. "And vampires."

The vampire on screen skimmed the information on the papers. "Just as I thought. You fuckers know full well Ducare isn't holding up the agreement we made when we allowed a vampire governor. Our people were supposed to be taken care of."

Our people. The Falcyran vampire thought of the shifter next to him, and the humans among his group, as his people. Did the Orders matter less in Falcyra? Harlow didn't know what to make of what she saw, but her chest ached at the thought. She turned her attention back to the video now that the vampire was moving again, shouting to his companions.

"Get them all out. Search every room and then burn it all down." He looked back at the camera. "This is your final warning. Help us, or we will make you pay."

"Pause the video, please," Riley asked.

Nox looked to Finn who nodded. Riley examined something on the screen, something she couldn't see. Axel rubbed against Harlow's leg and she made a soft sound, coaxing him onto her lap. He chose Finn instead, flicking his tail in her general direction and purring loudly. Finn almost immediately relaxed, as Axel rubbed his face against Finn's chest. The cat was being aggressively affectionate; he'd sensed Finn's distress. As Finn's body relaxed, so did Axel, who settled in on his cat-dad's lap, purring happily now as he made biscuits on Finn's leg.

Such a Daddy's boy, she thought.

Riley looked away from the screen finally, smiling at Axel, who blinked back at them slowly, now flexing his paws at the shifter who'd won him over by turning into a cat for a few hours each week. Riley always said they thought that if they had to have one form, it would be a house cat, and Harlow occasionally found them napping together in the sunshine.

Riley pointed to the screen, at a blurry image on a bookshelf near Ducare's desk. "Can you zoom in on this?"

Nox nodded, typing a few commands into the computer. The screen showed a framed photo of Ducare sitting on a boat with Connor and Aislin McKay. They were smiling and holding drinks. It wasn't a pleasant revelation that they were friends, but Harlow didn't know why it was significant.

Riley turned to Enzo. "Isn't that dress from your spring collection, for the season?"

Enzo nodded. "Yes."

Riley looked at Finn, who was vibrating with fury. "He can't claim he doesn't know what's going on in Falcyra if he's been taking photos with Ducare. He's probably been to the orgies— and that's *our* boat."

Aurelia sighed, picking at her fingernails. "But he *will* deny knowing anything about it... Publicly anyway..." she trailed off, frowning.

Selene sneered. "The cowards. All of them."

Next to her, Aurelia shifted uncomfortably, averting her eyes from Harlow's careful gaze.

"You can keep playing it," Riley said.

Nox pressed play. The camera swiveled out of the office and down the hall where several of the Humanists practically carried humans to the elevator. Some were fighting their rescuers, swearing violently.

One sobbed as she beat the ground with her fists. "I was promised immortality. *Ducare promised me.*"

"Get her up," the harsh-voiced vampire barked. Harlow heard the exhaustion in his voice, saw it in his eyes. Whoever he was, he was at the end of his rope. "I mean it, Berith," the vampire said. "Help us. Get Connor to change his mind, or I will make Nytra sorry. Our people have suffered enough."

The footage ended, static filling the screen.

Thea clapped a hand over her mouth. "I knew I recognized him. That's Jareth Sanvier."

"Sanvier?" Enzo asked. "Is he House of Remiel?"

"Not exactly," Thea answered. "He was born in Falcyra. He just came here for uni. There are rumors he is Berith's natural son."

It was rare for vampires to be born, not made, but it did happen occasionally—once every few hundred years, as their fertility was even more sluggish than the Illuminated's.

"Why does no one know this?" Selene asked.

Thea shrugged. "Jareth hates the House of Remiel, from what I remember. He was a year or two ahead of me. Did you know him?" Thea turned to Alaric, who shook his head. Thea shrugged. "I remember him saying he hated Nytra a lot. It made a lot of people dislike him."

Nox took a deep breath. "That's not all. As we finished the decryption, Indi picked up on a rumor making its rounds through our sources: Connor hired a hit on Berith and the rest of the House of Remiel higher-ups."

Everyone took a collective sharp breath in. "For what?" Enzo asked.

"Because he betrayed them with the Mark Easton thing," Riley replied, avoiding Harlow's eyes. "And all the research into Gene-I."

Indigo's forehead wrinkled. "That might be the real reason, but the chatter says it's because the House of Remiel was being pretty open about thinking the Illuminated have lost control."

"Are they all dead?" Aurelia asked.

Nox grimaced. "It's hard to say. No one's seen much of them, so at the very least they're in hiding. Jareth was clearly trying to get this message to Berith though."

"Naming a child something that rhymes with your own is the height of poor taste," Cian said.

Normally, everyone would have laughed, but the mood around the table was somber. Indigo blinked back tears. "Why would the Illuminated let things be this way in Falcyra? What happened to 'no poverty'? And if Berith knows, who else does?"

Again, Aurelia looked uncomfortable. Selene turned to her wife. "What aren't you saying?"

Aurelia shook her head, conflict on her face. "We all knew. All the heads of the Orders. We all knew what Ducare was up to. The way he'd let things go. It was made clear that taking any action would put not only ourselves at risk, but our families."

Selene's eyes went wide as she took Aurelia's hands. "My love," she breathed. "I can't believe you've been carrying this around and I didn't know."

It was clear to Harlow that Selene forgave Aurelia, and she saw on everyone else's face that they did as well, but she saw the flicker of unease still in Aurelia's eyes. The others began talking, discussing the video, but Harlow watched Aurelia. As Selene comforted her, Harlow's sense that she was uncomfortable dissipated. Perhaps she'd been mistaken, or perhaps Aurelia was simply ill at ease because she'd admitted to a fact that could get them all killed, if the Illuminated learned she'd told.

"Where's Meline and Larkin?" Harlow asked Indi, who was getting up to grab a hanky from her purse.

Indi dried her eyes and glanced towards the back stairs. "I think they're both still asleep. Meli was up really late last night reading the new Wesley Arden book, and you know Larkin these days…"

Harlow smiled at Indi's comment about Meli, who was on a steady diet of *very* sexy sci-fi romances, which were all the rage on the bookish socials. But Larkin was another story. During the day, she seemed happy enough, but everyone noticed she'd been sleeping later and later as the summer wore on. Harlow was just as glad neither of them had watched the footage with the rest of the family. Axel wound around her legs asking to be held. She picked him up, whispering, "Go get your Aunties up and see if they want breakfast."

The cat trotted off, disappearing up the back stairs. He loved living in this enormous villa with all his favorite people. While everyone talked over what seemed like endless possibilities about who might control the Humanists, Harlow made coffee and tea. Riley joined her, working in silent concert to lay out a spread of pastries, cheeses and cut fruit. Indi disappeared upstairs with Nox's laptop, returning a few minutes later with red eyes.

"They both need a little time," she whispered to Selene, who nodded as Aurelia took their breakfasts to the terrace.

Everyone was going about their day as usual, which didn't surprise Harlow. Her family had become rather used to living double lives. In public, they pretended to go on with life as usual. In private, the frequency with which they discussed the various atrocities committed by the Illuminated and the Order of Night was growing. There was a palpable sense that the time they had left to live their normal lives was winnowing, and so they transitioned quickly from things like the video they'd just watched into a perfectly normal summer day, full of mundane plans. Whatever was coming with the Illuminated and the Order of Night was getting closer, but no one could determine what action to take yet.

Finn often said they were still in the information gathering stage, but Harlow worried they were missing something vital, and the Vault hadn't yielded the information they'd hoped for. Harlow poured herself another cup of tea and looked around for Finn. Enzo and Riley were already on the terrace strategizing about a luncheon meeting with a realtor for Enzo's new retail space, and Indi snuggled into the crook of Aurelia's arm, looking exhausted and very young. Finn must have gone to the bathroom, as he popped out of the back hallway near his office. He looked to be headed down to the Vault with Nox and Alaric, who were going to analyze the footage on what Harlow assumed would be a granular level.

Finn brushed a kiss to her cheek as he passed by her. "Are you headed to the Citadel today?"

Harlow checked her phone to see if there was news about *The Warden* being ready to scan, but there was nothing. "Not today."

She hadn't told him about the book yet... It was important, but she needed to bring up *The Warden* delicately, and now was not the time.

Shifting focus might be best. They could talk about the book later. "Where is Petra this morning?"

Finn averted his eyes. "I'm not sure... She had a date last night."

Harlow made a pleased little noise, a smile lighting her lips. "Really? She didn't text me."

Finn swallowed hard, his expression changing. Harlow's stomach flipped as he looked away. *Was Petra upset?* They'd gotten along so well since she'd explained her behavior in secondary to Harlow a few months ago and the thought that Petra might be angry with her turned her stomach.

Finn waved Alaric and Nox on. Nox was on the phone with Ari, who was presumably still in Falcyra, and Harlow caught a snippet of their conversation. "—I'll look into it, send anything you find over. See you soon." Finn took her elbow gently and drew her into the back hallway, where there was a little nook that looked out over the lemon arbor, with a view of the bay.

"So, Kate wanted to talk to you about this yesterday, but you wouldn't come out with us..."

What did Kate have to do with anything? Her heart stumbled over a beat as she understood. "Oh," she mumbled. "Oh... *Oh*."

A smile played on Finn's lips, and the flip in Harlow's stomach went deeper, morphing into another feeling entirely.

The uncomfortable feeling that she got thinking about Petra and Kate dissipated as Finn's lips curved. Her skin heated as she became acutely aware of him, as though noticing him for the first time. He looked delectable, still in a pair of low slung, light joggers and an old band tee. His hair was standing up in all directions after he'd shoved his fingers nervously through his hair a thousand times while they'd watched the footage. It was his only tell, as far as she knew, and she only saw it when he was comfortable, and with family.

"Are you okay with this?" Finn asked. "I get the impression things are very new with them, and they were reluctant to tell you until they were sure they liked each other."

Amidst her growing arousal, Harlow felt a stab of something she couldn't quite identify, maybe a little jealousy, followed quickly by protectiveness for Petra. The haze of desire that was flooding her system clouded the feeling as her skin flushed. She stepped closer to Finn, by instinct, but tried her best to stay focused on the conversation at hand. "Does Petra know Kate's not interested in monogamy?"

Finn's eyes hooded slightly as he breathed her in. He was having the same trouble concentrating that she was. He cleared his throat, obviously trying to focus. "She's not super into it either, from what I gather, though I think they might be serious about each other—or they will be when Petra knows you're okay with it. She's worried."

Harlow frowned as her hands skimmed over Finn's chest of their own accord. "Then why didn't she talk to me about it?"

Finn brushed a loose strand of honey colored hair from her face. "You haven't been exactly... open... to hanging out with Kate this summer."

Harlow's eyes fell to the floor and her hands, which had been tracing the lines of his pectoral muscles, stilled. "That's not because I'm still interested in her."

Finn's arms tightened around her waist. "It's okay if you're a little jealous. I know you and Kate had something special."

Harlow's eyes flickered up to Finn's. His voice was so gentle, but she could see he was crawling out of his skin with anxiety. She threw her arms around his neck, and he lifted her, setting her onto the heavy chest of drawers that was tucked under the window in the nook. They were face to face now, the same height.

"I'm not jealous—well, that's not true—" Finn's arms tightened around her and she felt him steady his breathing. Was he panicking? She rushed to add, "I was jealous that the two of you are better friends than I am with either of you."

"What?" The word came out in a bark. He looked genuinely confused.

"Every time we hung out, it was so clear. The two of you have a ton in common. I didn't want to intrude on your friendship." He was staring at her in disbelief. "I just make things awkward," she added.

"Harls," he breathed as he kissed her. "*You* don't make things awkward. It's just awkward to figure this stuff out."

"Oh," she responded. Riley and Enzo had both talked to her about this kind of thinking and she'd been working on it, but sometimes it was still hard to remember that not everything was her fault.

He hugged her tight. "Kate is a good friend, but you are one of the *best* friends I've ever had. You always have been."

"I'm not your *very* best friend?" she asked playfully, feeling the weirdness that always followed episodes like this dissipate.

Finn's head dipped towards her ear as he yanked her forward, pulling her body into tight contact with his. "I don't fuck my friends in front of packs of fox shifters."

Harlow bit her lip as his hand slid under her pajama top, his fingers grazing the bare skin of her back. "They really saw everything?"

He laughed in her ear, his breath sending chills through her. "I don't think they saw much, but they definitely heard us."

"Sorry I fell asleep," she murmured as his hand skimmed her side, grazing the curve of her breast. Her nipples hardened in response and she arched into his chest as he kissed her neck.

Their friends and family were just in the other room. She was ravenous for him now, but they had things to do today. He pulled away, seeming to think the same thing. They were both breathing hard, and he shook his head slightly. She slid off the counter and walked back towards the kitchen. They needed a measure of space before they both became frenzied with lust. Already her head was clouding, and it was hard to think of anything but him.

An arm snaked around her waist, and Finn pinned her against his body. The hard length of his cock pressed into her ass as he dragged her with immortal speed through the back hall, into his little office. Inside, with the door shut and the lights still off, he kept her pinned to him. "I don't know how I'm supposed to go downstairs and think, with you smelling like this."

She wrinkled her nose. "So weird."

He kissed her hair, then her temple, his voice low as one hand slid down the front of her body. "It's not just your wet pussy, though that smells so good I can hardly think. It's your skin, your blood, your magic. You smell like rich amber, and silken pleasure... I want to sink my cock, my teeth, my fingers—anything I can get inside you—I want in."

With those words, his finger tucked into the waistband of her pajama bottoms, pushing them down over the generous curve of her hips. "That smell," he breathed as she spread her legs, bending over to brace herself on the bookshelf next to the door. "That fucking smell. I want it all over me."

His fingers teased her entrance from behind, and he groaned when he found her wet and eager for him. Two fingers slid into her as he gripped one hip with his other hand.

"Won't Nox and Alaric wonder where you are?" she asked, desperately not wanting him to stop.

"No, it's obvious where I am."

"Why can't we behave?" she asked, spreading her legs a little wider to steady herself.

He halted. "Fuck," he swore, in a tone that did not suggest arousal.

"Please don't stop," she begged. For some reason, his tone didn't deter her. Her body's needs had taken over.

He pulled her against him, pinning her to his body once more, but this time immobilizing her. She thought she might burst into flames, she needed him so badly. His fingers spread over her bare belly as he moved his other hand away from the breast it was cupping. He was panting hard behind her.

"What do you feel like right now?" he asked. Again, his tone was strained. He wasn't asking to arouse her further. This wasn't bedroom talk. She tried to focus, but the pressure of his cock between her ass cheeks was so delicious she could hardly think, and she wiggled her hips a little in frustration.

"If you do that, I'm going to lose my focus and fuck you," he groaned. "I need you to think for a minute and then I promise I'm going to make you come as many times as you need."

The promise was enough to tide her over, for the moment anyway. "I feel like if I don't get you inside me soon, I'm going to die," she said honestly.

"Like you're going to *die*?"

Harlow nodded. She'd spoken impetuously. The feeling of his hand on her belly was distracting, but she was honest. "And once we get going... I can't stop now... It's like—if I don't have more of you, I won't live."

"Fuck," he said again. "*Fuck*."

"What is it?" she asked.

"The fervor. I don't know how you could have it. It's not

really possible. Or at least it shouldn't be, because you're not Illuminated."

Harlow wiggled her hips again, spreading her legs so his cock slid between them. "What's the fervor?"

"Bad girl," he moaned, slapping her ass lightly. "I told you I'd make you come as many times as you need, but we *have* to talk about this."

"Talk while you fuck me," she begged, maneuvering so the head of his cock fitted against her entrance. She felt his thighs clench behind her. He was struggling not to thrust into her. He allowed the head of his cock to enter her, the proud ridge of it massaging her flesh as he spread her ass cheeks wider.

She glanced behind her. The dim office light showed the reverence on his face as he watched his cock slowly sink into her. His voice was a low, restrained growl. "The fervor happens when Illuminated resist the urge to Claim one another. I've been feeling the effects for a few weeks now, but it shouldn't be possible for you to. You can't bite me back—the Claim can go only one way between us."

"It feels like this for you? Like you'll die if you don't have me?"

"Yes," he said, sliding deep inside her as he pulled her against him. One hand rubbed her clit, and the other went softly around her neck, his thumb putting gentle pressure on her throat as he slowly thrust into her.

"I think about you constantly," he growled in her ear. "The last few days, all I've wanted is to taste you, your sweat... your blood. I know it's wrong, after what happened, but I can't stop thinking about it."

Harlow gasped with pleasure as the pressure on her throat increased ever so slightly, but his confession didn't scare her. She'd been thinking of it too, but she hadn't wanted to admit it to herself. The primal urge to Claim and be Claimed seemed to override both their good sense. He sank to the ground, pulling her down with him. When she was steady on all fours, he thrust into her harder a few times. The wet sound of him sliding in and out of her thrilled Harlow.

He pulled out of her, leaving her hollow with need. "We have to stop and actually talk about what this means."

"Now?" she asked, turning to face him.

Finn nodded, getting up, pulling his joggers on as he went. His face contorted with worry, or disgust, she couldn't tell which in the shadows. He'd shed his t-shirt at some point that she'd missed. In fact, the last few minutes were a blur. She remembered what they'd been talking about as Finn rummaged in the little fridge behind his desk for a glass jug of water. He poured some into two glasses, handing one to her as he sipped his own.

He sank into the club chair across from his desk. She stepped toward him, but he shook his head. "Don't. I need to regain composure, and I need you to hear me."

Harlow stopped, feeling momentarily hurt. Some whisper in the back of her mind recognized the desperation in his voice though; he was serious about all this. A blessed string of logic threaded its way through her: this was real. Whatever the fervor was, it was riding them hard, and after what had happened in the Vault, there was no question it could be dangerous. She pulled her pajama bottoms up, then sat on the edge of his desk, a safe distance away.

"The fervor can drive people out of their minds, and if I'd had any idea you were experiencing it too, I would never have tried biting you in the Vault the other day. This is too big an anomaly. It shouldn't be possible."

She let out a noise of frustration. "But it's fine for you to feel like this?"

Finn sighed, putting his glass down on the corner of his desk. "No, it's not. I slipped up the other day, but it won't happen again. I have more experience getting shit like this under control than you do."

A dark look crossed his face, one she knew was reserved for memories of his father he didn't speak about. The most she'd ever heard him say was that his father had been brutal about training him to fight as a child. Connor McKay believed in the old ways of the Illuminated, unlike many of his peers, and he'd trained his son to be a soldier, just as he had been on their home world, wherever that was. The training, from what Harlow understood, was little more than abuse a good portion of the time.

Her mind traveled over the conversation she'd had with Cian after the incident. There was little doubt in her mind that this was all connected, that some Illuminated secret was tied to this very issue—and that at some point, Connor and Aislin had terrorized Finn into keeping it, no matter the cost to himself. The thought of it sickened her. How had he turned out so well with parents like them?

Cian. Cian Herrington had loved him. And then Alaric and Petra, and eventually Nox and Ari. They'd been his family. They'd shaped him to be the good man before her, who was fighting with his unquenchable desire to keep her safe. If he felt half as tortured by the fervor as she did, then she knew he was nearly wild with desire right now.

Her instinct was to go to him, to stroke his hair and comfort him, to make love to him until all these memories and worries washed away, but even her smallest movement towards him caused him to grimace, so she leaned back on the desk, holding her hands up in surrender. "I hear you," she said. "Is there any way to stop the fervor?"

Finn's eyebrows raised. "If you were Illuminated, we'd Claim one another and it would recede. But—"

"Since I'm not, you're worried my fervor will drive me out of my mind."

His head fell into his hands, muffling his words. "Yes. I did this to you. Because I'm selfish. Because I couldn't stay away from you."

A lump formed in Harlow's throat. She hated to hear him say things like that. This was a complication, but they could get past it. "Is there any way to slow it down and give us some time to figure this out?"

There was a long pause, and Harlow closed her eyes, feeling both her heartbeat and her shadows, which gathered at her fingers, softly soothing her. Some of them extended from her hands, wrapping around Finn's too, as though she took his hands in hers. Finn looked up, smiling faintly.

"That feels nice." The crack in his voice confused her. She pulled the shadows back, but he shook his head. "Not sexy-nice. Nice-nice. Comforting."

"Everything keeps getting more complicated," she murmured.

He sent a bit of his own magic swirling back to her, intertwining with her shadows. "It doesn't matter how complicated it gets. We'll work it out."

Harlow believed Finn. With every thread of her being, she believed him. And if they needed a little space to get their heads together, she'd give it to him. "Go on downstairs and find out what's going on. I'm going to go grab a lemon scone and some tea from The Gate. Want me to bring anything back for you?"

The Gate was their favorite coffee shop in the neighborhood, and Finn could consume half a dozen of their lemon scones in a sitting, so it surprised her when he shook his head. "No, but enjoy yourself, okay?"

And then he was gone, just a breeze and an open door. Harlow's heart ached deeply, but she went upstairs to get dressed, texting Petra on her way. Now was as good a time as any for the two of them to talk.

CHAPTER NINE

Petra Velarius looked like sunshine embodied, her bronze skin contrasting with the tight cotton mini-dress she wore. As she entered the shady courtyard garden at The Gate, she pushed her sunnies on top of her head, sending her mane of wavy dark hair flying backwards. Harlow already had two of The Gate's signature tea lattes waiting, and a plate of lemon scones on the table she'd grabbed in the corner. The scent of the bergamot in the tea wafted through the air as a breeze crept through the courtyard.

Petra sat down, her eyebrows raising as she crossed her arms. "Finn is such a snitch. Are you mad?"

"Mad that you didn't tell me," Harlow said, keeping her voice even. She was terrified that Petra was angry with *her*, and her heart was beating out of her chest. "It's fine if you and Kate are interested in one another."

"No, it's not." Petra glared at her. "I picked up your sloppy seconds. Somebody who was carrying a torch for you still last spring."

The words stung, but Harlow understood them. Her own inner landscape sounded like that far too often. She pushed the plate of scones to the side and took both Petra's hands in her own. For a long moment, she simply stared at her friend. The music from inside the coffee shop drifted into the courtyard, mingling with the sound of the fountain and birds singing. *Nothing could be more peaceful*, Harlow thought.

In moments like these, the threads that made up the world, reality as they knew it, were more than conduits for aether. The peace of the courtyard flowed through her, changing the riot of emotion in her, thread by tiny thread. As her own mood calmed, the invisible threads that bound her and Petra together, stronger than ever now because of their growing friendship, smoothed out. Harlow had always sensed threads with her second sight. That was as easy for a sorcière as breathing. But ever since she'd manifested, her sense of the threads that wove reality had become more acute. Her shadows purred with the pleasure of reaching into them. She wasn't using magic, and yet this moment was magical.

Petra's expression finally softened enough that Harlow let go of her hands. "I don't think that's fair to either of us, but especially you."

Petra sipped her latte, her face a perfectly cultivated mask. Harlow had seen this version of Petra thousands of times. It was a kind of armor—the illusion that she was shallow, so no one would see her true depths. Her voice was bone dry when she replied, "Fine. But I'd be mad if I were you."

"Would you?" Harlow asked, a tease in her voice. Humor and gentle teasing were surefire ways to break through Petra's outer shell, she'd discovered.

A cool breeze blew Petra's hair into her drink and she spent a moment blotting foamed milk out of her tresses. Harlow shivered. Autumn was just around the corner. When Petra's hair was deemed clean enough to disregard, she sighed, her protective mask finally dissolving, revealing the true Petra. "I just... It took us so long to be okay with each other. I feel like I might have fucked up."

The threads between them sang with life-giving aether, strengthened by nourishing truth. Harlow took a deep breath, drinking in the heady sensation of being able to feel the energetic compound behind mundane reality. It was odd. She rarely felt this so acutely with Finn, and given their conversation this morning she had to wonder if perhaps the fervor masked this ability with him. What a disappointment *that* was... she could only imagine what it would be like to sense this with Finn. She turned her focus back to Petra. "Do you like Kate?"

Petra nodded, a smile playing at her lips. "I really do."

"And she likes you?"

Petra's smile got wider. "Yeah."

"And you're giddy and excited all the time?"

The full-bellied laugh that spilled out of Petra was everything Harlow wanted for her. The threads between them practically thrummed with the beautiful energy of this moment. "Yes, I am. It's great."

Harlow reached out and grabbed Petra's free hand, giving it a squeeze. "Then how could I be mad?"

Petra brushed a kiss to Harlow's knuckles before releasing her hand. "Thank you. That means a lot."

"You deserve to be happy," Harlow added.

After everything her parents and the McKays put her through, Petra deserved to be blissfully happy for the rest of her life. Harlow just hoped that Kate was able to give her friend whatever she needed. Whether that was forever, or just a few months or years, Petra deserved to have the best of every relationship experience she could have after the way her parents had treated her. Harlow was honored to be a part of Petra's chosen family, and she wasn't going to let the potential awkwardness of this situation get in the way.

Petra took a long drink of her iced latte. "What do they put in everything here to make it taste *so good*?"

And just like that, things were fine between them. Harlow had four sisters and Enzo, and it had never been this easy to make up when things went wrong. But Petra was different. For all her bluntness, which could be irritating, the other side to it was this; she didn't linger long on bad feelings. Harlow enjoyed this feature of their relationship immensely. She smiled as Petra scarfed down scone after scone. No one could resist the allure of The Gate's lemon scones.

They chatted for a while about a podcast they both listened to that was being turned into a television show. Harlow's muscles relaxed as she listened to the utterly mundane sounds of the coffee shop. There weren't many people here right now, as it was just after the morning rush. Perhaps it was the aetheric link she'd just experienced with Petra, but her sense of connection to the threads was strong this morning, affecting her deeply. Something prickled at her back, sending a bizarre chill between her shoulder blades. She turned slowly to find the Ultima from the library watching her, though she glanced away quickly enough when she saw Harlow turn.

Today she wore a fashionable shift dress and heels, and she sat at a table with another woman, who faced away from Harlow. The other woman was human, but there was something odd about her, something limenal in nature that Harlow couldn't quite put a finger on. The Ultima wore that same stern expression as she had at the library, and Harlow wondered if it might just be the way her face looked. Their eyes met for a moment, and the warrior murmured something to her companion.

They both rose to leave. When they passed Harlow and Petra's table, Harlow got a good look at the Ultima's companion. The young woman was stunning, with muscular arms and a grin that could melt hearts. She flashed it at Harlow as she passed, and a younger version of herself practically swooned. Her hair was short, though not as short as the Ultima's, with a spectacular fade. Her skin was the same rich brown as Petra's. A tattoo on her wrist caught Harlow's eye; it looked like a compass.

The two exited the cafe and Harlow felt momentarily guilty; her heart was beating fast at the sight of the human. She was probably a few years younger than Harlow. More the twins' age, but still... As her heart settled, she smiled. It was fine to be attracted to other people. Finn wouldn't have minded at all, she knew. But a weird flutter lingered in her stomach.

"Someone doesn't wear heels often," Petra said softly as the sorcière warrior and her companion faded out of sight. "She was wobbling something fierce."

Harlow hadn't noticed that at all. In fact, the guardian had looked rather graceful to her, but Petra was probably the expert on such things—or just being petty. Either way, the flutter in Harlow's stomach calmed. She checked to make sure the warrior and her companion were gone and then leaned forward. "I think they were watching us."

"The one looking at us recognized you," Petra said. "The human was just flirting."

Harlow ignored the comment about the human. "The one in the dress is a guardian at the Citadel. One of the Ultima. She's checked me in a few times."

Petra frowned. "Oh, yes, I suppose that could be it." She glanced away quickly. Ever since Petra had broken free of her parents, she'd been almost allergic to lying and deception in personal situations. As it turned out, her emotions were perpetually written on her face, and now she looked supremely uncomfortable.

"What is it?" Harlow asked.

Petra shook her head, her lips pressing into a tight line, like she was refusing to speak.

"Spit it out, Velarius," Harlow chided. She couldn't help but smile as Petra pulled her phone out of her purse and unlocked the screen, so clearly relieved to be asked to tell the truth.

"She might have recognized you from this," Petra said.

Section Seven was pulled up, and there was Harlow on the pinned post. The photo wasn't terrible. In fact, she thought she looked nice, but underneath the caption read, *Harlow Krane can dress it up as much as she wants. We know the frump will return. Click through to see Harlow's twenty worst fashion blunders.* Harlow sighed deeply; there were nearly three thousand comments already. Yet *another* article that rehashed the incident at Gastro Lupo, which the Krane sisters had dubbed "The Great Pineapple Debate," followed it.

"For gods' sake," Harlow said. "We were just arguing about getting pineapple on pizza. Finn has the worst taste in toppings."

"Yeah," Petra agreed. "Pineapple should not be hot."

Harlow grimaced, shuddering.

"Have you been checking it lately?" Petra asked, her voice careful in a way that made Harlow's stomach turn. "Section Seven, I mean."

"No," Harlow sighed. Of all the gossips, Section Seven was the worst, and the cruelest to her. "I kind of hate to give them the views."

Petra nodded, but she looked worried.

"What is it?" Harlow asked.

Petra shrugged, but then seemed to change her mind. "They've started running old content about you from the season. They're picking apart everything about you and Finn's relationship…"

"And?" Harlow prompted when Petra trailed off.

"They're implying that the two of you look like you're faking things. That Finn probably feels sorry for you or something."

"Wow," Harlow breathed. Mean content had always been a part of Section Seven's brand. She was far from the only person they wrote about this way, but it was hard not to feel singled out. "Well, they're not wrong about the fact that we faked it for a while. I suppose it was only a matter of time. Are the stories popular?"

Petra nodded, pushing the plate of scones towards her. "I think your sisters didn't want to mention it to you, but they've been in the 'top likes' category for the past week."

Harlow took a scone, grimacing. "Thank you for telling me."

She wasn't wholly sure she was grateful as she turned the thought over in her mind a few times. *Why did they have to be so cruel about her?* She hated having drawn their attention like this. It would mean being followed more frequently, and she had to admit, it just *hurt* to be scrutinized so closely, to have so many people saying things about her, speculating about her life.

"Distract me," she said, passing Petra's phone back to her. There was no need to dwell on Section Seven's bullshit; they were the way they were, and nothing was going to stop them but something else being bigger news. "Tell me more about you and Kate. How did you meet?"

A slow smile spread over Petra's face. "We met here at the start of summer and kind of hit it off. It's not a very exciting story, really. We just had coffee that day and have been a thing ever since."

Harlow was positive there was more to the story than that, but she understood why Petra wasn't giving her details. She would have done the same if the roles were reversed, but she hoped that eventually Petra would share more. They were careful with each other, after so many years of snide comments and uncomfortable encounters, and Harlow didn't mind it a bit. She trusted Petra, and that was what counted.

Before Harlow could say anything else, she was interrupted by a familiar voice. "Harlow, Petra!"

Harlow turned to greet Meline. "Hi, you."

Meline looked like she'd been crying. Her eyes were red, a sharp contrast to her pale skin, and her hair was pulled into a tight ponytail. The dress she wore was pretty, but she didn't have a single accessory on, nor was she carrying a bag. Petra gave Meline a once-over, noted the same uncharacteristic lack of accessories that Harlow did, and got up from the table. She pulled up another chair, giving Harlow a knowing look that said, *I'll give you two a minute*, and went to order Meline her usual cup of black coffee.

Meline sunk into the chair Petra procured, looking dejected. She took the last of the lemon scones, but didn't eat it. She just sat there, staring at the scone, not saying a word. It was, perhaps, the most subdued Harlow had ever seen her.

"What's wrong?"

Her sister shrugged, then sniffled as though she was suppressing a sob. She mumbled something Harlow couldn't make out.

"I can't understand you, silly."

Meline looked up, her eyes puffy, and said, clearer this time, "I am useless. Those people are in trouble, and I'm fucking *useless*."

Although Meline had been vague, Harlow couldn't help but glance around. The coffee shop was still empty. Meline had many talents, but none of them had been particularly helpful this summer, and when Ari was gone, which was most of the time, she'd retreated further into herself than Harlow had ever seen. She faked it well when she went out, but Harlow had noticed that she was quieter than usual when they were alone with just family.

"You aren't useless," Harlow said. "But I understand why you feel helpless. I do too. Especially after this morning."

It was true; the video footage made Harlow feel ineffective, like nothing she was doing meant anything. She could understand why Meline felt as she did. While they were here in Nea

Sterlis, essentially on a luxury vacation, people in Falcyra were fighting for their lives.

Meline picked at the scone angrily, with a long, perfectly manicured nail. "I want to be helping. Not pretending to have a social life. Even Larkin has been helping the maters with covert networking schemes. I'm not even good at that. All I know how to do is run socials and shop."

"*Meline*," Harlow implored, not knowing what to say.

Meline shook her head, biting her bottom lip. "You don't have to convince me of something else. I know it's true."

Harlow's phone buzzed. It was Petra, from the line inside the shop. *Ari's back from Falcyra. Might cheer her up.* Petra's keen ears probably caught the whole conversation. She glanced over her shoulder, and Petra's eyes were full of understanding.

Another text came through. *I know how she feels. Before the Knights, I was just like her. She needs a purpose, Harlow. Talk to Finn.*

I will, Harlow texted back. To Meline she said, "I just got a text. Ari's home. Do you want to go see him?"

Meline shook her head, looking away. "No, he'll be disgusted by me."

This broke Harlow's heart to hear. She hadn't realized Meline was struggling this much, and felt guilty about it. She tried to reassure her, "He will *not*."

Her little sister looked her straight in the eyes. "Why wouldn't he be? He's off doing important things while I hang out here getting my nails and hair done. Shopping. Dinners. *Useless bullshit.*"

Harlow's chest ached with each sharp word Meline spoke against herself. "Arebos Flynn thinks the world of you, Meli, as does everyone who knows you. And there's *nothing wrong* with liking to do things like getting your hair and nails done."

Meline rolled her eyes, but Harlow saw her jaw relax a measure. She obviously wasn't torturing herself out of some desire to stir drama. Meline had always shied away from dwelling in negativity, which is why it affected her so deeply when she couldn't break free of a mood. Indi was the opposite, seeming to enjoy yearning and aching a bit more, but Meline liked for things to be straightforward, and she embraced happiness easily.

A slow smile quirked the corners of Meline's mouth. She looked so much like a young Selene in this moment that Harlow felt like she was looking through a window to the past. Harlow saw both herself and Mama in her sister, and the connection was so intense it throbbed in her chest. There it was again, that sense that her connection to the threads was refining somehow, changing shape before her.

Meline interrupted her thoughts. "Ari really does like me, doesn't he?"

Harlow nodded, taking one of Meline's hands and kissing her palm. "You are wonderful, Meline. Everything you've done this summer has been really helpful. You know that, right?"

Meline glanced at her. "I'm a good distraction."

Harlow nodded, smiling. "You are at that, my beautiful bunbun." Selene always called the twins that, her beautiful bunbuns. Meline cracked a grin as Petra handed her a cup of coffee, but tears still threatened in her eyes. Petra went wide-eyed, and Harlow realized that for once, she was going to have to guide the conversation, as Meline was too caught up in her head to do so, and Petra didn't really *do* girlfriends.

She wracked her brain, trying to think of something to talk about that wouldn't take them deeper down the sad-spiral each of them seemed poised to slide right into. Television was safe, wasn't it?

"Did either of you catch the *Knight's Own* spinoff last week?" The vampire drama was on summer hiatus, but a new show had just aired exploring one of the side-character's dramatic exploits.

Within a few minutes the three were chatting amiably about

the soap opera, and the new romance novel Meline had devoured the night before, which apparently featured a sexy monster love interest. Both Petra and Harlow added it to their StoryTracker accounts and listened with rapt attention as Meline recounted some of the juicier bits.

Content as Meline appeared, Harlow recognized it for what it was: a finely honed act. Her sister wasn't satisfied, and things would change. Harlow had never met someone as strong-willed as Meline. Once she figured out her purpose, she would be unstoppable. As another chill, damp breeze blew in through the courtyard, Harlow felt unsettled, despite the pleasant turn the day had taken.

Things were changing, as they should. It was time they all grew up and faced the truth of the world they lived in head-on, but Harlow wished she could slow time down a little. Every second of peace and pleasure these days felt like they might be the last for a long while. A prickle of excitement skittered through her, chased by a vague sense of foreboding.

CHAPTER TEN

The last week of Août passed in a blaze of heat and as soon as the month turned—in fact, nearly the exact moment Septembre began—the rain started. Nea Sterlis' summer of society events and beach days waned, and the tourists all went home. Section Seven let up on Harlow and Finn just enough for them to go out in public more frequently, and though speculation continued that their relationship might be on the rocks, it looked like attention was waning. When a wolf-shifter heiress threw over her longtime alpha lover for a rabbit shifter, Section Seven dedicated their content to discussing the ins and outs of The Order of Masks' social mores.

While that offered some temporary relief, Harlow knew better than to get comfortable. Someone on Section Seven's editorial team had a thing for her, and they'd likely turn back to their nonsense when the uproar over this latest scandal died down. Besides, she had other distractions. She and Finn could hardly keep their hands off each other. He'd fucked her in nearly every room of the villa, and just last night she'd gone down on him in the bathroom at the market.

In the grip of fervor, and a desire not to push Finn too hard to talk about the past, Harlow forgot about *The Warden* until she received an email from the library telling her that her hold was about to expire. She and Finn were cuddled in bed, both scrolling on their phones, when the email came through. She noticed *The Warden* wasn't listed among the books whose hold was about to expire.

"Shit."

"What is it?" Finn asked, looking up at her over his glasses. He was using her belly as a pillow and she'd been playing with his hair.

"My hold at the library is about to expire. One book is missing. I meant to tell you about it…"

She hesitated, not sure if this was a good time to talk about this. They'd been having such a peaceful evening, and things had been good between them, the incident in the Vault firmly in the past. She knew that discussing *The Warden* would bring it all up again, and though she knew she couldn't keep putting this conversation off, she wanted to hold on to this moment of peace between them.

He was clearly still reading an article about woodworking when he responded. "Yeah, what was it called?"

"*The Warden,*" she replied.

Finn glanced up. "*The Warden*. Like Ashbourne the Warden?"

Harlow nodded. "Yes, I found a book in the library that claimed that Ashbourne was a member of a race known as the Ventyr, and that in some alien war he fell in love with a girl from an enemy house… Her name was Lumina—"

Finn sat up. "The Ventyr? Are you sure?" He'd gone ghoulishly pale. "*That* word was actually used in the book?"

Harlow's brow automatically furrowed. "Yes…" Finn's hands shook. She'd been right. This was connected to whatever had happened in the Vault. Harlow sat up as well, pushing herself off the pile of pillows she was reclining on, praying to Aphora to smooth the way between them. "What is it?"

"Did the book mention the Anemoi?" Finn asked, his voice hollow.

Harlow nodded. "Yes, they were one of the houses in the book. House Anemos and House Thuellos. They were enemies who had to work together to imprison elemental creatures called the Ravagers, and Ashbourne fell in love with a girl from the Anemoi house, and.... Finn, what's wrong?"

He'd sprung away from her like her words were poison, his chest heaving. "All that was... in a *book* at the *library*?"

Harlow was utterly confused. He seemed panicked by this information. She got up and moved towards him, but he threw his arm out in front of himself. "Harlow, you read that book in the library? *When*?"

Harlow thought back. "The night of the fox shifters, it was that day."

"And you haven't been back to the library since, have you?" He paced like a caged animal.

"No." She reached out, trying to catch his hand, but he was just out of reach. "What's this about?"

Finn's hands glowed, and his bright power flashed through the threads of aether surrounding them, into the wards on the windows and that surrounded the villa proper. *Why was he checking the wards?*

"Nothing like that should exist," he said, his voice quiet but dangerous.

This was the Finn people both feared and admired, the one that got him his way wherever he went. She marveled at how different he was from the softer version of himself that had been resting on her belly a few moments ago. He sank into one of the chairs that sat in front of the fireplace. It wasn't lit, of course, it hadn't cooled enough for that yet. Harlow moved to sit in the chair opposite his, folding her legs underneath her.

"Why not? What does it mean?" The fearsome Finn was dissolving before her. Now he rocked slightly, back and forth, as his face went blank. Like he was somewhere else, lost deep inside himself. "Finn?"

He didn't hear her, that much was clear. She slid to the floor in front of him. He'd buried his face in his hands and was shivering. "It was so cold in the basement," he murmured. "So cold."

Her heart skipped a beat. He'd only talked about something like this once before. Long ago, when they were children, he had told her and Enzo that sometimes Connor locked him in the basement as a punishment. But what did that have to do with *The Warden*, the Ventyr, or House Anemoi? Whatever it was, this was the thing that Cian had warned her from pushing him to tell. She needed to keep her head now and be careful not to push him too hard.

"Finn," she said again, as she tried to take his hands. He wouldn't budge. "*Baby*," she said, softer this time. His fingers, which were digging into his hair, loosened. "Baby," she said again, dragging the syllables out soft and slow, as his arms fell around her. She rose quickly, winding her arms around his neck, pulling him to the floor in her arms.

He buried his face in her neck, his hands clutching her tightly. His humanoid alternae fell away, and he was naked in front of her, in his true form. For the first time in weeks, there was nothing even mildly arousing about his naked body. All she cared about was the shake in his shoulders and the hot tears seeping into her shirt.

Harlow felt for the surrounding threads, the way she'd done instinctively at The Gate with Petra, but though she sensed them, whatever had happened there wasn't happening now. Once again, she had the unnerving sense that the fervor was blocking this new ability and she had to fight her own frustration to focus on Finn.

She held him tight. Even without being able to connect through the threads, she could help Finn. She had to. "Do you want to tell me what happened in the basement? If you don't want to, you don't have to, but I'm here."

His voice was deeper in his true form, and now it shook as he nodded, his chin quivering. "I told. I wasn't supposed to tell about the Ventyr, but I told..." Finn was murmuring now, nearly unintelligible, but she caught one phrase, his shoulders shaking as he choked out, "Cian... My father beat Cian... I thought he'd kill them... But I promised. Promised we'd never tell... and that I would take the punishment instead."

The story was tumbling out of him in such a confused manner that she had trouble understanding it at first. From what she could gather, Finn had nearly died from the beating and the cold, while Cian was forced to watch. Apparently, the point of this abominable endeavor was to drive home that if either spoke about the Ventyr again, they and anyone they associated with would be swiftly killed. The only reason Connor had not executed Cian was that he seemed to believe they had no interest in the knowledge. She'd always known that Connor McKay was a monster, but she'd never imagined *this*.

Inwardly, she raged. No parent should ever treat a child this way. "That shouldn't have happened to you."

Harlow wasn't entirely sure what he was talking about, but at least he was talking. *Why did he know about the Ventyr as a child? And why was this such a problem for Connor McKay?* She watched Finn's wings flex behind him, and then tuck into a tight bundle at his back. *A winged race—more powerful than gods— who could conquer and inhabit multiple worlds.*

She wrapped her arms closer around Finn, holding him as tight as she could as her mind raced ahead of her. Could it even be possible that her suspicions about *The Warden* had been correct? The conversation they'd had on the train the night they came to Nea Sterlis played in her mind.

The Illuminated are hiding on Okairos.

Hiding from what?

From the rest of our people.

The author of *The Warden* had gotten it all wrong. The Ventyr weren't more powerful than the Illuminated, the Illuminated *were* the Ventyr. At the very least, *The Warden* was a story about who the Illuminated *might* be. Whether it was accurate could be impossible to say, especially if Finn didn't know the truth of it... but the Ventyr were very real. The implication of this information was terrifying. The Illuminated were more powerful than they seemed—and they seemed omnipotent as it was.

Finn stilled in her arms, calming some. He looked up at her, eyes feral with fear. "Did you tell anyone about the book?"

"No," she said, cupping his face in hers. "No, I wanted to see it again and get a copy to show you and Cian. I thought it was one of the pseudo-histories, like the ones Mother collects."

His head shook vigorously. "It's not. I haven't heard that exact story, but everything else—it's all true. The Ventyr, the two warring Houses. The Ravagers... It's why they came here. Something about Okairos was different, hidden from all that. *Safe.* It's why the secret is so important." Finn's words tumbled out of him in a frenzy, as though he was pushing them towards her as fast as he could, while every instinct in him told him to stay silent.

Her first reaction was icy terror, and then white-hot fury ripped through her veins as the full magnitude of what Finn had endured sunk in. Connor McKay deserved to be torn apart, piece by piece. Her skin was too tight. Finn had only been a little boy, telling the only person he was safe with a dangerous secret. *He had just... been... a... little... boy...* Her thoughts were thick and stilted, as though time had slowed to a crawl.

Finn looked as though he moved in slow motion. He was gripping her arms, saying something to her she couldn't make out as rage engulfed her. *Now* she felt the threads between them. As she looked down, her second sight saw them... and something else. She saw where her shadows and his light intertwined, and those led somewhere *beyond*. Her second sight slid over them, and she was out of her body before she knew what was happening, racing along the threads as though they were a pathway she could travel, a road of sorts.

Harlow didn't expect what came next so much as she launched into it headfirst. She was thrust out of her own reality, deep into the heart of the limen—the heart of Nihil, where shadowy magic gathered, raw and unbridled. She counted fifteen guardians of the prison, clear as if she stood in front of them. She counted them again. Weren't there supposed to be seventeen?

But no, there were just fifteen. They appeared to be sleeping inside tight, coffin-like chambers, but she sensed their sharp intelligence. Though their eyes were closed, they were not asleep, but in some sort of stasis, in a grand chamber at the center of what she assumed was the prison—Nihil. The heart of the limen pulsed behind them, an enormous knot of life-giving dark power: the aether that filled not only the threads of reality on Okairos, but made magic possible everywhere, in all worlds.

The wardens were winged, just as Finn was, their skin varying shades of subtle blues and greens. Unlike Finn's true form, they were taller, and grander somehow, their features more severe. Harlow wondered if it had something to do with their proximity to the heart of the aether, which flowed around them, into them and out of them. The aether was more alive here than she'd ever seen it and the wardens were absolutely breathtaking in their power.

As the shadowy magic moved, she saw where the missing wardens *should* be: there were two empty chambers. *Two of the wardens were missing? What did that mean?* A sharp burst of fear sliced through her.

Seeing the prison for herself, it hit home what a dangerous gamble it was to house any elemental being that ostensibly fed on aethereal energy so near its *actual* source. As she looked around, she understood the risk. Her spirit body was a pure vehicle for her second sight, which meant she saw the threads of power here more easily than she would in the waking world.

The guardians—the wardens—channeled aether into the great web that was the prison itself; not a physical building exactly, though it had form, but a spell so complicated she could barely track the intricate threads that bound the place together. As she examined the spellwork, she saw that the wardens themselves were the conduits for its power, all that stood between the prisoners and what they likely wanted more than anything in all worlds.

As if by instinct, Harlow traced the dark source of magic; it made up the very walls of the chamber, spreading into vast spaces that she sensed, rather than saw, in her spirit form. There were countless smaller cells, but four that were vast. One was empty, but the others were occupied. Her curiosity piqued, she tried to sense what was inside them from the outside, but could not tell.

Harlow wasn't sure what she could do in this space, but she badly wanted to see what was inside those chambers. She pressed into one, sliding between the walls of the spell easily in her non-corporeal form. It was a little surprising that her presence didn't trip any wards, and she wondered if being a Strider made her somehow invisible here. As her second sight adjusted to the chamber, she recoiled in horror. The thing imprisoned there was nothing like any elemental being she'd ever read about, or could even conceive of.

Its attention moved slowly, but she felt when it turned towards her. She was but a speck of dust in comparison with it, and yet, it sensed her. Its size was inconceivable, and though she could not make out its form, her spirit understood that it was a thing of nearly pure malevolence, which should not be possible —all things were a mixture of what she understood as good and bad, even elemental creatures. She froze in abject fear as it laughed. The thing was *sentient*.

Hello, little bird.

Its words were not words. They were bloody shrieks and tortured wailing. They were little more than an impression, but one that filled her with despair. She pulled away from the Ravager, for that was what it had to be, as quickly as she could, but she felt it in every fiber of her being as she re-entered the stasis chamber.

See you soon, it called after her as she retreated.

Harlow's spirit form threatened to pull apart from panic. It was vital that she regain control of herself, as there was no guarantee that her consciousness would reassemble in her body on Okairos if she disintegrated here. She stumbled towards the wardens, thinking to steady herself nearer to the knot of aether they guarded.

The largest of them opened his eyes, which glowed with the same light as the Illuminated's. There was no doubt that, whatever power the Illuminated had, they were one and the same with the Ventyr. There was something regal in his expression, as well as deep sadness.

"Strider," he whispered, a smile forming on his impossibly beautiful face. His features were stronger, more rugged than Finn's, but there was a resemblance between them, she thought. Some hint of affinity.

When he spoke again, he had a voice that would have sent her to her knees, had she been in her corporeal form. "Go home, child. It is not safe for you here." His hand stretched out before him, and the shadows he channeled from the heart of the limen surrounded her, pushing her backwards, out of the dark world at the center of all life.

Her eyes flew open. Finn was staring at her. He was back in his alternae, his jaw slightly slack as he took her right hand in his. Her entire arm was covered in black, iridescent feathers. The feathers dissolved before their eyes, melting into her shadow magic, which flowed around her ink-stained hands.

"You started to shift," he said.

"How long was I gone?"

Finn glanced at the clock. "Gone? What do you mean?"

Had no time passed? How was that possible? "I was angry," she replied. "And then... I think I was in Nihil. I think... I think I *saw* Ashbourne."

"You saw him?"

She nodded. "And the generals. They were like you... I must have been hallucinating."

He shook his head. "You weren't."

"The Illuminated are the Ventyr," Harlow said.

"Yes," Finn replied, his shoulders slumping.

"That's not all I saw," Harlow choked out. She did her best to describe the Ravager, but no words could capture its terrible essence.

Finn rose far enough to slide back into his chair, dragging her with him into his lap. They were silent for a long time, breathing in time with one another. When he finally spoke, his voice was weary. "No one can ever find out that you know this, Harls. Promise me you won't tell anyone else."

Part of her railed against the idea of having another secret, of keeping a secret for the Illuminated. But when she thought about the fact that Connor McKay had beaten his only son within an inch of his life for just telling Cian, literally the most trustworthy person ever, that the Ventyr *existed,* it made more sense. She had no trouble imagining that Connor, or any of the elder Illuminated, would kill her and anyone they thought she might have told about all this. This was a secret they wanted kept at all costs.

As much as she hated to admit it, after coming in such close contact with one of the Ravagers, if there was any possibility that what Finn had said was right, that somehow Okairos was safer than other realms—hidden somehow—then keeping this a secret made more sense than telling. It excused nothing about the way the Illuminated had operated here for the past two thousand years, but she could agree that if Okairos was beyond the reach of those creatures, and the rest of the Ventyr, then maybe secrecy was necessary.

"All right," she agreed.

"Stay away from that book."

She nodded, but he took her chin in his fingers. He didn't grip her hard, but his hold on her was firm. "Promise me."

"I will," she whispered. He didn't need to explain further. She already understood. Children were precious to the Illuminated, and Connor had tortured Finn to drive his point home.

He pulled her tighter against his chest, playing with her hair. Both of their breathing slowed. "The Ventyr are dangerous, Harlow. They have a limited ability to travel between worlds, but when my parents came here, they were looking for easier ways to do so, and not to explore or create alliances, but to serve their endless desire to conquer."

"Isn't that what they did to us, though?" Harlow asked. She didn't want to make Finn feel bad. She understood he was nothing like his parents, but there was something she didn't feel he was acknowledging.

"Yes," he agreed. There was no *but*. "I don't think my parents' generation knew any other way to behave. If it matters at all, I think they love Okairos and want to protect it."

Harlow let out a derisive huff of air, rolling her eyes. "That's one way to put it."

"They're evil. I know that... I'm just not sure they ever had a choice to be any different."

Harlow thought of the noble expressions on the guardians' faces. The way Ashbourne had looked at her when he sent her home. It was *nothing* like Connor or Aislin McKay, or any of the older Illuminated. "Are you sure that's true? The wardens were different somehow."

Finn's bottom lip quivered and his eyes fluttered shut. "No," he said, voice hoarse. "No, I'm not." He stared into the dark fireplace.

She stroked his cheek, pressing kisses to his cheekbones, his brow, then finally his lips. "I understand why you need to believe there could be good in them."

He glanced at her, visibly cringing at her words. "Do you?"

She kissed him again. "You're the only good thing they ever did. *You* are what's good about them."

His eyes fell to her engagement ring, which he touched. "You are what's good about me."

She shook her head. "That is not true. *You* are what's good about you. You, Alaric, Petra... You're all good in ways they aren't. The three of you *chose* something else."

Finn's jaw clenched, as though he couldn't quite trust what she said.

She gripped his chin now, a mirror of what he'd done to her before, turning his stormy eyes to hers. "It is a *choice* to be good —to do good—one you make every single day despite them." His eyes misted as she spoke. "I'm so fucking proud of you."

"You are?" he asked, his voice breaking over the words.

"I am," she replied. They stared at one another as her words sunk in. "Everything you are, everything you've done, everything you've *endured*... I am so proud of you."

He shook his head, a smile playing at his lips. "What did I do to deserve that kind of love?" he murmured. The look in his eyes was full of gratitude she didn't want.

"Nothing, sweet boy," she said, pressing yet another kiss to his lips. "You never had to *do* anything for me to love you this way. It's not something you can earn." The blush blooming on Finn's cheeks sent heat through her. He looked so damn *happy*. "It's not something you can lose, either."

He hugged her tight. "I love you, Harlow," he breathed into her hair as he lifted her, carrying her to bed.

CHAPTER ELEVEN

The next day felt like autumn, a Nea Sterlis autumn, mild and blessedly sunny; but a storm was raging out at sea, though the weather reports said it was unlikely to come ashore. From the terrace off the kitchen, the view of the imposing clouds was menacing. Harlow sat outside, sipping her last cup of coffee for the afternoon. If she drank much more, she'd be unlikely to sleep.

The household was all out at their scheduled activities, she and Axel the only ones left at home. Even Larkin had gone to the pool with the twins and the Wraiths. They'd asked her to come along, but Harlow was still shaken from her trip to the limen. Thea knew something was wrong, but when she'd pressed her about it over breakfast, Harlow had snapped at her, which started one of their silent wars.

Harlow hated to keep a secret from her family, particularly Thea. She'd worked so hard to mend her relationships with them, after everything that happened with Mark, and having to keep a secret so monumental from all of them bothered her. A heavy thump caught her attention. The auburn cat was back, and it rubbed its face against her calf.

"Hello there," she crooned, patting her lap. She wasn't sure if the big feline would consent to be held, but she felt like offering.

It didn't take her up on the invitation, instead leaping onto the table next to her, staring into her eyes. Its expression was fiercely intelligent, as though any moment it might open its mouth and speak. She chuckled at her own foolishness.

"May I scratch your ears?" she asked politely, stretching her fingers towards him.

He bumped her hand with his head and she gently rubbed behind the massive ears, feeling the muscles in the cat's neck as it strained towards her, purring. "Aren't you sweet?" she crooned.

It glared at her, pawing her hand away as if to say, "Don't underestimate me."

"You are very fierce," she said. "Obviously."

Axel chirped from the doorway and the red cat jumped down from the table to bump noses with him. The two of them leapt onto the wall and disappeared down a steep ledge that ran along the sea wall to the next terrace over. Harlow couldn't watch. Though she knew it was probably safe for a cat, Axel was her baby and she hated to watch him navigate such spaces.

She waited a moment, then rose to peek over the balcony at them. They were facing away from her, watching something intently below. She followed their gazes, but saw nothing. The red cat turned, its topaz eyes alight with awareness and it looked straight at her and yowled, then looked back at the spot below where Axel's gaze affixed. Harlow saw nothing at first.

The red cat hissed just as Axel growled. Both cats' fur stood on end, their tails doubling in size. Harlow peered again at where their attention was affixed. She took a few deep breaths and then engaged her second sight. Sure enough, the threads were disturbed, just in the spot the cats were looking. There was something there, rendered clumsily invisible by spellwork.

"Not so clumsy if I missed it the first few times I looked," she muttered.

Harlow marked the spot where the disturbance was. It was near the door to the beach below, bouncing against the villa's ward. If she could get down there before whatever it was disappeared, she might be able to get a better look at the thing. She rushed down the stairs that led to the seawall level. Footsteps followed her, and she glanced behind her.

Finn grinned at her, caught sneaking. His hair was still damp. He'd been surfing earlier in the day and had made a trip to the market. His hands were full of groceries. "Hey there, gorgeous. Where are you off to in such a rush?"

"Axel and his cat friend found what's probing us. Somebody's made whatever it is invisible, rather badly, but still... It's at the beach door."

Finn set the groceries down. "Okay. And you're going to look?"

She nodded, urgency filling her. "We should hurry before it gets away."

Finn grabbed her arm. "Let's take this slow, okay? Whatever it is, it might be a good idea to pretend we don't see it, don't you think?"

Harlow rolled her eyes. "Or we could grab it and take it apart."

They stared at each other for a moment, both thinking. "Something about the Great Pineapple Debate has been bugging me," Finn said.

Harlow threw her arms up in the air. "What in seventeen hells does that have to do with anything? You want to argue about pizza right now?"

He snickered. "No. Though you're wrong. It's a superior topping."

Harlow glared.

"No, what's been bugging me was the angle the video was

taken from. Like the camera was on the ground," Finn said, taking her hand and kissing it.

Harlow couldn't remember the video itself. She tried to avoid watching anything Section Seven posted. "What's weird about that?"

Finn pulled her towards the beach door. "Even if a person had taken the video, it would be odd for the camera to be on the ground. Maybe table height, but the angle was strange."

Harlow couldn't really see the significance, and she was worried they were going to miss whatever the thing was altogether.

"How did you catch sight of it, if it's invisible?"

"My second sight caught the spell. If I'd known what I was looking for, I'd probably have caught it sooner. The cats hissed at it."

Finn nodded. "Cats see through spells easily. Did you know that?"

Harlow sighed. "Of course."

"Okay, okay," he said, drawing her toward him, wrapping his arms around her waist. "So, think with me for a minute. What if we have a fight in front of it and see what happens?"

He had a point. If Section Seven, or one of the other gossips was utilizing some kind of surveillance device, then having a fight in front of it might trigger some kind of reporting. It was the kind of thing she wasn't used to thinking yet, but of course he was. She smiled, agreeing. "And then what? Just let it go?"

Finn nodded. "You use your second sight to see if you can get a better look at it, but we'll be having a fight about something."

"Like what?" she asked as his hands slid under the light sweater she wore. It had been chilly in the house all day and she'd pulled one of his sweaters on over a bathing suit. She'd meant to go swimming this afternoon. The warm days were numbered, after all.

"Did you have to be wearing this?" he asked, his fingers grazing over her hips, tugging at her bikini bottoms. "It's going to be very distracting to be rude to you while you're wearing something so hot."

"Focus," she laughed. "Was anyone with you today when you surfed?"

His forehead wrinkled. "Kate, of course. But we ran into some of her friends on the beach. Some kind of bird shifters, swans maybe?"

Harlow's heart leapt. "Was one of them Leto Vipointe?"

Finn nodded. "Yeah. She wouldn't stop touching my arm."

Harlow snickered. "This is almost too perfect. Kate and I used to argue about that girl all the time."

Finn frowned. "Because?"

"Because she's a hideous flirt!" Harlow smacked his arm. "You are so oblivious sometimes."

He shrugged, kissing her nose. "I think about you a lot. It doesn't leave me a lot of room for noticing other people that way."

His face was so open and earnest that Harlow had to kiss him. She raised up on her tiptoes, pressing her lips to his. "I'm really sorry about this, okay?"

Finn started to say something, but she threw the door open and stalked out onto the beach. "Don't follow me," she sneered, her entire countenance changing.

"Harls," Finn pleaded as he followed her out. "What's wrong?"

She spun, letting out a dry laugh. "Like you don't know."

He looked genuinely confused, shaking his head. This was perfect. She was facing the door now, and her second sight locked onto the device. It was a tiny drone, with a camera affixed to it. Invisibility spells were hard to cast, and though this one was fairly good, it wasn't anything like what Nox and Ari could do. The drone was easy to sense now that she had it in her sights.

"Leto Vipointe? Really?" Harlow tried to inject as much jealousy as she could into her words, remembering the way Kate and Leto had flirted at a party when they first started dating.

Finn shook his head, the picture of confused innocence. "Who?"

Harlow strode forward and poked him in the chest. "The swan shifter you were flirting with at the beach this morning. I've been getting messages all day."

Finn captured her hand in his. "I honestly don't even remember who you're talking about. Could we go inside and talk?"

Harlow groaned loudly. "You're just going to keep following me until I agree, aren't you?" This was exactly the kind of thing Section Seven should eat up. Finn being the dejected good guy, her the shrill bitch.

He hung his head, his shoulders slumping. "Can we please just talk?"

"Fine," she snapped, practically stomping back into the villa.

When the door was firmly shut, they rushed to a hidden window in the back stairwell that looked out over the beach door. "Is it still there?" Finn asked.

Harlow shook her head. "It's gone. Now what?"

Finn shrugged. "Now we wait. If the footage appears, we'll know who's been probing us."

Harlow snickered. "I can think of a few things I'd like probed."

Finn gave her a helpless look. "The groceries are melting. I got gelato from Moretti's."

"By all means," Harlow laughed. "Let's take care of that, and then *you* can probe *me*."

He tossed her over his shoulder in one fluid motion, pressing a kiss to her exposed ass cheek. "And we can eat gelato after."

She squealed with delight as he stroked the back of her legs. When he set her down next to the pile of groceries, he pressed a kiss to her forehead. "We make a good spy team, Krane."

Harlow smiled as she picked up a few bags. "That we do, McKay." She smacked his ass with one of the bags. "Get going."

Finn cheated and simply whooshed away, his laugh echoing as she trotted up the stairs after him.

CHAPTER TWELVE

T here was no sign of their "fight" on the gossips, but the next day brought the threatening storm closer to shore than had been predicted. New reports suggested hurricane gales were possible, but that the storm itself would likely still miss them. Everyone's phones blared Nytra's severe storm warning shortly before dinnertime. All across the city, storm shutters closed and people went into their basements to wait things out. The entire family was making their way downstairs with books, laptops, and tablets, but Harlow wasn't sure where Axel was and she needed to check in with Enzo before they shut the front door. All summer, he'd alternated between staying at the villa and with Riley.

She was on the floor, looking for the cat under his favorite chair, when Enzo texted her back. She could hear Finn shaking treats upstairs, calling for his "little baby kitten." He'd probably find him first, so she sat back on her heels to read the text. *Safe at Kate's. Petra's here too.*

Enzo and Riley had been so busy coordinating the sale of the new retail space that they hadn't had much time for socializing as the summer wound down. Harlow was a little jealous that Finn, Enzo, and Petra were all spending so much time with Kate. This hadn't been an issue before everything with Mark happened. Logically, Harlow *knew* Kate had nothing to do with what happened with Mark, but she found herself less trusting overall these days and she was frustrated that Kate had inched back into her world, person by person, until she had no choice but to have her as part of her life.

You'll stay put through the storm? Harlow replied.

Of course. We're spending the night. See you tomorrow.

"Come *on*," Thea said, pulling on her arm. Axel was in her arms and she pointed to the last open window, the one Ari was busy shuttering. From their vantage point, Harlow could see the terrifying way the sea lurched towards the shoreline. It was clear why there were no buildings close to the beaches, and why the majority of homes were perched high atop the cliffs of Nea Sterlis. Everything about the bay was different in the green light of the storm.

Rain hit the windows, blown by the high winds, and then all was quiet as the villa's storm shutters closed in place. Finn came running down the stairs, and he activated the shutters that closed the front door. "All in, right?"

Harlow nodded, taking Axel from Thea, who disappeared downstairs. "Enzo and Petra are with Kate and Riley."

Something flickered across Finn's face, almost like he was confused for a moment. Harlow had to wonder if he was seeing what she did, that Kate was a bigger part of their lives than either of them had noticed. Something banged against the shutters at the back of the house. Something big. Axel yowled piteously.

"We need to get downstairs," Finn said, taking Axel from her.

Fittingly, he was wearing his *Cat Dad Extraordinaire* shirt today, and Harlow chuckled a little, despite her racing heart. She was terrified of hurricanes and tornadoes. Finn took her hand, and she followed him to the Vault, where everyone gathered in various states of undress. They'd been getting ready for dinner when the storm rolled in, fast and unpredictable. Nox pulled a few bins out of a closet in the Vault's common room.

"There's a bunch of sweats in here," she explained. "And tactical stuff, but we bought emergency clothes a few years ago, in case we had to lock the house down."

Everyone started digging through the bins, handing one another clothes. Harlow had been wearing a robe when the storm swept in and was chilly now, so she took both a sweatshirt and some sweatpants. They all had the Haven logo on them.

"Are these merch?" she asked with a laugh.

Alaric snickered. "Yes. Cian designed them, but we never sold any of them, so all the samples came down here."

Indigo shrugged. "I think they're smokin."

Cian raised an eyebrow.

"She thinks they're cute," Meline explained. "It's slang."

Cian shrugged. They were dressed in a luxurious cream-colored cashmere tracksuit, which Selene was wearing a twin of. Aurelia glanced between them. "Have the two of you been shopping together?"

"Yes, Li-li," Selene said with a sigh. "*Online.*"

"Every night before bed, with wine," Cian added.

Everyone was joking and chatting. Larkin was arranging snacks on the table and Nox got cards out as Thea and Alaric sat on the floor, wrapping themselves in blankets. Axel curled up on Thea's lap and it seemed like the twins were settling in with their ereaders, along with Finn, who stretched out with his feet on Aurelia's lap. She had a book about ancient shifter iconography that she raised so Finn could get comfortable.

They were all chatting, their conversation a comfortable buzz as Harlow stood at the doorway of the room, gathering up the last of the shed pajamas and robes into an empty bin. Only Ari was missing, but she'd seen him come down. She finished pulling a set of wool performance socks on and then stuck her head out into the hallway. A light was on in the office he shared with Nox.

She padded down the hallway to see if he wanted tea. The heavily-muscled shifter hunched at his desk, staring at a screen that she couldn't see, because his desk faced the door. The room was eerily quiet for Arebos' usual tastes. He typically had loud rock music playing, as he said it helped him concentrate—and he hated to wear headphones.

Now, the office was silent, a sure sign something was wrong. Half of Ari's long, ebony hair was pulled away from the sharp planes of his face, and his hand covered his usually smiling mouth. Arebos Flynn was one of the most incorrigible teases Harlow had ever met, constantly making jokes and flirting. It was rare for him to look so serious. The sounds of happy family life muffled as she shut the door.

"What is it?" she asked. They'd told the Wraiths and the other Knights about their subterfuge with the drone. Perhaps the footage was airing. "Has someone released the beach footage?"

Ari startled, his narrow eyes worried. He shoved a piece of hair behind one of his pointed ears, pointing at the computer screen in front of him. "No, nothing on that yet. It's Falcyra. Things are getting worse."

Harlow trailed around the piles of Nox's books on the floor. The Wraith had been obsessed with theories of surveillance all summer and collected tomes on everything from cutting edge tech to the ethics of surveillance culture. Harlow didn't know Nox well yet, but she was impressed with the vigor with which she explored her own position in the shadowed world of espionage. When Harlow made it through the maze, she caught sight of Ari's screen, and her breath caught in her chest.

The footage was playing on a loop with the sound off, in three-times speed, but that didn't make it any less horrific. Falcyra was *burning*. The vampires were killing humans by the dozen and it looked like the humans were revolting.

Harlow closed her eyes. "I thought the Dominavus were sent to handle this."

"They were," he replied. "But even they can't be everywhere. They get one riot calmed, and another crops up elsewhere. Falcyra has fallen to chaos."

Finn poked his head in, his excellent hearing having drawn him toward their conversation, no doubt. Alaric was behind him, followed by Thea. Soon, the whole family crowded behind Ari's desk, watching the awful footage.

Ari slowed it to normal speed, and the sound turned back on. The humans were overpowered, but the vampires and the Dominavus were outnumbered. It was sheer carnage on both sides. Nox went to her desk, murmuring something to Ari about sending her the footage as she went. She pulled the footage up on her super-powered computer and ran a scan.

"Rakul Kimaris isn't in any of this footage," she said.

"You can't know that yet," Alaric reasoned.

"No, but I'm willing to bet on it," Nox replied with a smile that showed she knew more than she was saying. Harlow was continuously surprised by the things that Nox and Arebos could find out about people—she with her near-magical ability to navigate technology and he with more traditional means of reconnaissance.

Nox tied her mass of jet-black hair back and began typing furiously, squinting a little at the screen. Indi handed her a pair of glasses and the wistful look they exchanged elicited a fake gag from Larkin, shot in Harlow's direction.

"She's right," Ari added, pointedly ignoring Larkin's antics. "I caught something this morning, but I've watched that footage a dozen times. He's never with the Dominavus, and it's not like you could miss him."

"What did you catch?" Larkin asked.

"I think he's back in Nytra," Ari replied, glancing at Larkin, who squeezed his shoulder as she passed him, plopping down on the couch behind his desk. The office was too small for this conversation, but no one seemed like they were willing to go elsewhere.

Nox nodded. "He used a little known alias at Cerberus, just last week," Nox said. "CCTV picked it up."

Ari glanced at the information his sister pulled up and added, "It's an odd one: Vivia Woolf."

The teacup Cian was carrying clattered onto its saucer. Harlow noted the nearly imperceptible shake of their fingers and made eye contact with Finn. He saw it too.

"What is it?" Finn asked.

Cian's mouth pressed into a grim line. "I haven't heard that name in a very long time. What makes you think Rakul uses it as an alias?"

Nox frowned. "It's in the Vault's records as being associated with him. I haven't ever seen an instance in which he actually used it."

"Associated?" Cian laughed. The sound was harsh and tears filled their eyes. "Yes, that name is *associated* with Rakul."

Everyone went still. Cian Herrington was nothing if not perpetually serene and in control. Sometimes their humor was dry and acerbic, but they never appeared as they did now.

Unhinged, Harlow thought to herself. She made eye contact with Indi, who nodded, understanding her older sister's expression immediately. Indigo whispered something to her twin, who then whispered to Ari.

"Let's give Cian some space," Indi said, ushering Nox out of the office. Nox protested, but Indigo shook her head. Harlow watched as Nox's fingers brushed Indigo's as they left the room.

They were like courtly lovers from an old story. Something about it was achingly sweet to watch. Meline and Ari left as well. Selene and Aurelia followed, dragging Thea and Alaric with them.

Larkin gently pried the teacup from Cian's hand. "I'll take this," she murmured.

Cian nodded, looking lost as Larkin left. Harlow led Cian to the small couch behind Ari's desk and slid onto the couch next to them. Their head was in their hands and their shoulders shook. Cian was obviously in pain.

Finn sat in Ari's chair, leaning forward as Harlow's hand went to Cian's back. "Are you all right?" she whispered.

"No," Cian choked out. "No, I am not."

"What does that name mean to you?" Finn asked.

Cian covered their face with their hands. "Vivia Woolf was an Argent."

Finn's breath caught. "Rakul's alias…"

Cian nodded. "Yes, Vivia and Rakul were bonded."

"What happened to Vivia?" Harlow asked, knowing the story couldn't possibly have a happy ending, not with the dark look on Cian's face.

Cian tossed their hands in the air, frustrated somehow. "To be honest, I don't know. I believe she's dead, but Rakul would never, or *could* never, say."

Finn tensed, but his voice was gentle. "There's something you're not saying, old friend."

Cian ran a hand through their hair, sending it spiking up in all directions. "This secret has protected the few of us left for nearly two thousand years…" Cian trailed off, looking distraught.

While she'd never describe Cian as stoic, she expected a well of stillness in their persona that she could depend on. This version of her friend was unsettling, worrisome.

"We would never tell anyone," Harlow said, trying as hard as she could to keep her voice even. Every part of her stood at attention. Whatever Cian was keeping from them had to be monumental to get them so worked up.

Harlow's sense of the threads in the room clarified. Tension snapped like an electrical current through them and Harlow's second sight sensed the connections between the three of them. They were strongest between Cian and Finn, but she was connected to them as well. Both glanced down at her.

"It's nothing. Just another weird development with my Strider abilities."

Relief spread through Cian's countenance, but Finn looked concerned. He'd been more worried than ever after her strange "trip" to the limen, given the way she'd partially shifted.

"Whatever it is, you can tell us," Finn said, reassuring the firedrake. For the moment, he seemed to have refocused on the problem at hand.

Cian reached toward Finn, their brow furrowed and mouth tight. The two of them grasped onto one another's forearms. It was a silent pledge, Harlow understood. A confirmation of a life-long commitment between the two of them, deeper than any bond of simple friendship. They'd made promises to one another, binding promises, and Finn was a good enough leader to remind his friend that those promises would be kept forever. Harlow couldn't help but swell with pride.

Cian let out a long sigh. "The Argent were here before the Illuminated, as were many of the Heraldic Order."

The silence in the room rang in Harlow's ears. It was one of the basic tenets of life with the Illuminated. They had created *all* the immortals on Okairos. What Cian was saying undermined everything Okairons held as truth. She glanced back at Finn to see his reaction. *Had he known this already, the way he had with the truth of* The Warden? The open shock on his face told her everything she needed to know.

"And you?" Finn asked, his words clipped.

"Born not from the Illuminated, but Argent parents, about fifty years before your people came here. We age very slowly and truth be told, I remember little of the world before the Illuminated came."

A long silence passed. Cian was older than most of the Illuminated on the planet. Many things made sense that had simply been mysterious about Cian previously. Their strange mix of youth and antiquity, in particular. Harlow's mind raced past those revelations and towards the historical implications of what Cian said. "Were there sorcières here? Vampires?"

In an uncharacteristic movement, Cian pushed both hands through their short hair, mussing it in a way that still looked perfect. "There were magical practitioners before the Illuminated, but not like sorcières. They worked aether differently, with more subtlety. As for vampires, they didn't exist before the Illuminated, but there were the Vespae..."

Harlow had read about the Vespae in books of old Falcyran folklore. They were creatures of legend, humanoid in some ways, but like swarming or hiving insects in others. Their sting was said to immobilize an immortal's access to the aether, a tall tale. "They're not supposed to be real," she mused.

Finn and Cian both raised their eyebrows in an identical expression that proved Cian had essentially raised Finn. She grinned at them, tempted to boop each of their noses, the way she would with Axel, but she restrained herself. "The tales I've read seemed tailor-made to scare children."

Cian nodded. "The lore is pretty accurate. Probably because for a long while in Falcyra, a nest or two would crop up—deep in the mountains, but still it made sense for people to tell their children the stories."

"A safety precaution," Finn mused.

"Yes. They were intensely territorial and once they'd decided to make a home in a given area, they wiped out all humanoid life. There weren't many of them for a long while, so the best line of defense was avoidance. When the Illuminated arrived on Okairos, the Vespae were growing in numbers, expanding their territory. A swarm working together could slaughter whole towns and cities in a single night. Humans didn't stand a chance against them."

The sheer thought of it was terrifying. Even now, humans had the means to at least make a stand against immortals. The riots in Falcyra were proof of that. Despite everything, their numbers won out over immortal strength, but the Vespae sounded like they might present another kind of problem.

Cian continued. "My people were the single line of defense against the Vespae for centuries, but there were few of us, spread thin across the planet. We were leaders, royalty in most places. The Empress Lofrata herself was an Argent. We protected our people the best we could."

Cian's head lowered, sadness in their eyes. Finn gripped their shoulder, attempting to comfort the Argent. "But it wasn't enough?"

Cian shook their head. "No. It wasn't enough—they overran us. For most of our history, the Vespae had been a problem, but a manageable one. And then their numbers swelled. When the Illuminated came, Lofrata accepted their offer of aid, never believing the price we would all pay for it. She was the High Empress, ruler of all—and they executed her..." Cian's voice broke over their next words, as Harlow's heart shattered in her chest. "... and my parents, along with all the heads of state with Heraldic blood. A few of us—children, mind you, the oldest were adolescents—were spirited away, kept hidden."

Harlow reached out to hug Cian, but they shook their head. This was painful, and they needed to finish. "When the Order of Masks came into prominence, we could reintegrate into society more fully. Many of our children were weaker than we were, and they presented differently when they shifted than we do. The Illuminated believed that their own remarkable genetics generated *our* children."

The scorn in Cian's voice cut deep. It was remarkable that they could stand to be around any of the Illuminated.

"What does all this have to do with Vivia Woolf?" Finn asked, his voice gentle. "And Rakul?"

"Vivia was Lofrata's daughter, the heir to the most powerful draconic power the world has ever known. The daughter she had with Rakul Kimaris was remarkable, but wholly different from both her parents. Inasa was pure shadow, a creature of the limen."

Cian paused as their silver eyes lit on Harlow and held fast. "Inasa Kimaris was the first Feriant, and she paired with a sorcière, and her daughter…"

"… was the first Strider," Harlow breathed. "No wonder she could shift. With both Illuminated and Argent blood, as well as her sorcière half, she must have been very powerful. But why the Feriant? Why a bird and not a dragon?"

Cian smiled sadly. "No one ever knew."

Finn leaned back, eyes shrewd and analytical. "That's how Rakul knew what Harlow was. His own grandchild was like her. What happened to them? To Inasa and Vivia, and the first Strider?"

"Inasa died in the War." Cian's eyes filled with tears. "Caitriona, the first Strider, died later. She was a good friend. We grew up together."

Harlow was willing to bet that Caitriona Kimaris was more than a friend, but she wouldn't press on what was still clearly an open wound. "What happened to Vivia?"

Cian shook their head. "I don't think anyone ever said, and we scattered so quickly that information on what happened to everyone became hard to keep track of."

There was so much grief in Cian's voice, but they turned

towards Finn, steadying their breath. "Your father was the one to execute Caitriona. He had an obsession with her. They were left... alone... for days before the execution."

Finn paled, staring at Harlow. "Why didn't you tell me this sooner?"

Cian stared at their hands. "I should have. But just like your secrets have kept you safe, so too have mine." They glanced at Harlow. "But I should have told you both when you were seventeen. I should have known."

Harlow took one of Cian's hands. "How could you have? Even my own parents didn't know what I was—and they were watching for the signs in all of us."

Cian wiped their eyes. "I worried it might be one of you and when Finn loved you... I... I should have seen this all coming. Connor won't stop until he has what he wants from the two of you." Cian paused, their mouth a thin line. "Caitriona had a disorder that Argent sometimes get. Her bleeds were painful, debilitating. She was infertile."

Harlow's breath caught as a wave of nausea washed over her. Her chin quivered, as what Cian was saying became clear. "That's why Connor killed her."

Cian nodded, tears flowing down their face freely. Finn looked as though he might burst into flames. His eyes glowed fiercely with that cold, lethal light that only appeared when he was incensed. His fists clenched tightly, and he obviously held his breath.

Harlow didn't want to push either of them harder on any of this, so she left her questions about all the specifics of Cian's story for another time, and got to the point. "So what does Rakul using Vivia's name at Cerberus mean?"

Finn spoke. "It's a message."

Cian nodded. "I think we have to assume so."

The implications of all this pieced together. Her heritage was part Illuminated, part shifter, and part sorcière. Something tickled in the back of her mind, some connection she felt just about to make, but Finn interrupted her train of thought.

"Someone has to go back to Nuva Troi to find Kimaris and ask him about all this," Finn said in a hollow voice—looking beyond her at Cian. "Whatever he wants, I don't think we can afford to ignore him. He wouldn't leave the Dominavus alone in Falcyra for no reason."

Cian regained some composure. "I agree. It might be valuable for you to spend some time with your father, to gauge his level of concern with you and Harlow. Connor will play this carefully, and we need to be a step ahead for once."

The sound of Finn's teeth grinding together made Harlow's skin crawl. "Then I have to go back. If we have any chance of getting the upper hand, the window is surely closing."

"I am sorry, Finbar. I should have told you all of this sooner," Cian said.

Finn sighed. "I understand why you didn't. I only wish we didn't have to guard ourselves so carefully. Secrets are our way. That won't change."

"We will go back to Nuva Troi then," Cian said, standing.

Harlow saw the way they were looking at one another. "No," she said, shaking her head. "I'm coming too."

Finn's response was sharp, his voice jagged and rough at the edges. "No. You will stay here with Alaric and your family. Where it's *safe*."

"You don't get to decide that for me," Harlow argued.

"I do," Finn said, standing. "You were sworn into the Knights and I'm your commander. It's not a request. It's an order. You will stay here."

Harlow stood. "Fuck you, McKay. You don't get to boss me around. I'm coming to Nuva Troi."

Cian stepped away from them carefully, backing out of the

room. "I'll leave you two to discuss this. I'll plan for our trip, Finn."

Finn nodded. "Do that. Make arrangements for *two* of us."

Cian nodded once, then disappeared.

"Why are you cutting me out of this?" Harlow hissed.

Finn growled. "Didn't you hear what Cian said? You are the descendant of a pairing that should not have been possible. That my parents did *everything* to stop. You've met Rakul Kimaris. Do you think there is any instance in which he'd work for my father after he killed Rakul's family—unless they had some way of *making* him stay loyal?"

Harlow was stunned into silence. Put that way, it didn't make much sense.

"He's sneaking around, leaving a trail of breadcrumbs for us to find... Whatever Connor has on him to keep him loyal, it's not something small. Until I know *exactly* what's happening here, I don't want you anywhere near Nuva Troi."

Harlow saw his point, but they had to make this time count. The sense of foreboding she'd had for weeks culminated here, she was sure of it. "Fine. But we have to be clever."

Finn relaxed a measure, one eyebrow quirked. "You have a plan in mind?"

Harlow paused for a beat. "I think so, but you won't like it."

Finn's head fell back, and a laugh escaped his beautiful lips. Harlow was confused until he said, "All my Knights' best plans start with those exact words. Tell me what I won't like." He pulled her closer to him so that her head rested against his chest, his arm curling around her.

"This all started with us pretending to be together to draw them out..." she began.

Finn pressed a kiss to her forehead. "Yes, and it worked."

"Sort of," Harlow agreed. "It got them to back off Antiquity Row, but we also gave them what they wanted... *us*."

Finn's entire body tensed. "You want to take it away?"

She craned her neck to look up at him. "Yes. Let's make it look like we're about to break up and see what they do. Section Seven has them primed, and our little show for the drone supports it."

His eyes darkened as his forehead wrinkled in thought. "Section Seven will rip you apart if we do this right."

Harlow swallowed hard. "I know. I can take it."

"You won't be able to tell anyone, not right away anyway. Not until we know what that probe was about. Anything that even hints that we might try to trick them could be a risk."

"I know," she whispered, her fingers curling around the arm draped around her waist. It hurt to think of deceiving her family this way, but they had this one chance.

"Then we'll get it set up. I'm going to tell Cian so they can be our go-between if we need one, but that's it. It'll only be a week, maybe two." He shifted a little against her, his breathing relaxing as he thought things over. "I think we have to assume the drone might not have been from Section Seven. It could very well be a decoy."

Harlow pulled away, looking up as Finn's arm dropped away from her. "What would the point of that be? Misdirection?"

"Yes. It's one of my father's favorite ploys. Send something just clever enough to draw everyone's attention, but clumsy enough to be discoverable... And then while everyone's trying to figure that out..."

"Send in the real probe," Harlow finished.

Finn nodded. "We'll have to be very careful about this, Harlow. There can't be even one slip up."

For the first time all summer, Harlow felt like they might be getting somewhere. Like all the weeks of frustration and failure might lead up to a win. "Let's do this then. Let's trick Connor McKay again."

Finn pulled her closer again. "We can do this. We can win." He kissed her, his mouth desperate and warm against her own.

Harlow wound every part of her with what she could of his. She let her shadows out, sending them through the threads that bound them tighter with each passing moment until his light responded, twining in amongst the darkness as they made wordless promises to one another. Vows that could not, would not, be broken by subterfuge or deception.

CHAPTER THIRTEEN

The next day dawned blessedly clear, though the temperature had dropped significantly. Harlow had to wear one of Finn's sweaters with a pair of leggings to get coffee together. The sun was warm, but the air smelled like fall, or maybe it was simply the myriad evergreen needles that had been strewn about by the storm crunching under their feet. They were walking back to the villa when a ruckus from the bushes startled them both. A cheeky red squirrel ran out, chattering angrily.

Finn pressed a kiss to her hair, as he squeezed her shoulder tight in reassurance. "I love seeing you in my clothes," he said as he wrapped an arm around her waist.

She'd been about to text Larkin that The Gate was out of lemon scones and when jostled, her coffee and her phone both slipped out of her hands. "Shit."

Finn bent to pick up her phone, and she tried to grab the cup that was flying away in the breeze. Another noise from the bushes caught both their attention. It was a camera. They'd been followed to the coffee shop again. They were just getting past the overblown drama around the pizza toppings. And now this? Harlow lunged for the photographer, suddenly furious. She knew exactly how those photos would be used—another Section Seven spread, making fun of her. The shifter scandal in Nuva Troi was dying down, and the scavengers needed fresh meat.

Finn pulled her back as the photographer stepped out of the bushes, backing away, but slowly, still taking photos. She struggled against him for a moment and then relented. When she stilled in his arms he let her go, but surprisingly he didn't follow the photographer, or menace them in any way. Her heart skipped a beat. Usually he was so protective of her.

"Sorry," she muttered, an unpleasant feeling taking root in her gut.

"You did great," he replied, handing her phone back to her. She looked up at him and saw the concern in his eyes, though his face didn't change. "You did great," he said again, watching her carefully.

So this was it. The game had started. She nodded, letting her feelings show on her face. They had no idea who was watching, and this was their first opportunity to show their relationship changing, even subtly.

Harlow looked down at her phone. The screen was shattered.

"I'll get you a new phone," Finn said, and in those few words, she heard another step of their plan formulating.

"One of the fancy ones?" Harlow asked with a grimace.

"Yes," Finn laughed. "You'll love it."

She wrinkled her nose at him to show her displeasure, but brushed a kiss to his lips to show him she was okay.

"Do you want to go back for another coffee?"

Harlow shook her head. "No, it's fine. I'll just make tea at home."

His hand slipped into hers, warm and comforting. A sinking

feeling spread through her. He was leaving soon, and then she'd be here without him, and there would be more moments like these. More times when he treated her in ways that didn't feel good, so they could lure Connor into giving something away. He seemed to be thinking along similar lines, and they didn't talk much the rest of the walk home.

When they entered the villa, Meline was standing in the front foyer, shaking her head as she stared at her phone. "Sorry about your coffee," she said, obviously reading about the encounter on one of the gossips. "Did your phone break too?"

Harlow rolled her eyes. That was fast. "Yes."

"Bummer," Meline replied, taking Harlow's elbow. "Can me and Ari talk to you two?"

Finn nodded. "Sure. Let me go give Larkin these croissants."

Meline shook her head. "That's gonna be disappointing. She wanted the lemon scones."

Harlow laughed, trying to banish the rush of anxiety she felt after the encounter with the paparazzi. She hugged Meline as they walked together into the villa's ridiculous formal living room. Ari and the maters were already seated, and everyone looked uneasy.

"What's going on?" Harlow asked as she found a seat. She hated this room. All the chairs were too hard to get cozy in. She'd asked Cian if she could turn them into better chairs, and they'd screeched something about heirlooms and respect for historical artifacts.

"It's time for us to go home, dear," Selene said as Harlow attempted to make herself comfortable in a stiff armchair covered in a blue satin stripe.

Aurelia nodded. "We've been away for too long already, and you know that autumn is our most important season at the store."

Harlow had been expecting this for a week or two. The

maters had done all they could in Nea Sterlis, talking with the sorcière and shifters here that they thought they could trust about potentially confronting the Illuminated over the imbalance of power at the next Council of Orders, after the Winter Solstice. Neither Harlow nor Finn believed it would do much good, but they'd agreed to solve things as amicably as possible before other, more violent options were considered.

It was time for them to go home, and continue the work there, but she wasn't ready for her family to go their separate ways—even though it would be easier to pull off her ruse with Finn if the maters weren't here looking over her shoulder constantly. They took Section Seven and the rest of the gossips with a grain of salt, but if they saw her getting upset, they'd want to know what was happening.

Tricking Thea would be harder. Both Alaric and Finn had made it abundantly clear at breakfast that they thought it was best for both Harlow and Thea to stay in Nea Sterlis, at least until Finn and Cian could gauge what Rakul Kimaris was up to, and talk to the McKays and Velariuses both in person.

Harlow smiled sadly. "Okay. You're going home. I'll miss you so much."

Aurelia, who sat in the chair next to her own, patted her hand. "We will miss you too."

"Indi and Nox are going with them," Meline said.

Ari added, "Nox and I have connections in the city, and someone needs to help Finn and Cian with the intelligence side of things."

"Okay," Harlow said. They needed people in Nuva Troi to monitor Rakul's movements if they could find him, she knew that. She just wished her little sister didn't have to be a part of it.

Finn entered the room, plopping down on the loveseat next to Selene, slinging his arm around her shoulders. "So what do the two of you want to talk about?"

Ari and Meline glanced at one another, both looking

anxious. Ari spoke first. "You know I have to go back to Falcyra. We need eyes on the ground."

Finn nodded. "Agreed."

"I want to go too—" Meline said.

"No," Harlow responded, cutting Meline off. "No. It's too dangerous."

Finn held a hand up, then looked at the maters. "You think this is a good idea?"

Aurelia sighed. "Meline's power will manifest soon. She shows every sign of being an expert with glamour."

Selene added, "It runs in my family, and we've been sure Meli will be the same for some time."

"It's started already," Meline said. "It's a matter of days now, not weeks. Maybe hours."

If the maters were right, and they usually were, when Meline's power manifested, she would be capable of glamouring herself to look like almost anyone for short periods of time. And Ari could literally disappear. They would make an excellent team if Meline knew anything about being a spy.

"Ari has been helping me," Meline said softly. "I asked him to tell me about his job, and at first it was a game, but look…" Meline's fingers worked swiftly, pulling threads of aether in lightning fast strokes. Before Harlow could blink twice, Meline had transformed into a perfect copy of Wesley Arden, her favorite author.

It was a stunning piece of magic, as she hadn't even fully manifested yet. Typically, witches who excelled at glamour did best with people they saw every day. Meline stood and walked around the room. From every angle, the glamour was perfect.

"That's incredible," Finn said. "And no one knows you can do this?"

Meline shook her head. "I can hold it for a few hours now, but when manifested, I think I could go a few days without reapplying the magic."

"And how will we explain your absence?" Harlow asked. It wasn't that she wanted to burst Meline's bubble. She saw how much her sister needed this. How much she wanted to do something useful with her talents, rather than simply turning herself prettier and prettier for social events.

Ari grinned. "You know that silent retreat that everyone's been raving about on socials?"

Harlow shrugged, but Finn nodded. "Sure. The thing in wine country, where you get the private cabin for as long as you want, and it's basically a luxury hotel."

Meline smiled. "I announced to my socials this morning that I'm having a spiritual awakening. Apparently, Aphora has called me into 'beautiful silence' for at least a month, maybe more."

"I'll go with her," Ari said. "Out of sight of course. And we'll disappear in a week. The place has some seriously strict rules around privacy. Their contracts are magically enforced, so we should be good."

Harlow glanced between Ari and Meline. They were pleased with their plan, and it seemed like they'd thought of everything. But they didn't need her permission. They needed Finn's. He looked to her though, wanting to make sure she thought it was a good idea. She nodded once and Meline whooped with joy, throwing her arms around Ari.

As they left with Finn to make plans, Harlow turned to the maters. "Are you sure she's ready for this?"

Aurelia smiled, but her eyes were sad. "My darling, we learned long ago never to clip our girls' wings when they were ready to fly."

Selene brushed a kiss to her forehead as she and Aurelia left to go pack. Axel passed them on their way out and hopped into her lap. At least he wasn't leaving her. Thea and Alaric would be here still, and Enzo and Petra of course, but they were busy with their partners. She wondered if Larkin planned to go home as well.

Where *was* Larkin? Harlow picked Axel up and walked through the house. Larkin's favorite terrace was located just off the library, as it was sheltered by trees and quieter than the ones overlooking the bay. Also, there was a hammock, and Larkin was a sucker for a hammock. Sure enough, her sister was napping on the terrace, the hammock swinging gently in the breeze.

Harlow grabbed a blanket from the back of one of the chairs in the library and let Axel down. He followed her out to the covered terrace. Larkin opened her eyes. "Hi, the croissants weren't awful. Thanks for getting the lemon ones."

Harlow smiled. "Brought you a blanket." Axel jumped into the hammock, landing on Larkin's chest. "And a cat."

"And a sister," Larkin added, scooting over. "Hop in with me?"

Harlow got in, covering herself and Larkin with the blanket. It was just cool enough on the covered terrace to need it. When Axel was settled between them and they rocked gently once more, Harlow asked, "Are you going back to Nuva Troi with the maters? Or are you running away to Falcyra too?"

Larkin smiled. "I'm staying here with you and Thea. If that's all right, anyway."

"Of course it is. I'm happy you're staying."

"Me too," Larkin said, but she didn't *look* particularly happy.

"Is everything okay?"

Larkin forced a smile. "Yeah. I've been sleeping poorly for the past few weeks, that's all. Maybe my bleed is coming. I haven't been tracking it very well."

Harlow made a non-committal noise. The sound of the waves far below the terrace soothed her, and because everything was chaotic, she needed all the soothing she could get. Larkin went back to her book. Axel purred, setting a deep rhythm as the hammock swung. Harlow woke to Finn carrying her upstairs.

"Put me down," she murmured sleepily. "I can walk."

"You can, but I'd rather carry you," he assured her. "We're going to train for the next few days. You need the extra rest."

She was tempted to grumble about it, but the resolve in his voice was firm. So she snuggled into his chest and drifted back off. They didn't have many days left together, and she didn't want to spend them fighting.

CHAPTER FOURTEEN

The next few days made Harlow deeply regret not arguing with Finn about the training. He'd seen her shift, at least partially, so they knew she *could*. But nothing happened, no matter what they tried, and they certainly weren't going to try anything including biting again, so they settled on honing her abilities with her shadows. Finn taught her how to make weapons from mundane objects, and she practiced launching them at all manner of targets.

She tried knives, javelins, and a variety of sharp, pointy objects, but arrows seemed to be her favorite projectile. When she got the hang of making them, they flew true, at least sometimes. Finn was proud of her. She could tell from the way his eyes shone whenever she struck one of the dummies he tossed into the air for her to hit.

On the day she hit half of them, he grinned. "We don't have time for you to learn hand to hand combat techniques before I leave, but I feel better knowing you can protect yourself."

Harlow snickered. "I can protect myself half of the time, you mean."

He slung an arm around her. "It's *progress*, Harls. And you'll keep practicing while I'm gone, right?"

Harlow nodded. "So, I guess it's time to work on the Feriant again."

Finn shook his head, his eyes on the floor. "Forcing it isn't working. I'm sorry I pushed you so hard earlier this summer. I acted like my dad."

"What?" Harlow was incredulous. "No. You didn't."

He looked away. "I don't know if I want to have children."

That was a surprise, but she understood exactly where the worry came from. "Okay," she said. "If you don't want them, we won't have them."

He looked up, shock on his face. "Just like that?"

She shrugged. "Just like that."

"Do *you* want them?" he asked. They'd never talked about this before.

She sat on the floor of the studio, hugging her knees to her chest. The truth was that it was impossible for her to imagine having children. She could imagine being an auntie to Thea and Alaric's children easily. In fact, it was a favorite pastime of hers to imagine what their babies might look like, but she never thought about her own. She'd barely spent a moment or two thinking about the same between her and Finn. "I don't think I really care one way or another. If you wanted them, I'd be happy to think it over, but if you don't, that's fine with me too."

He sat next to her, his shoulder pressing into hers. "Really? You won't be disappointed?"

Harlow laughed as Axel rolled on his back in front of the studio's mirrors, admiring his reflection. She'd never played at being a mother like Thea had when they were little. She'd spent her time imagining what her manifested powers might be, the books she might discover and restore, the person she might marry, but she'd rarely pretended to parent. Thinking about it now, she realized she'd never cared much about having her own children either way. "No. I have you and him, and probably a whole gaggle of little AlThea witchlings."

"*AlThea*?" Finn grimaced, squeezing her shoulders. "That is terrible. Who came up with that?"

Harlow fell into his lap, tweaking his nose playfully. "The kids on the interwebs, Finbar, who else?"

He kissed her. "So, just me and you for all eternity?"

"For all eternity," she agreed.

He sighed, and she saw a layer of the hurt he carried peel away. It left him a little raw, but she loved him more for it, if that were even possible. Axel lost interest in his reflection, and came to lie on Harlow's chest, and the three of them chatted aimlessly for long hours, until someone called them to dinner.

TWO DAYS BEFORE EVERYONE WAS SET TO PART WAYS, Cian popped into the studio in the Vault's subterranean gym, where they'd just finished a series of exercises meant to help focus Harlow's breath and mind. Even though Finn had suggested they stop trying so hard, Harlow still made at least one attempt every day.

It hadn't worked. Of course. She was still in her humanoid form, not a feather in sight.

"Have you tried the river?" Cian asked.

Finn's eyebrows raised. "No, I hadn't thought of that, but now that you mention it... It makes sense. Let's try it."

"What river?" Harlow asked.

Finn took her hand, helping her up from her seated position on the floor. She blushed as she rose, a tingle of desire flickering through her veins. Nearly every part of her was painfully distracted by him. The way the muscles in his chest and abdomen rippled as he dragged a shirt on didn't help things.

Cian made a gagging noise. "The two of you are *terrible*."

A giggle slipped between Harlow's lips, and Finn kissed them, muttering against her mouth, "I think we're pretty amazing."

His hand slid around her waist as he turned her, pushing her forward, after Cian, who was hurrying out of the gym. She followed them, acutely aware of Finn right behind her. He followed closely enough that every once in a while some part of him brushed her.

Her ass, her shoulder, the small of her back. Every touch was like a burning brand. Fervor raced through her, driving her into a near-frenzy when he tugged on her ponytail. It was meant to be a playful gesture, but her body responded immediately.

"Keep your hands to yourselves, please," Cian begged, clearly exasperated as they led them further back into a dark hallway behind the Vault's gym that Harlow had never noticed. There was a half-flight of stairs in the dimly lit hall, and then her feet hit what felt like stone, rather than marble tile.

"Are we headed deeper underground?" she asked.

"Yes," Finn said, keeping enough distance now that he wouldn't risk brushing against her again. He grinned when she looked back, and a piece of his dark hair fell onto his forehead. She nearly leapt at him.

He shook his head at her, but the bulge in his joggers gave him away. He was as far gone as she was. Fervor had them in its clutches, and they were embarrassing themselves, shamelessly, so it seemed.

She bit her bottom lip, and Finn growled. "Turn around, you merciless creature."

She did as he asked, flipping her ponytail at him with a seductive look over her shoulder.

He was at her back in an instant. His breath caressed her ear as he said, "When we're done here, I'm gonna pull that ponytail. *Hard*."

A thrill went through her, throbbing with molten heat in

her core. His hands gripped her hips, his fingers pressing into her soft flesh, an obvious clue to how he'd like to take her—the position in which the hair-pulling might take place.

"Would you like that?" he asked. Cian was gone from sight.

Harlow nodded, unable to speak.

Finn's voice lowered now to a quiet rumble. "These fucking leggings... And this tiny little crop top, are you even wearing a bra?" He pulled her hard against him, stopping them both from progressing further.

She tried to laugh, but she was too breathless to make much noise. His hands—his wicked hands—were everywhere, slipping underneath her top to find out if she was, or was not, wearing a bra.

"Bad girl," he said as his fingers grazed her bare flesh. He spun her around, pulling her tight against his heaving chest. "We were *supposed* to be training today."

His fingers wrapped around her ponytail and he tugged. She leaned into him as he exposed her neck. Harlow's eyes fell closed. Somewhere in the distance there was the sound of water, but she didn't care. All she wanted was for this moment to last. For Finn to stay right here with her, for them to go on with their engagement. To bond, and move into a new house. To be safe and *normal*, not faking a breakup.

But they weren't normal. Even now, they were driven by fervor, and as they dug deeper into the Illuminated Order's business, they ensured their lives would never be normal again. He sensed her breathing change and stopped. "What's wrong?"

She shook her head, squeezing her eyes shut.

"Harls, you're crying," he whispered. His hands were gentle on her now, pulling her close for comfort's sake.

"I don't want to do this," she said as she buried her face in his chest. "I don't want you to go."

His arms tightened around her. "I know. I wish everything was different..."

"That we could just be happy," she finished.

She felt, rather than saw him nod, since she'd tucked her face between his ridiculously large pectorals. He smelled so good she could eat him, but the fervor relented a little. Just enough for her to feel her emotions welling up, the dark sadness behind all the desire.

"Do you want to back out of the ruse? We don't have to do it," Finn said as he hugged her tighter.

"No," she whispered, though she knew he heard. "I just wish we didn't have to."

"Me too," Finn answered. He didn't have to say more. They both knew they'd go through with this. It didn't make letting it happen any easier.

In the dark of the tunnel, Finn's fingers laced through hers and they walked forward. There weren't any sconces on the walls here, but as her eyes adjusted, she realized there was light. Above them, thousands of bioluminescent insects crawled on the ceiling. Harlow was fascinated. They were delicately formed beetles, slow moving and peaceful, and they put off the mildest glow that was just enough to see by. The walls of the tunnel were smooth, as was the ground, though it didn't look to have been made by people or modern means.

"Where are we?" Harlow asked as the path curved sharply, descending even further into the earth.

"Under the Vault," Finn explained. The sound of rushing water filled the tunnel. "These tunnels were made in one of the prehistoric eras."

"Wyrms?" Harlow breathed. There was evidence that Okairos had long ago been host to enormous subterranean wyrms, who never surfaced, but wove through the many upper layers of the planet's surface.

"Yes," Finn said. The tunnel widened into a cavern, and the glowing insects on the ceiling of the tunnel were *everywhere* here. Harlow frowned—that wasn't quite the case after all. They were still only on the ceiling, but their reflection in the rushing river that took up most of the cavern floor was deceiving. The river looked like it was made of stars.

Cian sat on a rock near the river, grinning. "Welcome to the Pyriphle."

Harlow sounded out the word in her head, trying to find the source of the tickle of recognition she felt. *Peer-eef-lahy*—it was one of those ancient human words with far too many consonants in a row that sounded nothing like it was spelled. Her brain hit on it, *Pyriphle*. Human lore said that the river was the pathway to Akatei's domain. "The river to the underworld?"

"Yes, we think so," Finn said, watching Harlow closely. He and Cian were both watching her rather closely, she noticed.

"What do you think is going to happen?" she asked, raising her eyebrows.

Both of them laughed, and Finn let go of her hand. "We have some evidence that this river is connected to the limen."

"What kind of evidence?" Harlow asked, her interest piqued.

"It's more of a theory," Finn said. "Magic behaves strangely around the Pyriphle."

"The river doesn't respond to any of the magic that most sorcière and Illuminated use," Cian said.

"But I don't use magic like they do," Harlow said, following their reasoning.

Finn nodded, smiling at her in encouragement.

"Use your second sight," Cian urged, stepping towards the riverbank and dipping a hand into the water.

As the water slipped through their fingers and back into the river, Harlow engaged her second sight, until she saw the threads. They appeared as glowing filaments of golden light, filled with dark aether. The aether that flowed through them was what made magic possible. According to metaphysical theorists, on many worlds only a little aether flowed through the threads of reality—just enough to create life. Okairos' threads were more robust, according to them, more conducive to carrying aether, which made magic possible.

But the water of the Pyriphle was different; it wasn't made of threads at all—which was impossible. *Everything* was made of aethereal threads. But this water was made of the same substance her shadows were, the same substance at the heart of the limen. At the heart of Nihil.

And then the fifteen guardians flashed before her spirit sight. Two were still missing. When Ashbourne's eyes snapped open, she was flung back into the cavern. Harlow wasn't sure what had happened, if she had been to Nihil again, or if she'd just recalled her earlier visit, but something had changed in the cavern in the split second she'd been gone.

Time slowed to a crawl around her, as it had that first visit to Nihil. Though this time she moved freely, or so she thought. She walked toward the river, drawn to its dark magic. Her feet moved as though they had a will of their own, and before she knew it, she was sprinting towards the water, her body preparing to dive. There wasn't a single thought or strand of reasoning in her head. She moved on instinct and desire alone. Hands gripped her, dragging her back as time resumed its usual pace.

"What the fuck?" Finn yelled as he dragged her away from the river.

He was utterly panicked, she realized, as her mind raced to catch up with what had happened. *She'd run towards the river at full speed, hadn't she? Why?*

Harlow looked down at her arms, expecting to see feathers again, but this time her fingers had sprouted claws—no, talons. Both arms, to her elbows, were stained the deepest midnight blue.

"I'm sorry," she said, looking up into Cian and Finn's worried faces. "I don't think I was in control of myself."

Cian crouched down, running their knuckles across her cheekbone. "You're all right?"

Finn turned away, and she watched him take several deep breaths. "Yes," she said. "The water is different. It's made of the same substance as my shadows."

Cian pressed a hand to Finn's back as they stood. "She's fine, Finbar."

But Finn didn't turn. Harlow stood, Cian helping her up as she went. "I'm okay."

"How can I leave?" Finn said, his voice barely loud enough to make out over the rushing of the river. "How can I leave you? How can I be sure you'll be fine on your own?"

She took one of his hands, exhaling. "I promise not to come down here alone, but maybe you could start by *listening* to me."

He glanced back at her, catching Cian's chuckle just as she did.

"I won't come down here alone, but honestly, it's not affecting me the way it was at first, even now."

Finn turned. "And how was that?"

Harlow looked down at her hands, which were slowly returning to their normal color. The talons were gone. "It was like my shadows wanted to join with the river. They're made of the same stuff."

"And now?" Finn asked. His expression was drawn, but at least he was listening.

"Now they're calm." They were slithering around her legs, reaching out to touch him, as though in apology. When one tickled his palm, it glowed with his own power.

He glowered at her, at her shadows, but they were persistent. A smile played at the corner of his mouth. "Okay, I believe you."

Cian walked toward the tunnel. "Let's go back, just to be safe."

Finn took her hand, and they followed, talking as they went.

"The river might help me shift," Harlow pondered. "But I don't think it's safe."

"No?" Cian asked, casting a look back at her.

Harlow glanced up at Finn. "No. I don't like the idea that I wouldn't be in full control of the shift. When you get back, maybe we can try some experiments."

Finn squeezed her hand. "We can."

What were sure to be harrowing weeks ahead loomed like a spiral of anxiety and insecurity, just waiting for her to slide right down. She had to change the subject. "Have you ever tried to travel downriver, like by boat?"

Finn nodded. "Yes, a few times, but there's a waterfall about a mile in, and no instrument we've ever brought with us has ever been able to measure it. Something about the river messes with reality."

That made all the sense in the world to Harlow, given that there were no threads in the river, just pure aether.

Cian added, "Honestly, we just thought it was an interesting feature of the house. We found it rather recently when we expanded the Vault to make the gym. I'm sorry I didn't think of taking you down there sooner." The shifter paused. They'd re-entered the finished part of the tunnel, and now sconces lit their way, so it was easy to see the deep consideration on their face. "Are you sure about our trip to Nuva Troi? We could put it off and prioritize this."

Finn glanced at Harlow. She shook her head, and he squeezed her hand again. "No, we've decided. Plus, Father is expecting me now. It would be hard to back out without arousing his suspicions."

Harlow's chest tightened around her heart at the harsh tone in Finn's voice, the one reserved for discussing Connor. She squeezed Finn's hand, raising it to her lips.

"It's okay," he said, his voice gentling for her.

Cian nodded. "Good. In addition to everything else, we need

to try to suss out what he and Pasiphae are thinking about Falcyra. It's nearly time, don't you think?"

Finn nodded. "Yes."

"Time for what?" Harlow asked.

Finn smiled, but it didn't reach his eyes. Cian walked away, calling back to them. "I'm going to go look through my notes about the Pyriphle. Come find me when you're done."

Harlow's stomach felt as though it had dropped into freefall, or that someone had pulled a rug from beneath her feet and she was crashing to the floor in slow motion. The sense that everything was going to change was overpowering.

"You understand we are not the only operatives of the Knights, don't you?"

She understood that, vaguely anyway. She knew there were others, but not how they were organized or what they did. They'd been so focused on trying to figure out how to get her to shift again at the beginning of the summer, and then the fervor had taken over, she'd lost focus somewhat and hadn't asked the kinds of questions she usually would. Looking up at Finn now, she knew that falling in love had made her not want to ask those kinds of questions. She hadn't really wanted to know. But now she did. With him leaving, she *needed* to know.

"Tell me everything," she said.

CHAPTER FIFTEEN

They went to Finn's workroom in the Vault, which belonged to both of them now. The antique library table at the center of the room held both their notebooks and the fancy tablet that Finn had purchased for Harlow. The one she never took out of this room, if she could help it.

Finn perched on one of the stools that surrounded the table, gesturing for Harlow to sit on the one opposite him. When she sat, he stared at her for a few moments, then reached out to touch the soft curve of her jawline. She saw in his eyes that this was hard for him to tell her, and not because he didn't trust her. There was a sadness there that let her know he was about to bring her into the full scope of his world in a way he didn't much want to.

He still didn't understand. She wanted this—she wanted to know every part of him. This, the Knights, whatever their true goals were, this *was* Finn.

"You know that we've worked for many years to carve out places that the people most harmed by the Illuminated—by the Orders—could find safety, right?"

Harlow nodded. The Haven project was bigger than just the

cafes in Nuva Troi and Nea Sterlis; it was a shadow network of people who helped mostly humans, but often shifters and sorcière as well, when they'd been targeted by the Illuminated or the Order of Night. The Haven units provided immediate escape from imminent harm, but also helped people disappear, or at least relocate, when more complicated situations arose.

"While that's been one of our primary objectives, it's only a part of our bigger goal..." Finn trailed off, frowning, as though he couldn't quite figure out how to say it.

But Harlow already knew. It was obvious. "You're looking for a way to break it all. To break their reign for good."

Finn nodded. "We are, and we're just getting started, but this is the Knights' purpose."

A part of her had always known this was the mission. She just hadn't wanted to admit it to herself. It was too big to think about. The Illuminated Order was more than just the Illuminated. It was entire systems, nations. It was everything that Okairos was built on in this modern era. Breaking those systems down would take years, decades even.

It wouldn't be easy, and a part of Harlow understood that they might never see the fruits of their labor, not in their very long lifetimes, but she was in. Hope flooded the dread that had been collecting for weeks, amongst the constant stream of twisting turns and failures to find her footing with all this. She'd hoped for something like this to come along and claim her for years, and now here it was: purpose, paired with love and belonging.

Finn played with a pen on the desk, clicking it over and over. She pried it out of his fingers. "I'm in. All the way."

"You understand that the penalty for doing this kind of work is execution, right?" Finn's voice didn't waver, but his eyes dropped to the floor as he finished speaking.

It hadn't occurred to her how much he banked on being perfect until now. It wasn't just that he was a leader, or that he felt responsible for all the people who looked to him for guidance. He actually believed he wasn't worthy of love if he couldn't be perfect. What she'd always assumed was ambition, was actually something much more complex. He fought terrible internal battles, just like she did.

Harlow waited for a long moment to speak, until his eyes dragged back upwards to hers. "I want this. All of it. You, Haven —all of it. I don't have any questions about this. I'm sure. Are you?"

His eyebrows pulled together in an ever-so-slightly petulant frown. "*Obviously*."

Harlow raised her own eyebrows and shook her head, mimicking his petulance, but secretly pleased that he'd bounced back so quickly. "Well, me too."

She knew she couldn't heal the wounds that caused him to feel this pain to begin with, but she could be here for him, just like he was for her. It was good to see him unfurl a little, to trust her more—and not just with the Knights' secrets, but with his heart. As that well of emotion filled, Harlow's skin tingled with anticipation. The way his eyes smoldered for her alone was enough to send her into a desirous frenzy.

"So much sass, Krane," he purred leaning across the table to brush a kiss to her lips. "Please never stop with your smart mouth. I have so many things I want to do with it."

Harlow resisted the urge to fan herself as he sat back down; she would miss these snippy little back-and-forth battles. "So, what's our first step?"

Finn opened his laptop and turned it towards her. "We've been mapping out possibilities for three years. We knew that social instability had to be one aspect. The humans had to resist. Their numbers are too great at this point to completely control without eradicating them."

"Which the Illuminated Order would never do, because the Order of Night is their closest ally," Harlow reasoned.

Finn's expression darkened. "Yes, there's that, and—" He looked like he'd swallowed something too large for his esophagus for a brief moment.

"What is it?" Harlow urged. Whatever was causing that expression wasn't going to get any easier to say.

"Some Illuminated... Not me. Not Alaric or Petra—*ever*. But some of the older Illuminated... Enjoy human blood."

The room spun around Harlow. Of course she knew that the Illuminated had fangs, but unlike vampires they ate food. They obviously didn't need blood to sustain life. "Why would they?"

Finn's eyes fell to the floor. "Because it feels good."

While the feeling that the room was moving around her had stopped, Harlow's heartbeat throbbed in her ears, her nerves setting a ragged rhythm in her body she could not slow. "Like in the Claiming."

Finn nodded. "Yes, but the Claiming grounds us. It's intimate. Passionate, but it is meant to form a bond, much like the ways vampire families are bonded."

"Okay," Harlow said. That made sense. Not all vampires were like the House of Sorath or Remiel, both of which seemed unusually interested in growing power. Most vampiric houses operated more like families, sharing resources. "So what's wrong with that, and why is it such a secret?"

"Because it is addictive for us. And as such, a weakness. One my parents have." Finn's eyes darted away from hers. "It is also part of why I was so worried about the Claiming, and about biting you. There's a certain amount of any bloodletting that can open the door for those desires, and I was afraid of what it might trigger for me with you since you are not one of us."

Harlow nodded. "That makes perfect sense now."

They sat quietly for a while, each thinking private thoughts, processing. Harlow turned the conversation back to Finn's original confession. "So the older Illuminated won't be motivated to completely eradicate humans if they start to resist on a larger scale."

"Right," Finn agreed, grimacing slightly.

"That makes what's happening in Falcyra an opportunity for the Knights, right?"

Finn frowned. "In some ways, yes. But I want to know who the other players are in this. There's someone helping the Humanists—their money trail makes little sense. Nox chased it into multiple dead ends."

Harlow sighed, shrugging somewhat helplessly. It sounded like a difficult thing to try to find out to her. People were always manipulating money in exciting ways in novels, so she assumed the same was possible in real life.

"Nox is *really* good at shit like this," Finn said, twining a finger through her ponytail. "There should be *something*."

"Then she'll keep looking. She'll figure it out."

"She will." He glanced at his phone. "It's getting late. I'm going to leave my laptop here, and you can read all the files you want while I'm gone, okay?"

"I bet they're meticulously organized, aren't they?" Harlow teased.

He scooped her into his arms. "Just because you're the messiest person alive doesn't mean everyone else is."

"I'm not the messiest," Harlow argued. "Meline is worse."

Finn carried her upstairs. "I'm going to miss refolding all your laundry for the next few weeks."

As he kicked the door to the bedroom shut, she replied. "Me too, sweet boy. Me too."

CHAPTER SIXTEEN

The next morning, everyone left on the early train. Finn had asked Harlow not to get up. He thought it would make things easier on them both. So she stayed in bed, Axel in her arms, as she listened to the quiet sounds of her heart leaving her behind. She knew they were doing the right thing, but it didn't make things any easier.

Except, in some ways, it did. The further Finn got from the house, the more relief she felt. The fog that had cluttered her mind for weeks slowly cleared. She could feel his train leave and by the time she was feeding Axel and making tea, she knew he was gone. It was strange to be heart-achingly sad and full of relief at the same time.

Harlow found a box on the counter, with a note. *New phone, text me when you get it set up.*

After they'd made love several times last night, Finn had explained that her new phone would have a tiny flaw in its security system. Something that looked like a mistake in the extra security that went into all their phones that blocked them from prying eyes. If Connor was probing their security, he'd eventually find it. So while Finn's phone would remain secure, hers would not. Even despite the security system that Alaric and Nox had built for their tech, the Knights had a strict policy against using phones for any sensitive conversations. The security was to keep their private lives private.

She had been worried that if the phone's security was weakened, it might be hackable—turned into a listening device. There had been a rash of articles on just that fear in the past few years, but Finn assured her that the rest of the phone's security would be firmly in place, so that the text and call monitoring would be convincing as a glitch. Harlow would have to be careful to limit her phone and text conversations with her friends and family until Finn returned, which made her nervous. She boosted herself on the counter next to Axel and stared out the villa's floor to ceiling windows at the ocean. Then she got to work setting the new phone up.

When she was finished, she texted Finn. *How are you feeling?*

He saw it immediately. Like he was waiting for her message. *Sad, but also... better?*

Harlow couldn't help but sigh with relief. Some of the guilt she carried for feeling better eased. *Me too. It's okay.*

It is. We'll fix this and I'll be back before you know it.

There was a long pause, and she saw he was still writing something. *I got in touch with an old friend, Sabre LeBeau. Do you know them?*

Axel bumped her hand, then flopped over on the counter to show her his belly. She snapped a photo of him being cute and sent it to Finn, then responded, *Maybe? Who are they?*

A realtor. They're going to show me houses while I'm in Nuva Troi... for when we get back this fall.

This was a part of the ruse—the one she hated the most. Sabre LeBeau was one of Finn's exes and an affiliate of the Knights of Serpens. They were utterly trustworthy, and would be brought in on the ruse, but what they were about to do still made Harlow sick. The plan was for Finn to be seen about town with Sabre to get the gossips going. They hoped that was all it would take, but Harlow knew it might take further measures to lure Connor into believing that Finn and Harlow's relationship was truly in trouble.

They had agreed not to plan much else, to let the lies they told be spontaneous. Finn reasoned that they'd both done so well at improv nights as teenagers that they should have no problem with that now.

"We're *theater kids*, Harls," he'd said, wiggling his fingers in a showy dance meant to make her laugh. "We can do this."

She'd dissolved into giggles when he'd said it, and she smiled now, remembering that while this whole thing was bound to drum up old insecurities, under all his sexy broodiness, Finbar McKay was a theater kid, a history geek, and cat dad extraordinaire. And that he was *hers*. She tried to rub Axel's belly, but he nipped at her fingers, warning her to stop. She sent Finn another photo of her cat-trapped arm. Axel looked absolutely feral.

She had to ask something else about Sabre, even though she knew the answer. If they were being monitored she had to behave as though she was in the dark about Sabre. *Are they human?*

Yes, we met at Aphelion. They're back in Nuva Troi now. Cian's in a huff with the concierge about our seats. Gotta run. Love you.

Harlow locked the new phone. The camera on the thing was phenomenal; her photos of Axel looked practically professional. The cat bumped her arm, purring, and she pulled him into her arms for a hug. She needed the comfort. That conversation was just the first, and probably the most comfortable, of many that likely wouldn't be.

"What are you going to do today, baby boy?" she asked as the cat hopped down and perched in a windowsill, cackling at some birds in a cypress below. Just underneath the tree, she saw a flash of auburn fur. Axel's cat friend was back.

Harlow pressed a kiss to his head, and he pawed at her face, pushing her away. "Have fun."

The house was quiet. Larkin would sleep until mid-afternoon. She'd been up late in the Vault, playing her violin. Harlow had heard her come upstairs in the wee hours of the morning, when she'd been watching Finn sleep. Thea was probably already in the study, hard at work. She didn't much like spaces without windows, so she rarely worked in the Vault if she could help it.

Harlow wandered through the bright marble halls until she heard her eldest sister humming her favorite sonata. When she peeked into the study, she was met with a vision of magic. Thea's fingers pulled threads at a pace that was nearly too quick to watch, the filaments of aether shimmering at her fingertips. Her focus was trained on the book in front of her, resting in a cradle.

Thea had been hard at work all summer trying to restore the second image in the triptych from the Merkhov book, but though the snakes were easier to make out now, the details were still unclear. The first image had been easy enough to restore, but Thea's magic had snagged on the second and progress had stalled out.

"Any change?" Harlow asked softly, not wanting to startle Thea.

Her sister looked up. She'd lopped off her long, dark hair into a fashionable chin-length bob the first week they'd been in Nea Sterlis and it swished around her face in a satin curtain as she shook her head. "No, I can bring out the details in the scales, and I can see the snakes are positioned differently in this one, but it's the egg I can't get."

Harlow stood next to her sister at the library table, staring at the facsimile of the triptych from the Scroll of Akatei. The first, and only fully restored, image showed two snakes, one golden and one midnight blue, locked in a figure-eight pattern, consuming one another's tails. Inside the lower half of the figure eight was a luminous egg, surrounded by a protective film.

The second image seemed to show the same two snakes, no longer locked together, but united, protecting the egg, or so she and Thea thought. The part of the image that should show the rest of the two snakes holding the egg was still obscured.

"You brought the color out," Harlow breathed. "The snakes really are one now."

Thea nodded, wiping a thin sheen of sweat off her brow. "Yes, and see, they are golden and blue now, elements of both. I got it last night, but I can't get the egg."

Harlow looked closely at the image. "Is the egg… cracking?"

Thea nodded. "I think so… But the longer I work on it, the worse I feel."

With those words, Thea stumbled. Harlow caught her elder sister in her arms and led her to a linen-covered chaise and sat with her. "You all right?"

Thea nodded, and Harlow reached out towards the facsimile with her shadows. "What's making Thea sick?" she whispered.

Arebos had suggested to her that speaking to her magic might help direct it. He'd had some experience working with the Ultima, apparently, and they swore by something called "verbal manifestation." He'd thought it might help her, since the Striders of the Feriant Legion had also been warriors. She'd been testing it out. It worked well enough most of the time, but when she looked at Thea, there was no obvious clue to what was making her woozy.

Harlow looked closer, utilizing her second sight. Her shadows gathered around the book. She walked over to the table where Thea had been working, and sure enough, though it was faint, she saw it. There was an anomaly in the threads, so slight she could understand how Thea missed it. Her sister was most talented at fixing art, restoring it. Sometimes she was so focused on bringing out the best in something, she missed little details like this. Harlow moved around the book, using her second sight to look at it from several angles. There was most definitely something there.

"Did you test the book for spellbinding?" Harlow asked.

Thea rolled her eyes, clearly annoyed, despite her nausea. "Of course. I'm not a fool."

Harlow stepped closer to the book, turning her head as her shadows moved in and out of the aethereal threads that both surrounded the book and that made it up. Thea rose on shaky feet to stand next to her.

"Can you see it?" Harlow whispered, not knowing if Thea saw the same thing she did.

Her sister leaned forward, squinting. Her breath caught as she saw what Harlow did. "Oh..."

"It's so subtle," Harlow breathed. "Like it's a part of the book itself."

"Only a healer could have done a spellbinding like this," Thea said, her words slow and thoughtful. She looked long and hard at Harlow.

"What are you looking for?" Harlow asked as Thea lifted her wrists, examining them. One of Thea's talents, part of what made her restorations so sought after, was her ability to see traces of magic left behind, to identify them, and bring out their original intent. Now that she saw the spell on the book, she might be able to fix it.

"The magic used on the book. I've seen it before." Harlow looked into her sister's fawn-colored eyes. "On you."

Harlow glanced down at her wrists, at the place that had been injured the night she'd left Mark. "Kylar Bane."

Thea nodded. "I don't think this is a coincidence."

Harlow had to agree. "I don't think it is either."

"I'll talk to Alaric about it," Thea said. She scrunched up her face a little, pressing the back of her hand to her forehead, which bore a slight shimmer of sweat. "Sorry I snapped before."

"It's okay," Harlow reassured her.

Harlow's phone dinged loudly. She'd forgotten to turn the sound off when she activated it earlier. Both she and Thea startled and then laughed.

"I don't think I've had the sound turned up on my phone in years," Thea said as she took a few photos of the restoration with the camera reserved for such things.

Harlow scrolled through her settings, turning the sound off, smiling. "Me either."

The notification was a message from a librarian letting her know her book was ready to retrieve. Harlow frowned. She'd emailed the library back after Finn asked her to stay away and told them to terminate her hold. This email didn't state *which* book was ready to retrieve, and what's more something was odd about the email itself. Harlow had been requesting books all summer; she knew what the form email for this type of thing looked like, and this wasn't it.

Someone wanted her back at the library. She'd promised Finn she wouldn't, but after her two trips to Nihil, she desperately wanted another look at *The Warden*. If there was any possibility that this might be about the mysterious little book, she needed to know. It wasn't as though anyone would hurt her in the Citadel, after all. It was the most heavily guarded place in Nea Sterlis.

She'd made her decision. "I've got to run to the Citadel for a few hours," Harlow said.

Thea nodded absently, lost in re-examining the Merkhov book, apparently.

"Wake Larkin up, please," Harlow said as she brushed a kiss to Thea's cheek.

Her elder sister made a noncommittal noise and waved as Harlow went to gather her things. When she was ready, she stared for a moment at Finn's car keys, then left them behind. It was early enough in the day to walk while it was still cool, and the trip home in the sunshine would make an afternoon swim that much better.

The winding streets to the Citadel were quiet and fragrant. Occasionally, when the wind blew just right, the Citadel filled with the scent of the lavender fields located just outside the city. The sun was out as Harlow ducked into her favorite shaded back-path, covered by a lemon arbor.

The sounds of waves crashing against the shoreline were faint here, and she didn't have to look over the sickening drop down the cliff side that the switchbacks to the Citadel provided —just lovely, peaceful lemons surrounded by bushy rosemary plants and various succulents and blooming flora. Really, nothing in the world could be more pleasant. The sound of crunching footsteps in the pea gravel behind her caused her to look back. She was sick to death of the paparazzi, and was going to give them a piece of her mind.

But there was nobody following her. No paparazzi anyway. A large hound, low to the ground, with long ears and enormous paws, was following her. She was tempted to stop and coo at it, but it growled loud enough for her to hear—and even at this distance, it was enough to have her back on her journey quickly.

When she glanced behind her, the dog had laid down in a shadowed doorway, big head on its paws. It didn't follow her, and its eyes drooped sleepily. Perhaps she'd just startled it. She popped her earbuds in and listened to the audiobook for the monster romance Meline had enjoyed so much as she walked on.

She was only a little sweaty when she reached the library, but the cool atrium had a drinking fountain. The Ultima from the coffee shop was nowhere to be seen. In fact, there was no one at the desk at all checking reader cards.

They must be on shift change, she thought as she approached the retrieval desk. There was a different sorcière working than the last time she'd been here. This one was younger, closer to her own age, and wore a disgruntled expression on her pale face.

"Hi," Harlow said softly. "I got an email about a retrieval?"

The witch looked up, her eyebrows raised in such a way that made it look as though she didn't believe Harlow.

"I actually had sent all my books back, but..." Harlow trailed off. The glare the librarian was giving her was cold enough to freeze lava.

"Reader card," the librarian demanded, not bothering to lower her voice. A few patrons looked up, annoyed at the disturbance.

Harlow handed her the card, and she scanned it, then swiveled in her wooden chair, rolling it backwards a few inches towards the rack that held retrievals. The witch pulled a book out of a basket and handed it to Harlow.

"You must have forgotten you requested this."

Harlow stared at the book in her hands for a brief second, then nodded. "Thanks."

The witch's forehead wrinkled and then she shrugged, sighing a dismissal. Harlow went into the reading room. The same seat she'd sat in dozens of times before this summer was open. She sat down in it, her forehead wrinkling in confusion. The book she held was titled *The Warren.*

Was this some kind of joke?

The Warren was a classic children's book about warring clans of hare shifters. Aside from the fact that the plot of the book was in some ways disturbingly similar to that of the story she'd read in *The Warden*, she couldn't see what the meaning of this was. There was nothing to do but examine the book itself, she supposed.

Was it possible there had simply been a mistake? She supposed there was, but this felt like a message. Awareness that someone was watching her crawled over her skin. Casually, she looked around. No one was looking at her. When she glanced back at the book, she saw that something was written on the back of the retrieval slip. Seven words.

The Gate. One o'clock. Don't be late.

Harlow glanced at her phone. It was nearly noon. She had time to glance through the book casually, but she practically knew the story by heart. It had been the sillies' favorite as children, and she and Thea both had read it to all three of them dozens of times, and Larkin still fell asleep to the audiobook many nights. The real information was this message.

The noise of the room disappeared as she placed *The Warren* on the cradle and began to look through it. As she'd suspected, there was nothing particularly special about this edition, but the illustrations were lovely, all the same. Comforting as that was, the sense that she was being watched did not abate, and Harlow's pulse raced.

I shouldn't have come here, she thought, panic rising in her throat. *I made a promise to Finn, and I broke it.*

Why had she been so arrogant? The first day Finn was gone, she'd done the very thing he'd expressly asked her not to.

Always defiant, aren't you, Dollface?

Mark had said that to her once for "talking back" to him when he was berating her. He'd then proceeded to give her the silent treatment for a week. Harlow wished she hadn't thought of Mark. Memories of their relationship, of the way he'd influenced her emotions, of the night she'd killed him—all came flooding back.

Her breath came in shallow gasps, and her sundress felt too tight, like the fitted bodice was restricting her lungs. She glanced around the room, careful to appear as casual as possible. No one was looking at her, nothing was amiss. She tried to tell herself that she was imagining things and to just calm down—but that didn't work.

Harlow's heart fluttered into a rapid drumbeat, pounding in her ears. Her skin was overheated, and her hands were clammy. She wiped sweat from her brow, feeling chilled as well as hot. There was no way she could sit here any longer—whether or not someone was actually watching her, she was panicking. Harlow gathered her things quickly and dropped the book off at the retrieval desk.

"Thought you were scanning it," the grumpy witch said, not looking up from her computer.

"It turned out to be less informative than I'd hoped," Harlow replied, her heartbeat accelerating.

The witch looked up at her and Harlow wondered if the irritation on her face could be more than just grumpiness as she asked, "Will you need it again?"

Harlow shook her head. "Not right now. I'll call it up again if I do."

She stepped away from the retrieval desk slowly, and the librarian never broke her gaze. The look of irritation was replaced with something steely, evaluative and shrewd. Something in the other sorcière's face frightened Harlow—was she the one who was watching her? What purpose would that serve? Harlow turned, concentrating on taking slow, even steps as she left the library.

When she got past the courtyard and into one of the narrow alleys that led downward and out of the Citadel, she picked up her pace. Thoughts raced through her. Was there any possibility that she wasn't overreacting? That the librarian could have been the person watching her somehow? But that made no sense. The sorcière had been in Harlow's line of sight the entire time and had never looked up from her computer. Still though—that look she gave Harlow as she was leaving.

"Maybe you just looked like an unhinged yew elf," she muttered to herself. Her heart slowed to a more normal pace. Enzo's breathing techniques came in handy right now. She fished her headphones out of her bag and popped them in, calling Enzo.

"What's up?" Enzo asked as he answered.

"Are you busy?" Harlow asked, checking her phone to make sure she was taking the best route to The Gate.

"I'm walking," Enzo said, sounding a little breathless. "Up seventy thousand stairs to meet a supplier. You all right?"

Harlow paused. She *was* all right—she wasn't sure what was going on, but she wasn't losing it. "I'm okay. I'm going to grab some tea at The Gate. Do you want to go for a swim?"

"Gods, yes," Enzo laughed. "I'm going to be a sweaty mess after all these stairs and we won't have many pool days left, I wager. Meet you at the Grand Plaza when I'm done?"

Harlow wished they could just go swimming at the villa, but the pool at the Grand was gorgeous and she hadn't been all summer. "Sure. See you in a few. Love you."

Enzo made the sound of kisses and hung up. She felt better, clearer, after even that short conversation. Harlow switched on her audiobook to keep her company on the rest of the walk, but her mind wandered almost immediately. This wasn't the first time since the House of Remiel fire that she'd panicked somewhere and overanalyzed her interactions with others.

Enzo had been teaching her to interrupt herself when her thoughts spiraled into something unproductive and then reevaluate, so she tried to concentrate on the audiobook, but it was almost as if the narrator was speaking a language she didn't understand. She had to back the book up twice before it made sense again.

As her breathing slowed into the rhythmic pace of her walk, she evaluated her emotions. The sense that she'd been watched at the library and that the librarian had been acting strange was less urgent now, but it was apparent to her that something *had* been happening there. She wasn't imagining things simply because she had unresolved feelings about killing her ex.

Harlow rounded a corner and found that she'd already arrived at The Gate. She hardly remembered the walk from the library at all.

It was often like this after she panicked; the twenty or thirty minutes afterwards sometimes got a little fuzzy for her. Soft jazz played on a speaker and there were people tucked into various corners of The Gate's garden, reading or sipping delightful beverages. A quick check told her she was about ten minutes early, and she might as well get in line for a drink.

CHAPTER SEVENTEEN

There was a line three deep in front of her, so she didn't bother to shut off the audiobook. It was starting to get good, and Harlow understood why monster romances were all the rage with Meline's generation. Harlow was half in love with both of the love interests already, and any moment they were about to fall into bed, which promised to be beyond satisfying. She wished she were at home, instead of in the coffee shop, but anything to keep her mind off what had happened at the library was a welcome distraction.

Suddenly, the sound of the narrator's voice gave way to a song she'd never heard before. The singer crooned about going your own way, and Harlow felt transported to... *somewhere else*. The song felt familiar somehow, but also strange. What *was* this music?

The person in front of her turned around, a quizzical look on her face. It was the young woman who'd been with the Ultima the last time she'd been here with Petra and Meline. She was about as tall as Harlow, with brown skin, and luminous, long-lashed eyes. Her hair was short, cut similarly to Kate's, but with a closer undercut and longer on top, grazing her high cheekbones in a way that nearly made Harlow blush.

The young woman took a white earphone out of one of her ears and seemed to listen before flashing one of the most dazzling grins Harlow had ever seen. "Were you, perhaps, listening to an audiobook just now?"

Harlow was reluctant to pull her own earphone out, afraid the music would stop, but she nodded. "Am I listening to your music somehow?"

The woman leaned forward, and Harlow noticed she smelled of vetiver and moss, and something otherworldly—she *reeked* of raw aether. Until this moment, Harlow hadn't recognized that Nihil had a smell, but the woman definitely smelled like the heart of the limen, or perhaps just the limen itself. She couldn't be sure.

The woman appeared to listen momentarily, then smiled again. "Yeah, somehow our signals must have gotten crossed."

"What *is* this?" Harlow asked. "I need this album."

The woman smiled, then shook her head, fiddling with her phone. "You can't get it here, unfortunately. Besides, it's a cover of the original."

"Who sang the original?" Harlow asked, as her audiobook mysteriously returned.

Harlow thought she said something like Fleetfoot's Tracks, but wasn't sure. The woman was already ordering her drink. Someone touched her arm, and she startled, staring up into Rakul Kimaris's amber eyes. He didn't look a day older than he had when he pulled her off the Ledge. Harlow's heart beat wildly again. *What was he doing here?* He was supposed to be in Nuva Troi.

"Come sit," he urged, pulling her toward a table in the corner.

"I wanted tea," she responded, her head spinning.

"You can order some when we're done," he said. His voice

was urgent as his forehead wrinkled into a deep frown. "It would be better if we weren't seen together."

She whispered, "Did you send me the message in the library?"

"Yes," he muttered. "Please, let's sit. I don't have much time."

She followed Rakul to a table in the corner. He was casually dressed, in a pair of dark tactical pants and a black tank top showing the tattoos that covered his ridiculously muscled brown arms.

Rakul Kimaris made Finn look positively puny in comparison, at nearly six foot seven feet tall and at least thirty to forty more pounds of muscle. His long, dark hair was twisted into a messy bun and he was exactly as swoon-worthy as she remembered him. She glanced at the attractive person she'd been standing behind in line and wiped a bit of sweat off her forehead. This coffee shop was filled to the brim with dark-haired beauties today.

She sat across from him, waiting for him to speak, trying not to remember the giant crush she'd had on him for years as a teenager, until she'd developed feelings for Finn, that is. He seemed to struggle, so she began. "Why did you ask me here?"

He shook his head. "Listen, it's not going to be easy to explain this. There are things I'm not capable of telling anyone..." he trailed off, his brow wrinkling and his amber eyes narrowing in frustration.

Harlow's head tilted of its own accord. She was thinking about what he might mean, but when she did it, his eyes softened. "Such a hatchling."

There was a slight disturbance in the threads around him, as though they constricted somehow. Her second sight was engaging more easily than ever these days. Now she saw it, fascinated. "Someone *bound* you."

He neither moved nor responded. In fact, he was frozen, as

though he could not react to her question. Even if she had not somehow developed the ability to see a spell in the threads, it would be a giveaway that someone had done one of the most terrible spells in existence on him, on *Rakul Kimaris*. That in itself was telling.

Spellbinding an object was one thing. But to bind a *person*—that was so forbidden that the Order of Mysteries had never needed to make an ordinance against such spells. To bind anyone's will was such a grave violation of their personal sanctity that Harlow felt the shock reverberate within her enough to feel cold, despite the close air in the shop.

"Okay," she said. "Okay, so *that* happened. I understand."

Rakul's body relaxed. The only way to circumvent a binding that was specifically directed, as Rakul's seemed to be, was to speak neutrally—stop asking questions of any kind. Quickly, Harlow puzzled together what she knew about the situation. Obviously, Rakul was able to use the full range of his Illuminated power, and from the way he was struggling, she assumed he could remember what he was not allowed to speak of.

That meant that one of the Illuminated had done the binding, rather than a sorcière. If one of her own had done it, he simply wouldn't remember what he was not supposed to. But the Illuminated had never been good at complex spells, and it took a very special, very talented witch to cast a binding as intricate as the one that would have been needed for such a task. This was more like a blunt instrument—a gag—and she wished to Akatei that Enzo or Riley had come with her today. Perhaps they would have been able to discern more.

Rakul glanced at his watch. "We don't have much time."

Harlow wanted to say, "You asked me here," but instead she asked, "What happened to the copy of *The Warden* I was looking at?"

Rakul sighed. "It disappeared. I was the one who sent it to you to begin with, and when I returned for it—it was gone."

187

"So the story of Ashbourne and Lumina, it *is* important."

Rakul did not answer, frozen once more.

Harlow decided to try an indirect approach. "Do you think one of the librarians is involved somehow? Could one of them have taken *The Warden*?"

"It's possible," Rakul said, glancing around. "But the book isn't important now. You read the story, didn't you?"

Harlow nodded. "I did."

"So you have to start look—" Rakul tried to continue, but his skin reddened, as though he were being choked.

"Shit," Harlow swore, fumbling for anything that would distract him. "Do you like cats?"

Rakul's eyebrows raised, but the flush drained quickly from his skin. "I'm more of a dog person... Thank you."

There were so many ways she could go with this, but they didn't have much time. The way she saw it, there were two important things about the story of Lumina and Ashbourne: that the Illuminated had some extremely dangerous Elementals imprisoned in the limen, and that they'd used their own people to guard them for eternity. Either could be tied to the reason why Rakul wanted her to see *The Warden*, and why he was bound, or both, she supposed. But it might be easier to talk around the binding if she knew which it was.

"What do you know about imprisoning an incorporeal creature?" she asked.

Rakul's forehead wrinkled. "Not a lot, from a technical perspective. Spellwork isn't really my thing."

Vague, she thought, *but he's not choking*. So this wasn't more *specifically* about the imprisoned Elementals. "Right. But let's say you wanted to find where they were being kept, specifically. Would you know where to look?"

Rakul nodded, looking uncomfortable. "The underworld," he choked out.

So even referring obliquely to Nihil might be dangerous. But why? "Have you ever been there?" she asked. It was a risky question, but she might as well try.

"To the human underworld?" Rakul asked, raising an eyebrow.

"Sure," Harlow agreed. "Let's call it that. Have you been?"

"Once," Rakul choked out.

They'd hit gold. She pushed him further. "Is there a way to get there from here?"

Rakul gasped for breath loudly enough that a few patrons turned. He collected himself quickly, shaking his head. "No more about that," he pleaded, his voice hoarse.

So this was what he wanted her to find out. How to get into Nihil. *But why?*

"So I need to find the way to the wish-granter," she said, trying to keep her wording vague; she wasn't sure how the spell was tripped.

Rakul nodded, rubbing his throat. He was clearly afraid to say more. "Be careful. The Sistren of Akatei cannot help you." He choked again, frowning.

They were getting closer. Harlow turned what she knew about Rakul Kimaris over in her mind. When her memory hit on the fact that he'd been one of the original Knights of Serpens, she paused, her magic fluttering inside her like an excited moth. "Do I have access to the information already?"

Rakul did not move. His face turned red, and it was obvious that he couldn't answer. The Vault. There *had* to be something in the Vault. Rakul looked at his watch. Harlow sensed he wanted to leave, but she had to ask about the fervor. "Have you ever met anyone like me—a sorcière—who experienced..." She looked around and then whispered, "the fervor?"

Rakul's cheeks turned a little pink, but otherwise he didn't react. "Yes. You must be Claimed."

"It's safe?"

Rakul shook his head, looking frustrated, but managed to say, "No."

She didn't want him to be hurt by the binding, but she had to ask. "Will it kill me?"

Each word he said sounded forced. "No... will.... change...." Rakul doubled over, clutching his neck.

Harlow struggled to think. "What's your favorite pie, Rakul?"

He glanced up at her, face pained. "Lemon meringue."

"I'm sorry," she breathed. "I'm so sorry."

He nodded. "I wish I could help you. I thought if I had you here in front of me that I'd be able to just—" His face crumpled, and he buried it in his huge hands.

"Shhh," Harlow soothed, touching his arms. A tiny bit of her shadow magic wound around his fingers.

He glanced down at it and smiled. "It's been a long time," he said, almost as though he was speaking to her magic itself. "I'm sorry I can't help you more."

Before Harlow could answer, a barista called out, "Morgaine Yarlo, order's up!"

The person from the line stood. She'd been waiting at a corner table and as she fetched her coffee and a bag that probably held a pastry, her gaze caught Harlow's and she winked. As she left the shop, Rakul's nostrils flared, and Morgaine grinned at him, a rakish look on her face that Harlow swore looked like a *dare*.

"That one smells of aether," he growled, nearly standing to follow.

"What of it?" Harlow asked.

"I need to go. If you want your questions answered—all of them..." He paused, then forced out a few more words. "Find the Warden—by whatever means necessary. He can help you."

Harlow knew better than to question Rakul Kimaris. He looked positively lethal at the moment, even though he rubbed his neck as though the binding was chafing him. She hoped Morgaine Yarlo, whoever she was, had a good head start. Rakul looked as though he might take his frustrations out on an unsuspecting victim.

"All right."

Harlow held out her hand, and he took it, kissing her palm as though she were an intimate, rather than someone he just met. "Thank you for meeting me, little bird." Her heart nearly stopped. The creature in Nihil had called her that as well. Rakul stood. "The next time we meet, it may not be as friends. Please remember today if that happens."

Harlow nodded, squeezing his large hand in hers, hoping to give Morgaine a little time to get wherever she was going without Rakul's interference. "I understand. Thank you. I'll figure this out, Rakul. I *promise—all* of it."

She hoped he understood. If there was a way to break the binding that he'd endured, she would find it. She thought he understood her as he nodded solemnly, kissing the back of her hand now, with chaste gratitude. Then he was gone, faster than even the typical Illuminated could move; but he was not the typical Illuminated, after all. Harlow ordered one of The Gate's signature tea lattes and a lemon scone to go, then walked home, deep in thought.

CHAPTER EIGHTEEN

The air was sultry in the sun, but in the shade, it was almost too chilly to be wearing a swimsuit. The beach at the Grand Plaza was emptier than Harlow had seen it all summer. After receiving a text from Enzo that Riley would join them, Harlow scored one of the coveted cabanas overlooking the infinity pool. It shocked her when the concierge told her one was open, even this time of year. Typically, she needed one of the twins to get such treatment, but she wasn't going to question her luck.

Enzo claimed not to care about things like the exclusive cabanas at the Grand, but she knew he secretly loved this kind of luxury, so she ordered a spread of delicious food and settled in with a magazine. She would have preferred loungers on the beach, which was blissfully empty and quiet right now, while the cabana level was nearly full. Still, with everything she'd had going on in the past few weeks and Enzo's hard work on the new retail space, she'd had almost no quality time with her best friend.

She liked Riley Quinn a lot, but she would have preferred to spend time alone with Enzo today. She was trying to adjust her attitude, but the various immortals chatting loudly in their cabanas were making her grumpy. The food came just as Riley and Enzo arrived, and their delighted smiles washed any irritation she felt away.

They wore matching swimwear that Enzo had designed. The only difference was that Riley also wore a new robe in a stylishly clashing print over their tiny briefs. "I am jealous of this," Harlow said, gesturing towards the billowing magenta fabric that featured whimsical winged cats.

Enzo grinned and dove into his beach bag, pulling out another robe, in a similar fabric, this one midnight blue with snow leopards. "It matches your suit."

Harlow let out a delighted noise as she took the robe from Enzo. It was exquisite, of course, with generous sleeves and an extra long hemline. Her swimsuit, which had been a hit on some of the gossips earlier in the summer, was made from a midnight blue leopard fabric, and the two would be divine together. It had been the only positive attention she'd received from the press all summer, and if they saw this, they might run another positive story about her. Harlow hated that she wanted that so badly, but with everything they were bound to say about her when her ruse with Finn really got going, she did.

"Put it on," Enzo urged, pulling her from her lounger.

"Your new supplier is phenomenal," she cooed. "These fabrics are to die for."

Enzo grinned. "The Grand thinks so too. They'll be carrying both the suits and the robes in their shop next spring."

The contract was a big one and would help fund the new retail space. Harlow listened to Enzo and Riley detail the progress they'd made in the past two weeks, proud of her best friend. The way they talked, finishing one another's sentences— the sweet way that Riley beamed when Enzo got excited about the new suppliers they'd contacted this summer—it was everything Harlow wished for her best friend.

When each of them had a plate piled high with food, the

conversation died down to a supremely comfortable silence. Harlow's heart swelled a little, and again, she wanted to hold tight to the sweetness of the moment.

"Not to get too serious," she said, keeping her voice low. "But I've been having this weird feeling lately—like anything that's good might disappear at any moment."

Enzo and Riley nodded simultaneously, giving one another a knowing look.

"You're going to say it's the trauma of what happened in Nuva Troi, aren't you?" Harlow responded, trying hard for a dry laugh that didn't quite land.

Riley shrugged. "Sure. It's probably a little of that. But, with the shit in Falcyra, and with what happened in Nuva Troi today, why wouldn't you feel that way?"

Harlow frowned. "What happened in Nuva Troi?"

Enzo's eyebrows raised. "You don't know?"

"No, what happened?"

"There was a bomb in the subway, on one of the school lines," Enzo said.

Harlow's heart skipped several beats. There were two lines in the city that were devoted to children and teachers during school commuting hours, to make sure they were able to get to and from school on time with supervision.

"Which one?" Harlow asked. They were, of course, largely divided by geography. Since humans in Nuva Troi didn't live in the same parts of the city as the Orders, for the most part, the two lines were separated.

"Ours," Riley said, clearly as uncomfortable with the distinction as she was. "There were no casualties. According to the Crisis Management Unit, the bomb malfunctioned somehow and went off sooner than it was supposed to. There were injuries, but no deaths."

Harlow thought she might throw up. Someone had targeted *children*. She glanced around at the other cabanas. No one was paying any attention to them. "Was it, you know... the Humanists? Or—" She didn't look at Riley, but the "or" just slipped out.

Riley sighed. "Akatei's tit, Harlow. The Rogue Order has morals. We would never target children."

"Sorry," she muttered.

"Don't be," Enzo replied, giving Riley a pointed look. "It's not like you've been briefed on what the Queen is up to."

Harlow sensed a conflict between the two of them, and she didn't want to be in the middle of it. Riley looked around, glaring at Enzo as if to say, "Anyone could hear you."

Enzo stuck his tongue out and pulled threads quickly until the sound of the others at the pool muffled into eventual silence. "Better?"

"Better," Riley said, kissing Enzo's nose. "And for the thousandth time, when I'm at liberty to brief Harlow, I will."

Harlow frowned at Enzo. "Does that mean that *you* know what's going on with the Rogue Order?"

Enzo looked uncomfortable. "I know some things. Not all."

"Are you defecting?" she asked. Her tone came out too blunt, but she genuinely wondered. Would Enzo give up his legacy as the future of the Order of Mysteries for the Rogue Order and its mysterious goals?

"No," Enzo replied. "I can appreciate the Rogue Order's purpose, and try to collaborate with them without abandoning my people, Harlow. It doesn't have to be one or the other."

"Of course," Harlow replied, chastised. She wasn't sure how to feel. Of course neither of them owed her any explanation, but this was awkward.

"If it were just you, Harls, we'd have already told you," Riley said, as though that explained everything.

"Just me? What does that mean?"

Riley sighed, exasperation written all over their face.

"Oh," Harlow said. "You don't trust Finn."

"Or Alaric or Petra," Enzo added, as though that would help.

"And it's not that we *mistrust* them," Riley explained. "It's that we're not done vetting them."

Harlow set her plate down. She wasn't hungry anymore. "Why didn't you just ask Finn whatever you want to know?"

Riley smiled. "We didn't have to. He's offered us a lot of information already. But he and the others are still Illuminated. It's safest for us to be sure of them by independent means. Finn understands."

That was an interesting way of putting it. "He *understands*?"

"Sure," Riley said with a grin. "And his confidence that we'll trust him and your Knights eventually is either very reassuring, or chilling, depending on how you look at it."

She turned to Enzo. "And what do you think about all this?"

Enzo grinned. "I know Finn's heart." He patted Riley's hand. "I think it will all turn out fine."

Riley's smile was a touch tight, but their brown eyes were relaxed and clear. "I hope so. We would like to be allies, Harlow. But surely you understand that we all need to be cautious."

She supposed she did, so she nodded. The conversation made her feel a little foolish for trusting Finn so easily. For just believing everything he'd told her, after everything his parents, and the rest of the Illuminated had done.

Enzo took her hand. "Stop that. You *know* Finn. Neither of us would let you or your family continue on with him or Alaric if we thought they were a threat to you. You know that, right?"

Harlow glanced between Riley and Enzo. Both smiled at her. "I think so."

Riley leaned over, taking her other hand, and Enzo's both. "This is about alliances, not personal stuff. It's complicated."

Harlow nodded, as though she completely understood. On a cognitive level, she did. The Rogue Order was mysterious, a shadow organization that the Illuminated allowed to go about their business largely because they thought they were silly—nothing more than a haven for immortals who didn't like the way their Orders operated.

Finn had explained to her that Connor and Pasiphae actually thought the Rogues were useful in keeping immortals who felt like outsiders from aligning too closely with humans, as the Rogue Order had a reputation for scorning human members. Apparently Connor's view was that, "They believe themselves an edgy 'alternative' to what we've set in motion, when in reality, they simply replicate our ideals in different packaging."

But Finn and Cian suspected they might be more than that, though they struggled to probe deeper into their organization. Even Nox and Ari had hit dead ends with the Rogue Order. Petra and Thea had a believable theory that if they were as silly as Connor supposed they'd have recruited the Wraiths at some point, since most shifter clans were prejudiced against those with "outlier" alternae, like Riley and the Wraiths. But neither Nox nor Ari had ever been approached.

Thea thought it was likely because of their loyalty to Finn, and that the Rogue Order was protecting their secrets closely. Petra thought that something about the Flynns scared the Rogues. Harlow picked her plate of food back up and took a giant bite of dolmades. The Grand's were some of the best in Nea Sterlis, and she wasn't going to waste them.

Enzo's spell kept the commotion outside the cabana from getting in, but she saw the paparazzo anyway, as one of the vampires in the next cabana was striding toward them with purpose. Their camera was pointed right at Harlow.

"Shit," Enzo swore.

Riley rolled their eyes. "Time to go."

"We didn't even swim yet," Enzo said, sounding disappointed.

Harlow put her plate down, as she finished chewing. Her

temper was rising, but she attempted to stay calm. "You stay. I'll go. It's me they're after."

It was clear that the photographer meant to get closeups of her eating, not photos of her gorgeous swimsuit, or new robe. If they were going to obsess over everything she did, she wished that it might be something pleasant, at least occasionally.

"No," Enzo pleaded. "Look, security's getting them."

Harlow shook her head. "I just want to go home and call Finn."

Riley got up and hugged her. "It's okay. They shake me up too."

She brushed kisses on each of their cheeks and gathered her things. Enzo showed her the way the robe's belt worked to close it into a stylish summer gown, and she left without going to change back into her street clothes. She considered calling a cab, but the day was fine, and the weather tomorrow called for rain, so she walked home, turning the day's events over and over in her mind.

On her way home, Petra texted her, *Don't let this send you into a spiral. Come out with me and Kate tonight.*

Don't let what send her into a spiral? She rolled her eyes and swiped over to Section Seven. There she was, shoving food in her face. The caption read, "Finn McKay's been back in Nuva Troi for twelve hours and Harlow's already stress-eating."

"Fatphobic fucks," she muttered.

It was a distinctly human thing to use thinness as a metric for attractiveness, and Section Seven often shied away from making such commentary, since they wanted to stay on the Orders' good side—but apparently she was fair game since they hated her so much. The photo had been out for nearly an hour, and there were only about a hundred comments on it.

She did the thing she knew she shouldn't and opened them up. Quite a few were from immortals saying that Section Seven had gone too far. Apparently, it was fine when they were speculating about her relationship and diminishing her character, but immortals didn't want humans deciding what made a person attractive or not. Harlow tried hard not to hate them all, her eyes stinging with tears.

Then the comments were all gone, and when she clicked out of them, the post itself had been removed. Finn had offered several times to ensure that Section Seven stopped publishing so many hit pieces on her, but they'd eventually agreed that his interference would only stir up more trouble in the end.

But she knew the disappearance of this post was his way of protecting her from afar, doing what he could before the real maelstrom started, to give her some peace. He couldn't stand that they wrote such terrible things about her, and their relationship, while they praised him like he was a god. She tripped over the sash of the robe, into a bench, and just about dropped her new phone. Her heart skipped a beat.

"Careful there." A hand steadied her, and she looked up into the warm eyes of the young woman from the coffee shop. What had her name been? *Morgaine*.

"Thanks," Harlow said. She probably shouldn't have been trying to walk and read her phone at the same time. There was never a time when she wasn't a bit off-balance, but that certainly didn't help things.

"No problem," Morgaine said.

Harlow looked down, Morgaine had clearly been sitting on the bench Harlow had run into. Her drink and the remains of her pastry sat next to a sketchbook. Morgaine had been drawing a gorgeous dark-haired girl with pale plush cheeks and a pretty mouth.

"Did you draw that?" Harlow asked, pointing to the sketchbook.

Morgaine nodded, gesturing for Harlow to sit down. It was a little unusual to be invited to chat with a stranger on the street, but Harlow felt oddly at ease with Morgaine.

"It's really good," Harlow said. "She's beautiful. Did you dream her up?"

Morgaine grinned, a faint blush coloring her cheeks. "Sometimes it feels that way."

Ah, so they were involved. Something about knowing the beautiful girl in the drawing and this gorgeous creature were together was downright comforting. Outside all the strange drama she was surrounded by, there were average humans, like these two, falling in love and swooning over one another.

"How long have you known each other?" Harlow asked.

Morgaine thought for a moment. "It feels like forever, but a little over a year."

"And you've been together the whole time?" It was altogether too easy to talk to Morgaine. Harlow liked the way it felt, just to randomly make a friend like the fate of the world wasn't currently in the balance.

"Not exactly. She was involved with someone else when I met her. Bad timing." Morgaine winked.

"You won her over though, didn't you?" Harlow laughed.

"I won them both over," Morgaine said, stretching her long legs out in front of her.

"Nice," Harlow commented.

Morgaine snickered. "Not like *that*. Though if I were into guys, Fenric might be okay. He's one of my best friends now, though."

"Wow." Harlow was impressed. "And your girl..."

"Echo," Morgaine prompted.

"Echo... She's okay with that? They're friends too."

Morgaine nodded. "Yeah, pretty much." There was a deep sadness in her eyes.

"You miss them," Harlow said after a moment.

"I do," Morgaine said.

There was a long pause between them and Harlow almost got up to go, but Morgaine spoke again. "I hope you don't mind me saying this, but the social media here is fucking rotten about you."

Social media? Harlow had never heard anyone refer to the social apps quite that way before, though she supposed that was what it was. "Yeah... You recognized me, huh?"

Morgaine nodded. "And from the coffee shop."

Harlow remembered that Rakul had been interested in Morgaine. She smelled faintly of aether still, which was odd. "Do you practice magic?" Some humans did, after all, though it was forbidden, and quite difficult for them.

Morgaine shook her head. "Nope. Never had any penchant for it." She glanced down at her phone and saw the time. "I've gotta run. It was nice running into you, Harlow."

"It was," Harlow said as Morgaine packed her things up.

"See you around," she called over her shoulder, as she jogged off.

Harlow leaned into the back of the uncomfortable bench and smiled to herself. This is what she was working for—nice people like Morgaine and Echo, who didn't deserve to have their lives controlled by the Illuminated. Whatever went on in her personal life, in Section Seven and the other gossips, this was what mattered. Making the world a better place for people like them.

CHAPTER NINETEEN

arlow debated whether or not to tell Finn that she'd
seen Rakul. She worried he would insist on coming
back to Nea Sterlis, and they needed whatever information Finn and Cian could dig up about the McKays in Nuva
Troi. After some thought, she emailed Cian about the entire
interaction over a secure server in the Vault. She wasn't taking
any chances that someone might find out she'd spoken to Rakul.
He was in enough danger already, just for having had coffee with
her, and their conversation had crossed a line. She knew there
would be no explaining if people like the McKays found out.

When Cian emailed back that they'd take care of things with
Finn, Harlow enlisted Thea to help her search the archives in the
Vault for anything that might give them more information
about Ashbourne and Lumina—in addition to the Ledge and
Nihil. She was careful not to tell Thea about the Ventyr, or
anything that might lead her to make the connection between
the people in the story and the Illuminated, but she told her
enough of the story so that she could help.

She'd already broken her promise to Finn not to go back to
the library, and she had no desire to put her sister in more danger

than they were already in, but she needed the help to get this done as quickly as possible. Despite all that, they looked for three days, and came up shockingly empty in terms of new information. They found various accounts of the geological formation of the Ledge, and the usual children's stories.

And of course they came across stories of the Ravagers, in one form or another. Stories of epic destructive forces were common, especially in human fiction and folklore. But nothing they found shed new light on anything. Nothing any different from what they'd known going in, even after careful probing. It was odd not to find even one significant deviation.

"I didn't expect we'd find exactly what we were looking for," Thea said as she filled the electric tea kettle in the Vault's common room with water. "But it's suspicious to find *nothing*. The Knights have been meticulous with records of the other gods, and so many legends."

From her spot on one of the blue couches, Harlow nodded. "It's definitely suspicious."

Thea scooped tea into the teapot, musing, "When Alaric gets back from Santos we can ask him to help us look."

Alaric had gone to handle a leak at the Velarius family compound on the exclusive island off the coast of Nea Sterlis. Harlow made a noise to show she'd heard, but she was lost in thought as Larkin came down the stairs, looking rumpled from sleep. "What are you two doing?" she asked.

Thea smiled brightly, too brightly in fact. "Making tea."

Before they'd left, the maters had asked that Larkin not be roped too deep into the intrigue brewing around them. Selene had been worried enough to caution, "I think with her awakening about her asexuality that she needs time to come to terms with herself. Let's try to give her that time."

So Thea and Harlow had done just that for the past few days, letting Larkin sleep as much as she wanted, and only telling her the bare minimum of what they needed to in order to keep her from prying further. But it was easy to see she was getting annoyed.

Right now she looked about ready to roll her eyes. "Pour me a cup then."

Thea smiled brightly and got another mug out for just that purpose. "We need more oat milk down here. Wanna go fetch some, littling?"

Larkin plopped down next to Harlow. "Not really."

Thea sighed, doing her best impression of Selene, and then just as Mama would have done, she went upstairs to do it herself.

"Be nicer to Thea," Harlow murmured as Larkin snuggled in next to her.

"You two are keeping something from me. Why should I be nice to either of you?"

Harlow sighed. "Mama asked us to let you rest. After everything that happened—with the fire, with all your ace stuff..." Harlow trailed off as she felt Larkin tense.

"When you figured out that you like all genders, was it confusing?"

"Yes, sort of."

"Did you just stop doing everything?"

Harlow saw where her youngest sister was going. "No, of course not."

"So tell me what's going on—"

Harlow was about to answer, though she wasn't sure exactly what to say, when Thea came back downstairs, without the oat milk she'd gone up for. She stared at her phone in a fairly uncharacteristic way for her as she rushed down the steps.

"What's going on?" Harlow asked, worried that something might have happened to the maters or Alaric.

"Open up Section Seven," Thea breathed.

Harlow and Larkin both got their phones out. Larkin made a little noise, and her countenance immediately tensed as she glanced at Harlow, whose app was taking a moment to load. She cleared a few open windows and when it finally loaded, she understood what they were reacting to.

The pinned post was a photo of Finn, arm in arm with a luscious brunette with luminous brown skin, dressed in couture. The headline read, "Nuva Troi's consummate playboy returns, looking at Midtown brownstones with fashionable Sabre LeBeau." The first line of the caption read, "It's time for another round of #HarlowKraneIsOver."

She bit her bottom lip, glancing up at her sisters. "I'm okay. Sabre LeBeau is our realtor. Finn's looking at brownstones for us —for this fall when we go back."

Larkin nodded. She loved Finn and would never want to think the worst of him. "You forgot the oat milk," she said to Thea. "I'll go get it."

Thea nodded and when Larkin had disappeared upstairs, Thea turned to her. "This article says Sabre LeBeau is one of Finn's exes."

Harlow kept her composure as well as she could. "Really? Interesting."

"Did you know he'd dated them?"

Harlow shrugged. "I guess."

"And you don't have any problem with the two of them spending time together like this? They look pretty cozy."

Harlow glanced at the photo again. Sabre LeBeau was wearing sky-high heels, and they were walking down a set of steep stairs, wet with rain. "He's clearly helping them with the stairs. Being *polite*. The gossips like to stir up drama."

Thea didn't look convinced. Inwardly, Harlow groaned. Thea wasn't going to let this go. "You know as well as I do that Section Seven loves to trash me—it's like a sport for them and Sabre LeBeau is a human. They're gorgeous, fashionable, and glamorous. Everything I'm not. Of course Section Seven is going to make it into something it isn't."

That *did* seem to make sense to her sister. "You're right,"

Thea said. "Partially anyway—Sabre LeBeau isn't 'everything you're not,' they're who they are—"

Harlow interrupted, "I just meant Section Seven *thinks* I'm not those things. I don't need a pep talk. Can we talk about something else, please?"

Thea's expression clouded with something Harlow desperately hoped wasn't pity, but she nodded as she changed the subject. "Do you get the impression that all the information about Ashbourne and Lumina is *purposely* missing?"

Harlow considered that they couldn't find anything at all related to the Ledge of Wishes or how it came to be. In her experience with mythologies, that wasn't how it worked. There were always seeds of different stories that grew and transformed, proliferated, shapeshifting as they went, but remained recognizable.

The fact that there was a sorcière legend about Ashbourne the Warden, and no stories about who he was or how he came to be, was more than suspicious, it was impossible. "I think someone—probably one of the Illuminated—scrubbed Ashbourne and Lumina from as much as they could."

"But why?" Thea mused.

Harlow would rather she not ask that question. She was about to try to distract her sister when a clatter came from the stairway, where Larkin had dropped the carton of oat milk, which was now rolling down the stairs. Axel followed close behind her, seemingly disappointed that it hadn't shattered and spilled all over the floor. Larkin rushed to pick up the carton before it burst, while Harlow and Thea looked on, startled.

When she'd picked up the milk, she looked up at her sisters, her face a flurry of conflicting emotions. "Are the two of you talking about Ash?"

Thea glanced at Harlow, fear in her eyes. "*Ash*?"

Larkin nodded, coming in the room. "Ashbourne the Warden. Are you talking about him?"

Harlow felt how tightly wound Thea had become, and reached out to squeeze her sister's arm, a silent plea to calm down, lest she terrify Larkin. Thea's shoulders relaxed, slightly, and she looked like she was in pain. Harlow's head shook. She had no idea how Thea had kept her relationship with Alaric a secret for so many years. She was typically an awful liar, and this was more evidence of that fact.

"Yes, we're talking about Ashbourne," Harlow replied, getting up to take the oat milk from Larkin. "Why do you ask?"

Larkin gave Thea a worried look, as Harlow poured milk into their mugs. "I just—wondered."

Harlow bumped her shoulder to Larkin's. Larkin looked back at Thea, who had her knees drawn to her chest and a truly strange look on her face. "Don't mind Thea, bun. She's pretending to be calm about this."

Larkin snorted and Thea let out a little noise of frustration. Harlow took her eldest sister a mug of tea and the three of them curled onto the couch together. "We're looking for stories about Ashbourne. Do you know where we might find one?"

Larkin stared into her mug, as though it was the most interesting thing in the world. "No, I don't know where you'd find *stories* about Ash."

Why was she calling Ashbourne, Ash? "Okay, well what *do* you know then, pal? Obviously you know something."

As Thea tensed into an even tighter ball, Harlow's chest felt like it might burst from the overwhelming amount of tension between the three of them. She was relieved when Larkin finally spoke. "It's hard to explain, but Ash is my friend."

"He's your *what*?" Thea screeched. In Selene's absence, Thea often took on the role of Over-Reactor in Chief.

Larkin's face scrunched up as she leaned away from Thea. Harlow stared at the ceiling. A family of five sisters could be a lot sometimes, even if only three were in the room. "Could we maybe—take it down a notch?" Harlow asked.

Thea sighed. "Explain, *immediately*, why you're friends with an ancient immortal and no one knows." She sounded remarkably like both of the maters; Harlow was impressed.

"He speaks to me in my dreams..." Larkin whispered.

The faraway look in Larkin's eyes twisted Harlow's stomach. Thea glanced at Harlow. When Larkin was little, the Order of Mysteries High Council had believed that Larkin might be a seer, because she often dreamed true, but she'd stopped before she turned eight, the true dreams simply disappearing. Everyone had forgotten about it, or at least it had seemed that way.

"Do you mean you have dreams *about* Ashbourne?" Harlow asked carefully.

Larkin shook her head. "No, they aren't dreams *about* him. He's *there* and we talk."

Thea drew in a sharp, deep breath, every trace of annoyance replaced with deepest worry. "You walk realms in your sleep?"

It was a highly valued but rare talent—so much so that Realm Walkers, like Striders, were thought to be extinct. It made a certain kind of sense that Larkin might have a special ability, one specifically related to the deeper magics, as her own Strider abilities were. What they'd learned from Cian about the origins of Striders made it seem possible that out of five sisters, at least two of them might have anomalous manifestations of magic.

But this revelation made Harlow more than nervous; it terrified her. If Larkin walked realms, there was no doubting why she'd kept it a secret from even her family. The last Realm Walker had died in Illuminated custody, kept imprisoned for their entire life, in servitude. Times had been different, but there was no doubt in Harlow's mind that the same could happen today.

Larkin let out a breath. "Yes. I stumbled into the limen when I was eight, and there he was, almost like he was waiting for me... except he was as surprised to see me as I was him."

Harlow wondered how he'd gotten free of the chamber in Nihil, but she didn't interrupt.

"And then I saw him lots of times when I walked realms. It was like we kept running into each other. Each time, he had that same look, like somehow he'd been waiting for something, but was surprised it was me."

"Interesting," Thea said. "And what did Ashbourne the Warden have to say to a child?"

Larkin rolled her eyes. "He's not some creep, Thea."

Harlow hid a smile when Thea gave Larkin her best Selene-stare, but she felt a measure of relief. It wasn't that she thought the immortal had done anything to her sister; in fact, from her only encounter with him, she'd guess he was lonely more than anything else. There had been a moment before he sent her back where it seemed he was relieved to see another person.

"Ash warned me about what would happen to me if I kept 'dreaming' the way I had been. About the Illuminated."

"How did he know who the Illuminated were?" Harlow asked. Larkin didn't know that the Illuminated had another form, not yet anyway.

Larkin sighed. "He's one of them. You know how the Illuminated are supposed to shift? Well they shift into great big winged people, with sparkly skin."

Thea muttered, "It's not sparkly. It's *illuminated*."

Larkin's eyebrows lifted, creasing her forehead with exasperation. She turned to Harlow, giving her a pointed look.

Harlow shrugged. "I *guess* there's a difference. They do that in their humanoid alternae anyway. You know, all the glowing."

Larkin pursed her lips, teasing. "It's definitely *sparkly*. You have sparkly boyfriends."

"It's not as ridiculous as you're making it sound," Thea insisted. "Besides, I'm *bonded*." Her voice had a shrill edge to it that suggested she was getting defensive. They could be here all day.

Larkin's response was a hysterical screech that Harlow supposed might be a laugh. Harlow wished her sisters didn't have such a propensity for high-pitched noises; it was disconcerting. "The point is," Larkin said when she quieted, "I can't believe the two of you kept all this from me. It's rude."

Thea folded her arms across her chest. "There are lots of things that the Illuminated keep secret. Things that are dangerous for people to know. This is one of them."

Larkin snorted. "I meant I literally can't believe *you* could keep this a secret. Harlow, I can believe. You? Not so much."

The two of them looked as though they might start fighting, so Harlow changed the subject. "You talked with Ashbourne in Nihil?"

"Nihil? Is that the prison?" Larkin asked.

Harlow nodded. "Yes, there's a chamber, where the guardians sleep, or are in stasis or something."

"Sounds like someone *else* is keeping secrets," Thea said as she poked Harlow sharply in the leg.

Harlow tried to stay casual about it. It wasn't exactly that she'd meant to keep it all a secret from her sisters, but that she hadn't gotten around to telling them yet. Sorting out what was a secret and what wasn't was complicated these days and she was worn down by the idea. Reluctantly, she admitted, "I may have been to Nihil. Twice."

Thea looked as though she might start screeching again. "Why the hells wouldn't the two of you tell me these things?"

"You should talk," Harlow responded. "You were a member of the Knights for how many years? With a secret *boyfriend*?"

Thea rolled her eyes, as though that were nothing in comparison with an ancient immortal friend, secret talents, and traveling to the limen. Anyone with sisters understood this was the way it was; you thought you knew them because you saw them every day, and then one day they'd change on you, morphing into someone else entirely. Sometimes the change was mundane. Sometimes it was life-altering, but the best thing to do was roll with it.

Larkin stuck out her tongue, then directed them back to the conversation at hand. "I don't think I've ever walked in the chamber you're talking about, but maybe the other parts of the prison. Sometimes there's just nothing but Ash when I arrive, and he's saddest then. But the rest of the time, we meet in the limen itself, not the prison. Ash and the other guardians can manifest in the limen in astral form. Kind of like a break from their responsibilities."

Thea held up her hands. "You're going to have to back up and tell me everything the two of you know."

Harlow recounted her visits to Nihil in close detail, along with her experience with the Pyriphle. When she'd finished telling about how quickly she'd started to shift near the heart of the limen, Thea nodded. "Yes, that would make sense. Because your shadows are aether in its purest form, before it fills the threads, and the Feriant is tied to your manifestation, contact with the heart would make it easier for you to shift."

Larkin nodded along, the exaggerated look on her face making it clear she was mocking Thea's academic tone. "Yes, Professor Krane."

"Shut up," Thea said, now poking her youngest sister playfully. "Does that all line up with what you know?

Larkin's face fell into seriousness. "I guess so. Though I don't know much about all of it, not the way you do. Mostly Ash listens while I talk."

The loneliness in her little sister's voice tugged at Harlow's heartstrings. Sometimes she forgot that Larkin was so young, and that she'd never made friends the way the twins had. She wondered why Ashbourne wanted to speak to Larkin. As her sister talked more about him, Harlow thought she understood; he was lonely too.

The other guardians were resentful of Nihil, and though they'd all been friends once, they were tired of one another now. Some of them hated each other, from the way it sounded.

And Ashbourne, he felt guilty about it *all*. Harlow wished Finn were here to hear this. She thought he'd understand how Ash felt.

When she finished talking, Larkin looked exhausted, but Harlow had to ask her something. "Does he ever say anything about someone named Lumina?"

Larkin smiled sadly. "No, not specifically, but I've gotten the impression there's someone he worries about."

"Okay," Thea said, pushing a piece of hair out of Larkin's face. "Do you know where he is? Or rather, how to get to him in the waking world?"

Rakul had said that if they wanted all their questions answered that they needed to "find the Warden." The more she tried to understand all of this, the more it felt like a web. Threads connected to one another and then dropped off when she didn't have enough information, but they spiraled out from one another, regardless. Harlow wondered what was at the center of it all. The deeper in she went, the more she got the sense that she was missing some wider view.

Larkin's head fell to the side as she thought. "Other than what we already know? Not really... I don't know how to get to Nihil. Not even my way."

"What happens when you visit his realm?" Harlow asked. "As opposed to the other places you've met, I mean."

"I just *arrive*. I rarely see anything but Ash... I think he wants it to be that way. The prison isn't safe."

"I should think not," Thea said.

Harlow's body remembered the Ravager, and its terrible voice. *Hello, little bird*. She shivered, glad that Ashbourne had kept her sister safe. Even in her astral form, she was vulnerable.

"Has he ever talked about what he guards there?" Harlow asked.

Larkin shrugged. "Not really."

"And you can't dream walk on purpose?" Thea asked.

Larkin shook her head. "No, I'm sorry. If I'd had a teacher, I probably could, but I'm pretty bad at it, I think."

Harlow knew how that felt. She wished she'd had anyone like her who could tell her what to do as a Strider. "Have you ever been anywhere else, besides being drawn to wherever Ash is?"

Larkin smiled. "A few places. The limen is interesting. It presses up against all worlds, of course, and sometimes there are doors to other places. Occasionally, I come across one and just watch."

"Watch what?" Thea asked.

"The world on the other side," Larkin said with a dreamy smile. "There are some really beautiful worlds."

It was hard not to ask questions about that, but they needed to stay on topic. "You don't go through though?" Harlow asked, uncomfortable. A theory was beginning to form in her thoughts, and she didn't much like it.

Larkin pushed some hair out of her face, her mouth screwing into a tight knot. "No. In the limen, I know how things work. My astral body is predictable. Once I stuck my hand through one of the doors and it felt strange. I'm not sure what might happen if I moved into a whole other realm."

Harlow nodded. "Have you ever seen anyone else there?"

"Anyone like me, or Ash?" Larkin asked.

"No," Harlow said slowly. "Have you ever seen anyone in the limen who was actually *there*."

Larkin shook her head. "No people, but occasionally an animal will wander in from the doors. I saw a fish swim in from a door that was underwater once. I tried to throw it back, but I couldn't become corporeal enough to touch it. It died."

Harlow nodded. "Because it wasn't underwater anymore."

Larkin's face scrunched up. "No... I mean, yes, it probably would have... but something came out of the aether and snatched it up.... It disappeared."

"Weren't you worried about your own safety?" Thea asked, sounding anxious.

Larkin laughed. "No. There are creatures in the limen, of course. It's a world of its own, despite how it layers between so many worlds. But they're semi-corporeal and have no interest in the non-corporeal."

Harlow raised her eyebrows.

"They don't care about my astral form. I think they see me, or sense me anyway, but they're not interested in me in the slightest."

"What are these creatures?" Harlow asked.

"I don't really know," Larkin said. "I don't see them very often, and they use the clouds of aether to hide in. Some seem harmless, like the ones who took the fish. I think they were just hungry... But others..." she shook her head. "They could be dangerous to corporeal beings."

Harlow swallowed hard. "Okay."

Thea watched her, likely recognizing the face Harlow was making intimately. She'd certainly seen it dozens of times over the years as they solved the mysteries of the texts they'd restored together. All that seemed like a lifetime ago now.

Harlow knew how the Illuminated got to Okairos, and knowing it terrified her. If they'd come through the limen, then more of them might be out there. Finn had said the "journey" was dangerous. Wherever they came from, if they found their way here, they would most certainly change things, and *not* for the better.

CHAPTER TWENTY

The next morning, as Harlow readied herself for brunch with Enzo and Riley, Thea entered the bathroom. "What do you know that you're not telling?"

Harlow set the curling iron down. There was no need to burn herself because she was distracted. Thea turned the iron off and began pulling threads to shape Harlow's hair into her usual waves. Like Meline, she was talented with glamour. "Well, are you going to tell me?"

Harlow stared at her sister in the mirror. In so many ways they were different. Thea was so beautiful she nearly always got her way. It made her blunt and insistent at times like these, when she felt someone wasn't immediately giving into her every whim.

"No," Harlow said. "I'm not."

Thea glared at her. There was no malice, or even anger in it, just sisterly frustration. "Why not?"

"I promised Finn I wouldn't tell anyone. Not even you. Some of what I know is dangerous."

Thea finished working on her hair and turned, sliding onto the vanity countertop so she faced Harlow directly. "Is this about who the Illuminated really are?"

Harlow nodded. Thea was clever enough to figure things like this out on her own, and they'd certainly been skirting the issue in their research for days. She'd wondered when Thea might figure it out. There was no need to try to lie, but she wasn't going to give anything away.

"I know," Thea said. Her fingers fluttered out, checking the wards on the villa, adding an extra layer of sound protection to just the surrounding space. "I know about the Ventyr, the Anemoi and Thuelloi."

"What?" Harlow whispered, afraid to speak aloud, even here. "Alaric told you?"

Thea nodded. "A long time ago. Back when we were trying to find information about the Striders, I came across a little volume of poetry. Quite obscure, just a few printings—they were numbered. The verse was quite bad, really. No artistry to it."

"And it was about the Ventyr?" Harlow asked.

Thea tucked her hair behind her ears, nodding. "About an endless war between a winged race of people, and an Emperor who wanted too much. He wasn't satisfied with the two planets he'd managed to conquer, so he used his children, twins, against one another to open portals to other worlds. It had a disastrous result—the witches of one world cursed them—throwing all sorts of things off balance in the worlds they'd accessed."

Harlow was acutely aware of the blood rushing through her veins as her heart beat faster. It was a disconcerting feeling to be so sensitive to everything going on in her body still, despite Finn's absence. "You confirmed with Alaric this was about the Illuminated?"

Thea's mouth pressed into a grim line. "The Ventyr. He swore me to absolute secrecy, and I never told anyone. We never even talked about it again. But all this has brought it up again. You know how they got here, don't you?"

Harlow closed her eyes. She wished to all gods that Thea

didn't know any of this. Now she had to worry about her, in addition to everything else. Still, it was easier that she knew. Harlow hated keeping secrets and having one less to worry about eased her burden. Finally she nodded. "They got here through the limen."

Thea bit her bottom lip, humming softly, as she often did when she was puzzling through something. Harlow had heard her make the same noise thousands of times in the workroom at the Monas over the years. "Yes, that's what I think too. Are you worried that somehow they'll find their way here? The rest of them, I mean."

"I can't really help but think they might." There was so much to be worried about these days. Admitting that she was worried about her fiancé's ancient ancestors coming to Okairos and making everything worse was awful. The complications just kept piling up. Thea didn't look concerned though.

Harlow threw her hands up in the air. "That would be bad, don't you think?"

Thea shrugged, grimacing. "Yes, but I'm not sure that's even possible at this point. It's been over two thousand years. Don't you think if they were coming they would've done it?"

Harlow tended to agree. "Yes, but what if what the Merkhov text shows will make magic accessible to everyone, somehow also brings the Ventyr here?"

She'd asked Finn about this before and he'd agreed with her; since awakening magic was what the Illuminated were sent here to do, it might somehow signal to the rest of their people, the Ventyr, where they were.

Thea's brows knit together. "I think that's a real risk. Whatever we find out with the Merkhov text, with the Scroll of Akatei, I think we'll have to weigh the risks pretty carefully."

Harlow's heart was heavy. "I have to get to brunch. We can talk about this later. Obviously, I don't think it's a good idea to talk to Larkin about this."

"Because Ashbourne and the guardians are Ventyr, right?"

Harlow nodded. "Exactly. That, and I came in contact with what they're guarding, Thea. It's worse than anything you can imagine. They're not like what we've been told the primordial elementals are like. They're sentient."

"What?" Thea snarled. "Sentient? Primordial elementals are..."

"Supposed to be more like animals, or worms, I know. And maybe they are like that, somehow—in form anyway—I don't know. I couldn't actually see it. But it spoke to me, and it said we'd see each other again soon."

Thea pursed her lips. "It was messing with your mind."

"Two of the guardians are missing. I don't think we can afford to ignore the threat."

"Fuck," Thea swore. "*Fuck*."

Harlow pressed a hand to her sister's shoulder. "My thoughts exactly."

"Every time I think it can't get worse it does," Thea muttered, her elegant fingers fluttering as she waved Harlow away. "Go to brunch. You might as well."

The foreboding she'd gotten used to reflected back at her, in her sister's eyes. "I'm sorry, Thea. I don't want this to be how it is."

Thea brushed a kiss to her forehead, dissolving the extra sound protection around them. "I know you don't. Go to brunch. I'm going to take another pass at the Merkhov."

RILEY'S HOME IN NEA STERLIS WASN'T AS GRAND AS the Herrington villa, but realistically, not many places were. Still, it was very nice, a flat in a beautiful modern building, with views of the sea. By the time Harlow got there, it was raining and chilly, so the three of them ate in the cozy kitchen, rather than the terrace. Riley had been decorating, spending the summer at the famous Nea Sterlis flea markets, picking up charming oddities. Harlow was impressed with their eclectic grasp on home decor, and the stories they had about each item they'd collected.

It was a pleasant enough meal, but Harlow was distracted. Her conversation with Thea had been disturbing, and to make things worse, in the cab on the way over Section Seven had run another story about Finn and Sabre. Apparently, they were *also* at brunch, which meant their ruse was in full effect. She'd texted Finn, the first of her queries that was meant to indicate jealousy and suspicion, and he hadn't answered her yet, which put her on edge.

"So," Riley said. "Are we going to talk about it?"

"What?" Harlow asked.

"About this idea that S7 has that you and Finn are on the rocks," Enzo chimed in.

His calm expression was slightly strained, around the eyes— he was reading her. She could only imagine the dread and anxiety that were coming to the surface. He'd read them as being about Finn, but in reality, they were about this, about lying to the people she loved. She'd just gotten Enzo back, and now she was keeping something huge from him, something that would make him worry for her, and maybe even hate Finn.

Harlow rolled her eyes, trying to affect a casual air. She had to try to diffuse some of this to soften the eventual fallout. "There's no truth to it. Sabre is our realtor."

"Who Finn used to *date*," Enzo said, emphatic. He was definitely reading her high levels of anxiety. "That really doesn't bother you?"

"They went on like five dates three years ago," Harlow tried her hardest not to sound defensive, but didn't make much headway. Trying to deceive two empaths was anxiety-producing. "Decided they were better off as friends, and that's how things have been ever since."

"And now Sabre's helping you buy a house?" Riley asked, one eyebrow raised. They looked suspicious enough that Harlow knew they knew she was lying about something. "And you're not even *there*?"

Her ability to stay calm was deteriorating with every passing moment. She'd known this was how it might be, but the reality of it was different. "Do the two of you *want* there to be a problem?"

Enzo shook his head, giving Riley a look that said, *we should give her space*. "No, Harls, of course not."

"We just want to make sure you're okay," Riley said, their voice gentle.

Both of them clearly sensed her distress, and it was infuriating that it was working in the ruse's favor. The more worked up she got, the more they believed something was truly wrong between her and Finn. She would have a lot of explaining and apologizing to do when this was over.

Harlow drew in a long breath and gathered her thoughts, but her emotions took over and the words spilled out of her, unbidden. "And yet, the tone of this conversation makes me feel like things are very much not okay. Is there something about Sabre that I should find threatening? Because they're so attractive and glamorous and I'm just *me*?"

The room was so silent Harlow could hear the wards on the building humming, ever-so-slightly. Enzo's lips pressed into a tight line. "You know that's not what we're saying."

"I know." Harlow swallowed hard. *Where had all that come from? Did she really feel that way?* She stared at the ceiling for a moment, trying to stay calm. "Of *course* I'm sensitive about the things the gossips are saying. It hurts, especially when I'm trying hard and they still hate everything I fucking do."

They were staring at her now, slightly aghast at her outburst. Harlow took a beat, examining her hands, her ring, for a brief moment before saying, "I trust Finn, okay?"

No matter that he was taking his sweet time answering her text. Even if it was fake bad news, she hated waiting for it. She glanced at her phone. Both Riley and Enzo caught the direction her attention had traveled in. The look they shared nearly broke Harlow's resolve to stay calm. There was nothing in the world she hated more than being pitied.

Luckily, a knock at the door saved her from further conversation. Riley got up to answer. Enzo tried to take her hand, but she snatched it back from him. He had that look in his eyes that said he wanted to talk about her feelings, and she just *couldn't*. Not right now. "I don't want you to comfort me, okay? Nothing is wrong."

"Okay," he said. "I believe you."

"Do you?" she asked, hating the high pitch of her voice.

"No," he replied. "I don't. There's something wrong, but whether you're upset about this Finn stuff or something else, I can't tell."

Harlow's jaw clenched so hard it ached in the back of her neck. She reminded herself again that this was the plan. This was exactly what they'd meant to happen. If they were convincing Riley and Enzo, they were likely to be convincing anyone else who was watching.

"I know that face," Enzo whispered. Harlow made a silent plea to Aphora, wishing hard that Enzo actually knew what was happening. Tears filled her eyes as he said, "I'm here if you need me, all right?"

"I know," she said, finally taking Enzo's outstretched hand. "Just give me some time, okay?"

Enzo nodded and squeezed her hand, just as Kate and Riley entered the room. "Sorry to interrupt," Kate said brightly. "I borrowed a book from Riley and thought I'd return it on my way to the beach—but the WaveReport just said there's a possibility of a storm moving in."

Kate's usually brown hair had gone a bit red from her

summer in the sun, and she was tan, with a few freckles sprinkling across her nose. Her linen shirt was unbuttoned past the point of what the gossips would consider decent, showing her bikini. It irked that she looked so good, casual and at ease, when Harlow was so uncomfortable.

"I asked Kate if she wanted to stay for brunch," Riley said. Their face was cautious, as though they were worried Harlow might get upset. She wasn't that bad, was she?

Harlow tried her brightest smile, but Kate raised her eyebrows incredulously. "Don't strain yourself, Lo," she said as she sat. "It's just brunch. I won't bite."

The air in Riley's apartment felt sticky and hot, all of a sudden. Harlow shifted uncomfortably in her chair, feeling as though she might be drowning. This was supposed to be something fun to do, something to distract her from missing Finn, and she wanted nothing more than to bolt. Of course she'd known there would be friction around all this, she'd just expected it to go differently.

Riley brought out an epic spread of toppings and freshly made bagels, as Enzo and Kate chatted about the science of growing grapes at the vineyard. It was so boring Harlow nearly yawned, but the food looked delicious, so she focused on it instead. No one spoke directly to her for the rest of the meal, though both Enzo and Riley exchanged several furtive looks that did little more than agitate her further.

When they were finished eating, Harlow went to the bathroom to text Finn again. *Are you ignoring me?* Her heart beat a little faster as she waited. His read receipts were on. She saw the moment he saw her text, the little dots cascading that indicated that he was answering, and then nothing. Her hands shook as she washed them, but she steadied herself enough to go back to the living room, where everyone was having tea. Or rather, Enzo was drinking tea while Kate and Riley made coffee in the kitchen.

"I'm gonna go," she said.

Enzo gave her a close once-over, but only nodded in response. Harlow glanced towards the kitchen, meaning to say goodbye, but Riley and Kate were deep in conversation with one another, speaking in soft voices. She prayed they weren't talking about her and Finn, but the way they startled when she walked towards them made her sure they probably had been.

"I'm going home," she said. "Thank you for a beautiful meal."

"Did you walk here?" Kate asked.

Harlow's chest tightened. "No, I took a cab."

"I have my car, want me to drive you back to the villa? Petra and I are supposed to have a date later anyway, I can see if she wants me to pick her up early."

Harlow's immediate instinct was to say no, but after talking to Morgaine, she'd been determined to try harder and things had gone badly enough already. She took a deep breath and nodded. "Sure, shoot her a text."

Kate did, and almost instantly received a response, which Harlow tried not to be jealous about. "We're a go. Come on, I'm parked out front."

Harlow hugged Enzo and Riley, trying to ignore the concern in both their expressions. She supposed that as soon as she left, they were going to have an extra analytical conversation about her, determining that she was jealous of Sabre, and likely jealous of Kate and Petra. If so, they wouldn't be altogether wrong. Kate chatted easily about Petra and the vineyard as they made their way to her car and Harlow did feel jealous, but not for the reasons Enzo and Riley might have guessed.

The skies opened up then, and the mild drizzle she'd arrived in shifted to a torrential downpour. Kate and Harlow were soaked in an instant. They ran the rest of the way to Kate's car, laughing from the shock of being so quickly drenched. They were still laughing when they shut the doors to the SUV.

Kate had purchased the rugged little SUV when they were in college. It was banged up and about a million years old, but like the Woody, an absolute classic that she refused to magically restore. She always said that the Illuminated and Order of Mysteries used magic to fix things that weren't broken, and loved the SUV for what it was.

Harlow reached for her seatbelt, but it was stuck. A faint memory that it had always been broken came back to her, followed by some less innocent memories about the back seat. Harlow blushed.

"You remember the trick to get it to go?" Kate asked. The question and tone were innocent enough, but a flush colored Kate's cheeks that made Harlow wonder if she'd had the same thought.

Harlow shook her head, unable to trust her voice. Kate leaned over and pulled gently on the seatbelt, her face close to Harlow's. It was a friendly enough moment, but it made Harlow nervous all the same. How was she supposed to act natural when they'd had sex in every seat of this car, and on the hood, and once on the roof? It wasn't that she missed those times, but just thinking about them made it awkward as Kate handed her the seatbelt.

"This is weird for me," Harlow said, her voice shaking slightly.

For once, Kate was serious. "It's weird for me too. I'm not sure how to act."

A long silence passed as Kate started the car, pulling away from the curb and into the light traffic. Nea Sterlis was so much easier to navigate by car this time of year, Harlow might actually start to get comfortable driving again.

"I really like Petra, and we have a good understanding about things."

Harlow nodded. "I'm glad." She stared at her hands, at her ring. The pause was so long that awkwardness set in.

She was about to say something about how happy she was for the two of them—she *was* happy for them, after all, but Kate spoke. "It wasn't your fault, you know."

"What wasn't?" Harlow asked.

"The way things ended. I was wild about you."

Harlow sighed. "We don't have to do this, Kate."

Kate rolled her neck, an exasperated laugh filling the car as she pulled over, into a parking lot overlooking the ocean, one of Nea Sterlis' dozens of scenic overlooks. "I kind of think we do. *I* need to. We never talked about it after I told you I was leaving."

"What was there to *say*?" Harlow said. She didn't realize she'd been angry with Kate all this time. "I couldn't do things the way you wanted, and you couldn't do things the way I wanted. It was all a mistake."

Kate shut the SUV off. "That's not fair. It wasn't all a mistake. I *loved* you."

The words hit hard. They'd never said them while they were together. It had been implied, but the fact that Kate leaned heavily towards non-monogamy hadn't worked for Harlow and though there hadn't been anyone else at the time, the mere thought had scared her, kept her from saying all she'd felt at the time.

"I loved you too," Harlow finally admitted. It felt good to say it, even if that verb was in the past tense. She'd spent the whole summer working hard on healing, and she knew this was part of things. Being honest now was important to her, because this was obviously keeping both of them from fully moving forward—and it was time. With Finn and Petra involved, it was beyond time. "But you left and Mark showed up... and I know it's not fair, but if you stayed he never would have done all those things to me, because I never would have left you. I would have figured it all out."

Kate's mouth fell open, and then she shut it. "I know. I *know*, Lo. Don't you think I know that? It's all my fucking fault.

Everything that happened to you..." A sob choked off the end of her sentence.

Tears wet both their cheeks as their words hung in the air. That wasn't what Harlow had meant at all. The stress of the day had made her emotions a jumble, and her words had come out all wrong. "It's not. None of it was your fault. I know that. I'm just *so mad* that I let it all happen."

Harlow's chin trembled with grief. Snot was running down her face and she buried her face in her hands. She was too far gone to care what Kate thought about how she looked. The lid was off the box she shoved her feelings down into now, and she couldn't get it back on.

Kate's arms went around her, stroking her hair. "It was *his* fault, Lo. Not yours. It was always all his fault. I'm glad he's dead."

Harlow pulled back a little to look at Kate. Something about the way she said it made Harlow think she knew more about what had happened at the House of Remiel than she was supposed to. She'd never found out where Kate had disappeared to that night.

Kate pulled a hanky from her pocket and wiped Harlow's face off. "You're all puffy," she said, smiling as though she thought it was cute. "All I meant is that he was so obviously an asshole, and you deserve better. Finn is a good man."

Kate hugged her again, and she smelled familiar, like sunshine, wood sage and salt air. Long ago, this would have ended with their clothes off, but now—now Harlow was just grateful Kate was here. She'd forgotten how the best part of *them* had been their easy friendship. The rest was fleeting, but maybe that could last.

She let her arms go around Kate too. "I missed you," Harlow mumbled into Kate's shoulder. "I missed you so much."

When they let go, Kate said, "I missed you too. Can things be better with us now? Could we *try* to be friends at least?"

Harlow shook her head. "We don't have to try. I think we're already there." She smiled through her tears as Kate's face lit up.

Harlow felt the joke coming before it came out of Kate's mouth. "Really? That is so good, because Petra hates *Pretty Little Firestarters* and the final season is about to start."

It was her way of smoothing things over. Of making intense emotions easier to digest, and Harlow didn't mind it a bit. It felt good to laugh. "The Illuminated have terrible taste in television. Finn doesn't like it either."

Kate fished another hanky out of the console for Harlow and started the car again. They chatted about their shared love for the nighttime soap opera the rest of the way home. It felt like a new start, made more poignant by the fact that the rain let up and the sky cleared. When they pulled into the villa's half-moon driveway, Petra was sitting on the front steps, staring at her phone.

As they got out of the car, she looked up. "Did the two of you finally make up?"

Kate nodded, grinning, but Harlow saw the caution in Petra's eyes. "What is it?"

Petra glanced away from them, cheeks flushing slightly. "Section Seven."

Kate took the phone from Petra's outstretched hand, swearing at it. "Those fucking assholes. It wasn't like that, babe."

"I know it wasn't," Petra said simply. "They're obsessed with breaking Finn and Harlow up."

"Do I even want to see?" Harlow asked as she took Petra's phone from Kate. The question was rhetorical, of course; she was already reading. Photos of Kate fixing her seatbelt certainly looked like they were getting intimate in front of Riley's building, and the ones at the beach overlook were even worse. The headline read, "Finn McKay is gone for mere days and Harlow's replaced him."

"Their headlines aren't even clever anymore," she said. How

were they getting all these photos taken and out so quickly? They had to be using more of the invisible drones. But why weren't they publishing the footage of the fight at the beach then? Inside her bag, she felt her phone vibrate. She glanced at it, then took Petra's hand. "Are we okay?"

Petra surprised her, pulling her into a hug so tight that Harlow could barely breathe. "Yes," Petra said into her hair. "Of course we are."

Harlow hugged Petra back. In so many ways, she was the easiest person Harlow knew. If she were mad, or worried, she would say.

Petra let her go and grinned at both Harlow and Kate. "Besides, you're the ugliest crier I've ever met. Your face is all splotchy. You and I both know you wouldn't have been sobbing if you'd been doing what Section Seven said you were."

Kate protested. "Hey, I've made girls cry because it was so good."

Petra bit her lip, taking Kate's hand. "Prove it."

Harlow groaned. "I don't need to hear that."

Kate dragged Petra to her side, glancing back at Harlow. "You gonna be okay? We could stay?"

Harlow's phone buzzed again, several times in a row. "No, I'm fine. Have a good time."

She watched as they drove off, then sat on the steps herself. She had no idea if Larkin and Thea were home, but she didn't want to do this in front of them. Her phone vibrated yet again as she opened it. Several texts from Finn awaited her.

Not ignoring you. At brunch.

Everything okay?

What's going on with you and Kate?

Are you ignoring ME?

Harlow waited for her read receipt to show up and took a few breaths before responding. *Nothing's going on with Kate. Section Seven's just being Section Seven.*

She watched as he read her message and then began to write his own. He was obviously writing and rewriting, because it took a while for him to respond. *Okay. They're jerks.*

Harlow's chest tightened. This was hard. She could feel him wanting to say more to comfort her, and her intense desire to be comforted, but they couldn't do that. Not if they wanted this to work. So she asked what they'd agreed would be one of their code questions: *Yeah. Any good properties?*, which meant, "How are things going with your parents?"

The answer was quick this time. *At least one good lead, but it won't be on the market for another few weeks.*

Harlow's heart beat faster. So the game had truly begun. His parents were buying what was happening. They'd agreed to be subtle at first. *Want to call and talk it over?*

His answer was immediate. *Not a good time. We can talk when I get home.*

And that was that, the code was over, he was back to being dismissive. *All part of the plan*, she reminded herself. Harlow locked her phone and closed her eyes. *I can do this*, she thought as she breathed deep.

"Are you sitting on the porch because Section Seven is at it again?" Thea asked.

Harlow glanced over her shoulder. Thea and Larkin were standing in the doorway.

"Yeah," she said, getting up. "I could really use a cup of tea."

Larkin came around to help her up. "No shortage of those here."

Thea hugged her as the three of them walked into the villa together, closing the door on the outside world.

CHAPTER TWENTY-ONE

T he next week brought rain, and not much else, as Thea tried to break the binding on the Merkhov text. They didn't see much of their friends, and Harlow wondered if maybe her behavior at brunch and the Section Seven onslaught had gotten to them. Every text she sent was met with friendly responses, and on the surface it seemed like they were busy, but she couldn't stop going over things in her mind. *Had she given too much away? Did they suspect she was lying?* She knew she was probably being paranoid, but worrying over every little thing she said was an old habit that she couldn't quite shake.

It wasn't as though there weren't plenty of other things to hold her attention. She helped Thea with extra research on breaking complicated binding spells and used the Vault's resources to find a whole host of training exercises that had names like "Lucid Dreaming for the Intermediate" and "Astral Projection for the Advanced Practitioner." She and Larkin watched them together in Cian's office, since it had a big screen television, and laughed at the retro-vibes of the videos that had been digitized from videotapes.

The videos weren't entirely pointless, vintage as they were. The principles were solid, and Harlow and Larkin worked together nearly every day to improve Larkin's control over herself when dreaming. Harlow secretly hoped that she was helping herself as well. She could use some increased control over her mind, and the tutorials seemed to focus on that idea a lot.

"I'm just like the heroine in Meli's sci-fi romance book," Larkin quipped one morning over iced coffee and toaster waffles.

The two of them had just finished the seventh installment in "Astral Projection for the Advanced Practitioner." They sat at Cian's desk in the Vault, which faced the big screen TV. Axel had taken the opportunity to stretch out in front of them, sure he was the main event, rather than the instructional videos.

"I thought it was a monster romance," Harlow said as she put the video back in its case, searching for another. There were two or three more in the series, but they seemed to have misplaced the next one.

"Oh, there's that one too, but it's a trilogy about three psychics who fall in love with different creatures—this one is about a dream walker and she falls in love with a mafia enforcer," Larkin explained.

Harlow turned. "And you... liked this book? The one with the cat-people was super spicy."

Axel rolled onto his back, purring at Larkin, who rubbed his belly as she laughed. "Would you believe it if I said I liked the story?"

"Whatever turns your key," Harlow said, laughing along with her sister. "I don't think that's why everyone else is reading them though." She found the missing video and set it up.

Larkin popped the last bite of her waffle in her mouth, shrugging. "We can all appreciate different things about romances, Harlow. This one's got great found family vibes."

Harlow plopped back in the chair next to Larkin, giving

Axel's ears a scratch as she settled in. "So how are you like the main character? I haven't read that one."

"She walks into people's dreams and solves their deepest mysteries," Larkin explained.

"And you're going to do that?" Harlow asked, not quite seeing the connection, since Larkin wasn't exactly going into a dream world, but astral projecting into a real place, albeit in her sleep.

Larkin shook her head, taking a long drink of her iced coffee, draining it of the last precious drops. Then she grabbed Harlow's, right out of her hands. Harlow rolled her eyes, letting her sister jack herself up on caffeine if she wanted to. For whatever reason, it had the opposite effect on Larkin than it had on most people; it seemed to calm her more than anything.

"No, see, she and the love interest form a connection in the dream world, one they can't seem to make in the waking world, on account of the fact that they're both so damaged and broody, of course."

"Of course," Harlow agreed, snickering as she snatched her coffee back. The days of iced coffee were coming to a close, and she didn't want to miss one scrap of them, even if they were locked deep underground in the Vault.

"Well, I can connect with Ash in the *real* limen, and hopefully I can solve the mystery of where you can find him, since that's what Rakul said you had to do." She smiled smugly, raising her eyebrows and kicking her feet up on Cian's desk. "And then I'll be the hero of the story, just like the girl from the book."

Harlow smiled. "I would love that so much. It seems like everything keeps going just a little wrong, you know?"

Larkin nodded. "It feels like that sometimes. Things are really complex, you know? Maybe we're making more progress than we think."

It was a nice way to think about things. Harlow kissed

Larkin's cheek, dragging her sister into a one-armed hug. "There's like three more of these astral projection videos. Guess if you're gonna be the big hero, we'd better watch them, huh?"

Larkin sighed in mock-exasperation. "Every hero has their training montage. This is mine."

They cackled hard as the credits started rolling. Cian's computer flashed a notification. "Keep watching," Harlow ordered, pointing to the screen. "I don't want you to miss any part of your big montage moment."

Larkin stuck out her tongue as Harlow scooted closer to Cian's computer in her rolling chair. The notification was from Cian, so Harlow clicked into it. It was a message for her, sent over the secure line from Haven in Nuva Troi: *I see you're watching movies in my office. Clean up after yourselves and get that cat off my desk.*

Harlow stuck her tongue out at the camera she knew was placed above the TV and rubbed Axel's belly before reading on.

While Finn's been off looking at brownstones and brunching, I've been doing some digging in the Order of Masks' archives. Merhart Locklear approved me for some of our more classified material last week, and I found this. It appears to be a crypt from about two hundred years ago.

Look closely at the inscription.

Hope you're well.

C

Harlow clicked on the attached image. It was an engraving of a cemetery, full of beautiful headstones, statuary, and large gated crypts all in a row. There was an inscription on the most prominent of the crypts: "The world between worlds waits just beyond knowledge. Beware what lies—" Harlow couldn't read the rest, as the inscription seemed to wrap around the crypt.

The first line was familiar somehow though. She opened up the private search engine that Nox built for the Vault's digitized archives and typed it in, leaving the unfinished line out. Larkin paused the instructional video to read over her shoulder. "That sounds familiar, doesn't it?"

"Yes, I'm searching." The search engine that Nox built for the Vault's archives showed it was ninety percent through its scan. One answer came up, in a rather common prayer book published by the Sistren of Akatei.

Larkin and Harlow both leaned in, right as Axel sat up, directly in front of the computer screen, blocking their view. Larkin dragged him off the desk and into her lap, where he grumbled before crawling into her hoodie, which she held open for him.

"You'll spoil him," Harlow said absentmindedly.

"Good," Larkin replied as the scan of the prayer book flashed onto the screen.

There it was, the inscription to the book, right after the ornate title page.

The world between worlds
waits just beyond knowledge.

"I mean, that's an obvious reference to the limen," Larkin said. "Which I guess makes sense. Akatei is supposed to govern it, after all."

Harlow nodded. "So you're the one who was obsessed with the nekropoleis as a kid. What do you think this means?"

Larkin thought for a moment. "Well, lots of crypts are entrances to the catacombs beneath them and operate as family altars. It was a popular way to build them about six or seven hundred years ago, but kind of went out of style during Grandmama's time, because there were a series of cave-ins that made the catacombs in Nytra unsafe."

"Okay," Harlow replied as she chewed on the thought. "So could there be some sort of entrance to limenal space in a catacomb?" She thought of the Pyriphle, and the strong feeling she'd had that it connected directly to the world between worlds. It made sense. Maybe this was how they'd find Ashbourne.

Apparently, Larkin thought so as well. "It could. What else is there for us to look at?"

"There's nothing else. It was just on this random crypt, and here in this prayer book." Harlow said. "I don't even know how we're supposed to know if this is even in Nea Sterlis."

Larkin pointed to a figure in the drawing. At first Harlow thought it was a leopard, or other big cat, but as she looked closer, it looked more like a dog. "Is that a dog?"

"Either that or a panther," Larkin said. "Doesn't really matter. I've seen it before."

"Where?" Harlow asked.

Larkin made a face, shaking her head as she chuckled. There was one historical site in Nea Sterlis that Harlow had refused to visit all summer. She hated going anywhere where the unquiet dead tended to congregate. Unlike most sorcière, she did not find communing with the dead to be peaceful, or even helpful. It was mostly just creepy, and Nea Sterlis' nekropoleis was one of the most haunted in Nytra.

"No," Harlow whined, drawing the word out to several syllables. It was terribly obvious, of course, but she didn't have to like it.

"I guess we know what we're doing tomorrow," Larkin said, looking at her phone. "It's too late to go today. The ghasts will be out in an hour."

Harlow grimaced. Nobody went to the nekropoleis after dark. Ghasts weren't fundamentally dangerous, but unlike most other spirits, they could touch you. Most people, even those that enjoyed chatting with dead people, found them disconcerting. Luckily, they only came out at night. "Let's leave early tomorrow, this could take a while."

Larkin nodded. "See if Thea will take a break. She could use some sun." She gestured towards the television. "I'm gonna finish watching this, but I could use a snack."

Harlow let out a bark of laughter and messaged Cian back

with their plans, then went upstairs to make her spoiled sister a snack and convince Thea to go with them to the City of the Dead.

❧

"WELL, AT LEAST IT'S NOT RAINING," THEA SAID, smiling cheerily. The air was crisp, and she wore a dress that made her look like she stepped out of a murder mystery set in Nea Sterlis about seventy years ago. As many of them had been filmed in this very nekropoleis, it was fitting.

The City of the Dead was pretty enough in the daytime, but even now there were spirits lurking everywhere. The spirit of a human woman, wearing a tattered gown that trailed the ground, passed by them screaming noiselessly and then disappeared as she walked straight through a wall. It wasn't raining, but that didn't make Harlow any happier to be "skulking around the cemetery," as she'd put it at breakfast.

They'd asked Enzo and Petra to come along, but neither had been available. Harlow was starting to worry that they all might be mad at her. She brushed the thought aside and took a quick selfie with her sisters to calm her nerves. There was a hedge of late-blooming *lantana camara*, and the riot of crimson flowers was too pretty to miss.

She posted the photo onto her socials, with the caption "Sister day!" and a little skull emoji. It felt disrespectful to the spirits, but she was trying to get someone's attention, after all. Paparazzi were absolutely forbidden from entering the nekropoleis, so there was no danger of being followed today. Besides, they were all back on the rabbit shifter love story again. As much as she hated it, she had to keep them interested in her, so posting a photo some place they were expressly forbidden from entering was sure to get them interested.

"Should we split up?" Larkin asked when Harlow was finished on her phone. "It might make things go faster."

She hadn't been able to remember exactly where she'd seen the dog-panther-leopard statue, so they were set to spend the day here. Harlow dreaded the idea of searching through the nekropoleis alone, but it made sense.

"Sure," she said, making a face.

Thea hugged her arm. "Don't be like that. The ghasties won't get you for at least another six hours. We've got plenty of time."

Harlow rolled her eyes at Thea, shrugging her off. The whole family knew Harlow was scared of spirits and loved to tease her about it. "It's fine. I'm fine. Let's split up. Text if you find anything."

Thea and Larkin both nodded, and they went their separate ways. If you could ignore the fact that at nighttime the place was quite literally crawling with the spirits of unhappy dead people, who behaved in all manner of disgusting ways—showing you their deaths, spitting up various insects, and generally scaring the shit out of you—in the daytime the nekropoleis was quite pleasant. Just a few restless ghosts milling around. *Absolutely nothing to worry about.*

The architecture of the tombs was varied, but many of them were ancient, preserved by magic, and the nekropoleis was famous for its long-blooming gardens. Plants that were beginning to go dormant elsewhere in the city in anticipation of the autumn rains were still blooming here, giving the City of the Dead the intoxicating scent of a spring garden.

Harlow's phone buzzed, and she fished it out of her purse. Despite the lovely architecture and plants, she desperately hoped one of her sisters had found what they were looking for. A decapitated vampire carrying its own head had been following her for several minutes and she already wanted to leave. The sooner they found what they were looking for, the better.

Instead, it was Finn. Her hands went immediately clammy as she unlocked her phone.

Probably shouldn't post your location on socials if you want Section Seven to leave you alone.

That was it. That was all it said. No hello, how are you... Nothing. He was turning the screw tighter, taking the ruse further, she knew that. But after all these months of learning to trust him and herself again—the cold condescension stung. She shook it off and took a deep breath before responding. *Paps can't get in here.*

He saw immediately and responded. *Still, I'd expect you to be more careful.*

Harlow's eyes narrowed as she read Finn's words over and over, puzzling through them, trying to figure out the best way to respond. On instinct, she looked at his socials. Nothing. Then Sabre's. Sure enough, there was a selfie of the two of them. On a rooftop, poolside at the Ambracia Palace, posted twenty minutes ago.

She took a screenshot and sent it back to him, no message. He saw, then began typing. Then stopped. Then began again. Then stopped. She waited, but there was no response. The minutes ticked past. The headless vampire still appeared to be following her. Now it was tossing its head around, playing with it. It set Harlow even further on edge, despite the prevalent thought that day-spirits couldn't actually see or sense the living, but were simply going about their own post-death existence.

To distract herself from the vampire-spirit, which seemed to be going the same direction she was no matter which avenue she turned down, she checked Sabre's socials again. They'd posted several stories. Harlow clicked into them, and sure enough, there was Finn right next to them at the pool. Sabre was wearing a tiny bikini that showed off all their curves, and their hair was pulled into a perfectly coiffed ponytail.

Harlow touched her own messy bun as her jaw clenched.

She watched the stories as she walked, not bothering to look around her. She'd had quite enough of the headless vampire. In Sabre's stories, a waiter brought out a feast of late-summer delicacies. Finn's phone was in his hand, but he watched the waiter setting the food down between him and Sabre with rapt attention as they popped a bottle of sparkling wine and said in what Harlow could only describe as a sultry voice, "Here's to us! A most excellent team."

Harlow closed the stories and opened her text messages. *Cheers to your most excellent team. Is there something for me to be celebrating, or are you and Sabre just having fun?*

It was an undeniably petty response that she was immediately embarrassed by, despite its likely effectiveness if anyone was monitoring them. She stared at the message, cringing so hard her shoulders and neck ached. She'd felt that jealousy, that pettiness, right to the core of her being and it was awful to recognize it.

There was no response. No read receipt. Just silence. Harlow's heart thumped hard in her chest, her throat suddenly dry. She dug in her bag for her water bottle and took a long drink, suddenly dizzy. *Could she unsend the message?*

Her phone buzzed.

"Please let it be Larkin or Thea," she said aloud.

No such luck. *Calm down. It's just some sparkling wine.*

Harlow locked her phone immediately to keep from responding—she was actually mad at him. She'd always had a penchant for jealousy and her hackles were up, much as she desperately wanted to be cool about this, like a girl in a spy film. Instead, her back teeth gritted together unglamorously, and she flushed with rage. She stared up at the sky, hoping to soothe herself by looking at the clouds, but the sky was perfectly clear. As her eyes fell back towards the nekropoleis, she saw the dog-panther-leopard they were looking for in the distance.

Her heart leapt. She rushed toward the statue, having to navigate several small alleyways before she found it. She tried climbing onto a few of the crypts' front steps, but she couldn't see the tomb from Cian's message. She opened her maps app, grabbed her exact location and texted her sisters. It would be better to look together.

Harlow sat down on the steps of a crypt to wait, scrolling through all of Sabre's socials, making herself needlessly miserable. *Why am I doing this?* she thought to herself. Finn showed up in a few images, looking tanned and relaxed, and her heart ached. She missed him terribly and hated how this was going.

I should just call, she thought. *Hearing his voice might help.* Her fingers hesitated over his name in her phone, her chest constricting. Footsteps saved her from having to make a choice.

"You found it!" Larkin said, a broad grin lighting her face.

"Yep," Harlow said, faking brightness. Thea shot her a suspicious look. "But I can't find the tomb from the image from here. Any ideas about where it might be? I'm hopeless with directions in this labyrinth."

Thea looked up at the statue and opened her phone to look at the original image. "Come," she said, already walking.

Harlow and Larkin followed their elder sister through several twisting paths. Thea looked up and back at the dog statue, high above them the entire time. When Harlow was fully lost in the maze of crypts, they stepped out onto a broader avenue and Thea smiled. "There you are."

A magnificent crypt rose above them. No, not a crypt. It was a small, very ancient temple of Akatei, and above the front the words from the image were still visible, though the building was in surprisingly poor shape, as though no one had bothered to maintain it for some time.

The words were as they had been in the image, *The world between worlds waits just beyond knowledge. Beware what...* Harlow and her sisters walked around the side of the building to read the rest: *lies beneath the Alabaster Spire.*

"The Alabaster Spire?" Larkin said aloud. "What's that?"

Harlow shrugged. "I've never heard of a building in the Citadel named that. It has to refer to something in the Alabaster Citadel, don't you think?"

Thea nodded. "It must. You're right, there's no building named anything like that, but that doesn't mean there never has been. We could look."

Harlow nodded, but she'd hoped for more. Above their heads, clouds were rolling in on a chill wind. "Let's go home before it rains."

Larkin snapped a few photos of the temple, and even shook the front doors, which were securely locked and warded. "Can't get in."

"It's progress," Thea said, sounding encouraged.

Harlow tried to let her sister's optimism outshine the text conversation playing in her mind as they walked home, but she couldn't shake the darkness creeping in.

CHAPTER TWENTY-TWO

Harlow spent the next morning with Larkin and Thea, combing through the Vault resources for mention of any "Alabaster Spire." Nothing turned up. Larkin messaged Nox, but got no response.

"They're probably all busy with the shop," Thea said. "I think we've done what we can for today. I'm going to work on the Merkhov for a bit before Alaric gets home."

Harlow wished she'd go paint instead. Thea had a way of focusing on a problem so closely that other things—things she loved to do—disappeared from her life until she'd solved it. She typically ended up irritated and exhausted, drained for days or weeks. But Harlow knew better than to say anything about this. Thea would just scowl and do whatever she wanted anyway.

Larkin got up from her perch, stretching. "I'm going to go try my astral projection meditation again. I'm making some progress; yesterday I projected into the upstairs hall bath."

"Useful if your astral body has to pee," Thea said.

The three of them laughed, but Harlow thought hers sounded hollow. She couldn't shake the feeling that time was slipping away. After her sisters went upstairs, she looked at her calendar—where had the summer gone? It was nearly the equinox. At home, the Order of Mysteries would be getting ready for their annual feast and rituals. She texted the maters to find out how things were going at the shop. She, Thea, and Larkin video conferenced nearly every day on the secure line in the Vault, but she wanted to check in anyway.

Selene sent back a few videos of the Monas, bustling with customers, just as Thea had assumed. Indi and Nox were working the front desk together. Indi's hair was cut in a sleek ear-length bob, and her outfit was a slightly more femme version of Nox's tech-goth style, with an edge of glam that was all Indi's own. She hadn't been posting much to socials, except for the Monas account, since they'd returned. Indi had always over-compensated for her intense dislike of being thought of as "the shy twin," and Harlow was glad she was finally doing things her own way. Nox and Indi waved at the camera, leaning towards one another in a way that warmed Harlow's heart.

Her heart ached for Nuva Troi at the beginning of autumn, the Monas, and her family. The past few days had been terrible, and all she wanted to do was curl up in Selene's lap and watch trashy reality TV. The city would be cooling off finally, the leaves would turn soon. Was she just supposed to stay here and rot? What were they even doing here still? Rakul Kimaris was back in Falcyra, Cian had told them late last night, and Alaric was returning from Santos this afternoon. Maybe she could convince them that they should just go home.

Whatever the plan for the ruse had been before, was it even working now? Without much communication from Finn or Cian to let her know that their little game was working, it felt like nothing but a painful exercise in misery. Harlow trudged upstairs to find Axel, who was curled up on the couch in the library. She snuggled in next to him and practiced making the uncomfortable couch into something cozier and slightly more modern. Cian hadn't sworn her off the furniture in this room, after all.

Her shadows danced with pleasure at being used. She hadn't tried to turn into the Feriant for days. The longer Finn was gone, the less she wanted to try. A little frustrated growl escaped her throat. She didn't miss the fervor one bit, but since he'd left, everything seemed so dull.

This is how it starts, she thought. *You depend on them too much, and then lose yourself.*

Her shadows shimmered around her, begging to be used. She got up, tucking Axel into a blanket, full of every intention to go down to the gym to see what she could manage on her own. She passed through the foyer and glanced outside when movement on the driveway caught her eye: Alaric's car pulling up in the driveway.

"Hubby's home," she called to Thea as she headed towards the Vault. Though the study looked out onto the front drive, her sister was probably too engrossed in her work to notice the love of her life arriving.

"No, no, no…. shit," Thea swore. There was a clatter from the study. Harlow slowed her trajectory towards the Vault, turning back to see what was wrong. Thea rarely swore like that, and certainly not because of Alaric. Her feet moved faster as she heard her sister repeating the words over and over.

"What are you doing?" Harlow asked. Her sister was flailing, trying to find a place to hide the Merkhov book. But Thea didn't have to answer. Harlow saw out the window, and swallowed her panic quickly, as she watched Alaric help his mother out of his car. Pasiphae Velarius was *here*.

"What is she doing here?" Harlow hissed.

"I don't know. I missed a text from Alaric…" Thea looked up, throwing her hands in the air. "Stall them, please, while I make myself presentable."

The Merkhov text was nowhere to be seen, but Thea was

still wearing her pajamas. Harlow nodded. "Go, go... I'll keep them busy."

Thea was halfway up the stairs when she stopped. "Is Larkin in the Vault or her room?"

"Her room, I think," Harlow said. Alaric and Pasiphae were headed towards the house. "Go check and text me."

Thea ran up the stairs in record time. Harlow popped into the hall bath under the stairs and pulled a few threads of aether, trying to spruce up her hair. Luckily, she was wearing one of her favorites of Enzo's new line of dresses, so she didn't look terrible, but she hadn't bothered with makeup or her hair today. The best she could do was fix her flyaways and apply a bit of color to her lips before Alaric and Pasiphae came in the front door.

"It's been a while since I've been here," Pasiphae was saying as Harlow stepped out of the bathroom. "I don't think Cian has ever been particularly fond of your father."

Or you, Harlow thought.

"Hi," Alaric said, his voice tense and face drawn. She'd never seen him so obviously anxious. Usually he was cheerful and friendly, but now his broad shoulders were tight and his jaw was squared so hard she thought he might burst. Whatever reason Pasiphae had for being here wasn't good, or innocent.

"Hello," Harlow said, attempting her best Selene-voice—the one Mama always used for company. "I'm so glad you could visit us, Madame Arch-Chancellor."

She held her hand out to Pasiphae, who took it and smiled. "Please. You may call me Pasiphae. We're practically family, after all." She glared at her son for a moment, then poked him in the ribs. "Cheer up, darling. I'm going to be making that jab for years to come."

Alaric attempted a smile, but it didn't reach his eye. Pasiphae patted his cheek. "Sons who elope must expect such treatment from their mothers. Daddy didn't mind, of course," she said, more to Harlow than Alaric.

Harlow laughed, surprised at how easy it was to fake it in front of Pasiphae. "The maters feel the same as you." She paused for a moment, listening for Thea's possible entrance, and when she heard no sign of her sister, said, "Please, won't you come inside and I'll make some tea. Thea should be down in a moment. She's helping Larkin with some delicate spellwork."

Pasiphae raised her eyebrows as she followed Alaric down the long winding hallway to the conservatory. As villas in this area of town went, the Herrington's conservatory was small, but it was a gorgeous addition to the house, having been built about a century ago from wrought iron and seeded glass; it was a totally different style than the original house, but charming all the same.

Cian didn't have the patience for taking care of indoor plants, and for security reasons hiring one of the expensive gardening services in Nea Sterlis was out of the question. So the conservatory was unusually bare, containing only a small rattan table that sat in the center of the room. For her own preferences, Harlow liked the lack of furniture. The rough limestone tile in the conservatory had been laid in a beautiful starburst pattern.

The family hadn't used it much for entertaining all summer, preferring to be in places where they could all gather, but the table was big enough for this small group. Besides which, the conservatory was cut off from the rest of the house at the end of a long hallway, with its own bathroom, making it nearly impossible for Pasiphae to go wandering off. Alaric had done some quick thinking to get them in here, rather than the formal living room right off the foyer.

"I'll go make the tea," Alaric said as Pasiphae sat. His words came out too fast, too desperate.

"All right," Harlow said, not knowing how else to respond. Alaric was so often at his ease that she was thrown off by this version of him.

When he'd left, Pasiphae smiled, gesturing to the seat next to hers. "I'm afraid my visit has put my son quite out of sorts."

Harlow forced another smile. "It's natural that he would be nervous. He wants you and Thea to get along."

"Yes," Pasiphae agreed. She also smiled, but Harlow noticed that like her own, it didn't reach her eyes.

Something in her pocket buzzed several times. She was getting a call.

"Please, don't ignore it on my account," Pasiphae said, not a note of malice in her voice.

Harlow stood, inclining her head respectfully. "One moment."

She stepped away from the table. It was Finn. She opened the conservatory door and stepped outside. "Hello?"

"Hi," he said. His voice was distant, like they had a bad connection.

"What's up?" Harlow asked, not really knowing how to begin. "Did we find a place?"

"Maybe," he said, but didn't elaborate. She couldn't tell if something was wrong with the connection, but his words sounded clipped. Harlow thought quickly, but his demeanor was so disconcerting that she couldn't put her thoughts together.

"Oh," she said, fumbling for the right words. "I just thought that the drinks on the roof might be to celebrate—"

"No," he cut her off. "We were just having a bit of fun. For gods' sake Harlow, are you going to make every conversation we have about Sabre?"

"Every conversation? We've barely spoken since you left."

Something crackled, a bit of static, perhaps, but it didn't mask the agitation in Finn's voice. "Whose fault is that? You're always busy with Thea."

Thea. Did this have something to do with Thea? Harlow paused, glancing at the open conservatory door and wondered if he knew Pasiphae was here. "I can't really talk about this right now," she said, not trying to keep the shake out of her voice as she lowered it a measure. "We have company."

His laugh was dry, acerbic. "Seems like you're social now that I'm gone."

That stung, but Harlow swallowed her hurt. "When are you coming back?" Finn was silent. "Are you still there?"

"Yeah," he said, sounding exhausted. That was real, she could feel it in her bones. This was wearing him out too. Something in her heart sang a little to know that he was struggling as much as she was, that they were still in this together.

Some of her vitality returned, and she added a little edge to her voice. "I asked when you were coming back."

"Yeah..." There was noise in the background. A muffled voice. He was covering the phone. "Sorry, Harlow. Now isn't a good time."

"You called me," she said.

"I'll call you later," he said, and the line went dead.

Harlow wanted to collect herself, but she felt eyes at her back. When she turned, Pasiphae was standing right behind her and had clearly heard every bit of the conversation with her keen Illuminated hearing.

"I—" Harlow began to explain.

"You don't have to explain a thing, my darling," Pasiphae said, striding forward to take her arm. She led her back to the table in the conservatory. "I've been bonded to an Illuminated man for quite some time."

Harlow nodded, her face heating with embarrassment. This was no time to let her guard down, no matter how humiliating this was. She had one job now, and it was to help get Pasiphae out of the house without incident.

Pasiphae's expression was shrewd as she smoothed the fabric of her skirt, just so. There was a glint of strategy in her eyes that made Harlow suspicious. "This is how they are, Harlow. *Fickle.*"

Could this be the reason Pasiphae was here? To check on *Harlow*? In all their plans, they'd focused mostly on Connor, and by association Aislin. They'd never talked about whether Pasiphae might be involved.

"Everything is fine," Harlow said, careful to keep her voice smooth and her face calm. Pasiphae would get nothing from her.

Pasiphae laughed. "Oh, you will make a wonderful wife for Connor's son. I'd hoped Finn might turn out a modicum better than his father, but they are the same, through and through, chasing tail all over Nytra."

Harlow kept her face very still; this was no time to argue. The ruse was working. Pasiphae believed that Finn and Sabre's interactions were real. She forced even, steady breaths through her lungs as Pasiphae continued. "There was a time when I thought I might have bonded with Connor McKay, but the way he treats Aislin? No thank you. I prefer my cuckolding to be quiet. Discreet."

Now *that* was interesting. Leopold Velarius was practically insignificant. He never came to events, and was rarely seen. According to Alaric he was mostly interested in birding and golf. Apparently, he was also bedding people outside his bonding.

"Everything is fine," Harlow repeated, trying not to react to the information Pasiphae had given her.

"Yes," Pasiphae said. Now the smile reached her eyes. "You *will* be one of us, won't you, witchling?"

Harlow wasn't sure what that meant, but she lowered her eyes. She hoped Pasiphae read it as respect, but she simply didn't want her to see the fury burning in them. "I hope so," she replied.

Pasiphae took her hands. "Look at me, child."

Harlow composed herself before dragging her eyes to meet the ancient immortal's. How old was Pasiphae? Her eyes were dark pools of mystery, and her skin glowed faintly with the pleasure she seemed to derive from this moment.

"You are humiliated now. But you will find ways to push back, subtly of course. You will marry, and give Finbar a family, and in return, you will be one of the most powerful women on Okairos. This is what you want, isn't it?"

Harlow dropped her eyes again. There was no way to respond to that. Honesty certainly wasn't an option, and she didn't trust herself to lie at the moment. Not with the level of fury coursing through her. But still, despite that anger, a thrill of victory hummed through her. She and Finn had not only deceived the Illuminated, they'd revealed that whatever Connor's machinations were, Pasiphae was also involved.

Pasiphae let go of one of her hands, her fingers curling around Harlow's chin, as though she was appraising her. "You're not like your sister. Thea is lovely, and the perfect wife for my Alaric. Docile and always so *appropriate*. But you have a fire in you I recognize. You will make Finbar McKay pay for every time he embarrasses you, won't you?"

Harlow nodded once. It was the furthest thing from what she wanted, but it seemed like it served her best to let Pasiphae think the anger in her eyes was for him.

"All that rage," Pasiphae said. "You come to me when you're ready to make him pay, my darling, and I will teach you the ways of an Illuminated wife."

Footsteps in the hallway signaled that Alaric and Thea were on their way. Harlow let a thin smile spread over her face. "Thank you," she said. "I would be grateful for your help."

"Of course you will be," Pasiphae said, standing. Thea and Alaric entered, a vision of newly bonded bliss. Thea wore a pastoral-inspired floral day dress that skimmed the floor of the conservatory and Alaric carried tea, which he set down as Thea kissed Pasiphae warmly.

"Now, what spellwork does young Larkin have going?" Pasiphae asked as she took a cup of tea from her son.

Harlow barely listened as Thea explained Larkin's most

recent project. She'd created a spell that allowed musicians to hear their compositions played by multiple instruments at once as they composed. When it was perfected, it would be a major contribution to the Order of Mysteries' body of work.

That much was not a lie, but the fact that Larkin was upstairs working on it obviously was. Harlow couldn't concentrate on any of that though, so consumed by anger as she was. She didn't touch her tea once for the hour that Pasiphae stayed. When she finally got up to go, Harlow said the mere politest of goodbyes.

"I'll be back in a bit," Alaric said as he kissed Thea goodbye. He'd agreed to take Pasiphae to the Velarius' flat across town. "Should I pick up gelato on the way home?"

"That would be nice," Thea said, her eyes softening as she squeezed his hands.

Gelato was nearly always Alaric's way of apologizing for some minor infraction he thought he'd committed. It was more of a joke than anything most of the time, but Harlow saw the real apology in his eyes now, and Thea's acceptance.

When they were gone, Thea's shoulders slumped and Larkin appeared at the top of the stairs, cradling Axel in her arms. "Is she gone?" Larkin asked.

Thea nodded as Larkin made her way down the stairs. The three of them went into the kitchen together and began the work of making a sheet pan of frozen pizza bites. It was at least an hour 'til their usual late dinner time, but they needed the sustenance after Pasiphae's visit. The ritual of making snacks in times of trouble was a Krane family tradition.

"She ambushed him in Santos," Thea explained. "Apparently, she insisted on coming back with him. She'll be here for a week."

Larkin made a face. "She's terrifying. I listened in on the old intercom. Did you know it still connects to the conservatory? So convenient for spying on you all." She waggled her eyebrows at Thea, and Harlow cringed. She wondered how many times Larkin had caught her older sisters screwing like bunnies this summer. She and Finn had done it there at least twice.

Harlow's phone buzzed, and she dreaded the idea it might be Finn. When she made her way across the kitchen to look at her phone, she realized it hadn't been hers after all.

"It's me," Larkin said, pulling her phone from the pocket of her sweatpants. "It's Meline. She and Ari are leaving tomorrow for Falcyra—everything is set up there. We won't hear from them again until they establish a safe connection and get new phones."

"Tell her we love her," Thea whispered, her face drawn as she put the pizza bites in the oven.

Harlow yanked both her sisters into her arms. They squeezed each other tight in a three-way hug. Thea had tears on her cheeks. Harlow wiped them away as they pulled away from one another. The three of them settled into the table in the alcove, flipping through the stack of magazines and catalogs Selene collected wherever she went. They sat quietly for a while, while the kitchen filled with the tantalizing scent of melting cheese.

"She'll be okay," Harlow assured Thea.

"I know," Thea sniffled. "Ari won't let anything happen to her. I just hate that we're not together."

"Me too," Larkin said, her voice breaking a little. "We haven't been apart like this since Harlow left us for..." She glanced at Harlow and then quickly added, "I'm sorry. I didn't mean to bring Mark up."

Harlow kissed Larkin's cheek as Axel rubbed her ankles with his face. "It's okay. I hated being apart from you all then, and I hate this now."

The little kitchen timer rang and Thea pulled away from the group to save the pizza bites from burning. When all three of them had a plate, she asked, "Isn't *Pretty Little Firestarters* on tonight?"

"You want to watch it *live*?" Larkin asked, slightly horrified by the idea.

Thea smirked. "Yes, because I'm *old*, and remember when that was the only way you could watch something on TV."

Larkin shrugged as she walked towards the study. "You said it, not me."

Alaric walked in the front door, with a bag of gelato from a place near the City Center, not Moretti's, which Harlow thought was a mistake. "What are we doing?" he asked, raising his eyebrows

Thea nodded towards the kitchen. "There's snacks on the baking sheet. Put the gelato in the freezer."

"And?" he asked, clearly wanting to know the rest of the plan.

She swiped a kiss to his cheek. "*And*, we're watching *Pretty Little Firestarters* in the study. Come with us."

Alaric's smile was a light. He was literally glowing. "I love you," he said, before practically running to the kitchen.

"You let him off easy," Harlow joked as they settled into the little couch in the study.

Thea glanced at Harlow, a concerned look on her face. "What did he need to be let off for?"

Harlow shrugged, a little embarrassed, despite the fact that Thea seemed genuinely confused, not snarky. "Nothing, sorry. Bad joke—it's been a long day."

Thea patted her knee. "You'll get some good rest tonight and feel better tomorrow."

Alaric entered with a plate full of frozen snacks and snuggled into the couch next to Thea. Harlow's heart ached deeply, despite the minor victory she'd achieved with Pasiphae, but she pushed the feeling down. This would all be over soon. Finn would come back and things would go back to normal. She couldn't pay attention to the episode, no matter how hard she tried. She'd picked up her phone on the way to the study, and it buzzed now. Kate.

Petra finally admitted PLF is good. She said to tell you that next week you're coming over for a watch-party.

Harlow gave the message a little heart and texted Petra. *So you finally caved.*

Petra wrote back immediately. *If you can't beat 'em, join 'em. LU.*

Enzo was next, apparently she'd missed a plot twist in her misery and he had a long theory that he explained in about fifteen consecutive messages.

Missed it tonight, she wrote back. *But I'll watch tomorrow and we'll dish.*

No one was mad at her. She'd been being paranoid. They were all just busy with their own lives, and hadn't been obsessing over her at all. Why did she do this kind of shit to herself?

"Because you're insecure, Dollface." She heard Mark's voice like he'd spoken aloud. But of course he hadn't. Mark was dead, and she was imagining things. "I'm going to bed," she said, getting up. If hallucinating Mark speaking to her wasn't an indicator that she needed to be done for the day, she didn't know what was.

"The episode isn't over," Larkin said, confused.

"It's your favorite show," Thea said as the show came back on.

"I know, but I'm tired—" Harlow started to say when the sharp blare of an alarm interrupted the scene-setting music of the nighttime soap. A screen that read "Breaking News" flashed, and a new anchor came on the screen.

"We have news tonight from Falcyra that Austvanger has fallen to a group of rebels calling themselves 'the Humanists.'" The human anchor paused, pressing a finger to the device in her ear. "One moment, please, we're going to our correspondent in Falcyra."

"Shit," Alaric said, whipping his phone out. He glanced at Harlow, a silent query passing between them about whether or not she'd heard about this from Finn. She shook her head once. He nodded, turning back to his phone. "I can't believe Mother let this get onto the news... Someone at the station is going to lose their head."

Harlow wished he were exaggerating, but it seemed possible that someone could, indeed, lose their life for a report like this. Sure enough, his jaw clenched as his phone rang. Though he stepped outside the study, they could all hear Pasiphae on the other end of the phone, screeching about not being able to get through to Nuva Troi. Apparently, there were so many calls into the city, hers wasn't getting through and she wanted Alaric to do something about it, immediately.

He poked his head back in the study. "I'm going downstairs to get in touch with Cian."

Thea trailed after him, but Larkin stayed. Axel wandered in and curled up between them as the correspondent in Falcyra came on the screen. She stood in front of a mass of burning buildings. "Nytra?" she asked. "Nytra, do you have me?"

Someone spoke in the background, and she continued, "I'm told we've lost connection to our Nytra office, but that I am on air. This is the scene in Austvanger tonight. The city is burning, and the House of Sorath and Governor Ducare are no longer in control. We aren't sure what will happen in the days to come but the last three weeks here have been hell. Tonight is the first time our signal hasn't been jammed getting out of the country."

The correspondent went on to describe many of the things they already knew, and some more personalizing details about the people affected on the ground. Stories that would move a Nytran audience about schools being bombed, and mass executions without trials.

"Wow," Larkin said. "Honestly, after getting a really good look at the way the Illuminated have suppressed information, I'm shocked this is airing."

Harlow nodded. "Yeah, me too."

"Pasiphae is totally freaking out right now, huh?" Larkin asked, her eyebrows raised mischievously. She was covering up how upset this made her, and Harlow couldn't really blame her. It felt as though the world was spinning out of control, just beyond their grasp. They were forced to watch, unable to do much to change any of it yet.

Harlow attempted a laugh, but the sound was dry as a bone in the nekropoleis. "I bet she's having a shit-fit. Poor Alaric."

Larkin snickered, but Harlow couldn't seem to laugh with her. Thea was wrong—she wouldn't sleep well tonight at all. Harlow felt like she might never sleep again.

CHAPTER TWENTY-THREE

T he next day, Pasiphae went back to Nuva Troi without so much as goodbye. No one was sorry about it, but Alaric and Larkin got to work mobilizing as many aid units as they could muster in Falcyra and Harlow worked on communicating with Cian and the rest of the Haven team, both in Nuva Troi and Nea Sterlis. Their assumption was that the Illuminated would instill martial law in the next few days to control Nytran humans from attempting something similar, and that they might need more support.

Not surprisingly, she didn't hear from Finn, but instead got a notification from Section Seven—which just *had* to make the day worse—just as she was leaving to help Petra at the Alabaster Way house, Haven's more extensive safehouse in Nea Sterlis. Thea and Larkin both shook their heads when their notification came through, but neither made eye contact with her. Harlow knew this was getting old, and no one really knew how to address their bullying at this point.

Section Seven had the audacity to mark the news as "breaking" in the midst of everything going on and used a push notification for it. The headline read, "Harlow Krane is officially over.

Finn McKay spotted canoodling human beauty Sabre LeBeau at the White Oak last night."

Harlow clicked through to the article. Finn was, indeed, hugging Sabre LeBeau, who had their face buried in his neck. She closed her eyes, her jaw tightening as the muscles in her back tensed, drawing her shoulder blades together. For a brief moment, everything hurt.

"I need to get to the Alabaster Way house," she said.

"Okay," Thea replied, her voice soft and soothing. She reached out to touch Harlow's arm.

Harlow stood. "I'm fine, okay?"

"You can't just keep saying that," Thea said.

"I can," Harlow said. "Because it's true. I'm fine, and I need to get over to the AW house to see if they need help today. Humans are going to need help, Thea."

Her sister didn't meet her eyes. "Of course. You should go."

Harlow scooped Axel up and hugged him, grateful for his rhythmic purrs against her chest. "See you when I get back, baby boy. Naps on the terrace?"

He blinked his golden eyes at her, as though agreeing. She deposited him in Larkin's lap and left the house quickly. The safehouse was only a twenty-minute walk away, so she set out on foot. The day was the coldest they'd had since arriving, and Harlow wished she'd brought a jacket. She was already dressed in a pair of loose pants and a light sweater that fell off her left shoulder, but she shivered in the breeze.

Her phone rang. She'd turned her sound on after last night's announcement, not wanting to miss any more breaking news, should it come through. Still, it startled her into picking up without seeing who it was.

"It's not what you think," Finn said on the other end of the phone. Harlow's heart pounded. They'd promised not to call unless it was absolutely necessary. So this was necessary, and she had to keep her wits sharp.

"What do you think I think it is?" Harlow asked. It wasn't hard to sound agitated; this was nerve-wracking.

"Don't do this," Finn hissed. There were voices in the background.

"Are you with *Sabre* right now?"

"No, my parents."

So this was for them. Even more nerve-wracking then. "Even better," she bit out.

"I can explain everything."

Harlow turned a corner and walked into the park to take the shortcut to the Alabaster Way location. "Oh, I'm sure you can."

"I *can*," Finn said, and there was a plea in his voice that broke her heart a little. "I'm coming back on the morning train. Tomorrow. Meet me at the station?"

"Whatever you say," she said, hanging up. It was an instinct to do so, but if they were looking for a fight between them, her hanging up would prove she was angry with him. But he was coming home. Tomorrow.

Her heart hammered an unsteady beat in her chest as her vision blurred with tears, and she ran straight into Morgaine Yarlo. "Sorry," she said immediately. "I—I didn't see you." It was as though the girl had appeared out of nowhere.

"No apologies necessary. I blend in a lot of the time."

Harlow very much doubted that. As she calmed down, she wondered if Morgaine might not have the money for a hotel here in Nea Sterlis. "Hey, do you need help? Like a place to stay or something?"

Morgaine smiled bashfully. It was a sweet expression. "No, I'm staying with my friend Samira. You know her, I think—I was with her the first time we saw each other at The Gate."

"The Ultima?" Harlow asked, momentarily distracted from the horrible conversation she'd just had with Finn.

Morgaine nodded. "Yeah. She lives on the next block over. I was out for a run."

Harlow looked at what she was wearing: leggings, sneakers, a sweat-soaked t-shirt. Morgaine hadn't appeared out of nowhere, she'd just come around the corner Harlow was turning, and Harlow hadn't been paying attention, as usual. Her distractedness was going to get her into real trouble someday if she wasn't more careful.

"But thank you for the offer, Harlow. That was really kind of you."

Harlow shrugged. "It's no big deal."

Morgaine fell into step next to her. "Kinda seems like it might be. That's some wild news you all got last night."

The way she said it was oddly distanced, like it hadn't happened to her too. But it was obvious Morgaine was just visiting Nea Sterlis. Maybe she wasn't from Nytra, or even Falcyra, but somewhere further away like Castel des Rêves, or Avignone. Most humans didn't travel so far away from their home countries—many weren't allowed to, as humans had to submit to the Travel Advisory committee before leaving their home countries, unless they were rich enough to buy their way out of such things. The compass tattoo on Morgaine's arm made it pretty clear what her priorities were though, and Harlow got the feeling the young woman could talk her way in or out of pretty much anything.

All Harlow could think to say was, "Yeah. It seems like the world is going to pieces."

Morgaine let out a wry laugh. "Seems like the whole universe is, doesn't it?"

It was an odd thing to say. Harlow wasn't exactly sure what to make of Morgaine. "Have you been in touch with Echo? Is she okay?"

Morgaine looked confused for a moment.

"I just assumed she's human, like you—and you know things are probably about to get a bit difficult..."

"Oh, yeah," Morgaine broke in, as though just realizing how

being human might be a problem in this political climate. "Echo's fine in that regard."

That seemed unlikely. All humans would be especially restricted now, targeted even more than usual. "But you haven't had a chance to talk to her?" Harlow asked, pressing a little harder.

She was worried about the two of them, despite not having met Echo. Morgaine's lack of concern for both their safety was naïve at best. At worst, it could get the two of them killed. Humans were often like this. Since they seemed to regard immortals as benevolent celebrities, they didn't realize the danger they were in until it was too late. Harlow liked Morgaine too much to let her make reckless choices.

"No, not yet," Morgaine said, her voice sad. "Hopefully soon." She glanced down at her phone. "I've gotta run. See you around."

Before Harlow could say another word, Morgaine had resumed her jog and was out of the park. Her phone rang. She was not ready to go another round with Finn right now. Luckily, it was Thea. "I broke the binding on the Merkhov. Come home. Now."

Her sister was out of breath, panting hard. "Where's Alaric?"

"I'm here," Alaric said, clearly having taken the phone from Thea. "She's all right. I've got her, but you need to get back here."

Harlow sighed as she hung up, texted the coordinator at the Alabaster Way house that her plans had changed, and headed back home.

THEA HADN'T JUST BROKEN THE BINDING, SHE'D shattered it. When Harlow got home, she was stretched out on the couch in the study, an ice pack pressed to her forehead. Larkin sat next to her, holding a big glass of water with a straw.

Harlow rushed to Thea's side, just as Alaric entered the room with a plate of nachos. It looked like enough food for four people. Using magic always took energy. Breaking spells took more, and it was likely Thea was ravenous after breaking the binding on the book.

Harlow raised her eyebrows at Thea. "Are you going to share those?"

"If you're lucky," Thea said, struggling to sit up. "Go look at the book first, please."

The sound of chips crunching followed Harlow across the room, where the Merkhov book sat open on its cradle. All three of the triptych images were perfectly clear now.

The first showed two snakes, locked in a figure-eight pattern, each consuming the other's tail. In the lower half of the eight sat an egg, encircled in a protective film of some sort. In the second, the snakes had become one, but they still protected the egg. Now that it was restored, Harlow saw that the egg was indeed cracking, and the protective barrier had been pierced. The swirling lines that were meant to represent aether and the Illuminated light were fully intertwined in this image.

But the next image was something else entirely. There was no more egg at all, but an image of a fierce bird, with feathers of deepest midnight, encircled by a single serpent. "Oh," Harlow breathed. "*Oh...*"

In the first image the snakes were biting *one another*, and then they became one, and then separate once more: the serpent and the raptor. The triptych wasn't about what a Strider and a Knight might *create* if they had a child, though the egg had certainly been misleading. It was about how to make the Feriant shift happen. A Strider needed a Knight—or perhaps even just one of the Illuminated—to activate them. And the egg wasn't a baby, but representative of intimate energy, as well as of life and hope.

The Claiming. It had to be that the Claiming was the trigger. But that didn't make perfect sense, Cian had said many of the former Strider-Knight pairs had been platonic. Intimate energy could be platonic though, she reasoned. The way the Orders were raised to focus on romantic partnerships as primary obscured that as an obvious line of thinking, but of course familial and platonic relationships could be intimate as well.

But then why had biting her worked in the House of Remiel, but not here at home? The thought was distressing. To avoid thinking about Finn and spiraling out, she moved onto ramifications. She understood why Kylar Bane had gone to so much trouble to hide this information. If the Feriant were strong enough to kill an incubus, they would be strong enough to fight the Illuminated. This was incredibly dangerous knowledge.

She turned to look back at her sisters and Alaric, who sat in a perfect row on the couch, all three munching on nachos. "You didn't save me any," she complained.

Larkin shrugged. "Alaric can make more."

Alaric rolled his eyes in mock-annoyance, but he got up to do as Larkin suggested, flashing a smile as he left the room. He was happy to give the sisters a moment or two to think things through together, that much was clear.

"It's not a baby at all," Harlow said finally, letting the knowledge sink in.

"No," Thea agreed.

"Do you think this is how I'll make the shift?" Harlow asked after a long moment.

Larkin's head tilted to the side. "Seems like it. Is that going to be a problem? With the Claiming and you and Fi—"

Thea shot her youngest sister a glare so deadly that Larkin flushed with embarrassment. Clearly, they'd agreed not to move too fast for Harlow, given the weirdness with Finn. "It's none of our business, of course."

Both of them averted their eyes from Harlow's, the threads between them tightening in Harlow's second sight, taut with the tension between them.

Alaric returned with more nachos, interrupting the possibility of more discussion. Everyone snacked quietly for a few minutes, but Harlow saw the glances they were giving one another, even Alaric, who'd overheard their conversation. It was unbearable. Finn was coming home tomorrow, but she didn't think she could take another minute.

She broke into the uncomfortable silence. "Are we positive that the wards on the house are good? That no one can hear what we talk about?"

Alaric and Thea exchanged a look. "I check them every day," Alaric replied. "And before you ask, I set up an extra set of triggers for things like the drone, even Axel's new friend. Anything that touches the wards, or puts any pressure on them in the slightest is recorded and analyzed now. Even the elder Illuminated don't have this kind of security."

When Harlow met Thea's gaze, her sister nodded. "It's true. You can trust Alaric, you know that, right?"

Harlow laughed, but the sound was hollow, without humor. "That's not what this is about... It's about me and Finn."

The room went silent and still, as though everyone was afraid to move.

"Our relationship isn't in trouble," she began. Larkin raised her eyebrows, tensing. Thea looked as though she might want to argue. It hit her: they'd heard her talk like this before—about Mark, during the worst times, when she was constantly defending him to everyone. The reverberations of that relationship just kept echoing through her life.

"We faked all this to draw the Illuminated out. Sabre is in on it and everything," she said quickly, wanting to move past this stage. "We're okay. This has all been a ruse, but I can tell you now, because he's coming home tomorrow."

Alaric let out a harsh breath, and his face crumpled. He covered his face with his hands. "Thank gods," he murmured as Thea rubbed his back, her perfectly groomed eyebrows pulling together in a knot of concern.

Larkin was misty eyed, and when Harlow made eye contact with her, she smiled. "That's good. That's really good."

"I couldn't figure out why he was behaving this way," Alaric said, his chin quivering slightly. "I thought I'd failed him somehow."

"No," Harlow breathed, sorry beyond belief that their actions had hurt their family so much. "No, you didn't do anything wrong. And if he were here, he would tell you how sorry he is, I'm sure."

Alaric laughed. "He wouldn't. He's our commander, and you had a mission; he wouldn't apologize for not compromising it... The real question is did it work?"

Harlow nodded. "We won't know the full extent until tomorrow, but I think your mother showing up here yesterday was an indicator that we've convinced them."

Everyone looked slightly confused.

"She spent the entire time you were gathering Thea and the tea convincing me to let her help me become what she termed 'an Illuminated wife.'"

Alaric's face twisted slightly in disgust. "I'm so sorry, Harlow. That was so far out of line..."

Thea drew a breath in. "It's not just Connor and Aislin who want you to have the baby..."

Larkin covered her mouth, looking at Alaric with pity. He shook his head. "I'd be lying if I said I was surprised. I just... I hoped she was better than this."

"Of course you did," Thea said, her arms going around his neck. They leaned into one another.

"So we need to make preparations for his return," Alaric said. "We'll need to decon him pretty thoroughly."

Harlow's face scrunched in confusion.

"He'll have to be decontaminated for surveillance spell-work," Thea explained. "We'll get everything set up. The two of you can use the carriage house until we're sure he's clean."

There was a small cottage at the entrance to the villa that no one used. Harlow knew the place.

Alaric nodded. "Good thinking. We can get that set up now, if you want."

Harlow breathed a sigh of relief. She'd still have to talk to everyone else, but it felt good to have this out in the open.

"Is there anything else to discuss about the scroll?" Larkin asked. "If not, I can go do an initial sweep of the carriage house and..."

Larkin continued, describing an herbal tisane that could be used for ritual cleansing. Harlow hardly heard her. Something bothered her about the Scroll of Akatei—the document the triptych originated from. She needed to see it again to be sure.

"Thank you, Larkin." Harlow held up a finger, as Larkin finished speaking and Alaric and Thea both made ready to get to to work. "But before we get moving, Thea, do you have the rest of your scans of the Scroll of Akatei?"

Thea got up and pulled an envelope from a drawer in the table the cradle sat on. She pulled the scans out and spread them across the table. Harlow looked at where the triptych was meant to fit into the Scroll.

"What are you thinking?" Thea asked, examining the same spot Harlow looked at.

Harlow pointed to the formation of Heraldic creatures that included the Feriant. There was one of each type of creature. "What if these don't represent single creatures?"

Alaric nodded. "They might represent a collective of fighters. An alliance of sorts."

Thea's breath caught. "There could be other Striders. Others capable of turning into the Feriant."

The thought was dizzying. If there were, then they might actually stand a chance against the Illuminated. "But what about the rest of this, the humans in the tree? The firedrake? What does it all mean?"

Thea stared at the Scroll for a few long moments. Harlow could feel her thinking as Larkin moved to stand next to them, leaning on the table with her head perched in her hands. She too seemed to think deeply about the story the Scroll might tell.

Larkin pointed to the humans that had broken out of their shells after the firedrake's awakening. "Something about all this has to do with the firedrakes."

"Or a very specific firedrake," Thea mused. "We should talk to Cian about this. Are they coming home with Finn?"

"I don't know," Harlow replied. "I didn't get a chance to ask."

Alaric checked his phone. The family calendar, Harlow presumed. "Cian is coming later this week. They have Haven business to wrap up in Nuva Troi."

Harlow nodded. "All right then. We have a strong lead here, between the Merkhov and what we found out in the City of the Dead. We just need to find out where this Alabaster Spire used to be and find Ashbourne..."

Alaric frowned. "I think it would be wise to be cautious about that advice. We don't know what Kimaris' intentions were, and until Larkin can actually speak with Ashbourne, I think we should be careful."

Harlow nodded. "You're probably right. But the Claiming?"

Thea grinned. "Have at it, love."

Alaric gave two, very dorky, thumbs up. "Seems like the way to go!"

Harlow smiled, but it was hard to laugh along right now.

CHAPTER TWENTY-FOUR

When the train pulled into the station, Harlow thought she had herself pretty well composed. But as Finn stepped off, every bit of their history, their love, the hurt, and the fervor hit her at once. He was clean shaven, his longer hair slicked back, wearing a blue button-down shirt, tucked into a pair of perfectly pressed trousers. He looked nothing like the Finn she loved, and as his stormy eyes met hers, they held a warning.

He moved towards her, deliberately slow, his square jaw clenched tight, the slightest tilt of his head causing her gaze to drift behind him. Connor McKay stepped off the train, directly after his son, stern, handsome, and trussed up in a three-piece suit. Harlow's blood nearly boiled to see him, but she realized that like Pasiphae, his being here was a victory.

"Hello, Harlow," Connor said, using a bit of Illuminated speed to stand next to her just as Finn reached for her hand. "My son has behaved abominably for the past few weeks, and I am here to make sure he puts things right."

The elder McKay's voice was smooth, placating. He obviously had experience with this kind of thing, placating women.

No doubt he spoke this way to Aislin all the time, but Harlow wanted none of it. If she could shove him back on the damn train and send him back to the city, she would. Instead, she just stood there with no clever comeback, no thought in her head but how she might murder Connor McKay.

Finn started to say something, but Connor held up a hand. "My boy. You fucked up with Sabre, and embarrassed Harlow deeply. You will apologize, make amends with one another. I will see you both at dinner this evening. I expect you'll have solved this by that time."

He took Finn's elbow and drew him aside. Harlow barely caught what Connor whispered to Finn. "Claim that little bitch and be done with it, Finbar. Do your duty, and you'll get your way with the human."

Harlow looked down at her shoes as she listened. They were a pair of vintage leather boots that were glorious with the dress she wore, also vintage, from an estate sale she and Enzo had been to a few weeks ago. She'd taken every effort with her appearance. Her heart ached to hear Connor McKay's words. He didn't know his son at all.

"See you in a bit," Connor said before walking away.

"He's going to his hotel," Finn explained.

Harlow nodded. Neither of them moved a muscle. Heat built in her chest, and then slid down her spine, straight into her core. She hated the buttoned up look he wore now, the conformity of it, the way he looked like his father. But the high of having won just a few inches back from Connor and Pasiphae was intoxicating, stoking the energy of the fervor higher with every breath she took.

"I am sorry for everything that happened in Nuva Troi while I was gone." Finn's voice was flat.

"Sounds like it," she bit out, turning toward the car. There was every possibility they were still being watched. Besides, this felt like a game now, and the heat building between her thighs made her *very* motivated to play. "Come on. Let's go home."

Finn grabbed her arm. The gesture was more violent looking than the actual gentle press of his fingers into her flesh. His body heat filled the space between them and Harlow didn't even bother to fight the fervor. She let it rage through her, flooding her scent.

"I would like it if you'd accept my apology, Harlow." The harsh tone of his voice didn't match the silent plea in his eyes, or the bulge growing in his trousers. He adjusted himself, nostrils flaring as he scented her true feelings, no doubt.

"Fine," Harlow agreed. "I accept. I'll just forget about Sabre, and the fact that I've barely heard from you for weeks. I'll accept that apologies like these are just 'how it's going to be.' That's what I'm supposed to do, right? Just be grateful you're lifting me up out of my low state and keep my mouth shut."

Everything they'd said and done when he was gone was horrendous. But this heat building between them was delicious. It was like a reward to know that she could stand here, smarting off to him, proving to the Illuminated that she wouldn't be cowed so easily, and turning him on. Because there was no doubt in her mind, Finn was aroused.

"I can think of better uses for your mouth," Finn growled, yanking her into his arms.

"I bet you can," she snarled back, every bit as feral as he was. She would tear his clothes from his body right here if he let her.

Finn's voice was low and dangerous. "Get in the car, now."

His fingers pressed into her waist as he pushed her towards the waiting Woody in the parking lot. There were only a few people around, but Finn's grip on Harlow's waist was firm as he pushed her against the car, lifting her dress as she wrapped her legs around his waist.

"That's my good girl," he purred. "Say you accept my apology."

"*Actually apologize*," she hissed.

He dropped her, shaking his head as he reached into the pocket of her dress to fetch the car keys. His fingers dragged up her hip from inside the pocket, lighting a fire within her that wouldn't be stopped for anything now.

"Get in the car," he commanded as he got into the driver's seat.

She did as he asked, her heart pounding ferociously, her teeth practically aching from how tightly her jaw was set. They drove in silence for a few minutes. Finn pulled her phone from the console, and tossed it out the window, into the ocean, as they curved up the steep road toward the villa.

When the window closed she sighed with relief, but Finn shook his head. They still had to make it through decon. She let out a needy sound and his free hand stroked her thigh, sending the fire in her into a blazing inferno. Still, Finn said nothing, but kept the tease of his fingers moving up her thigh, closer and closer to the spot she needed him, through her dress.

He took a sharp left turn in the villa's driveway, pulling off to the carriage house that sat in a wooded grove. A blazing bonfire crackled merrily in front of the little cottage. Finn stripped out of his clothes immediately. Alaric had assured her that Finn knew the rules of decon well, and sure enough, he threw his clothes directly into the fire. A bundle of herbs went in next, and the two of them pulled threads, using sigil magic to set his clothes fully ablaze. They were ashes in moments.

Harlow took the waiting glass jug of the ritual tisane that Larkin had prepared and poured it over Finn's head. The fragrant herbs that made the spell work perfumed the air as water dripped over the planes of his face and down his muscled chest. She pulled threads of magic from the air, as well as directing her shadows to find any trace of foreign magic that might be hiding on or in Finn. She tried not to stare at his body, at his proud cock, standing at attention for her.

"You're clean," she said when he did not react to the water, or her probe. Her voice broke over the words. He was wet, water droplets still running through the rivulets of his various muscle groups, but it was the look on his face that undid her.

The raw love and fear in his eyes had her leaping into his arms. He caught her, yanking her up his naked body as his mouth crashed into hers. The kiss was desperate, fervent, nearly violent with the intensity of passion between them.

"I'm so sorry," he murmured against her mouth. "I'm so fucking sorry."

"Me too," she said as the sobs she'd been holding in since the moment he left came spilling out of her. "I knew. We agreed. But it felt too real sometimes."

And it had. All the arguments, well-positioned as they'd been, weren't scripted. They'd agreed it was best to improvise, and some of them had hurt more than others. She'd known he'd push her buttons and dig into things that were well-known insecurities for her, but she hadn't anticipated how real it all would feel. How truly heartbroken she'd been at times.

His arms tightened around her, as he held her effortlessly aloft. "I know, baby girl. I know. But it worked. We've got them worried, and despite everything going on at home, he's here. I don't know why, but he's here."

"Let's go inside. My sisters and Alaric are finishing with a second round of advanced wards in the villa. Alaric is going out to the bay this time, just to make sure."

He glanced over her shoulder at the cottage. "They did this already?"

Harlow kissed Finn's face about a dozen times, thrilled to be back in his arms. "Yes. We're alone and it's safe. I have so many things to tell you."

He detached her legs from around her waist, scooping her into his arms. "I don't really want to talk right now, do you?"

His kiss was gentle, persuasive. "Not really, but I have—er, some pertinent information."

Finn laughed, his real laugh, the one she loved as he carried her into the carriage house. No one had used it for several years, as it was mostly extra space for guests now, but there was a huge, comfortable bed upstairs, and she'd changed the linens on it herself this morning. When he dumped her in the bed, he stood at the end, smiling that slightly crooked smile, looking devious as seventeen hells.

"There's quite a few buttons on your pretty dress," he said. "I'll give you until I'm done unbuttoning them to catch me up. Deal?"

Harlow was unable to focus as she watched his cock. "Sure." She slid to the end of the bed and pulled him toward her. "But first, tell me a few things."

Finn's eyes fell shut as she stroked his cock a few times. Her hands were soft and loose as she asked, "Did you miss me?"

His eyes opened slightly and his fingers ran gently through her hair as her mouth closed around him. "Yes," he moaned. She took him deeper into her throat. This wouldn't be possible in his true form. When she pulled her mouth off his cock, swirling her tongue around the head of it for good measure she asked, "Did they read all our texts?"

He nodded, pushing her hair out of her face. "Yes, they read them all. Cian couldn't get a good bug on them, but they tracked where the information was routing to, and it's definitely Connor's people. Pretty sure the texts were the clencher."

"So they believe you want Sabre as your lover?"

"My dad at least thinks I fucked them while I was in Nuva Troi, especially after the Section Seven shit." He crouched down, and she made a little noise.

"I was playing with that."

The kiss he initiated was sweet, slowing things down, rather than advancing them. "I know, but I need you to listen. I am so sorry for what Section Seven put you through. When we decided to do this, I knew they'd be cruel, but the comments... Harls. I'm so sorry."

She nodded, swallowing her sadness. He was here now, and things were fine with them. They had been the instant he'd stepped off the train, and she'd felt how much he'd missed her in that first shared look. "It's okay. I don't care what anyone else thinks, as long as I know what's true."

"When this is over, I'm going to set this right. They won't be able to publish shit like that about you anymore."

Harlow stroked his face, running her fingers over the lines of his cheekbones, his jaw, and his lips. "You are wonderful, you know that?"

He turned his face away from her. "I don't deserve that." His expression was tortured. "All I've ever wanted was to keep you safe, but everything I do gets you hurt somehow. I fucked up your life again."

It would be so easy to agree with him, to be angry about the ways his status had made him unaware of how differently they would be treated, but he already saw it. He already understood, and she still wanted him. She still wanted to be *here*, and it seemed a miserable way to go about their relationship to constantly be keeping score on who'd made more mistakes.

With everything they'd already been through, she didn't want to spend their time together arguing about who'd screwed up the worst. She pulled him down on top of her. "Fuck me up then, McKay. Fuck me up forever."

"What?" he asked, looking confused.

"Claim me, now. Do what your dad asked and make me yours."

His brows narrowed with worry, but she felt the effect of her words pressing into the core of her as she wrapped her legs around him. "We don't know if it's safe," he said.

"It's not safe. It's never going to be safe. But it's the key to me shifting—Thea broke the binding on the triptych."

He sat back, straddling her. She reached for him and he pinned her arms above her head, his head tilting. In the dim light of the cottage bedroom, he looked alien—a beautiful predator, ready to consume his prey.

"Shift," she urged. "Shift and I'll tell you."

His glamour fell away and the creature who caged her body was magnificent, his skin lighting from within. His hard cock pushed between her legs, pressing against her now-throbbing clit through her dress. Six huge wings flexed behind him, enormous as they unfurled from the tight bundle at his back.

"If you Claim me—if we Claim each other—I will be able to shift into the Feriant permanently."

"How?" he asked.

Harlow shivered at the sound of his true voice. "Think about what Cian told us. My heritage is part Illuminated and part shifter, as well as part witch. When you Claim me, I believe it will trigger something in me that will shift into what I'm truly meant to be. Like a magical chemical reaction."

He seemed to be thinking. The planes of his face were sharper in his true form, harsher and almost painfully beautiful. "The snakes were biting *each other*," he said, finally.

She nodded, rocking her hips a little so that he pushed harder against her. The effect was immediate; she felt him tense, holding all that Ventyr strength back that she wanted inside her, *now*. "And in the subsequent images, the snakes become one, which breaks the egg, and then the serpent and the raptor exist separately."

"Become one..." His eyes glowed with desire as it all fell into place for him. He looked down at her, his skin faintly glowing as he met the subtle movement of her hips with his own, creating a delicious tease of friction between them.

"Yes," she moaned, her back arching off the bed. The word was a plea from the depths of her soul.

He grasped both her wrists in one hand, using the now-free hand to slip under her dress, between her thighs. When his fingers met the silken hair between her legs he moaned. "What are you wearing under here?"

"Nothing," she whispered, meeting his gaze.

In a flash, he popped every button down the front of her dress, baring her to him completely. His eyes ran over her flesh. Every curve, every dip and fold of her body. He panted with need as he parted her legs wider with his free hand, teasing her with his fingers, dragging them lightly over the sensitive skin of her thighs and then away before giving her what she so clearly wanted.

Her scent filled the air and his fangs protracted as his nostrils flared. His wings went as taut as his cock. Every bit of him seemed prepared to take her but his mind. "You're sure?" he asked. "It would be hard to take this back."

He pulled back from her a little, as though he only now noticed that he had her pinned to the bed. In an instant, he freed her hands, seeming to want her to take the lead in this. She understood: there could be no doubt in his mind that she'd chosen this.

Harlow was more than willing to show him just exactly how much she wanted to be Claimed, and to Claim him in return. She raised up, pressing a hand to his chiseled chest, pushing him backwards into a seated position. He moved with fluid grace under her direction as she climbed into his lap, sliding out of her dress as she went.

He adjusted to cradle her as her slick folds slid against his massive erection. She raised her hips, positioning herself above him. As she sank down onto his waiting cock, they stared into one another's eyes. In this form, his eyes were dark, his irises nearly as black as his pupils.

She lowered herself slowly, letting every ridge of him caress her inside as he stretched her open, and when he could sink no further into her, she began to move, her hips undulating in a steady slow rhythm. He caressed her ass, never taking his eyes from hers as she ground her clit against him. The vibration she loved so much purred inside her, sending electric shivers of pleasure up her spine.

The pressure of his hands increased slowly as she moved faster, giving in to the pent-up passion she'd locked away for the past weeks. She reveled in the way her soft belly and breasts met his hard muscles, letting the intensity of need in his expression drive her. One of his hands slid up her back and into her hair as she neared her peak.

She let her head fall backwards as his fingers fisted into her hair, a primal growl emanating from his throat as she cried out with anticipation. His bite would take her over the edge.

"Claim me, McKay," she moaned, letting the fervor take her over.

His mouth opened as he drove hard into her, the slick results of the encounter making it easier for him to slide in and out of her. Her back arched as she fell slightly backward in his grip, her hard nipples meeting the cool air of the bedroom as his fangs grew longer. He struck in a serpentine moment, one that turned her into both predator and prey, she wanted it so badly.

The pain was momentary, followed quickly by euphoria that sent her tumbling over the edge into ecstasy. A symphony of limenal shadow and Illuminated light burst to life as he drank from her. Every nerve in her body was more sensitive than it had ever been and she was connected to not only him, but his magic, the golden source of his power, and when it too entered her, she changed.

The Claim between them would not be an unbreakable bond. Its power was to transform, for as his light became hers, so did her shadow become a part of him, and in this exchange, her own canine teeth transformed. She tasted the venom in her mouth, sweet and thick, and her body's only mission was to complete the transformation—to share it with him.

As his fangs retracted, he licked the twin wounds on her neck, and they closed immediately. He looked up at her face, his expression astounded.

"Goddess," he breathed.

She looked down at herself, at the way her shadows glowed now with their own dark light. Yes, she was a goddess. Whatever this was between them, it was no less than divinity. She pushed him down onto the bed, straddling him, in a fast, fluid movement which he met with no effort.

"I want to look at you," he begged. "Let me see you."

She leaned back as his hands skimmed her hips and ribcage, cupping her breasts. He pinched her nipples, lightly at first, and then harder as she whimpered with pleasure. One hand slid between her breasts and slowly over the gentle curve of her belly and then between her legs to her swollen clit.

She was stretched full of him and as he rubbed her clit, she bent backwards to let him get a better view of the place where their bodies merged. As she did, she felt the jerk of his hips, the increase in his pleasure at seeing her writhe for him, mistress to the power of his cock plunging deep within her again and again.

And then his eyes lifted, and for the first time he saw her new fangs, shining with venom as she cried his name. The fingers rubbing her clit migrated upwards, into her mouth where she tasted herself mingled with her new venom.

"You are magnificent," he breathed. "Every fucking bit of you." He thrust hard into her as he dragged her against him. "Claim me."

The scent of his blood, coursing hard in his veins, spurred her on. As her mouth closed around his neck and her new teeth, purpose-built for this moment, pierced his skin, they came together, their pleasure winding together in what felt as though it might be an endless loop of love and euphoria.

He roared with a ferocity she'd never heard as she pulled his essence into her, from his cock, his blood, his power, his love. They were, in that moment, truly one. She felt when the peak crested and began to fade. Warm, contented bliss came over her, and her fangs retracted. She remembered how he'd licked her wound clean and she did the same, elated at the fact that like her own wound his closed immediately, healed by some unknown power.

His arms went around her as their movements slowed. "That was nothing like what I expected," he whispered as she stilled above him.

"What did you expect?" she asked, cuddling into his chest. She was in no hurry to move and loved the feeling of him still hard inside her, as the wet mingling of their bodies seeped out of her.

"My father said it was the ultimate possession. Those are the words he used. That I would feel as though I owned you. And I knew that was skewed, that his perspective was skewed by his values, but it wasn't anything like that. We were one, but..."

She nodded, raising her head to look in his eyes. "Now we're both *more*."

He hugged her even tighter. "Will you shift for me?"

Harlow looked around the room. "I don't think this room is big enough for the Feriant."

His laugh was rich, free of burden. "I suppose not. Do you want to go downstairs?"

Harlow shook her head. "No, I want to go somewhere I can *fly*."

Finn grinned. "I think I know just the place."

CHAPTER TWENTY-FIVE

F inn shifted back to his humanoid form and teleported
them to a deserted cliffside overlooking the sea. Far, *far*
to the south, Harlow could barely make out the dotted
coastline that made up Nea Sterlis. The day was cloudy, a storm
brewing. When they'd both determined they were well and truly
alone, a grin spread over Finn's face.

He looked up, pointing to the sky. "Perfect cover for a flight,
don't you think?"

Harlow gazed into the churning clouds. She and Finn were
both naked as the day they were born, and she laughed at the
audacity of the situation, and the brazen, unbridled joy in Finn's
face as he shifted into his true form. He shot into the air, his
wings leaving her in a cool wake of air as he went.

"Can you catch me?" he called as he disappeared into the
mist.

He didn't doubt her ability to shift one bit, even after the
hundreds of failed attempts they'd made all summer, and that
confidence spurred her on. Harlow closed her eyes, and as she
looked for a place to focus her attention, her shadows guided her

to the heart of the limen, the source of all her power. The change was nearly instantaneous.

When she opened her eyes her vision was different: panoramic in nature, the colors more vibrant, and everything sharp and easy to focus on. When she shot into the air, she found she didn't have to *try* to fly; she already knew how. In her humanoid form, Harlow was frightened of heights. As the Feriant, she feared no altitude, climbing higher and higher, searching for her heart's mate.

When she spotted him, she caught up to him quickly. They soared through the clouds, climbing ever higher until they broke free of the storm and into the sun-drenched aerial landscape that lay beyond. She didn't know how long they flew, stretching their wings, riding currents of air, but she had never felt anything like it before. For the first time in her entire life, she was free.

In this form, there were no questions, no pressing worries; those existed in her conscious mind. She knew herself still, but as the Feriant she was purely focused on instinct, on the trust she'd worked so hard to build with herself, and her anxiety had no place here. For the briefest of moments, she wondered if she had to shift back, or if she might stay this way forever.

As Finn soared beneath her, flipping over so he could watch her fly, she knew she would change back. *Can you hear me?* she asked in her mind.

Yes, came his answer. She could sense the laughter in his voice, rather than hear it.

Do you think you could catch me?

He grinned, but his brows knitted together in a question.

If I shifted back, could you catch me?

Here?

Yes.

Suddenly, he understood her. *I'll catch you anywhere you fall.*

It was dangerous, and she knew it, but she trusted him. Beneath her he spread his arms open, and she shifted back, falling for the briefest of moments before his body met hers, his arms wrapping around her tight and secure.

She wrapped her arms around his neck as they soared higher, her mouth meeting his in a kiss so passionate, so full of joy, that Harlow understood the full scope of their bond, the depth of the Claiming. It was like he had said—there was no sense of possession between them. They were separate entities, powerful in their own right, but deeply connected now in a way they had not been previously.

Her legs wrapped around his waist as his wings carried them onto a current of warm air. They glided, supported fully by the wind, which caressed her bare skin, heightening every sense of pleasure she experienced: the press of his fingers in her back as he kept her clasped tightly to him. The feel of his tongue as it moved in her mouth. The way she opened for him as his cock pressed at her slick entrance.

She deepened the kiss as she lowered her hips. Here in the air, with nothing to press against, she would be the momentum that brought them pleasure as he controlled their flight. She bore down on him as he stretched her open, sinking into her as they kissed. When he was as deep in her as he could go, she tilted her pelvis and hips, moving them in slow, sensual circles, rather than pumping up and down on his cock.

He came quickly, clutching her tight. When his eyes flew open, he was out of breath. "My wings aren't used to all this flight."

She wrapped her arms around him. "Take me home."

He teleported and they reappeared in the bedroom of the carriage house, where he shifted into his humanoid form and flopped onto the bed. "I never did get you to sit on my face," he said with a wicked grin. "And you know how I hate not getting my way."

She stood at the end of the bed, his words lighting a fire in her core. She crawled up his body, leaving a trail of kisses as she went. When she finally straddled his face, he groaned, taking in her scent, mingled now with his own.

"I can't wait to bury my face in you," he said.

She steadied herself and his hands drifted onto the small of her back, grazing the dip of her hips, then latching around her thighs as he brought her down to meet his mouth. His tongue was warm and soft as she moved against it, his lips gently sucking at her clit, then licking in turns.

Harlow was careful not to clench her thighs too tightly or bear down too hard. His mouth on her was sublime, but she didn't want to smother him. He pushed her away from his face for a moment, using the opportunity to slide a finger into her, teasing her as he spoke.

"Ride my face, baby girl. Ride it hard. I want you to scream."

Then he slid down further, so she was leaning forward just enough that he could take her clit in his mouth, and slide two fingers into her from behind. The extra pressure of his fingers in her sent her into a frenzy as he licked and sucked her. Her thighs tightened around his face and she did as he'd asked and rode his face hard, getting exactly the pressure and speed she needed.

Her breasts were heavy with desire, her nipples hard, and she was greedy for more stimulation. She grabbed her own breasts with one hand, caressing their fullness as she fucked Finn's face. She'd never felt so powerful and cherished as she did in this moment, pinching her nipples, as her hips moved faster. Finn moaned, and she glanced backwards at the liquid beading on his cock. He was so hard for her, for the way she tasted, and the feel of her taking her pleasure.

Her free hand moved from her breasts to her belly, which hung in a way that would have made her insecure months ago, but now it was beautiful to her; she touched herself the way Finn sometimes did when he took her from behind, stroking the soft curve of her flesh as Finn feasted on her. She cried out as her fingers caressed her own soft flesh, coming hard as she moved against his lips and fingers.

When her orgasm waned, he slid out from under her and flipped into a kneeling position, pulling her back until she was on all fours in front of him.

"Yes," she begged. "Yes."

He drove into her, spreading her legs, gripping her hips. "I missed you so much," he growled. "I missed your scent when you want me like this. The way I can smell you from across a room and know you're thinking about me too."

He reached around her to touch her swollen clit again as she lowered onto the pile of pillows he'd been resting on. His body was heavy on top of hers as he moved slowly in her, his fingers rubbing her clit exactly the way she wanted.

Their movements were less dramatic now, but more fervent somehow, as she raised her hips to give him a better angle. He slid another pillow under her stomach and the position was so perfect she felt her release begin to build.

"Yes," he urged her. "Yes, come for me."

"Bite me," she begged. "Please."

Behind her, he pushed her hair off her neck, then an arm snaked around her front, pinning him to her chest as he drove his cock into her harder. His fingers rubbed wicked circles around her clit as she begged for more.

When he bit her, she came so hard she saw deep space. It was easy to understand how the Illuminated got addicted to this, how they used it to bandage over emotional wounds, rather than working things out between themselves. There was no doubt in her mind that was a danger she and Finn would have to watch out for as time passed, but the pleasure it brought them both now was evident in the way he moaned her name as his fangs retracted.

When they recovered enough to talk, laying in a boneless heap of entwined limbs and soft skin, they exchanged stories, comparing notes on the way their deception played out. "Sabre wanted me to tell you how sorry they are about the comparisons Section Seven made. They're enraged on your behalf," Finn said.

Harlow nodded, but couldn't quite find words at first. Finally she said, "Maybe we'll be friends someday."

Finn pressed a kiss to her temple. "You'd love each other. You have the same kind of huge heart. After the rooftop stories got played thousands of times, they were nearly inconsolable. I thought we were going to have to end the whole thing."

Harlow smiled through her tears. "Thank you for telling me that. There were times when I wanted to call it all off too."

Finn stared at the ceiling. "I punched a hole in the wall at my parents' house when the photos of you and Kate came out."

"I'm sure that helped them believe you," Harlow reasoned.

Finn glanced down at her. "I'm sure it did. But I wasn't faking it. Not all the way. Something in me worried... That maybe you'd remember that Kate is *fun*."

Harlow propped her head up on her hand so she could look at Finn more easily. "Yes, Kate is fun. That's a given. What's your point?"

He sighed. "I'm not really all that fun."

His face was so serious she had to laugh. "I had a pretty good time just now."

He shook his head. "I don't mean sex. I mean the rest of the time. I'm not funny like Kate, and apparently I'm 'broody' all the time."

Section Seven had called him "Nuva Troi's Brooding Bad Boy" and posted dozens of images they'd taken of him over the years where he looked intimidating or angry. Overall, the effect had been complimentary, or so Harlow had thought, but he looked genuinely upset now.

"Kate is a great date," she said, her fingers grazing his chin, turning his face towards hers. "But you are the love of my life. I don't need you to entertain me. I'm interested in everything you say and do."

His eyes softened as she spoke. "I am the luckiest person on the planet," he said, wrapping her in his arms and rolling on top of her again. "I will love you to the end of everything," he said as entered her.

They made love again and again, making up for the weeks they lost.

CHAPTER TWENTY-SIX

T he rooftop restaurant at the Grand was nearly empty. As this was primarily a tourist spot, and the tourists were well and truly gone from Nea Sterlis now, this was not unexpected, but Harlow felt extremely unsettled by being alone with Connor McKay on a rooftop. Finn took a call nearly as soon as they'd sat down and now the two of them sat across from one another in awkward silence.

Connor spoke first. "What do you do with your time, Harlow?"

Harlow frowned. "Are you asking if I have a job?"

Connor shrugged, expression blithe. "I assume you have causes you care for. You have a degree in history, I understand."

"I've always worked at my parents' bookstore. When I return to Nuva Troi, I assume I will go back to work at the Monas," she answered.

To Connor's credit, he wasn't one to dole out fake smiles, or pleasantries. "I don't think that will be appropriate for my heir's wife. Perhaps you'd like to go back to school. I understand you spent quite a bit of time at the Citadel this summer."

Harlow paused. It wasn't the worst idea in the world, but

why did he want this? Talking to Connor McKay was like playing three dimensional chess. He was on one level and she was on another. "Yes, I'd considered getting another degree in history, but if I'm not going to work in restoration at the Monas, I'm not sure why I would."

Connor smiled now, but it wasn't placating or kind, it was pure amusement at her lack of understanding. "Why work at all?"

Harlow frowned. "Regardless of how much money Finn earns or inherits, I plan to work."

"Of course," Connor said, chuckling. "You all do at first. Tell me about your summer studies. Which libraries have you visited most?"

Harlow sucked in a breath. Being alone with Connor McKay felt like all oxygen had disappeared from the planet. "I've spent quite a lot of time at the Sistren of Akatei Library recently." Likely, he already knew this, so why hide it?

"Yes," he said slowly. "Why so much interest in that particular library?"

So this was what he wanted to talk about. She didn't have to make it easy for him. "Well, aside from the fact that Akatei is the patron goddess of my Order, I confess, I just love the gardens."

It felt glib to say it, and she assumed this would annoy him since he was so interested in knowing what she was studying, but she did not expect the reaction that passed over his face. He'd been taking a sip of water when she spoke and now he nearly choked, spitting his water back into his glass.

"Excuse me?" he asked. His voice was quiet and deadly as he wiped his mouth. The calm that came over him was eerie, like he was laser focusing on her. She fought to keep control of her body, not wanting to give away that he was making her anxious.

"The gardens? I don't remember that facility having particularly impressive gardens."

Really, it didn't. The courtyard garden was pleasant enough, but nothing special. She'd just been trying to annoy him by not answering his question. She racked her brain for something to say. "It has a rather unique fountain though."

Harlow took a sip of her tea, hoping they might move onto another topic, but Connor's expression darkened further and his jaw was clenched so tightly a vein near his eye began to twitch. Harlow fought to keep up. Somehow she'd lucked into making him react.

She kept talking, babbling really, just to see if she could get him to react further. "It's Akatei pulling the first threads of aether, but the body positioning of the statue itself is atypical, and I believe there might be something written on her hands. Of course, I'd never blaspheme and get into the fountain to look, but it's a delightful little mystery."

His face was still now; in fact his entire body was still, too still. If she weren't here as Finn's fiancée, she would be terrified right now. Finn's footsteps announced that he was returning to the table.

"How interesting," Connor bit out.

Beneath the table, Harlow's shadows danced around her ankles, almost as if they were issuing a warning. It was unnecessary. Every bit of her base instinct was on high alert. Finn glanced at his father as he approached, and Harlow knew she wasn't imagining things when she saw fear flash in his eyes as he sat down next to her.

He affected a cold demeanor. "Sorry for the delay. One of my properties in Nuva Troi went up for sale this morning and we've had three offers. That was Sabre."

Harlow shivered at the way he let his tone soften to a purr around Sabre's name. Even knowing full well that it was all for show wasn't enough to keep her from reacting. Her eyes fell to the table, and she bit her lip, trying as hard as she could to keep her chin from quivering.

Across the table Connor smiled—*smiled* at her reaction, and sniffed the air as it shifted in the breeze. "You've Claimed her. How lovely." He set down his coffee and clapped a hand to Finn's shoulder. "Good work, my boy."

Harlow's skin prickled with fear. How could he talk about something so intimate, so personal, like it was something to celebrate?

Connor grinned at her as her eyes raised. "You'll find things easier to handle now, my dear. Finn will take care of you. Each time you suffer, he'll erase it with a bite. Won't that be lovely?"

Finn's smile dripped with arrogance as his hand drifted to the back of her neck, his fingers wrapping around her throat. "That it will."

She knew it was a show, knew this was all just a ruse, but fear mixed with arousal. Connor's nostrils flared, and he laughed, loud and hearty. "See, even now she wants it. Go give her what she needs, my boy. I'll order us a spread."

It wasn't a suggestion. He'd just commanded them to go fuck. Finn shook his head. "She's had enough for today. It would do her good to wait. I don't want her to get too greedy."

Harlow nearly gagged on Finn's words. It made her sick to watch him twist himself into this. How could this be what Connor wanted, when the real Finn was so *good*? She knew she couldn't reach for his hand, but a single tear slipped from her eyes, down her cheek and as Connor laughed again, throwing his head back in delight, she saw the flash of understanding on Finn's face.

He knew exactly what that tear was for—*him*. She wasn't humiliated by Connor, she was sorry for him. Sorry he couldn't see the wonderful man his son had become, despite him and Aislin. And she was sorrier still for the little boy that lived inside Finn, the one she desperately wished she could travel back in time and comfort. The one that Connor broke, time and again for his own gain.

Connor's phone rang, and he answered, stepping away from

the table. Harlow and Finn watched the delight slide right off his face, shifting quickly to fury. When he hung up his voice was sharp. "I have to handle this now. I'm sorry, Finbar. It doesn't look like I'll have much time for you this week. I need to handle things with the Falcyran ambassador. He's just arrived in port."

Finn nodded as he stood to shake his father's hand. "I understand. Please let me know if there's anything I can do to help."

Connor's eyes softened as he hugged his son. "Truly, my boy, *truly*, I am so proud of you. I worried you might not come around to my way of thinking, but I see now you have things well in hand."

Connor nodded to Harlow. "Do as Finbar commands, girl."

Harlow let her eyes fall to the table, and she tucked her chin in a semblance of a bow. "I will," she promised.

When the elevator doors closed, Finn went to the railing of the rooftop deck, watching his father get into his car and drive away.

"Why doesn't he just teleport?" Harlow asked from the table.

Finn turned, speaking softly. They were still alone, but he was forever careful. "Teleporting takes a lot of energy. It makes it harder to do other, smaller magics for a few days if we don't recover in our true forms, so we don't do it often."

"Oh," Harlow said, realizing how little she knew about the way the Illuminated used their power. "Can we get out of here?"

He nodded. As they walked to the parking lot, he made several attempts to make small talk with her, but she barely answered. Something was bothering her about her conversation with Connor.

"I'm sorry for how that all went," Finn said when they were safe inside the Woody. "I will be so glad when this part of things is over."

Harlow put her seatbelt on. A deep sigh shuddered through her. "When is that going to be, Finn?"

He started the car, but turned to look at her. "What do you mean?"

Harlow flexed her hand, gazing at her engagement ring. "How long are we going to pretend for your parents that we're like them?"

Finn leaned back in his seat. "Not long. Cian thinks we need to make moves soon to gather our people and find a way to strike back."

"They're weakened enough by what's happening in Falcyra?" Harlow asked.

Finn nodded. "They had to send a legion there, in addition to the Dominavus. The next step would be to invoke a military presence, and that will take time to assemble."

"The lower Orders will never agree to that," Harlow mused.

"The Order of Night might, but my father and Pasiphae seem to anticipate that if the humans rise up, there will be mass chaos."

Harlow nodded. "And what about the Rogue Order?"

Finn shrugged. "Connecting with Riley really hasn't benefited us much. We're no closer to meeting with them than we were before. I thought I had a lead on the queen when I left here, but it dried up almost immediately."

Harlow pushed a hand through her hair. "So it's just us against them? There aren't nearly enough of us."

Finn backed out of the parking spot, pulling into the street. "There's not. Our war with them will be hidden—in the shadows. It will be waged privately, not in big battles, until we can find a way to undermine them enough that we can gain allies."

"Numbers," Harlow added.

"Yes," Finn agreed.

"We have to enact the process the Scroll shows," Harlow said. "If we need numbers, we need to set magic free."

"But how?" Finn asked as they pulled into the villa's driveway.

Harlow shook her head. "I don't know, but I think Thea does." She held up her new phone, which she'd had on silent. *Come home as soon as you can. Scroll unlocked.*

Finn leaned over and kissed her. "It's finally all coming together."

$\approx$

ALARIC, THEA, AND LARKIN SAT WAITING FOR THEM IN the Vault conference room, with Petra and Enzo. As they entered, Thea was finishing getting them up to date about the truth about Harlow and Finn's ruse.

As Harlow sat, Enzo grabbed her hand. "I knew there was something else going on."

"I'm so sorry I couldn't tell you," she said.

Finn was making similar apologies to Petra, who shot a weary smile at Harlow that let her know they'd be easily forgiven. Still, she doubted they'd be allowed to forget this anytime soon. Harlow engaged her second sight to view the threads that connected them, and they appeared graceful and calm, with only small areas of tension. She was beginning to see fine details of color variation in the threads, and thought that soon she might be able to decipher what they meant.

"Where's Riley?" Harlow asked Enzo as they got settled into seats.

"They're off somewhere with Kate today. Something at the vineyard, with her sire," Enzo replied. "Sounded boring."

Harlow laughed, and it felt good to have a normal conversation after the past few weeks. "I know, right? Why does everything she does at the vineyard always sound so, so boring?"

Apparently, they were all feeling how the tension between them had loosened. Petra kicked her, but she laughed too. "Gods, is this a thing? I was actually starting to think that Kate was too perfect, and then she talked about the vineyard and the winery and I was just bored to tears. All the talk about the genetics of the different vines…"

"And the natural pesticide compositions," Enzo added. "But Riley thinks it's all fascinating."

Harlow shook her head. "Everyone has their flaws."

Axel entered the room and hopped into Petra's lap. The three of them laughed about Kate, as Alaric struggled to establish a safe line between Nuva Troi—with Cian and the maters—for a video conference. Finn got up to help, but as he did, some expression flickered across his face that Harlow couldn't quite pinpoint.

He stopped, looking back at the three of them. "It's kind of weird, isn't it? Kate is always so much fun to hang out with, but you're right, *nothing* about the vineyard seems at all interesting."

Thea interrupted them. "I'm afraid this is why we're having trouble connecting." She turned her laptop around and played a video. "I'm pretty sure Nox just emailed this to me, but it was sent so covertly I can't be sure."

She pressed play. The video wasn't long, shot from a rooftop in Midtown. The sky was hazy, or so Harlow thought at first. She realized quickly it was smoke. Far away, in the distance of the video, there was a strange sound, like dozens of bottle rockets going off at once.

"What's that noise?" Enzo asked.

Petra's eyes darkened and Harlow watched her fingers run through Axel's fur as he purred comfortingly at her. "Gunfire."

"Gunfire?" Larkin asked. "How is that possible? Only the military has guns."

The air in the room was suddenly close, too close. Harlow's skin prickled with a deep anxiety as the camera panned across the Nuva Troi skyline. Dozens of buildings were on fire—and that sound—gunfire. Now that Harlow knew what it was, it was everywhere.

"That's your place, babe," Thea whispered, horror written

on her face, as Alaric sat down. He took one of her hands in his. They were all thinking it: *where were the people they loved in all this?*

Everyone went quiet as the camera panned down to the streets, where hundreds of Illuminated warriors were fanning out of a building across the road. "That's the tactical building, where my mom and Connor have offices," Alaric said. "Its location is why I took the Midtown apartment..."

He trailed off as a voice spoke for mere moments and then cut off. Thea rewound the video so they could hear the voice. It was clear it was Nox this time. "Me and Indi got here, with the maters. The riots started yesterday." Her voice was clipped. Out of breath. "Nothing like Falcyra here. Illuminated struck back almost immediately, but the Humanists were prepared. Hundreds, maybe thousands dead by now—we're safe here, for now. I'll get as many out as I can before things get—"

The video cut off. All the relief Harlow had felt moments before was gone, replaced by the sense that the looming dread she'd been feeling all summer had finally reached its catalyst point. That this is what she'd been waiting for, or the start of it, anyway.

"What is she talking about?" Harlow asked, her voice raising an octave. "Are they safe there? Is my family safe?"

Enzo took her hand.

"Yes," Thea said, her tone soothing, but there was intense worry in her eyes. "They'll be safe there. For now, anyway."

"That's why he left dinner," Finn said. Clearly he was talking about Connor. "The call he got—it wasn't about the Falcyran ambassador."

"Can we get a message back to them?" Harlow asked.

Finn nodded. "We can route it through Ari and Meline in Falcyra. They should be able to get through easier than us right now, believe it or not."

"Already on it," Alaric said, typing quickly on his laptop.

"Where's Cian?" Enzo followed up. "Nox said she had Indi and the maters with her, but where's Cian?"

Everyone was quiet. "We have to assume they're at Haven, helping people," Finn said. "That would be their first priority."

The room was silent but for the sound of Alaric, typing furiously on his laptop. Thea watched him, her beautiful face tense with worry.

"Okay," Alaric said. "I've got Ari—on chat only. Can't get a secure video connection. From what he and Meli can tell, it looks like the Humanists struck the Order of Night's temporary headquarters in Nuva Troi first. The building burned—they were having a diplomatic dinner though, and several of the Orders' top officials were killed."

"Any Illuminated?" Thea asked.

Alaric nodded. "Yes. At least two that we know of. And they managed to blow the school line today. Twelve children were killed this time. They got the Order of Masks and Mysteries both —the central headquarters buildings are all destroyed. No death toll yet. They've been targeting Order leaders... Enzo, I'm so sorry—they burned your parents' former home to the ground. No word on the atelier or the Monas."

"Shit," Enzo breathed. "I mean, it wasn't their house anymore, but I grew up there..."

Larkin moved to sit next to Harlow, taking her hand. Thea glanced at her sisters, and Harlow saw real fear in her eyes.

"No wonder the Illuminated cut off communications. This is unreal," Enzo said. "Who are these people?"

"Ari has a theory about that too," Alaric said. He glanced at Harlow, looking worried.

"Spit it out," Finn commanded.

"Alain Easton. Ari and Meli think they've traced the money back to Alain. He's funding the Humanists' terrorism."

Thea read over Alaric's shoulder. "That's not all. Before she went dark, Nox finally got a lock on where that drone was transmitting the information. She sent it to Ari, who traced it back to several of the same signatures that allowed him to identify Alain Easton as the financial backer for the Humanists."

Finn's jaw twitched. "Shit."

Alaric sighed. "Yeah. This isn't adding up to anything good."

They'd been so elated this morning, so happy to have finally gotten a step ahead of Connor and Pasiphae, and now all the hope that had inflated Harlow's sails simply vanished. "Why didn't they tell us this sooner?"

Alaric shook his head. "It's not confirmed yet. They wanted to be sure, but in light of all this, Ari says he thought it was better to say what they suspect now."

"He's worried they're going to get cut off from us," Finn added.

"Yeah," Alaric replied, sitting back in his chair and covering his face. "And I have to agree. The Illuminated will lock everything down. They can do it. The simulations Nox and I ran last month prove it. They can shut everything down, even the dark web. We're talking about worldwide outages of *everything*."

Finn stared at his hands. "Connor calls it the 'Great Reset.' He told me about it last week. He said if the riots reached Nuva Troi, this would be the first step—sending out the legions— they'll give it a month, and if the resistance can't be quelled, they'll 'reset' Okairos."

Harlow's heart nearly stopped. "What the fuck does that mean?"

Finn's hands shook. "They think that if they take us back to a pre-industrial period for three to five years, they'll be able to control us by force."

The magnitude of what Finn was saying was hard to even think about. No phones, no internet, no cars—no hospitals or modern medicine—no electricity.... The implications were too big to even think about. Add the fact that such a move would amplify the Illuminated's abilities immeasurably, and it was impossible to imagine anything other than total and complete oppression of humans and the majority of the lower Orders.

"But—people will die," Thea said. "So many people will die."

"They'd rather start over than give up their stranglehold on power," Enzo said.

No one else said anything. It was hard to know what to say. While it had been disturbing to see what happened in Falcyra, everything had gone on so normally here in Nytra that it was hard to imagine anything like that could happen here. But now it was, and they were all caught in the middle of it.

The only thing Harlow could hear was her heart, beating wildly at the thought of being separated from the maters and her sisters while all of this was happening. There was no worse outcome she could imagine. She'd always thought that when whatever was brewing began, they'd face it together.

"Thea, what did you find out about the scroll?" Harlow asked, breaking the silence.

"I hardly think that's important now," Thea said.

Harlow glared at her. Why couldn't she see what was right in front of them? "It might be the only thing that's important now. If their plan is to take Okairos back by force, we have to set the aether free."

Everyone watched them. It was clear Thea didn't agree; her expression turned to one Harlow had seen thousands of times as a child. Indigo had once called it "Mini-mater," because Thea looked so completely assured that she was in charge. "We don't even know if that's safe."

Larkin finally spoke. "But letting them kill thousands of people is? They could kill more in their 'reset' and you know it."

"We don't even know if that's what the scroll depicts," Thea said. Her voice was even, but there was tension around her eyes.

"But you're reasonably sure it is, aren't you?" Petra said.

Alaric took Thea's hand. "Tell them," he urged. "I think

they're right. If there's any possibility that we could make aethereal power available to everyone, now is the time to take a risk."

Thea pulled her hand out of Alaric's grasp as her mouth twisted in a little knot. Finally, she sighed. "I was thinking about what you and Finn experienced last Spring at the opening night of the season. The way you were both shot out of our reality—something about it seemed strange to me, so I used the Vault's records to do some research on binding rituals—between this and the Merkhov, I've been woefully unprepared. Anyway, I pulled some advanced spellwork out of the Order of Mysteries' digital archives—"

"Thea," Harlow interrupted. If they let her go on like this, it could take her an hour to get to the point. "We don't need to know your entire research methodology. What did you find out?"

Thea glared at Harlow, wrinkling her nose in a rather pointed way at her younger sister before continuing. "The season itself is a massive ritual, as we already know. If I'm right, on opening night, the invitation takes a tiny bit of aethereal essence—core material that humans often call souls—from each of the season's participants via the invitations. It links them to the ritual for the duration of the season until the Solstice. Any magic they use during that time helps to power the spell."

"That would have to be a really big spell," Enzo said. He'd always been good at spellwork and ritual planning. "I mean, really big."

"What kind of ritual would need that kind of power?" Larkin asked.

Enzo clapped a hand over his mouth. "It has to be a vascularity of some kind."

Larkin's mouth twitched. "Don't they call those 'battery spells' now?"

Enzo nodded. "Yeah, that's the colloquial term for them. It's a way to channel large amounts of magic into a physical manifestation."

Harlow rubbed her forehead, trying to remember what Enzo was talking about. She'd never been particularly good at spellwork. So much memorizing. "A physical manifestation?"

Larkin bit her bottom lip for a moment, thinking. "Yeah, so a vascularity could be used for a lot of things. When the maters were young, people used them for things like keeping mines from caving in, or dams from breaking. They're workhorse types of spells with a physical presence that looks almost like a web of blood vessels, for channeling aether. It's why it's called a vascularity."

Alaric's eyes lit. "Yes, and as human engineering advanced, combined with both Illuminated and sorcière magics, we stopped using quite so many of those types of spells. They took a lot of power to manage."

"Right," Larkin said. "That's why people call them 'battery spells.' They need a battery of some kind to keep them going and steady. You funnel the power into the vascular tubes, and then you use some object as the battery that stores aether and dispenses it evenly. They have to be connected to one another to work."

Enzo's skin went grey. "An Archean vascularity works differently though. It uses organic matter as the battery." When everyone gave him a round of confused looks, he elaborated. "Either a creature, or a person. Likely an immortal if you were going to use a person, but I've read about instances where whales or other giant creatures were used. Intelligent brains act as a kind of computer for the spell, used to distribute large amounts of power, over long periods of time, at an even pace. If the season was being used as you posit, Thea, then it's possible the vascularity used in the season's ritual is Archean."

Thea's eyes went wide. "It could be... Oh... that makes more sense than what I originally thought..." She rushed to get her folder with the images of the scroll in it, and spread them on the table, tapping the image of the sleeping Argent. "I thought this was a metaphor, but I don't think any of this is metaphorical, not really."

Enzo shrugged as he traced the images with his fingers. "I'm afraid not."

"So the Argent is the battery for the spell?" Petra asked, horrified.

Enzo nodded. "Essentially—their nervous system is likely the conduit for the power, the base of the root—like a battery pack. And their brain controls the distribution of power. The harvest from the season's ritual is likely funneled into the fire-drake, and then stored to be used throughout the year."

"That is gruesome," Harlow whispered.

Enzo nodded. "It is. They fell out of fashion in the modern age because of their cruelty, but they are powerful spells."

"If they were used mainly in industrial applications in the past, what is this one being used for now?" Larkin asked.

"There are more theoretical applications..." Enzo trailed off, his eyes narrowing as he thought. "Such as using them as complex bindings, ways to create things like prisons or barriers."

Prisons or barriers? Like Nihil? Things pieced together. "Could it be used to create a barrier between planes of reality?" Harlow breathed.

"What?" Finn asked.

She turned to him. "You said when the Illuminated came here that they were meant to free aether—to make humans more powerful to fight in the wars they were fighting on their home world, right?"

Petra nodded, following Harlow's train of thought. "Yes, and that means there must have been a source of aether on Okairos somewhere—a big one that didn't exist on other worlds. Something special."

"Like Nihil," Harlow said. "The prison is built on the heart of the limen, the actual source of aether. I don't think you and Cian were wrong about the Pyriphle. I think the river *does* go right into Nihil—to the prison—and Ashbourne. We have a door to not only the limen here on Okairos, but the heart of *all* magic."

"Is that even possible?" Petra asked.

Enzo nodded. "It is. Metaphysics tells us that it's likely the limen opens and closes portals all the time. The problem is, they're not supposed to stay open. Of course, there are stories…"

"About what?" Petra prodded, clearly getting frustrated. Axel grumbled in her lap.

Thea sighed. "That there are anomalies. Portals opened to other realms that stay open, creating massive imbalances in the universe, allowing certain elemental energies to grow far beyond their natural size and power."

"Like the Ravagers," Harlow said. "Something made them uncontrollable."

"What are you talking about?" Enzo asked.

Harlow glanced at Finn. "You have to tell them the whole truth about *The Warden*. They need to know."

He nodded and recounted the entire story of *The Warden*, explaining that the Illuminated were the Ventyr, a race of beings so powerful they'd imprisoned the elemental embodiments of suffering in the universe. The reality of the Ventyr's influence in the world, their corner of the cosmos, was overwhelming enough.

Petra's eyes went wide. Of course she had to know much of this, but Harlow had gotten the impression the finer details of many things weren't told to Illuminated women. She smacked Finn's shoulder and Axel growled, protective of Finn. "You knew this and never told me?"

"It was dangerous to know. It still is," he explained.

"We can't open a portal to Nihil, Harlow," Thea said, horror on her face. "If this is right, about the ritual at the root of the season, we can't risk disturbing whatever spell the Illuminated did to create it. They were right to close it."

Enzo frowned. "We wouldn't have to open the source up completely, just remove the barrier—whatever's keeping the aethereal energy restricted."

Thea shook her head. "No, that's too risky. We have no idea what might come through with it, or who it might draw to us. It might send a signal of some kind to the Ventyr. We have no clue what kind of tech they have, or if they're looking for a way to get to Okairos."

"Would they even still care about us?" Larkin asked. "It's been two thousand years."

Alaric shook his head. "We're young, all of us. We don't really have perspective on how time will work for us, later in life. Two thousand years might not be much time for them."

Petra drew a sharp breath in. "Our parents act like our life-times have been nothing but a short blip—the Ventyr could very well still be looking for a way to conquer Okairos. I think Thea might be right."

Harlow sighed. "There's only one way to figure this out for sure, Thea. We have to find out where it is and go look. Now might be our only chance."

Thea threw her hands up into the air. "Well, that solves it then. We'll just figure out where the entrance to Nihil is."

"Beneath the Alabaster Spire," Larkin said, a faraway look in her eyes. She was obviously thinking about Ashbourne. She still hadn't had any luck getting in touch with him.

"The Alabaster Spire?" Enzo repeated. "Is that where it is?"

Harlow nodded, telling them about the inscription on the crypt. Enzo smiled. "Well then, that's easy enough. You should have asked me before."

A little scream built in Harlow's throat, but she tamped it down. Now wasn't the time to explain that she'd been paranoid while she'd been pretending that Finn might have been unfaithful to her in Nuva Troi.

Enzo continued, apparently oblivious to her expression. "Right around the time the Illuminated got here, there was an earthquake in this region and a bunch of buildings fell—at least that's the logical explanation. There's an old Sterlisian legend that at least one actually disappeared: the Alabaster Spire."

All of her frustration dissolved. Harlow thought back to dinner with Connor. "It was a part of the Temple of Akatei, wasn't it?"

Enzo nodded. "Yes, part of what is now the library. How did you know?"

Harlow met Finn's eyes. "Your father was very worried that I've been spending time there. When I mentioned the statue in the courtyard, he got very upset. There's an inscription on Akatei's hands."

"That's where we have to look first," Finn said. "Who's coming with me?"

CHAPTER TWENTY-SEVEN

The moons were waning and would soon go dark, and the night threatened rain. Getting into the library's courtyard was easy enough. Probably a little too easy, if Harlow was being honest with herself. Everyone else had stayed at home, to limit their risk of being caught.

Finn's fingers laced through hers, and she was so happy he was home, but that happiness was marred by everything else going on, and the risk they were taking, being here now. They'd been crouched in the courtyard near a potted plant for almost ten minutes while she and Finn both probed the building's threads for guards. It was an excruciatingly detailed task, and as the building was practically empty, it was also boring.

"There's one Ultima," Finn finally whispered. "She's at the furthest edge of the stacks now, in the basement. That gives you enough time to get into the fountain, read the inscription on Akatei's hands, and get back. I'll keep watch."

"Why do *I* have to get in the fountain?" Harlow asked, a little grumpy about having to get wet.

Finn kissed her nose. "You're a sorcière. I'm not. If there's any chance that the fountain might be a key to something big, it would make sense that it'd be warded. I might set them off, but if anyone is getting through without an issue, it would be a sorcière."

Harlow had to agree, but there was no guarantee that she would get through. She felt for wards, and found none, but that didn't mean they didn't exist. Many skillfully woven wards couldn't be detected until tripped, by even the most accomplished practitioners. There was only one way to find out.

"Okay, I'm going in."

Finn was right behind her as she darted into the courtyard. She took long strides through the fountain, trying her hardest not to make splashing noises. She'd never been good at muffling spells, but she summoned her shadows to cloud around her and Finn.

She climbed atop the statue's base. The statue of Akatei was half a head taller than her, so it took a moment to read what was inscribed on her hands, since the sentence was split up. It was written in old Sterlisian, but Harlow was well versed in Nytran languages. *When bonfires light the ridge... The way will open.*

That was it. That was all it said. Harlow turned to get down, and stopped, spotting the rest of the inscription. The words were written in the dark shadow of the statue herself. Because of the hedge that grew behind her, this was the only view by which they could be read.

"What are you doing?" Finn hissed.

"There's something written around the inside edge of the fountain, can you give me some light?"

"That's risky," he said.

"Okay, well, use your phone's flashlight then."

He tried it, but there wasn't enough light. Harlow sighed, and tried to get her shadows to illuminate more, but their faint glow wasn't enough to see by.

"The Ultima is headed this way," Finn growled. "Get out of there."

"Not until I read it."

He glared at her, but his hand glowed as he stuck it into the water, lighting the entire fountain in a gentle glow. *The world between worlds lies just beyond knowledge. Beware what lies beneath the Alabaster Spire, for all reward comes at a price. Awaken the Fifth Order and find freedom in unraveling.*

A harsh voice broke the silence in the courtyard, nearly sending Harlow tumbling from the statue. "What in Akatei's name are the two of you doing?"

Harlow recognized the Ultima—Morgaine had said her name was Samira. She wasn't dressed in her uniform though, and for a moment Finn looked confused.

"Get out of here. *Now*," Samira insisted. She stepped into the fountain, pulling Harlow down off Akatei, shoving her towards Finn.

"Don't come back here again," she warned.

In the bushes, something moved. Harlow searched for the source of the sound, but couldn't find anything. Finn's arms went around her. "The Ultima is coming this way. We have to go."

Harlow frowned, trying to wrap her mind around what was happening. *Wasn't Samira the Ultima he'd been tracking?* He seemed to sense her question and shook his head. "I didn't even see her coming."

"*Go*," Samira whispered.

Finn made the jump, and as the courtyard dissolved in her vision, Harlow saw the bushes move again. An enormous auburn cat—the one who'd been visiting Axel—leapt towards another creature, snarling. Samira lunged for the creature the cat was attacking, in an almost coordinated strike. *As though she and the cat were fighting together.* Just as the courtyard disappeared almost completely, Harlow caught the briefest glimpse of the creature's face. It was a dog.

CHAPTER TWENTY-EIGHT

They teleported straight into the Vault, much to everyone's surprise. Harlow couldn't be sure exactly what had happened at the Temple of Akatei. *Why hadn't she or Finn sensed Samira, and what had she been doing there? And what had happened right before they left? What was Axel's feline friend doing there and what was it attacking?*

The explanation for their sudden return sparked an argument, which Harlow tried to ignore as she thought. She needed a moment to process what she'd seen, and the bickering was distracting. Thea wasn't happy about them being caught, and she and Finn argued over what Samira had been doing in the library after hours, when she clearly wasn't on duty.

Harlow searched for a pen and wrote down the entire inscription for Alaric, who began running several searches on what he felt were the keywords from the inscription. She turned over the incident with the cat, trying to sort out what she'd seen. It didn't make much sense to her, but she was sure that Samira and the cat were working together somehow. The idea was beyond far-fetched. Of course cats were, as all animals on Okairos were, extremely intelligent. But if what she knew she had seen made any sense, that would mean they were somehow communicating to one another.

Larkin read the inscription several times and smiled. "The bonfires refer to the Hallowed Moon. That's an old Sterlisian tradition."

Enzo nodded. "She's right. And I agree that the world between worlds must be the limen—and 'just beyond knowledge' has to be the library, right?"

Harlow nodded, letting her thoughts about the cat go for now. "That's smart. Just beyond knowledge could be the courtyard, couldn't it?"

Thea and Finn had quieted now, listening as Alaric chimed in. "If the Fifth Order is supposed to be humans, then does that mean we have to do as the Scroll shows? Free magic?"

Thea gritted her teeth. "Perhaps, but the inscription is pretty clear that there will be a price to pay—an unraveling. That sounds sinister as fuck."

Harlow smiled at her sister's language. "Yes, but there's consequences to anything. Wouldn't the risk be worth it to be not beholden to the Illuminated any longer?"

She didn't expect Finn's response. "We've never known a world in conflict, Harlow. How can we choose that for everyone on our own?"

Her idealism fell away. He was right, and he was wrong at the same time. They *shouldn't* make this choice on their own. They shouldn't choose this fate *for* humans—whatever the Fifth Order awakening entailed, a group of immortals shouldn't be the ones who chose it.

But Finn didn't—no, *couldn't*—understand that humans and the lower Orders lived in a world full of conflict at all times. It was a quiet conflict, to be sure, but the silent screams she'd seen on the faces of her human friends every day of the years she'd spent with Mark shouldn't be dismissed so easily. Oppression didn't always look like riots in the streets.

It looked like humans making their monthly blood donations, having their reproductive choices micromanaged by people who had no business doing so. It looked like separate sectors of every Okairon city divided into Orders and humans, and a country like Falcyra that was allowed to prey on humans without interference. And that's why they shouldn't decide for the rest of the world. They had to find a way to get human input on this, and let them guide the way to change things.

"So we'll let the Hallowed Moon pass," Harlow said, finally.

Everyone was silent, but there were nods around the table.

"There's one every year," Thea reasoned. "Don't look so sad. Larkin, show her what you found tonight."

Larkin's smile was wary. "I've been curating Nox's monthly CCTV collection from Nuva Troi."

"Her what?" Enzo asked.

Alaric explained. "Nox has a program that collects anomalies in Nuva Troi's CCTV—things that are out of place. Stuff like graffiti before it gets cleaned, odd traffic patterns, sometimes even people who shouldn't be in certain places at certain times..."

Enzo nodded. "Okay. I get it. What did you find, Larkin?"

She turned her laptop around. Dozens of photos of five rings, looped together in a chain, played on loop on her screen. "This has been appearing in lots of places for the last month. Five rings—it could be the symbol for the Fifth Order." Some looked as though they'd been spray painted, others were worked into things like flyers, or other signs. "I refined the search once I saw the initial grouping—look at this."

Five images isolated on the laptop screen. "Those are all Haven locations," Alaric said.

"And they're painted on the *inside* of the windows, not the outside," Larkin said with a smile.

"So tell us what you think this all means," Petra said, grinning. She liked that Larkin had a theory.

Larkin smiled back at Petra, proud of herself. "There's a human resistance that *aren't* the Humanists already—and I think Cian is working with them."

"How do you know?" Finn asked.

Larkin enlarged the darkest of the images. The camera was focused on the glass of the window itself, but as it clarified, it was clear that CCTV had caught the actual moment this particular link had been applied. A hand pressed the appliqué to the glass. It was dark, and the image was fuzzy, but there was no denying it. The person in the window had a bright shock of silver hair.

Larkin played the video that still had originated from. It was hard to make out, but at the end the figure looked right out the window and a passing car illuminated their unique eyes, which reflected silver light into the dark.

"That's definitely Cian," Finn said. "Why wouldn't they tell us this?"

Harlow slipped her hand into his. "Maybe they started working with them more recently. Like while you were both back in the city. It was dangerous to share information then."

The lights in the Vault flickered for a mere second. Larkin turned her laptop around and frowned. "The internet's not working."

"That's not even possible down here," Alaric said, opening his own laptop. He shook his head. "Try it on your phones."

Thea was already on it. "It doesn't work."

Alaric raced to Cian's office. When he came back his eyes were wide. "The web and phone lines, even the hard lines, are down all over Okairos."

Finn picked up his phone, tried to make a call and then slammed it down on the table. They hadn't been able to get through to anyone in Nuva Troi since the email from Nox had come through, but calls to elsewhere had been working.

"Try Kate or Riley," he said.

Petra and Enzo both picked up their phones, but Harlow already knew they wouldn't be able to get through.

"Who did you try to call?" Harlow asked.

"My father," Finn answered as Petra and Enzo both shook their heads. "It's started. They'll cut off communication first and then impose martial law. Turn the TV on."

Larkin started to say she didn't think it would work, but when Petra turned on the conference room's TV, all channels were playing the same recorded message on loop.

Pasiphae Velarius sat in her pristine Nuva Troi office, smiling, her voice calm and steady. "Over the past few days, there have been a rash of terrorist attacks all over Okairos. As of now, martial law is in effect; all citizens are to be in complete lockdown. Provisions will be delivered to your homes.

"There will be no breach of lockdown restrictions. All those found in violation will be executed on sight. Please stay calm. This situation is temporary until all terrorists are in custody. Cooperate fully with all military officials in your area and we will get through this as we do all things: together. *Ab ordinae libertas.*"

"Bullshit," Finn said, but he sunk into the couch looking more lost than Harlow had ever seen him.

"We have to get my family out of Nuva Troi," Thea said, touching Alaric's arm. "Aurelia will be a target."

Alaric nodded. "I agree. I'll go back tonight and get them out myself. No one will question *me.*"

Thea shook her head. "You're not going alone. I'm coming." He started to argue, but Thea was firm. "I'm coming."

Alaric looked to Finn, giving him a helpless shrug. "You okay with that?"

Finn nodded, clapping his hand to Alaric's shoulder, and then hugging Thea in turn. "Be careful. We'll rendezvous in Santos on the equinox."

Thea and Alaric both nodded, but Harlow was confused. "What's on Santos for us?"

Finn's smile was wry. "A plane. Until we can figure out the best way to handle all this, we need to get everyone to one of our safehouses, preferably outside Nytra. The Illuminated have always been more protective of Nytra. We'd be better off almost anywhere else."

There was a long pause, and then Enzo stood. "I'm going to get Riley. If we're leaving, I'm bringing my partner."

Finn started to protest, but Petra joined Enzo, taking his hand. "I'll go with him. We can get Kate too, if she'll come." Finn opened his mouth—to argue, Harlow assumed—but Petra shook her head. "*Finbar.* You and Alaric trained me. I'm as deadly as either of you. Don't you trust me?"

Finn hugged Petra tight. "Of course." He pulled away from her, cupping her face in his hands. "You better be careful though. Don't do anything rash. Get in, get them out. If there are soldiers involved, no retribution, you hear?"

Petra nodded, clasping the hands that cupped her face, her eyes welling with tears. "I love you too, big brother."

They fell into a hug so tight Harlow worried they'd smother each other. They had to separate in order to safely be together again, but it hurt all the same.

"What are we going to do?" she asked, when the four of them went upstairs to prepare for their respective journeys.

Larkin raised her eyebrows. "Do we get to storm something? I've always wanted to storm a castle."

Finn shook his head. "No, we'll go to Santos and get the plane ready for them... But I've got to try to talk to my father first."

Larkin looked like she wanted to fight him on that, but Harlow touched her sister's arm. "He's right. If anyone can get through to Connor, it's Finn. Will you go get Axel's things ready to go?"

Axel meowed at the sound of his name, winding his lithe body around Larkin's feet. She scooped him into her arms and nodded. "Sure."

When she went upstairs, Harlow turned to Finn. "What about Cian?"

Finn handed her his phone. It was open to what should be an impossible email, given the circumstances. "That's why I have to get to Connor. I don't know how she did it, but my girl is a genius. Look at this."

It was clearly from Nox, just two lines that read: *Everyone at Haven safe—except Cian. The Dominavus took them.*

CHAPTER TWENTY-NINE

H arlow's hand flew over her mouth. Rakul had warned her that if they met again, they wouldn't be on the same side of things. This was her worst nightmare. They'd been caught. Cian had been caught. The punishment for sedition against the Illuminated was torture and death.

"No," she whimpered when she could form words. Then confusion set in. "How did they take Cian, but everyone else at Haven is safe?"

Finn sunk onto the couch. "I've been trying to puzzle that out for the past fifteen minutes."

Harlow sat next to him. "Why didn't you say something when the others were here?"

He shook his head. "They'll panic if they know Cian's been taken. They need clear heads to do what they're going to do. You and I are going to take care of this."

"Together?" Harlow asked, her heart lifting a little.

Finn's eyes softened. "Harls, you still have a lot to learn about combat, but I know you've got my back with my parents."

Harlow nodded. "Of course I do."

Finn gripped her shoulders. "Then I could really use your support tonight."

The look in his eyes was desperate. She hugged him tight. "Of course."

~

THEY SAID GOODBYE TO THEIR FAMILY IN THE driveway as night fell. Enzo and Petra teleported out. Alaric and Thea left by car, and when they passed out of view, Larkin, Finn and Harlow went back into the villa.

"Don't break the wards for anyone," Harlow warned. "Only Finn and I can get back in now, and you and Axel have to promise to stay inside."

Larkin rolled her eyes. "Sure, but last time you left me at home with the cat while you all went on a mission, someone set fire to the house."

Harlow smacked her sister lightly on the arm. "The cheek on you."

Larkin grinned. "A bit of gallows humor wins the day."

Finn didn't laugh. In fact, as they'd prepared to meet his father, he'd retreated further and further into himself. He kissed Larkin's cheek as they left, though. Harlow didn't press him to talk as they drove through the empty Nea Sterlis streets and parked in front of the Grand. Finn sat quiet for a moment before turning to Harlow.

"When I ask you to go to the car, do it without arguing," he said, his voice solemn. He wouldn't meet her eyes.

Harlow's heart thumped wildly. "What? Why would I need to do that?"

"I will need someone to drive me home," Finn replied, in a tone so dark she didn't dare ask another question. Whatever she'd thought they were here to do, she realized she'd been very, *very* wrong. Dread pooled in her stomach.

They got out of the car and went into the hotel. Finn's grip on her hand was tight, so tight she could tell he was holding back, trying not to hurt her. His skin had taken on a deathly pallor, and a bright sheen of sweat covered his forehead, despite the cool night air.

The clerk at the desk looked surprised to see them, which was understandable, given the lockdown. "Please let my father know we're here," Finn asked.

The clerk nodded, stepping into a booth behind the front desk where there was an internal intercom, rather than using the phone at the desk that probably didn't work now. Harlow knew better than to say anything here, but she wanted to beg Finn to get back in the car. Surely, whatever was about to happen here couldn't be the only way. Finn looked down at her, his stormy eyes wide with fear. That's when she understood. Wherever Cian had been taken, they'd never be rescued, never be found.

The Illuminated could do whatever they wanted with the Argent. Whatever was about to happen was their only chance to get Cian back in one piece. This was the real reason he hadn't told Alaric and the others what they were going to do. Alaric and Petra never would have let him come here. They knew better, but she hadn't.

Tears threatened in her eyes, welling at the hopelessness of the situation.

"Please don't," Finn whispered. "This is the only way."

She nodded, pulling herself together as well as she could. He was so fucking brave she couldn't stand it—couldn't stand the purity of his conviction and his devotion to the people he loved. He would walk through fire for any of them, she was utterly convinced.

What would he do if it were her that was captured? She pushed the thought away, knowing the answer. Finn McKay would destroy worlds to get to her. She didn't know what Connor would make Finn do to get Cian back, but whatever it was, it frightened him. The least she could do in this moment was to be as brave as he was.

The clerk called out to them. "You can go up. He's waiting for you."

The elevator ride was brutal on her heart. The silence between them was thick with unsaid promises. Harlow was afraid to speak, so she tightened her grip on Finn's hand. When the elevator door opened, he murmured to her, "Remember what I said. Don't argue."

Harlow nodded. She wanted to fight him, but she agreed anyway. The look on his face wouldn't let her argue with him now. The fear was gone, replaced by steely determination. Determination, she realized as he squared his shoulders, to be brave in the face of the only thing he truly feared: his father.

So she squared her own shoulders, lengthening her spine and smoothing her face into an imperious mask. It was one of Selene's best faces, she knew, and she wore it now with pride. The two of them didn't look so much alike for nothing, and she carried Mama's sheer audacity with her now, grateful that each muscle in her body knew this by heart.

Finn glanced down at her as they walked into the penthouse suite, and a flicker of pride shone in his eyes. "Great Raia." He kissed her palm. "You are a vision."

She gave him her best Selene-takes-no-prisoners smile, and she saw the emotion in his eyes retreat. The creature before her now was the Finn McKay people feared. Fearless, steadfast, lethal. They walked into the monster's lair ready to be brave, or so Harlow thought, but nothing could prepare her for the scene in the penthouse living room.

There was blood everywhere, but no bodies. No bones, no gore. Just blood pooled on the floor, splattered on the walls, staining the rich carpets and upholstered furniture. And all over Connor's face and hands. Clearly, he'd been feeding. On whom,

Harlow couldn't guess, but the scene suggested it had been more than one person.

He smiled politely at the two of them, but there was a feverish look in his eyes Harlow didn't trust. "I wasn't expecting guests," he said, his tone casual as he wiped his mouth with a hanky he pulled from his pocket.

"Where is Cian?" Finn asked, ignoring the carnage before them completely.

Probably best, Harlow thought. *We're here for a reason. Better to stay focused*.

Connor smiled. "Whatever do you mean?"

Harlow honestly couldn't tell if he was mocking Finn, or if he was confused by the question.

Finn's voice was steady. "Don't play games, Father. I know you took Cian from Haven."

"Ah, Haven," Connor said as he sank into a formal chair at the dining table.

"They've done nothing wrong," Finn reasoned. "Give them back."

"Nothing wrong? Your little plan to undermine my authority was ill conceived, my boy. I know you think you've kept your plans a secret from me, but I've always known you were helping humans." Connor paused, his head tilting to the side in mock-thoughtfulness. "What I can't understand is why you didn't just tell me what you wanted to do. There was no need to keep it a secret. I would have funded your efforts, happily."

Harlow struggled to keep her heart beating normally as Connor spoke. *He didn't know.* He didn't know the true extent of Haven, or that the Knights of Serpens were the ones who ran the project. Finn squeezed her hand slightly, a reassurance.

"Then you won't have any issue giving Cian back," Finn said. "If someone needs to be punished for the transgression, let it be me."

Connor laughed. "Always the hero, aren't you my boy?"

Finn said nothing in response, but he glanced down at Harlow. The gravity of his expression was a reminder that she was not to argue. Her chin quivered for half a second before she steadied it. This would be like when he was a little boy in the basement. She understood why she was here now—why he didn't want to come alone. Every fiber of her being fought against what would come next.

Connor's voice broke through the syrupy fear that clouded her thoughts. "Let's get to it then, my boy. Will you let her watch you take your punishment?"

"No," Finn said, not sparing even a glance for Connor. "Wait for me in the car."

"All right," she said, staring straight into his eyes. She'd promised not to argue, but she wouldn't be in the car, nor the lobby, nor even the elevator. Right outside the door; *that* is where she'd be when Finn had done what he needed to here.

Connor laughed as she turned to go, and the sound of his laughter enraged her, but Finn's eyes pleaded with her: *Let me do this. Let me save Cian*. She didn't let go of his hand until the very last second possible. Leaving him here, to whatever was about to happen, was unimaginable. But she understood why she was. He would do anything for his family. Anything.

And *she* would do anything for him. Including waiting right outside the door, no matter what she heard, no matter how much she wanted to rescue her love, she would wait for him here. She felt for the threads that connected them; trying something new, sending waves of her love down the ones connected to him. Harlow only hoped he could feel it now. As the door to the suite closed behind her, she understood with heartbreaking clarity that she wouldn't be able to rescue him, even if she wanted to.

The wards sealed around the door as it closed, the knob

searing her fingers the instant they went up. Even the connection she'd felt to Finn via the threads was gone now. Her teeth grit in fury as she stumbled backwards. Tears streamed down her face as she sunk to the floor. The wards were so good that even with her enhanced hearing there wasn't a sound coming from the suite.

Her eyes fell closed, and she reached for her shadows. They had to stay buried within her, but she needed their comfort now. She dropped deep inside her mind, finding the little portal within herself where her shadows originated from, a mere pinprick of a thing, deep in her second sight. They were there waiting for her, and as her spirit body approached, they sucked her through that tiny portal into the limen.

She wasn't in Nihil this time, or at least not the part where the wardens slept, but a quieter place. Raw aether pooled around her feet in billowing, midnight blue clouds. Her shadows joined their own kind, blending into their source, losing a bit of their individual sentience. This place was soothing in its darkness.

There was just enough light to see by here, flashes of lightning in the distance, dim through the thick clouds of aether. Nothing was familiar about this location. She seemed to stand on an abandoned city street. Strange architecture rose up around her as she walked, hallmarked by sinuously curving lines and glass arches; all with a sensual organic grace that was as beautiful as it was imposing. Some menace threatened this place, deep and pervasive, whatever it was. Harlow had never seen the like. There was no way this place represented anywhere on Okairos. The limen often reproduced bits and pieces of the worlds it touched for brief periods of time, but this was clearer than Harlow had imagined it could be.

A figure walked in front of her, a woman, Harlow thought, a bit shorter than herself, with generously curved hips and narrow shoulders. She couldn't make much else out about her, but she walked with purpose. Harlow followed her, curious about the soul within. Something about her burned brightly in Harlow's vision. Of course, there were no threads here. The limen was not the same kind of reality as Okairos. Everything here was pure aether.

Soft footsteps walked next to her, and Harlow looked up. The Ventyr next to her was immediately recognizable. He was taller than she'd imagined, standing next to her now. His long hair flowed freely to his waist and his wings moved slightly with him as he walked.

"Ashbourne," she said.

"Yes," he said. His body wasn't fully corporeal here. This was an astral projection. His eyes were fixed on the figure.

"Is that Lumina?" Harlow asked, going on a hunch.

He looked down at her, his head dipping as he did so. "I believe it might be, but I cannot tell."

"A curse," she mused.

"Indeed. But I wonder, little one, what do *you* see?"

Harlow looked hard at the figure ahead of them now. "Nothing distinguishable, but there is something familiar about her. Do I know her?"

Ashbourne smiled. "Yes... No... Perhaps."

Harlow rolled her eyes. "That's not much of an answer."

"Look again," he pleaded.

She did, and then she saw it again: the light within the figure. "There is a light in her, a dark light."

"Yes," Ashbourne said, his voice interminably sad. "I was afraid you would say that."

"What do you mean?" Harlow asked.

Lumina, if that is who she was, walked faster now, and they had to rush to keep up. As she rounded a corner, the scene changed. Now they were in a forest of tall conifers, and several figures fought against one girl. The same dark light shone within her that had in Lumina, except this girl was familiar to her. She recognized her face somehow, but she couldn't remember why. The girl was fast, her voluptuous body bending and weaving as she defeated each of her foes, seemingly without effort.

"Who is she?" Harlow asked. "Do I know *her*?"

She wanted answers. Why had he brought her here like this? She needed to be back in the real world, waiting for Finn.

Ashbourne shrugged. "Who can say? Perhaps an echo of someone you met once."

An echo? That made no sense whatsoever. "Why are you showing me this?"

Ashbourne laughed. "I'm not showing you anything, little bird. You are showing me."

"How?" Harlow asked.

"Your stories must be woven together somehow," Ashbourne suggested. "Whatever the reason, your time here must end."

Harlow opened her mouth to argue, but the winged god before her, for that was how he seemed to her—a god—shook his head. "He will need you. Do not come looking for me again. Not here, nor in the waking world. I do not have the answers you seek."

He was fading now; she could hardly hear him as she felt herself sucked back into her body. "Leave what's beneath the Spire be, little bird," she heard as she opened her eyes. "Let Nihil's guardians keep you safe."

Back in her body, in the hallway outside Connor McKay's hotel room, her tears had long-since dried on her face. She checked her phone—somehow an hour had passed. Where was Finn? She leapt up, about to pound on the door to the suite, wards be damned, when it opened.

Finn stood there alone, his face bloodied and swelling, his shirt soaked in blood. He stumbled forward, into her arms. Connor McKay stood behind his son, wearing clean clothes and a smile. "Have a good evening," he said as he moved forward to close the door.

Finn's weight was heavy on her, and he mumbled something. "Don't."

She couldn't help herself. As she adjusted his body, she looked back at Connor McKay. "You should be ashamed of yourself."

Surprise lit the heinous immortal's face. How long had it been since someone talked back to him? She knew she was playing with fire, but she'd never been very good at knowing when to keep her mouth shut. Even when things were at their worst with Mark, she'd get in one last word, seemingly just to see if she could make him angrier. That same foolishness had her in its grip now.

"I'll make you pay for this someday, Connor McKay. Mark my words, I'll make you pay."

Something like respect tinged the laugh that escaped Connor's throat. "I'll look forward to you trying, Harlow." He stepped forward. "It will be a pleasure to break you."

Finn roared, his broken body lurching forward. Harlow pulled him back, putting a little of her own magic into her grip. Connor laughed as he stepped back into his suite, shaking his head. "The two of you will learn the hard way then. So be it."

He shut the door and Finn stumbled. "Let's go," he slurred, his mouth too swollen to speak clearly. Tears rolled down her face, but Harlow nodded, helping Finn into the elevator.

SOMEHOW, HARLOW GOT FINN INTO THE CAR. ONCE they'd exited the Grand, she couldn't hold her fear back any longer, and it all broke loose in a torrent of sobs. Finn, damaged as he was, tried to comfort her.

"Be quiet," she begged, fastening his seatbelt. "Just be quiet until I can get you home."

He nodded, groggy. She hated to hurt him, but she shook his arm. "Stay awake... I think you need to try to stay awake, at least 'til you can shift."

Harlow knew that he'd heal faster in his true form, so she drove as fast as she possibly could. The streets of Nea Sterlis were empty. Her mind was thrown back to the night she killed Mark. Wasn't it just like this? Her driving him, broken and battered through town—her scared for his life. At least this time she knew what would help him.

Finn wasn't in any danger of dying, but somehow that made what Connor had done that much worse. He'd done it for the sake of doing it. Because something in him got off on hurting one of the few people in this world that might ever have truly loved him back. She'd meant what she said in the hotel; someday she would find a way to make Connor McKay regret his choices regarding his son.

They'd driven out of the city proper and were on residential streets now. "Shift," she whispered. It was only a few more minutes to the villa, but still, every moment counted. He didn't open his eyes, but his glamour fell away. He'd already started to heal, but now his progress was more rapid. His face looked better almost instantly.

His head moved in her peripheral vision. He was looking at her. "You really let Connor have an earful."

Harlow shook her head. "He deserved it."

Finn coughed, and she heard a soft crackling noise. He grimaced as he gripped his ribs, which were likely healing. "He did."

"Where is Cian? When do we get them back?"

Finn growled. "We don't. The Dominavus don't have Cian."

"What?" Harlow's voice was shrill, nearly a shriek. "Then what was the *point* of that?"

Finn groaned as another rib crackled back into place. "He had to punish me for lying about Haven. Said he went easy on me since it wasn't an exchange for Cian's life."

Harlow pulled the car into the driveway, but didn't drive up to the house. She wanted to be clear on what they'd just done before they saw Larkin. "So where is Cian?"

Finn shook his head. "I have no idea. Connor doesn't know."

"And does he know about the Knights? About what we're doing?"

His long arm snaked out, and he pulled her to him by the chin. He kissed her gently, then sighed. "No, he doesn't know."

"Then why the fuck did you let him do this to you?" Harlow sobbed, tears falling in hot streams down her cheeks.

Finn grinned that crooked grin. "Because he thinks I'm still under his control. That I'll submit, without even so much as an order from him."

"You planned this?" Now she really *was* shrieking. "Did you know he had no idea where Cian was?"

Finn shrugged. "No, I knew there was a possibility…"

"*What possibility?*"

Finn winced. "You really don't know?"

She sat back, slamming her head against the headrest in frustration. Her eyes fell closed as she sighed. She played with the pieces of everything they knew. Cian was missing. A witness said the Dominavus took them, but Connor said they didn't. *How could it be both?*

Her mind drifted to the creature in the bushes at the fountain—the one the auburn cat and Samira had fought. In all that had happened, they hadn't discussed it yet, but her suspicions were firming up now. There had been a dog following her that day on her way to the Citadel, and Rakul had said he preferred dogs over cats. She'd just thought he was distracting himself from the pain of the binding at the time, but now she understood.

Her eyes flew open. "The Argent powering the Archean vascularity is Vivia Woolf."

Finn nodded; he'd put it all together as well. "Rakul Kimaris has Cian, and he's going to get his mate back on the night of the Hallowed Moon. We've led him right to her."

Chapter Thirty

I t took Finn two days to recover, and much as Harlow had wanted to spend it in bed with him, she and Larkin moved all the family's private business into the Vault instead. There was only one possible plan: stop Rakul from using Cian to replace Vivia at the vascularity, rescue Cian, meet everyone at the plane on Santos and get to a safehouse. If Finn was going to be strong enough to teleport the five of them out, then he had to rest, and Harlow and Larkin had to ready the villa to be left for an undetermined amount of time.

The morning of the Equinox, they had all the windows open on the main floor. The rains had set in, so a chill autumnal breeze blew through the house. Axel sat on the kitchen counter, sniffing the air as Larkin and Harlow cleaned out the fridge.

She was throwing herself into menial tasks, trying to tamp down her frustration. *Why had she trusted Rakul so implicitly?* She was furious at herself for putting Cian in danger like this. If she'd just been a little more cautious, just taken a little more time to think, this wouldn't be happening.

"I kind of hate to do this to all these lovely condiments," Larkin said as she tossed a jar of expensive capers into the trash.

They'd made exactly a dozen different snacks as they'd gone through the food, and Finn was sitting at the counter eating a huge plate of nachos in his pajamas. He *looked* fine, Harlow thought, at least on the surface. But he'd been quieter since the night at the Grand. He smiled at Larkin's jokes, but he didn't laugh. All three of them were doing their best to make it to the Hallowed Moon in one piece, but none of them were doing well.

Harlow hadn't pushed Finn to talk about things, but she hadn't ignored it either. She left the door open between them; he just hadn't been ready to walk through yet. He was staring out at the rain now, lost in thought, and she reached out to grab his hand. He startled slightly, then his lips quirked up when he realized it was her who'd touched him.

His fingers wound through hers and he stroked her palm with his thumb. The movement was innocent enough, but a little tingle of desire flickered through her. She blushed. The fervor was gone now, but her primal need for him hadn't disappeared. Now was probably not the time though... His thumb moved down her palm again, slower this time, languorous even.

The breeze hit the bare skin of her shoulders and she shivered, feeling the sensation between her legs and in the heaviness of her breasts. Her breath quickened and when she looked up, Finn's eyes burned with the same desire she felt now.

Larkin made a gagging noise and Harlow whipped around. "Is something gross?" Thea was the one who was rabid about keeping the fridge cleaned out. It was totally possible something had gone bad since she left.

"Yes," Larkin said, rolling her eyes. "You two. Please, go get it on in private if you're gonna act like that." She laughed then. "Really, go—I've got the fridge... And the dishes... Please, I will do *anything* to get you out of here, even chores."

She popped her earbuds in and Harlow heard her turn the music up. A symphony played in Larkin's ears and she smiled, saying too loudly, "Couldn't hear a thing if I wanted to. Wards are up. Get going, lovers."

Finn smiled at Harlow. "She's right. Let's go upstairs."

She let him lead her up the stairs, and she watched every flex of his muscles, every step, with raptorial intensity. He seemed fine enough, but it wasn't his body she was worried about now, it was his heart.

When the door to their bedroom shut, she turned to him. "We don't have to do anything. We can just lay down together."

"I want to," he said as he drew her towards him. His voice heated as his fingers skimmed over her hips and waist. "I need to be inside you."

She felt his words everywhere and lifted her face, her lips parting. When his mouth met hers, his kiss was soft at first, tentative. As her hands roamed over his chest and into his hair, he groaned in her mouth, deepening the kiss. She felt his need as his tongue danced with hers, his cock hardening between them.

She pulled his shirt off, throwing it to the floor as she trailed kisses down his neck and chest, pausing to tease each of his nipples as she pushed his joggers down. His fingers combed through her loose hair as hers went around his cock. When she was on her knees in front of him she looked up at him.

His mouth was open and his fangs protracted as her mouth closed around his cock. He moaned softly as she took him deeper into her throat, breathing steadily through her nose.

"Yes," he moaned as she dragged him out of her mouth, using her saliva to wet her hand and stroke his cock. Again and again, she took him into her mouth, using her hands to create seamless pressure as she licked and sucked him.

He pulled her up towards him, pulling her sweatpants off as he pushed her onto the bed. His fingers drifted up her thighs.

"Why'd you stop me?" she asked.

One finger slid between her drenched folds. "Because I want to come here," he said as he pushed another finger inside her.

His glamour fell away and his fingers lengthened, filling her. He pulled them from her body and lowered himself onto her. As the head of his cock pushed into her, he propped himself up so he could look into her eyes.

"I love you more than anything in the world," he said, voice solemn as a saint, expression just as reverent.

Her fingers ran over the angles of his beautiful Ventyr features, sharp and angular. Still her Finn, but something more as well.

"I love you," she whispered back as he moved slowly inside her. Heat built as the friction between them sent ripples of ecstasy through her. Her back arched as her pleasure mounted, the glow of his desire winding with her dark shadows, which had emerged.

His fangs plunged into her neck as he thrust harder into her, and every nerve in her body lit aflame. When he licked her clean euphoria rushed through her, her orgasm playing like music over her body in waves as he watched her.

"Just like that," he murmured.

When her orgasm peaked, her own fangs emerged and as she screamed his name, she latched onto his neck, pulling his sweet immortal blood into her mouth. Her eyes fell closed as she enjoyed every inch of him. The sounds he made as he drove into her, while she in turn, impaled him, were beyond exquisite. It felt like they were floating. Each crescendo of pleasure was that much better than the last.

Harlow opened her eyes to find that, in fact, they *were* floating, his wings and their combined magic holding them aloft. Her fangs retracted, and she looked down at the bed, laughing softly. "That's new."

He grinned as they fell to the bed, their concentration lost. It was good to see him *really* smile again. They collapsed against one another, breathing hard from their encounter.

"Should we try to make some kind of plan for tonight?" she

asked. They hadn't talked about it much, just the bare facts, really, and what had to be done to prepare to leave the villa.

Finn shrugged, his glamour returning as he pulled her into his arms and under the covers. They'd opened the windows up here too and the rain had started up again outside. "I figure we'll go in through the fountain. My guess is that something about the equinox will trigger the door opening if we're in the right place at the right time."

"And then what? We'll just ask Rakul nicely to give Cian back?"

Finn's expression darkened. "I doubt it will be that easy."

"Do you think we'll need the Feriant?"

"I hope not. You and Larkin stay back, if you can. Help Cian get out."

Harlow shook her head. "No, Larkin can help Cian. I'm staying with you this time."

He opened his mouth, and she shut it with a kiss. "Don't argue," she said against his lips. His returning kiss accepted defeat, quite gracefully, she thought as she climbed on top of him. They had at least an hour before they had to be ready to go, and she wasn't wasting another moment of it.

CHAPTER THIRTY-ONE

T he three of them, with Axel in a compact backpack especially for carrying pets, made their way to Sistren of Akatei Library under cover of darkness. The rain had abated for the time being, but the night was cloudy. There were no fires on the ridges tonight because of the lockdown, and the usual local festival had been canceled.

They had to go slow, ducking into alleys and doorways periodically to avoid the Illuminated troops that patrolled the streets. "This is going to take forever," Larkin grumbled as they hid, crouched behind a stinking restaurant dumpster that hadn't been emptied since the lockdown began.

In his carrier on Finn's back, Axel growled, also unhappy. "Hush, bub," Finn ordered, and the black cat shut up immediately.

Harlow couldn't help but smile, despite the circumstances. When Finn looked back at her she mouthed, *Cat Dad Extraordinaire*. Somewhere in the distance, there was an explosion. Larkin jumped, hiding behind Finn's considerable bulk.

"What's happening?" Harlow asked, craning her neck to try to see past Finn.

He slipped out of the backpack, handing it to her. "Put this on." When she had Axel securely on her back, he bent to kiss her. "Stay here, okay. I'm going to see what's going on, and I'll circle back."

He tapped the analog watch she wore tonight. "If I'm not back in five minutes, I want you to head back to the villa and get to Santos on your own. Use the boat tied up at the dock."

"I'm not leaving without you," she whispered.

"I'll be back in five minutes," he countered.

She nodded. When he was gone, she took Axel's carrier off and gave it to Larkin. "If he is not back in five minutes, I will shift into the Feriant, you will stay hidden here, and I will go get Finn."

Larkin nodded. "I like your plan better."

Harlow smiled at her youngest sister and they huddled together as she watched the seconds tick by. The sound of gunfire drew closer and, above their heads, several bottle rockets went off. The quiet of the Nea Sterlis lockdown was shattered as people moved through the streets. Many had weapons made from a pale wood that caught the light.

She ducked back behind the dumpster, whispering to Larkin, "Some of them have white ash."

Larkin's eyes went wide. "What? How is that possible?"

Harlow shook her head, looking at her watch. Finn had been gone for five minutes and three seconds. She took a deep breath; she had no idea how white ash might affect her—if she were from a purely sorcière lineage, it would harm her, but wouldn't incapacitate her or kill her—but with the fact that she had Illuminated heritage, she couldn't say. Whatever the case, she wasn't leaving Finn out there to fend for himself.

"Move back a little," she urged Larkin. "I'm kind of... huge... when I shift."

Larkin nodded, her eyes wide and frightened.

"What are you still doing here?" Finn hissed as he ducked behind the dumpster. He was grinning like a fool; he'd known she wouldn't leave him.

She hugged him tight and the three of them huddled close. There were crowds in the street now. "I think the Humanists are here," Finn breathed. "A lot of them have white ash weapons."

Harlow nodded. "So what do we do? We'll never make it to the Citadel this way."

"If the two of you help, I think we can teleport to the library without much trouble, and it won't drain my resources much."

Larkin and Harlow both nodded as they took hands. Harlow dug deep into her well of power, drawing aether from the threads around them, as well as the pinprick portal into the limen within her. Finn shuddered a little as she directed her power into him.

"Not too much," he warned. "You need to be able to fight."

She smiled. "It's no trouble, McKay. I've got plenty."

His eyes widened with pride. "That's my girl," he said, and they blinked out of the alley.

The library's courtyard was dead silent in comparison to the chaos that had taken over below. Harlow's ears rang for a moment as she adjusted to the quiet, and the force by which they'd teleported.

"Everyone okay?" she asked Finn and Larkin.

Larkin nodded, but she looked slightly ill. Teleporting made nearly everyone sick unless they were used to it. Finn shrugged. "I feel great. To be honest, I'm starting to think you could probably teleport on your own now. How do *you* feel?"

Harlow shrugged. "Fine."

"No energy drain? No nausea?"

She shook her head. "No, I feel fine."

Finn shook his head. "We're going to look into that tomorrow, okay?"

She smiled. "Sure. Let's get going."

They made their way through the maze of flowers and hedges to the fountain. Harlow couldn't figure out what felt wrong with the courtyard until it came into view: it was the silence, of course. The courtyard had never been silent before, because of the running water from the fountain.

As they approached it, they saw that the fountain was still, and completely drained of water. "He's already here," Finn said, pointing to the staircase that the dry fountain had exposed.

"Darn," Larkin said, her voice dry. "I was really hoping we were going to have to answer some sort of obscure riddle to get down there."

Finn smirked, but then his expression grew serious. "Just like we talked about, okay? Larkin, you stay back and get ready to get Cian out. We don't know what kind of shape they'll be in. Harls, you're with me."

Harlow nodded. "Leave Axel on and run if things get hairy, okay?"

Larkin hugged Harlow. "We'll be fine." She hugged Finn too. "We'll get Cian and this will all be over fast."

Harlow knew that Larkin's extra-bright outlook was a coping mechanism. She was scared, and Harlow couldn't blame her. What they were about to do was probably stupid, and completely terrifying. Rakul Kimaris was a seasoned soldier, and Finn, while a talented fighter, was not.

They were all banking on the fact that Harlow's magic, and her ability to turn into the Feriant, might turn the tides of the fight, if it came to that. But both Harlow and Finn still hoped they could talk Rakul out of whatever he had planned and get them both out safely.

Harlow felt there had to be a way to free Vivia from the

vascularity, but they needed more time to figure things out. She just hoped Rakul could hear her. As they descended the dark stairs, Finn lit the way with a bit of magic.

"Let me talk to him first, okay?" she whispered as they took turn after turn.

Finn nodded, concentrating on the way ahead. "You can give it a try." He looked back. "But if it were you, and this was my chance to get you back…" He shook his head. "I'd be ready to kill anyone who got in my way."

"Why hasn't he come before this?" Larkin asked, her voice quiet behind them.

Harlow shrugged. "I don't think he knew how to get down here."

"I think the little temple in the nekropoleis was the original entrance to wherever we're going," Finn said. "I have a feeling they're connected somehow."

Harlow agreed. They were both temples devoted to Akatei; it made sense that somehow they were both connected to this place. Whatever was down here, however it got here, this all started a long, long time ago. She wondered if they'd ever really know the truth about what had made the portal, and why the Illuminated had contained it this way.

"Careful," Finn cautioned. "We're almost to the bottom. Let me see what's ahead."

Harlow looked up, but all she could see was stairs and Larkin. When Finn moved forward, his smile was tight. "It's really something down here. This must be a part of the catacombs under the temple."

When Harlow stepped off the last stair, she saw what he meant. The way was lit by torches with strange blue flames, and they cast a weak gray light onto the walls.

"Oh, that's just wrong," Larkin said as she stepped down after Harlow. "Who makes whole walls from people's skulls?"

"Our ancestors, silly," Harlow said, keeping her voice low.

Larkin grimaced.

"We should try to be as quiet as possible from here on out, okay?" Finn cautioned. Both sisters nodded in agreement and they made their way into the hall that stretched ahead. The ceilings were arched, and made from the same alabaster as the temple itself. Periodically, intricately carved stone plaques were interspersed between the skulls.

They depicted a story of sorts. In the first one she noticed, there were two winged people, Ventyr children. Though Harlow wasn't completely sure what was being depicted, she understood that the next few plaques showed them growing into adults. In different phases of their growth, different creatures and activities were shown, though to keep up with Finn, Harlow couldn't stop for long enough to examine them closely. The last that depicted the Ventyr pair showed one of them performing a ritual while the other looked to be asleep.

The final plaque depicted two rows of what Harlow assumed to be portals, and the Ventyr that had performed the ritual. In each one, horrible things were happening. Harlow couldn't stand to look for long. This vaguely reminded her of the little book of poetry Thea had found. Could this be part of the story that she'd read? Another set of panels began, but whatever they depicted was lost. Someone had destroyed each of them with a sharp implement.

The tunnel didn't smell musty, as she'd expected it to. In fact, it smelled distinctly like water. As they moved further along, Harlow heard the sound of a river, or more accurately, she felt its presence. The sound itself was quite faint, but the feeling amplified it in her mind. Could the Pyriphle run here as well? That might make sense, given Cian and Finn's suppositions about it. She paused for a moment and pressed the side of her head to one of the damaged stone plaques.

Finn stopped to watch her. "What are you doing?"

"Don't you hear the water?"

Finn gave her a quizzical look, tilting his head. "Sort of."

She drew back from the wall, surprised. "Really? You don't hear it?"

Finn shook his head, and when she turned to ask Larkin, her sister also indicated that she didn't hear the water. Finn took her hand. "Is it the Pyriphle? Do you hear its call?"

Harlow squinted. Somehow that made it easier to listen. Yes, she heard the rushing water, but mostly what she thought she heard was not a noise at all; it was the silent call to the limen, to the heart—to Nihil. Now that she recognized it, it was more than noise; it was a song, an invitation.

When the path branched in three directions, Finn was perplexed, but she was not. "It's this one," she said, pointing to the path that veered furthest left and downward.

He didn't ask how she knew. He obviously remembered all too well how she'd rushed towards the river in the cavern under the Vault. "Are you okay to do this?" he whispered.

"Yes," she said, with confidence she wasn't sure she had. What other choice did they have? Cian's life was at stake.

When the river's song sounded like it had a vocal accompaniment, she began to worry, but Finn turned. "Okay, that's chanting, isn't it?"

Larkin nodded. "Definitely."

Harlow shrugged. "Sure."

Finn kept moving forward, and as they rounded a sharp corner, he pushed them back, then peeked around. He motioned for them to stay silent and take a few steps backwards. He pushed Harlow forward and made the motion for Larkin to stay put. She nodded, understanding that she should stay here until someone brought Cian to her or called for her.

Harlow stepped forward and peeked around the corner. An enormous cavern with carved walls spread out before them.

Rakul Kimaris faced away from where she stood, and he was chanting over a huddled form, with a silver shock of hair. *Cian*.

But her focus could not linger there, due to the beautiful woman who was suspended in a grotesque web of aether at the other end of the room. The physical aspects of the vascularity were horrifying. It looked like a web of organic veins, pulsing with power, feeding into a firedrake. From what Harlow could see, removing the Argent would be nearly impossible to do from a purely physical perspective, as the vascularity itself was connected to her spinal column, and likely her brain.

Vivia Woolf's hair was long and silver, though her face was young. She was as pale as Cian, though they did not look alike otherwise. Her features were broad, with high cheekbones and a generous mouth. Vivia was tiny—very likely shorter than Kate, in Harlow's estimation. Her eyes were closed, but she did not appear to be resting peacefully. Every so often, a little surge of power in the vascularity jolted her, and she made a soft noise that echoed throughout the room.

Harlow motioned to Finn that she was going to approach Rakul, and he nodded. He would hang back for a moment and see how things went. He squeezed her hand reassuringly and then she stepped into the cavern, making sure to step heavily.

Rakul turned, his chanting dying on his lips. "I'll have to start over, little bird."

Harlow nodded. "You might have to. Could we talk first?"

Rakul sighed. "Please don't try to convince me to stop. You'll only be wasting your time."

"How can you even be down here, with the binding?" Harlow asked, respecting his wishes for the time being. She moved towards him, and though he eyed her warily, he did not make a move against her.

Harlow dared a glance down at Cian, who she could see now was bound and gagged, but conscious. They blinked once at her and nodded to show they were all right. There wasn't a mark on them; Rakul had been gentle enough, she supposed.

"They never thought I'd find my way back to this place, so it wasn't a part of the binding," Rakul said, shaking his head. "And until you started looking for it, I never thought I would either. But you led me right to it."

"Ashbourne can't help me, can he?" Harlow asked. "You just wanted me to find this place for you."

Rakul nodded. "Yes, I'm sorry to have lied to you about all that."

Harlow believed that he was sorry. The slump in his proud shoulders told the tale. "And you tricked us—didn't you? Using Vivia's name at Cerberus to get Finn and Cian to leave Nea Sterlis?"

Again, Rakul nodded. "Yes, I had to get Finn at least out of the way so the two of you wouldn't figure things out." Rakul paused, sorrow clouding his eyes. "I wish I could have helped you in some way. And I am sorry about Cian, but you'll find a way to get them out."

Harlow heard the pain in his voice; there was no doubt in her mind that this was wretched for him. He thought only of Vivia, and seeing her for herself, Harlow understood. She didn't want to leave the Argent here either. But what Rakul wanted to do was dangerous. They didn't know what could happen, and she wasn't about to let Cian be put up there in Vivia's place. "It's a risk taking her down, Rakul. We don't know what it might let out."

Rakul's eyes were full of pain. "She has been up there for nearly two thousand years. Don't you think she's had enough?"

Harlow stepped forward, reaching out towards Rakul. "Of course I do, and we'll find a way to help her, I promise, but it's too dangerous to let the vascularity go down for even a few moments."

He was shaking his head, losing patience with her. She saw

that and spoke faster. "Just give me some time, and we'll come back and close the portal for good, and she'll be free."

He quieted for a moment, staring at his love, and then his shoulders slumped in defeat. Relief washed over her. She stepped forward, reaching out to touch Rakul's arm. "I can work on getting the binding removed for you too, Rakul."

The vascularity pulsed with light, causing both Harlow and Rakul to turn. Vivia's eyes flickered open. "Don't do this," she whispered. "Do not break the spell, my love. You know I have to stay. This was my choice."

Rakul growled in fury, beating his fists to his chest. "But you didn't give *me* one. I didn't choose to live this life without you, nothing more than the Duke's enforcer."

Harlow's heart lumped in her throat as she reached out to comfort Rakul. She didn't know who the Duke was—maybe Connor—but the pain emanating from him was visceral.

A single tear marred Vivia's ethereal face. "I am still here. Still yours. And still committed to protect this world at all costs. You know what will happen if I fail. You must go."

The words the firedrake spoke seemed to drain all her energy. Her head drooped and she appeared to lose consciousness, though Harlow couldn't be sure. Rakul tensed visibly. She hadn't realized she was still touching him, and it surprised her when he launched into action. His arm pulled back from her touch, and he spun so quickly she didn't even see him move. He had hold of her arm before she could snatch it away, tossing her like a rag doll towards the entrance to the cavern. She slammed into something pliable.

Finn. He'd been rushing to her rescue. She tucked her body like she'd been taught and rolled, shouting, "Go!" as he crouched to check on her.

He sprung into action, shedding his glamour immediately. Rakul did as well, and they circled one another, Cian at the center. Finn lunged for Rakul, and Harlow could see it was a mistake the moment he did it, but she also understood why he'd taken the risk of letting Rakul get a hold of him.

Cian was left unguarded. Harlow rushed forward, dragging Cian out of the center of what appeared to be a sunburst, carved into the floor. As she dragged her friend out, she focused on loosening their bonds.

"Go," she said, pushing them toward Larkin's open arms as soon as they were free and moving.

She didn't wait to make sure they left, but turned back to the fight she could hear raging behind her. For a split second it looked as though Finn might be winning, but Rakul's body twisted like liquid, out of Finn's grip.

And in a movement Harlow's sorcière eyes could not follow, Rakul gained the upper hand, slamming Finn into the wall with such force he passed out immediately. Harlow cried out, rushing toward Finn with no thought for herself, and as she did, she caught sight of movement behind Vivia and the vascularity.

In the shadows, creatures were gathering, swarming, really. Harlow was immobilized by the sight of them. They were horrifying, vaguely humanoid forms. Their limbs were pale, and far too long, their hands and feet tipped with razor-sharp talons. Their heads reminded her a little of insects—perhaps it was the eyes, or the tiny mouths.

"The Vespae," Rakul said. "We locked them into the breach when we closed it. They were killing everything on this planet. The breach somehow made them stronger. It was one of ours that opened it, you know? Cut across all kinds of worlds, using his sister's power. Such a mistake."

Harlow listened to him, not knowing what to do. He was clearly in distress, and she didn't want to provoke him into more violence. "This is how the Illuminated manipulated the people here? They closed the breach and stopped the Vespae?"

Rakul laughed. "Yes, and the fools gave up all their power in the process. Did you know humans could do magic when we came here? It was incredible. Never saw anything like it on another world."

Harlow inched closer to Finn. He was breathing, but she didn't dare lunge for him.

Rakul stared at Vivia. "Make no mistake, we lost plenty of our own locking those creatures in with the Ravagers. It was a bloodbath."

Harlow had finally reached Finn. She bent down—his pulse was strong, and at her touch, he stirred. He would be fine. She left his side to try reasoning with Rakul once more. "Please. If you bring her down from there, it will let them loose on the world. Maybe even the Ravagers."

Rakul's expression was pained. "Yes, it will, and I am sorry for it. Close the breach with your Argent. My Vivia's time is served."

Before she could even think to shift, he'd tossed her to the side again, and she hit her head on the wall, hard enough to stun her. Finn came around just in time for them to watch Rakul Kimaris pull Vivia Woolf from the vascularity by force.

It did not want to let her go, but Rakul was determined, and the ritual he'd been doing had apparently loosened her enough that the vascularity stretched, pulling at her spinal cord. She let out an infernal noise, more than a scream, a sound of unbearable pain. Tears ran down Rakul's face as he pulled a sword from the scabbard strapped to his back. He sliced through the sinew of the vascularity, careful not to cut Vivia herself. Her screaming stopped, and it was obvious from the look on Rakul's face that he'd made the decision to free Vivia whether she lived or not. He gave Harlow a long, lingering look of sorrow—and then they were gone, teleported out.

Time slowed as the vascularity faltered. Without Vivia, it didn't have enough power to cover the breach. The Vespae whipped into a frenzy, surging against the weakening barrier.

"What in seventeen hells is going on here?" shouted a voice

in the distance. Connor McKay rushed into the chamber, pushing Cian ahead of him at the end of a white ash spear. Harlow's heart stopped when she saw the figures behind him: Merhart Locklear, Berith Sanvier... And her mother. *Aurelia*.

Aurelia was *here*, which meant she'd known about this place all along and never said a damn word. Her eyes locked with Harlow's and she shook her head slightly, mouthing "do nothing." Harlow's chest nearly burst with rage at her mother. *How could Aurelia have betrayed them all this way? How could she ally herself with Connor now?* Her chest shook with silent sobs.

Finn sat upright now, pulling Harlow with him. He glanced down at her, his eyes full of the same anger that rioted inside her. Their parents had let them down, brought them down. But they were together, and if they had to fight them all, she knew they would. They stood, ready to face them. Harlow made eye contact with Cian, who mouthed *Larkin is fine—hiding*. It was just like them to think about Larkin at a moment like this.

"Let Cian go," Finn said.

Connor started to say something, but Cian interrupted. "Finn. Stop. It's too late. They're gone, and there's no way around this."

Tears slipped down Finn's cheeks. "No," he pleaded. "You can't."

He fell to his knees in front of the one person who'd loved him unconditionally his entire life. Harlow thought her heart might break. Behind Connor, both Merhart Locklear and Aurelia clung to one another, fear written on their faces—maybe even regret for what was about to happen. Harlow had never hated anyone as she did Aurelia right now.

Connor sneered. "Get up, you coward."

Cian spun around, brave as ever. "Shut the ever-loving fuck up, Connor." They bent to hug Finn. "Let me do this, Finbar. I heard everything Harlow said. You'll figure out how to save me."

When they stood, Finn nodded. "We will."

Cian turned to Connor. "You were there at the beginning. I assume you remember how to get one of my kind up there."

Connor's lip curled in disgust, but he nodded, pushing Cian toward the vascularity. "Hurry up, we don't have much time. Aurelia, come and help. Merhart and Berith, we'll need you two as well when the spell begins. You understand?"

The vampire and shifter both nodded, and Harlow supposed it was lucky Berith hadn't been assassinated, after all. Finn reached for her hand and squeezed tightly. She held on for dear life, trying to spare herself the pain of looking at her mother in this terrible moment. Aurelia was clearly trying to catch her eye, no doubt to convey some useless apology for her part in all this. Harlow would not look. Instead, she looked straight into the breach, at the Vespae who pushed against the barrier.

An odd movement caught her eye. One of the Vespae had wings, ragged things that looked like shredded moth's wings, and it seemed to be pulling threads of aether just outside the vascularity. They were not brainless beasts then. The vascularity had broken down enough for one of them to manipulate reality on this side of the breach.

Connor saw it too, stepping back, his hands shaking. Connor McKay was *shaking*. "They have a queen—"

He seemed about to issue a warning when the vascularity simply dissolved. There was an enormous flash of light, accompanied by what might well have been a sound loud enough to destroy humanoid hearing, but might also have been merely a whisper.

The blast of power releasing into the world shifted something in the threads of aether so basic that at first Harlow wasn't sure anything had happened at all. And then she felt it: power flowed more freely throughout the threads, already more accessible and easier to use. Magic was free, but at what cost?

For a moment all was quiet and still but for the incessant buzzing sound the Vespae made with their tiny mouths, and then they tumbled forward in a writhing mass, rushing towards the tunnel on all fours. Harlow's body slammed against the wall, and she looked behind her to find Finn sheltering her with his wings.

"Where's Cian?" she shouted. "And Larkin?" She couldn't bring herself to ask about Aurelia or the others. A pang of guilt shot through her for it, but her anger at Aurelia was still too strong.

Finn craned his neck, and she could not see beyond him, but she heard the rush of myriad feet and her mind broke around the fear. There were thousands of those creatures, sentient and hungry, streaming into the world right now, and it was all their fault for not stopping Rakul. All the Orders' fault for not finding a better way to handle this. All Aurelia's fault for not just telling what she knew and allowing them to change this waking nightmare.

"Cian has Larkin," Finn said. And then all went blessedly, horrifically quiet. Finn stepped away from Harlow, letting her away from the wall. He stared at the breach, open and completely visible now that the vascularity was down. Berith Sanvier had disappeared, along with Merhart Locklear. To where, Harlow couldn't guess, nor did she care. Her mother stood alone near the cave entrance, pale and shivering, in complete shock. Harlow made no move towards her; in fact, she turned away.

Clouds of dark aether swirled beyond, disturbed by the Vespae. Finn stepped towards it, but Connor yanked him back. "Get the fuck away from that, boy."

Finn shook his father off. "Why?"

Connor shook his head. He looked so defeated, so exhausted, that Harlow almost felt bad for him. "There is still a barrier there—a one-way barrier of a sort. You could get through to the other side, but you would not be able to come back. It's why we built the vascularity. It made the barrier work both ways, to keep the power of Okairos limited, and to stop the Vespae, as we promised."

A soft laugh penetrated the barrier. "Yes, brother, you always keep your promises, don't you?" Ashbourne stepped forward, not in their astral body this time, but their true form.

CHAPTER THIRTY-TWO

"Brother?" Finn asked, astonishment on his face.

Connor sighed. "Yes, we are brothers. It has been a long while, Ashbourne."

"Since you closed the breach the first time," the Ventyr warrior reasoned. "Little bird," he said, nodding to Harlow.

Behind her, there was a rustling noise. People were talking. Harlow looked back and was surprised to find Kate, accompanied by Morgaine, and her friend, the Ultima, Samira. *What were* they *doing here?* They were deep in conversation with Larkin and Cian, arguing about something. Aurelia had moved towards them, but Larkin's glare kept her from moving closer. Morgaine was speaking quickly, touching Cian's arm for emphasis as they nodded. Whatever she was saying, Cian seemed to understand.

Harlow nodded to Finn, who turned as she slid her hand into his. "Why are they here?" he asked, obviously distracted. He was trying to keep tabs on his father, who had moved closer to the breach now, and was talking quietly with Ashbourne.

"I don't know," Harlow said, gripping Finn's hand harder,

unsure of where to turn her attention. She didn't understand what Kate was doing here with Morgaine and Samira—between that and what she'd seen her mother prepared to do, her mind spun. She froze, overwhelmed by the last few hours of terror and Aurelia's betrayal.

Perhaps that was why she didn't see Larkin break away from the little group, setting Axel down on the ground next to Cian. By the time her sister's movement caught her eye, it was too late. She'd moved too close to the breach, having spotted Ashbourne, and she hadn't heard Connor's warning.

"Larkin," she screamed, lurching forward, her hand slipping out of Finn's.

Her cry came an instant too late. Larkin stepped slowly through the barrier before Harlow could stop her. The void that opened up inside her sucked all air from her lungs, her heart stopping as she watched her youngest sister, her least-silly-silly, go somewhere she could not follow.

Ashbourne turned, his face a mask of horror as he saw Larkin on his side of the barrier. He shouted, rushing toward the barrier in protest, but he was not looking at Larkin. Too late, Harlow saw what caught his attention. Finn had leapt after Larkin, trying to stop her from crossing into the limen, but something about the breach was alive, and it sucked him through as well.

In one terrible instant, Harlow's world came crashing down around her. Her mind went blank as she ran for the barrier. Hands grabbed her, pulling her back. The rest of the world moved in real time, but she was stuck in slow motion as someone pushed her to the ground, begging her to stop fighting.

How could anyone expect her to stop fighting for them? They were her heart's home. Her family. Her responsibility. She wouldn't stop fighting for them, *ever*. She couldn't. It wasn't in her nature. Harlow didn't hear herself screaming, but her throat burned as she shifted. The strength of her wings knocked whoever was trying to stop her from rescuing Finn and Larkin backwards.

Beyond the breach, Ashbourne held Finn back as he screamed her name. Larkin kneeled on the ground sobbing that she was sorry, so sorry. Harlow felt sure she could bring them back, that the strength of the Feriant would carry the three of them back through the barrier, and so she crouched, ready to fly. Everywhere there were shouts, pleas to shift back, to *please just stop and think*. She ignored them. The only sound she heard was her own raptorial cry, as she launched herself towards the breach.

Something pierced her side, sending a shot of fluid pain blazing through her. She looked down as her avian body fell away. Wooziness came over her as several blurry figures surrounded her. From her vantage point on the ground, she saw Finn struggle out of Ashbourne's grip, only to be pulled back by Larkin. For her, he stopped, and Harlow could barely hear now, but she thought she heard Larkin say, "You'll destroy yourself. She wouldn't want that."

Their eyes met and even as whatever she'd been drugged with coursed through her she reached for him, and he for her. Harlow didn't know she was screaming until she was in Kate's arms. "Lo, Lo, *shhhh….* It's all right. They're gonna be okay, but you have to calm down. Sam, why isn't it working? It's not calming her."

"It was formulated for Kamaris. It should be working," Samira said, her voice floating somewhere above Harlow. Her vision was so dark and blurry she couldn't make much out. "But she's fighting it, and Majesty, she just might win."

Majesty? Somewhere in Harlow's mind, puzzle pieces moved, but she couldn't think of them now, she only wanted Finn and Larkin back. She held his gaze with hers, her lips moving now in a silent plea, *Come back, come back, come back.*

Everyone was trying to talk sense into them, but still he reached for her, and she for him. Vaguely, she saw Aurelia slide to the ground, covering her face and hands, wrapping herself in a tiny ball. *How had everything gone so wrong?*

In her peripheral vision, Kate moved to talk to someone Harlow couldn't make out. "Fine. Explain it to her, as best you can, but do it fast. We've gotta get them out of here."

Morgaine's face appeared, close to Harlow's, blocking her view of Finn. She fought it for a moment, but Samira was wrong; the drug was beginning to work and it stilled her body, no matter how her mind fought. She realized they were both lying flat on the floor, staring at one another now.

"Hi," Harlow said, her tongue thick with her continued sobs. "What're you doing here?"

"Hey there, bird girl." Morgaine's voice was low and steady. "Cian will explain it all to you later, but for now I've gotta know, do you think you might be able to trust me?"

Morgaine took hold of her outstretched hand, the one that still sought Finn. The compass tattoo on the younger woman's wrist glowed faintly with a familiar light. Harlow's second sight engaged, as if by instinct. Morgaine was using magic somehow, but it wasn't aethereal magic. It was like Finn's, made of light.

"Starfire," Morgaine explained, tapping the tattoo. "This is a conduit for celestial power, starfire, the sister substance to aether."

Harlow's second sight showed something strange about the girl. Though the celestial power of her tattoo gleamed with starfire, she herself glowed with the same dark light as the two women from her last trip to the limen had.

"Echo," she whispered, remembering how she knew the warrior girl's face. "I saw your Echo. In the aether. She was like me." Harlow wasn't sure what she meant by that—the drug was starting to make her mind cloudy—but it felt right. Somehow she, Lumina and Echo were all connected, similar somehow.

Morgaine nodded. "Yes, she's like you. We're all fighting the same thing, you just don't know it yet. The Ravagers. One of them is out already, and I'm here to make sure that its brethren can't escape."

The missing wardens. The empty space in Nihil. It probably all made sense, but everything was mixed up in her head. Whatever they'd given her was making it hard to think. She did trust Morgaine. But she'd trusted her mother, and that had been a mistake. The fuzzy thought occurred to her that she should ask questions, but she was too far gone to be clever. All she could manage was, "What will you do?"

"I'll close the breach."

"No," Harlow sobbed, struggling to rise. Somewhere in the distance, Larkin needed her, and Finn; her heart ached. She thought maybe she could hear him screaming for her, but her mind struggled to latch onto anything too far away. "My sister... Finn."

Morgaine made a soft shushing noise, stroking her hair back from her face. She spoke quickly. "I have to close the breach. It's what I'm here to do. But there *is* a way out of the limen, a natural portal in Falcyra, in the mountains. I will help them get there, but it will probably destabilize in a few days, once I close the breach. You *must* reach them before that. Do you understand?"

Harlow tried to nod, but didn't have much luck. "Why are you telling me all this?"

"Because I'm also here because of you," Morgaine said, reaching out to touch her cheek. "Because of your connection to the otham—I'm sorry—the aether. You will understand better later, but I'm here to pass a message onto you, as well as to close the breach. Will you trust me enough to carry it with you?"

Harlow nodded. "Yes, tell me."

Morgaine came closer and whispered words that were at once strange and completely familiar to her. Harlow nodded; it was as if Morgaine had unlocked a door that Harlow had been staring at her entire life.

"I don't think I'll remember," she replied.

Morgaine slid something hard and flat into her jacket, tucking it securely against her. "*The Warden*," she explained. "And I've written the message down for you. Find the missing bits of the book when you can. I have a feeling they can help you."

Harlow nodded, as her eyes drooped, threatening to shut without her permission.

Morgaine smiled as the enormous auburn cat who had been Axel's friend these past weeks brushed Harlow's face with his. Morgaine and the cat looked at one another, as though conversing silently, and the cat purred over her again, rubbing its face on hers in a comforting way.

"Do you understand what I've told you, Harlow?" Morgaine asked.

"I think so," Harlow murmured as her eyes closed further.

In her mind, she heard the cat speak, though of course that was impossible. *We knew you would, Strider. Walk with luck.* The cat bounded towards the breach and leapt through. Harlow couldn't see that far now, but she imagined Finn taking the great cat in his arms and giving it a snuggle. She was still weeping, her tears soaking the ground beneath her face, but she thought she might have laughed at that.

"I have to go now," Morgaine said.

Harlow nodded, her eyes threatening to close now. "Tell him I will find him," she mumbled before the drug her body had been fighting finally won its battle. "Tell him I will destroy worlds to find him if he doesn't come back to me."

"Let's hope it doesn't come to that, bird girl," Morgaine said, stroking her hair once more before she sat up.

"Will I ever see you again?" Harlow asked before her eyes closed.

"I'm not certain," Morgaine whispered as the girl who reminded her so much of her own dear Echo fell asleep. "But if we don't, please know that I believe in you, Harlow Krane. You'll do what needs to be done. Awaken them and prepare."

CHAPTER THIRTY-THREE

H arlow woke up with a start. Her entire body vibrated with phantom pain, and she was panicking. *Why was she panicking?* Finn. Larkin. The breach. A strangled sob clawed its way through her chest, rage at her loss, and the fact that she wasn't allowed to say goodbye, ricocheting through her. Her shadows welled inside her, begging to be let out, to take vengeance on anyone they could.

Soft arms surrounded her—they had been around her all along. "You're awake."

"Mama?" Harlow asked, sitting up. Selene held her tight. The two of them were curled up together on a big upholstered chair. Harlow was confused. She looked around, and it took her a moment to realize they were on a plane. A *big* plane.

A luxury jet, in fact. Instead of rows of seats, it was set up like a very long living room. Beyond where she sat, Indigo stared blankly at Nox, asleep on her lap. Next to them on the same couch, Thea and Alaric held hands, exhaustion written in the set of their shoulders. Enzo and Riley sat in a tight group with Cian, Petra, Kate, and the Ultima, Samira. Axel had been curled up next to Selene, but now came to sit on her lap.

Memories of what had happened in the cavern gripped her nearly as soon as she took a tally of everyone on the plane. *Finn. Larkin. Morgaine. Aurelia.*

She looked around for Mother, and found her sitting alone at the front of the plane, staring at the wall. Her clothes were rumpled and her face was dirty and tear stained.

"She lied to us all." Her throat was raw, from all the screaming, she assumed.

"She thought she was protecting us," Selene said, sounding lost.

"Has she always known?" Harlow asked.

"Apparently all the chancellors are told upon swearing in. It took the magic of each Order to keep the vascularity in place. They knew it was there all along, keeping Okairos... locked up." Selene's voice broke over her last few words. "And now... Larkin is gone."

"I'm so sorry," Harlow whimpered.

Aurelia's head turned towards them, tears flooding down her face as her chest shook. Across the plane, Thea and Indi both wept, watching the scene, clearly feeling as helpless and angry as Harlow did now. Her family was broken—shattered, like her heart.

"We'll never be the same." Her words sounded like a vow. Selene didn't answer her, but the pain in her eyes was enough to tell Harlow she understood the sentiment all too well. "What about Morgaine?"

Selene waved Kate over, rising. "Let Kate explain. I need to rest."

"No," Harlow said abruptly. Memories of the cavern were clarifying in her mind, and the last person she wanted was Kate. "I want Cian."

Cian was already walking across the plane, having seen that she was awake. Kate followed close behind. Thea walked across the plane, ignoring Aurelia as she passed her, and drew

Selene into her arms, guiding her to a seat between her and Alaric.

When they were settled, Cian folded their long limbs onto the seat next to Harlow as she sat up, taking her hands in theirs. "Where's Finn?" Harlow asked, ignoring Kate as she sat down in the bank of seats across from them.

"You know where Finn is," Cian said.

She did. "The limen."

Cian nodded. "That's right. We're on our way to Falcyra now to find them."

She deliberately ignored Kate, who sat forward, her elbows on her knees, her pretty face resting in her hands. Kate looked anxious and drawn. *Well enough*, Harlow thought. *That's the least of what she should feel.* She knew she was transferring some of her anger at Aurelia onto Kate, but they had both kept so much from everyone. It was clear Kate had known about the vascularity and what it did.

"Whose plane is this?" Harlow asked

"The Rogue Order's," Kate said, speaking softly. "We're taking you to our village where you'll be safe. It's close to where the portal Morgaine described is. We'll get them, Lo. I promise we'll get them back."

Harlow refused to look Kate's way. "And *she's* the Rogue Queen."

Cian's silver eyes housed an endless well of empathy. "Yes, she is."

"And you knew," Harlow said, resentment mixing with the focused fury in her chest. So many secrets. When would it all end?

"Yes," Cian replied. They would never lie to her again. She saw it in their eyes, a promise. It was too late for that now.

"You've been with them all along, haven't you? You're the one who gave Finn and Alaric the keys to the Vault, and set them on this path."

"When did you figure it out?" Cian asked.

Harlow shrugged. *Did it even matter now?* "I think I knew when we found the inscription on the crypt, I just didn't want to admit it to myself. And you," she said, pointing at Kate. "Did you know the whole time—about what the vascularity was for and where Vivia Woolf was?"

Kate nodded. "Yes, I knew. No one else on my Nea Sterlis team did, but I knew."

"And you didn't trust me enough to tell me all this?"

"I told you, Lo. It wasn't about trusting you. It was about protecting something greater than myself. If you had any experience with stuff like this, you'd understand."

The condescension in Kate's voice was too much. That she could justify not collaborating with this bullshit line of thinking was going too far. It was all too much: losing Finn and Larkin. Her mother's betrayal. Cian and Kate's secrets. The Vespae. Dear gods, the Vespae. Where were they now, and what were they doing to the world below as she flew away on a luxury jet?

The rage in Harlow's chest coalesced, winnowing to focus on Kate. She turned too quickly, her body moving with a speed she wasn't used to. In less than a second, she had Kate pinned to the headrest of her seat by the throat, her fingers threatening to crush her delicate esophagus. "I'd understand what, *Katherine*? That these are just the casualties of war?"

Kate didn't answer; her face remained calm as if she were reading her favorite book, which only made Harlow angrier. Samira rose, but Kate waved her away. "It's fine; she won't hurt me."

"Won't I?" Harlow snarled. Everyone had stopped what they were doing to watch, even Aurelia. Harlow knew she should stop. She knew Kate wasn't who she was really angry at, and Kate knew it too. It didn't stop her from saying, "Give me one good reason why I shouldn't." Her voice didn't sound like her own, and she liked it. She liked how strong she sounded. "Do you know I believed you? I believed you actually cared about me, but it was all about this the whole time, wasn't it?"

Across the plane, Aurelia covered her mouth with her hands, a small sob spilling out anyway. She knew as well as everyone else did that Harlow's words were for her as much as for Kate. Tears ran hot and fast down Harlow's face. This wasn't all about Aurelia. Kate had lied too. She glared at the woman she'd once thought she loved. "None of it was ever about me, was it? Just what I might be able to *turn into*."

To her surprise, Kate nodded. Harlow let her go, stepping back. "At first, yes. You're like Samira and the others. We'd been looking for you for quite some time. But you never manifested, and I thought I'd made a mistake. I wasn't queen then, but then Lou got sick."

It took Harlow a moment, but then she remembered: Lou was Kate's sire. "What does that have to do with anything?"

"The story I told you when we broke up about needing to go back to the vineyard to help Lou was true. She just didn't need help with the vineyard—she needed help with the Rogue Order. So I became queen when she couldn't be anymore."

"Congratulations," Harlow muttered. "Did you ever think that if you'd just *told* us all of this that we'd have helped you?"

"No," Kate said simply. "I *hoped* you might, but it's not that simple, Harlow. I am responsible for thousands of people. A whole network of rebels, of people that if the Illuminated got their hands on them—well, let's just say they'd make what you saw Connor do at the Grand look like child's play."

Harlow fell to the floor of the plane, her knees sinking into the plush beige carpet, her will to be angry suddenly dying. Cian dragged her against their legs, their arms going around her. They pressed a kiss to her forehead. "I'm so sorry I lied to you and Finn, sweet girl. I made a mistake. I thought I could convince Kate of our intentions on my own. I should have told you both everything."

Harlow stared at the wall, her arms limp at her sides. If any of them had just told the truth sooner, none of this would have happened. These secrets they all kept were a weakness. "If we get them back, I will consider forgiving the *two* of you," she muttered, hoping Aurelia heard. "Until then, leave me the hells alone."

"*When* we get them back." Kate stood as she corrected Harlow. "I *am* sorry, Lo."

Harlow laughed, a harsh sound. "If we don't get them back, I will *kill* you."

There was a long silence as Harlow's threat against Kate's life hung in the air. "She doesn't mean that," Thea insisted from across the plane.

"She does," Cian said, leaving Harlow's side. They reached back to touch her cheek, but they gazed at Aurelia as they spoke. "And I don't blame her one bit for it."

Cian and Kate walked across the plane together, leaving Harlow alone with her grief. She slept on and off for several hours, and when she woke again, Samira was sitting next to her. Axel was curled beneath them, his tiny snores a percussive white noise she found infinitely soothing. She stroked his back and he rolled over, pressing his paws against her thigh as he nuzzled into her leg.

"Go away," Harlow said to Samira, her voice flat.

"No," Samira said. "You can hate Kate and Cian, if you want. That is legitimate. But I will stay right here."

Harlow glanced at the warrior's face. She had a bright light in her dark eyes, something deeply humorous behind all that stern exterior. The Ultima kicked her feet up onto the footrest of her seat.

"Are you protecting Kate?" Harlow asked. "Worried I'll try to murder her here on the plane?"

Samira laughed. "I don't answer to her Majesty. I'm not a

bodyguard." The way Samira said "her Majesty" made it sound like a joke. Harlow liked the irreverence.

"Then who are you?" Harlow replied.

"A Strider, like you—a member of the Feriant Legion. And no one commands us. We answer only to ourselves." The Ultima's voice was soft and confident, her words seductive as she continued. "When we get to Falcyra, you will see what I mean."

Harlow turned towards the window, dragging Axel to her chest. "Perhaps," she said, as she shut her eyes against this terrible reality.

The Ultima started to get up, but a thought suddenly occurred to Harlow and she reached out to pull her back down. "Did Morgaine get the breach shut?"

Samira nodded. "Yes, her power is quite interesting. Not her own, apparently, just on loan for her mission."

"Saving us from the Ravagers?" Harlow asked. She wished she'd had more time to talk to Morgaine, to understand the world she'd come from, but Samira had spent time with her. From the sound of things, they'd have plenty of time to talk this over in the near future. Harlow remembered *The Warden*, and pressed her free hand to her side. It was there, tucked into her jacket's inside pocket still.

The Ultima grinned at Harlow's grip on her arm, her straight white teeth flashing. Harlow released her, and Samira settled in next to her once more as she explained, "Yes, the one her people call the Legionnaire is already out. It's why she became the bearer of starfire, to close the breaches between worlds. They were made by one of the Ventyr, a terrible mistake."

"Seems like they make a lot of those," Harlow said, bitterness edging her tone.

Samira smirked. "Isn't that the truth? They've been cavorting about the galaxy, fucking things up for eons. But some of them are sexy as fuck, yeah?"

Harlow's heart ached unbearably. "Yeah. Do you have a Ventyr partner?" It was not lost on her that they were calling them Ventyr, rather than Illuminated.

The dark beauty grinned, stretching her muscular legs out before her. "Yeah, Tomyris. We've been together for almost five years."

"Together-together?" Harlow asked cautiously. She didn't know if her heart could take the answer, or talk about romantic love right now, but she was curious all the same.

Samira nodded. "Yes, it's been rotten being apart this summer while I kept an eye on you." Her mouth fell open and she touched Harlow's arm. "I'm sorry..."

"It's okay," Harlow said. "I'm happy for you... That you'll get to see her soon."

"She'll love you," Samira said. "She's the warmest creature on this planet. Sweet to everyone with a wicked bite, if you know what I mean."

Harlow did, all too well, unfortunately. "I'm sure we'll be fast friends."

"You will," Samira assured her. She looked uncomfortable then, as though she knew the trajectory of their conversation had done nothing but pour salt into Harlow's very fresh wounds.

Harlow attempted to change the subject. She didn't want the Strider to go away. Right now, she might be the only person who truly understood the pain Harlow was in. "So, the Ravager that escaped to Morgaine's realm... What is it doing there?"

"As far as we know, it has taken hold of a vessel on her world, and its power grows."

"And the others?"

"Still imprisoned, but awake, after long years of slumber."

Harlow already knew that, from her visit to the limen. She didn't know if that was a usual thing for Striders to do, but she wasn't quite ready to talk about it yet. In fact, she was utterly exhausted. She curled back into herself, closing her eyes once more.

"Connor McKay got away," Samira said softly as she settled in next to Harlow, preparing to nap herself, apparently.

"Of course he did," Harlow grumbled before letting the sound of Axel's purrs lull her to sleep.

EPILOGUE

A frigid wind raked through Harlow's hair, pulling strands from the tight pair of braids that hung down her back. Though she was clad in thick gear that was spelled not to fall off her body when she shifted, the cold air still crept into her body, chilling her to the bone. Falcyra was perpetually cold in the lowlands, and here in the mountains it was even worse.

Harlow's muscles had hardened over the past two months, training and flying with the Striders. She thought Finn would be proud of the progress she'd made, and she knew he'd like the bulk she'd added to her generous curves. It was still hard to think about him and Larkin.

They'd followed the portal for weeks as it blinked through the jagged mountain range. But there was no sign of her sister or lover. One day, just as Morgaine had said it would, the portal destabilized and did not reappear. Yule would be here soon, and the air smelled like snow as she gazed down into the valley the ancient fjord sat in. Conifers covered the valley floor and walls, giving way to the rocky peaks she stood amongst now.

"They could have come through two stops back, or even

four," Samira offered, looking at their paper map. The world had been without power, without internet or phone for two months now. Harlow was surprised to find she didn't miss any of it much. She certainly didn't miss Section Seven. "Both times we didn't get there for days. High winds could have masked their tracks."

Harlow nodded, but her mouth was set in a grim line. It was hard not to lose hope. It had been nearly two weeks with no leads. Harlow dreaded going down into the valley, back to the settlement. Back to the people who loved her, who grew more worried about her with each passing day. They'd been lucky that Meline and Ari had caught wind of them, and now Harlow's family was nearly reunited, despite being broken in all the ways that counted.

With Finn and Larkin still missing, she hadn't spoken to Aurelia since the night they'd lost them. Her refusal to even listen to her mother was putting a strain on her family. Though they were incredibly lucky that so many of their friends and family were safe, Harlow couldn't bring herself to hear Aurelia out. She needed time, and the work the Feriant Legion was doing to keep her from losing her good sense.

From the Rogue Order's informants, they'd learned that nearly a million people, humans and the lower Orders alike, had been wiped out by the Vespae, who were reproducing quickly. The Humanists had all but disappeared in their wake, but Harlow didn't doubt they would re-emerge eventually. Especially now that humans could use magic. In the settlement, the sorcière had started a training program for interested humans, and nearly all of them attended one workshop or another, learning to pull the threads of aether as the sorcière did.

As Cian had once described, it was harder for them. They were not genetically disposed to it the way sorcière were, but many were growing skilled far more quickly than anyone had assumed they'd be able to. Harlow was learning not to underestimate humans' capability. She'd always known they were remarkably resilient, and they proved it beyond a shadow of a doubt now.

Despite the fact that she was still angry with Kate, she admired the work the Rogue Order was doing immensely, and she understood why the vampire had been so protective of it. While she was, indeed, called the "Rogue Queen," it was nothing more than a moniker. She was a figurehead, a bogey-man of sorts representing the ideal of the outcast the Immortal Orders feared most. In truth, the Rogues were led by a small council of elected representatives from each of the five groups of people that inhabited Okairos.

Samira perched on a rock, looking distinctly birdlike, even in her humanoid form. "Hey," she said, breaking Harlow's reverie. "You never told me what Morgaine whispered to you in the cave."

Harlow sat next to her. The sun had warmed the dark-colored boulder enough that it felt good beneath her, the heat seeping into her. "You don't know?"

"No," Samira said, shaking her head. "Even though we worked together when she came through the portal, she didn't tell me much."

Harlow had learned that Morgaine's mission was to close the breaches that one of the irresponsible Ventyr had made centuries ago. It was creating a kind of imbalance throughout the realms most closely connected to the limen. There would always be portals, Samira had explained; doors to other places, shortcuts across the universe. But largely, their natural state was to be unstable, appearing and disappearing without warning.

But since the Ventyr had tried to leverage the limen in the wars against one another, they'd wanted permanent doors, and in finding a way to achieve this, had wrought all kinds of trouble on many different worlds. Morgaine was meant to close those unnatural doors, the breaches, but she was also meant to deliver a message, to both Harlow and Lumina, on their respective worlds.

Harlow stared into the valley, watching the mix of humans and immortals working together. She turned to Samira. "Morgaine said this was a part of a prophecy from her world: *Awaken the Fifth Order and the seventh ward shall break, and in so doing balance returns. The terror of the Ravagers ends when gods walk the earth as mere denizens.*"

Samira grimaced. "Horrible things, prophecies. Always so vague and easy to misinterpret."

Harlow smiled; this was the usual perspective from the Order of Mysteries. Since so few sorcière were gifted with the Sight, as humans seemed more predisposed to psychic ability, foretelling was generally looked down upon. She couldn't fault Samira for feeling that way, but the words had ignited something in her.

"Awaken the Fifth Order," she said, gesturing to the scene in the valley.

Samira shifted on the boulder, and she squinted, as though trying to see Harlow's vision. She glanced at Harlow sidelong, shaking her head. "You don't think?"

Harlow nodded. "I do. I think they're the Fifth Order."

Samira bumped her shoulder with her own. "You mean *we*. *We're* the Fifth Order."

The last little piece of whatever Harlow had been trying to puzzle out about the message snicked into place. "Yes," she breathed, hardly able to believe it.

She'd found her place. And as much as she loved Finn, and was desperate to get him back, there was a part of her that knew she had to get here on her own, without his help. That knowledge was uncomfortable, and she sat in silence next to Samira, contemplating what it might mean.

A crackle came over Samira's portable radio. They were close enough to the settlement for it to reach them. A familiar voice,

Meline, said, "Samira, it's base. Do you copy?" Meline and Indigo had both taken to the communications team rather rapidly, and were often the voice at the other end of such communications.

"I copy," Samira responded. "We're headed back in. No luck."

"There's been a sighting. Sixty miles from stop four. A girl and a winged creature. Someone thought it was a Vespae queen with a hostage, but it could be them."

"Get me the coordinates," Samira said. "We'll head out now."

Meline sent a string of numbers their way, and Harlow tracked them on the map she'd unfolded in her lap. She nodded at Samira when she'd found the place. "Got it."

"We'll be back before dinner," Samira said. "And hopefully we'll have our people."

"Good flying, Warbirds," Meline said, and her transmission crackled out.

Harlow looked down on the settlement, with all its beautiful stone buildings and cobblestone streets, as she passed the map back to Samira. The area had once been a thriving resort town, perhaps three hundred years ago, but as legend went it was terribly haunted by poltergeists. There were none here now, but plenty of ghasts and other spirits, so the rumor probably persisted and largely kept people away from the region.

"We'll miss hand-to-hand again," she remarked, motioning to the two legions of soldiers lining up on the cleared fields beyond the settlement perimeter. Nothing grew in the winter, so they used them for training.

Samira laughed. "Like you need it. You took to fighting like a raven to wing."

Harlow's lips quirked up in a half-smile and she pushed the Ultima playfully. Sometimes she felt guilty for smiling, but Tomyris and Samira had urged her to try to find joy in these hard days, as much as possible. They reasoned that Finn wouldn't want her to languish in misery. "You just don't want me to kick your ass again."

"It was *one* time," Samira said, returning the smile. Harlow had been improving. She was by no means an expert, but with nothing to do but train, Harlow's gains had been rapid. Samira examined Harlow's face, looking worried. "Don't you want to find them?"

Harlow shrugged. "Of course, but it's not them. It never is."

There had been so many false starts, so many bad leads. She didn't want to give up, but her heart couldn't take much more disappointment.

"If you want to get back to Tomyris, I'll understand. I can go check it out on my own."

Samira bumped her shoulder. "I'll do one better for you."

She clicked a code into the radio and a musical voice answered. "I've got your location in my sights, lover. You headed home?"

"Nope, there's been a lead. Wanna come with?"

"On my way," the voice answered. Seconds later, Samira's partner blinked in next to them. She was a tall, muscular creature who rarely used her humanoid alternae. She was one of the Thuelloi, like Ashbourne, with mauve-colored skin and thick ebony hair that was currently braided into a crown around her head.

She planted a kiss on Samira's lips, her hand brazenly caressing her lover's ass. She then hugged Harlow, a little too hard. Samira hadn't been exaggerating about Tomyris; she was effusive in her affection, but could be absolutely terrifying in a fight. Harlow had watched her singlehandedly slaughter two dozen Vespae, the soldiers of a swarm that had tried to invade the valley only a week back. And yet here she was squeezing the air out of Harlow's lungs with the force of her friendship.

"Can't breathe," Harlow gasped and the Ventyr released her, laughing heartily.

Tomyris examined the map, pointing out possible routes to the coordinates Meline had given them, while Samira practically mooned over her lover's words. The two of them were disgustingly smitten with one another. Not all of the Striders' Ventyr partners were romantic, but like Finn and Harlow, Samira and Tomyris were in love. It was a little hard to watch at times, but it helped that they both were good friends. Harlow had always had her sisters, and Enzo, of course, but she'd never had a group of friends that were just hers. This new territory helped soothe some of the perpetual ache in her chest from missing Finn and Larkin, and the rift within her family.

"Shall we?" Tomyris asked. "Audata's making breakfast for dinner tonight and I want to be back by the time it's done."

Samira grinned and then shot into the air, shifting as she rose. Tomyris followed, yelling, "Last one there has to clean the waffle iron."

Harlow swore as she shifted, and then followed. *Hold on, McKay*, she thought to herself as she flew west into the setting sun. *I'm coming for you*.

Glossary

Akatei: Patron goddess of the Order of Mysteries.

Alternae: The non-humanoid form shifters turn into.

Aphora: Akatei's sister. Goddess of beauty, art and love.

Argent: A silver firedrake.

Bonded: Married

Firedrake: A heraldic shifter. Much like a dragon, a firedrake has the ability to breathe fire. It has two hind legs, and wings that can be used to fly, or operate as arms.

Heraldic Shifters: Shifters thought to be extinct that have humanoid forms and alternae that resemble mythical beasts. Often used in heraldic imagery to depict supernatural strength and nobility.

Incubus: A vampiric creature that feeds primarily off human and immortal fear and other strong emotions. Has the ability to manipulate emotions and is physically stronger than vampires and the Illuminated.

Limen: The space between worlds, the spirit paths.

Nekropoleis: A cemetery, often with temples to deities that govern the dead and underworlds.

Mater(s): A word that means "mother" or "mothers."

Nea Sterlis: A city in southern Nytra. Home of the Alabaster Spire and the Temple District, which are known as the "citadel of the gods."

Nuva Troi: A coastal city in the Midlands region of Nytra. Home to the seat of the Immortal Orders, functionally the capital of the world. All of the most powerful immortals have homes in Nuva Troi.

Nytra: The most powerful country on Okairos.

Okairos: The planet that *Dark Night, Golden Dawn* takes place on.

Paired: Being in a committed relationship. Being paired does not necessarily imply monogamy.

Raia: Mother to Akatei and Aphora.

Author's Note

I'll get real, real sappy in the last book about all the people who've made this series both possible and as good as it could be. For right now, let me just say a huge thank you to the people who sort me out when I'm writing: Kenna Kettrick, Holly Karlsson, Victoria Mier, Nicola Hastings, Chelsea Thomas, Sara McCormick, Maria Sclafani, Sarah Guthu. Y'all made this book what it is and I love you. Seriously, I could not ask for better friends. Also thank you to The Coven. Everything works better because of you.

The rest of this thank you is for *you*. You who are reading this. When I started writing *Dark Night Golden Dawn*, I thought it might do better than my other books, but you surpassed my wildest expectations. I'm sorry to leave you hanging this way, but please know that I know what genre I write.

I love you all, and I'm going to take you for an anxious ride of emotional damage, but I hope the tears on your face at the end of the series are happy ones.

Also By Allison Carr Waechter

THE OUTLAWS OF INTERRA TRILOGY

Vessel of Starfire

Sea Smoke

The Last Witch Queen

Gods Walk the Earth (forthcoming)

THE IMMORTAL ORDERS TRILOGY

Dark Night Golden Dawn

Beneath the Alabaster Spire

Awaken the Fifth Order (2023)

Printed in Great Britain
by Amazon

11209726R00222